WAR FROM JUNGLE TO DESERT

Pat Schneider

PublishAmerica
Baltimore

ISBN: 1-60474-926-1
PUBLISHED BY PUBLISHAMERICA, LLLP
www.publishamerica.com
Baltimore

Printed in the United States of America

TO: RANDALL

A TRULY GREAT
FRIEND AND A DAM FINE
FISHERMAN. HOPE YOU
ENJOY IT.

BEST WISHES
AND GOD BLESS

Lee Schneider

PART 1 - 1968

CHAPTER 1

High school was gone and college gave me heartburn. My high school year book called me Pat Taylor but for some reason people called me Shorty. I was not short but about average. College was not for me mainly because I never found a course or instructor I liked. The basic courses such as English and History came easy and maybe even boring. I was 19 years old and a fast car was my greatest desire. Chasing women came in a close second.

After a year and one-half of college I quit and found a great job selling cars. Uncle Sam kept a close watch on men not going to school that had a 1-A Classification. The Vietnam War was going full blast and Uncle Sam took everyone. Yes, Vietnam was not an official war but anytime there were bullets flying around my head, I considered it war. I never backed away from a fight and my strong desire as a survivor made me military material. I even kind of liked the idea.

I was the youngest of three boys and my two older brothers, Jeff and Andy, had already joined the Navy and Air Force. Three boys in the service were almost more than mother and dad could handle. Their every moment was waiting to hear from their boys. Letters were read hundreds of times and mother and dad traveled all over the States just to get a short visit.

Mother and dad lived on a farm, a small farm of 100-acres most of their lives. They were just country folks but had moved to Fort Worth, Texas looking for work in the 50's. My dad was a machinist working at a place that manufactured oil-drilling equipment. He never missed a day or was never late for work his whole life and he made a salary that was ridiculously low. My mother did not work but kept us three-boys in tow. We lived with little extra money to spend and my mother sewed our clothes, cooked and kept the house sparkling clean. We had great times, as a family and maybe being poor was a key. As kids, all three of us boys had jobs mowing lawns or just picking up soda bottles for the deposit. The only money we had to spend for ourselves was what we could make ourselves. Mother always taught us respect for the family and that meant no talking back and saying "Yes Sir" and "No Sir."

Therefore, when the draft notice came for me, my mother was a basket case. She could never understand how the Government could take all three of her boys to war. The evening news gave reports of how many soldiers were killed everyday and it was 50 to 200. That was the total focus of mother as she watched. My report date was only a few weeks away and I was not sure how to handle my parents when I left but I was soon to learn. It was time to get all my affairs in order at home that meant saying good-bye to all my girlfriends, selling my car, and clearing out the mess in my room.

It was August in Texas and that meant hot, 100-degrees hot. Maybe that would help me adjust to Vietnam. Everyone said it was hot, wet and humid. I packed a small bag of personal items and the day came to report to the basic training. A scene at the airport would be an under statement. Mother was crying and dad was holding her back as she tried to get on the airplane with me. I knew it would come to this and somehow I had my mind prepared. The plane left Dallas for Fort Bliss in El Paso, Texas with several mothers crying at the gate. El Paso, the land of no trees and many cacti was even hotter as we got off the plane. The only comfort was that our sergeant was there to greet us and told us that he would be our mother for the next six-weeks. I thought that was nice. Arriving at the fort we could tell everyone was happy because everyone was singing as he marched.

Daily the sergeant lined us up in front of the chow hall and gave us about a 10-mile run before breakfast just to work up an appetite. For an old guy the sergeant was in damn good shape. We were taught that our rifle was our best friend and taking care of our fellow soldier was top priority. The food in the chow hall seemed to get better or maybe it was those long runs on hot pavement. We did a lot of shooting on the rifle range and being from Texas and hunting most of my life I received an expert ribbon.

After making friends with a few of my fellow soldiers all the fun came to an end and we finished basic training. I was chosen for the infantry and that was not a surprise. Two days after basic training, I was on my way to Fort Ord, California for survival training. That also meant I was thrown out of the skillet and into the fire. More weapons training and how to survive in a jungle was my menu daily. Surviving with no weapons or any survival gear was one of the main topics and I knew if I made it through I would be sent me straight to Nam. I was taught hand-to-hand combat and knew how to fire most any weapon the Army had in its arsenal. After training, I was given a 30-day leave so back home to tell mother and dad that I was going to Vietnam, no fun.

The departure was even worse and I had a 16-hour flight to Vietnam to think about it. I do not like flying and this flight was like a tomb even on a commercial airlines. There were about seventy-five to a hundred soldiers on the flight. Some were going back for the second or third time. I grabbed an aisle seat, it gave me a little more security and I did not like looking out the window anyway. A black sergeant sat next to me. He was huge man of at least six foot-two. I introduced myself as Pat Taylor and asked his name. His reply was normal for a man that was going to battle for another year, "Sarge."

Believe me I called him nothing but Sarge. We talked small talk at first. He had a family in Mississippi and had been in the Army for twelve years. I tried to sleep but without success and finally the Sarge told me not to worry. I sat there, closed my eyes and they popped back open. I looked around and most of the soldier had that same glaze over their face. Some were trying to read, some trying to sleep, some just sitting twitching and one guy looked like he had been crying. We all were nervous, even the veterans. Not much conversation except for the occasional whisper was heard above the airplane's engines. Most of the men were no older than I and being sent to a jungle to do battle was terrifying.

I assume Sarge must have cared about his fellow soldier as he turned his face toward me and a stern look came across his face, "Let me give you some advice that might get you through this next year."

After all the advice that I had received in training, I felt there was nothing new he could tell me. I gave a second thought as his brow wrinkled meaning he was serious. "Staying alive takes a little common sense. Stay away from walking point and keep one eye on the point man at all times. He can help you or hurt you."

"What do you mean, Sarge?"

"Watch his moves. If he goes down, you go down. He's always the first to see trouble or get shot. If he goes down right, you go down left covering both sides. The most important tool you have is your eyes and ears. Pay attention to ever sound and movement. Walking along half a sleep will get you killed. Keep your eyes clean. Your eyes will save your life many times over. They will tell you which way to move before your mind will. Do as you see, not as you think. There is not enough time for reason with a bullet coming your direction."

9

I sat there soaking up his words and really had no idea what he was saying. Time would be a teacher and his words would remain for the remainder of my life. I had hunted deer and all kinds of other game most of my life and I knew about the eyes but deer don't shoot back.

The pilot gave orders to fasten seat belts for a landing. It was time. No one said a word, no one moved, and my throat filled with a huge lump. Surely all the others were not as nervous as me. I sure was not going to ask. The plane's wheel burnt rubber as they touched and no one even looked out the windows. As the plane rolled to a stop, I began to feel hatred. Fear seemed to turn to hatred. I took a quick look around and most of the men had the same look. Was hatred the sense that would keep us alive?

The plane stopped and the soldiers rose with pride and started toward the exit. The Sarge put his hand on my shoulder and said, "Good luck, Taylor."

I offered him the same and said, "I hope we see each other again, maybe even under peaceful circumstances."

I stepped through the door of the plane and air hit my face and I could feel and taste the smell of the country. It was the smell of bad soil, black water, and uncleanliness—death. I never got that smell away from me until I got back on the plane for the U.S. Still at times today the smell comes back to my memory. I turned to the young soldier next to me and asked, "Have you ever smelled anything like this before?"

"I'm not sure I have but it sinks like hell."

We walked across the runway wondering what now. We made a semi-formation of sort and a sergeant asked for our orders. The sergeant was about my height with a handlebar mustache and never cracked a smile. I am sure his only thought was, "Not another group of greenhorns."

I gave him my orders and we both took a long look at each other. Maybe he could tell the flight was not easy. He gave me one more look and said, "It's going to be a while before your chopper gets here. Why don't you lie down and get some sleep, Private. They'll call you when it is time to go."

He walked away and I threw my duffle bag on the ground and fell back against it. I pulled my hat over my face a bit and slept on and off for about an hour. I kept thinking about the many hours of training that I had completed and wondered if it would help at all in the foreign land. I sat up as the night was starting and took a quick look around, "I am not going to live through all this. I am not scared of dying but what about mother and dad."

I searched for a way and a reason then it hit me. North Vietnam had no right to kill and Russia had no right to provide supplies and weapons for war.

The more I thought about it the madder I got and that seemed to help. The anger made me fell mean and no one was going to kill me. If I was going down it would not be without one hell of a fight.

I waited and the night continued. It was quiet but off in the distance flares bombs exploded. It reminded me of the Fourth of July and that put a lump in my throat. I loosen my duffle bag using what little light there was and search for paper and pencil. I started a letter home to let my parents know I was okay. Just as I wrote "Dear Mother and Dad," the sky lit up and men screaming, "Incoming." There were no bunkers to hide. I was as scared as I have ever been in my life. I grabbed my bag and started to run with everyone else. I didn't have a clue were I was running. I saw a man-made wall about a hundred yards away and that seemed as good a place to be. Several other soldiers were headed for the same wall of sandbags. Bombs were exploding on the other side of the camp and the noise and flashes of light made me want to dig a hole right there. I made a dive for the sandbag wall and joined a sergeant. He said, "Get the hell down and grab the Claymore. Release it when I tell you."

I reached for the trigger and with an itchy trigger finger held it tight. Flares filled the sky, so many I could not count them. Other men filled the sandbag walls and I asked the soldier next to me, "Got any ammo?"

He handed me a clip, "Where is your ammo?"

"I just got into country about three hours ago and for some reason we were not issued any as yet. I guess they were afraid we would shoot each other on the plane."

"How did you end up in this bunker?"

"I just followed the crowd because I knew sitting out there on the ramp was not healthy."

"Private, you might make it back home, if you are lucky thinking like that."

Those words stuck with me and then I asked, "How often do they play these games?"

"Oh, not more than two or three times a night so just sit back and try to relax."

A lieutenant with a communications radio walking down the line of bunkers checking on G.I.'s stopped and took a look at me in shock. He turned and came to our bunker and looked me square in the eye, "By the looks of you, you are either ready to leave the country or you are in the wrong place."

"I'm new in country, Sir."

"Private, if any gooks get over the barbwire, you shoot the hell out of them."

"Yes Sir!"

The night continued and three or four hours went by with me waiting. Everything showed up except V.C. There were choppers, jets, tanks, and an assortment of trucks and jeeps. I was so tired that I could not stay awake and took a short nap with one eye open. It was breaking dawn and no more fireworks. The lieutenant walked by again and this time he acted like he knew me. "You, Private Taylor?"

"Yes Sir!"

"Get your ass to the central building. Your chopper leaves shortly."

"Lieutenant, where am I going?"

"Private, I have no idea, just go."

I picked up my gear and started to leave. The Lieutenant turned to me and said," Thanks for your help last night."

I nodded and started my walk back to the central building. As I approached the area there was another private sitting on his duffle bag. He was shaking all over as if he had fever. Maybe his nerves got the best of him and he finally was trying to relax. I approached him, "Want a smoke?"

He just stared straight ahead. I gave him a touch on his shoulder, "Hey, you made it through last night. Calm down, we have a long ways to go yet."

He kept staring straight ahead. A few minutes passed and I said, "You know you can talk or scream if you want. It won't hurt."

"It won't help."

"Why? It helps me at times. You need something?"

"Yes, a medic."

"Are you hit?"

As I spoke I noticed blood running down his neck. I kneeled down to make sure. Then I could see his whole side was bloody. I grabbed him gently and help him to lie down. He turned his face toward me. A huge piece of his skull was missing. I screamed as loud as I could, "MEDIC."

I pulled off my shirt to cover the wound as I keep screaming "MEDIC."

They finally came and lay him on a stretcher. I sat there with the blood on my hands and I started to shake. I had never seen a man with half his head blown off. I ran to the side and threw my guts up. I remembered this man everyday.

I kept telling myself that I could not go thought this. I had to keep my sanity and get home somehow. The sun broke the horizon as my first day in Nam ended. Only a year to go, God I missed mother and dad.

CHAPTER 2

A sergeant with a clipboard came walking into the area, "Taylor, get your shit together. The chopper will be here in ten minutes."

He called out five other names of men that must have been on the airplane but I had never seen them before. I was not sure were they had been all night. We nodded to each other as we picked up our gear. Two of the men were black and one of them looked like a brick wall, over six-foot and looked like a bodybuilder. The rest of us were just plain skinny and weak compared to him. I thought to myself, "Glad he is on our side."

We walked to the helicopter landing pad and was told to divide into two groups so we could load from each side of the chopper when it landed.

The procedure for a helicopter approach was for the chopper to radio the tower a few miles out. If there was not a battle going on at the time a flare was shot in the sky as an okay signal. If the pilot could identify the color of the flair correctly he was allowed to approach. The flair was shot and apparently the pilot got the okay. Within two minutes after the flair was shot the Bell Helicopter UH-1 Huey was landing between us. The dirt and rotor-wash blasted us. We threw our gear aboard and piled in. The Huey had no door and no one told us to buckle our seatbelts. As a matter of fact I did not even see any seatbelts. Two of us sat in the door with our feet on the landing skids as the Huey took off. The noise of the engine and transmission was so loud that talking without headsets was almost impossible. The sun was up the countryside looked beautiful from 1000-feet. So many colors filled our vision and it looked so peaceful. There was still a touch of red sky from the sunrise, which put the icing on the cake. The black man sitting next to me pointed down and said, "Me Cong Delta." At the time that did not mean anything to me but I would soon learn that the Me Cong Dealt was the hottest spot in

Vietnam. The North was moving to take Saigon and battles were continuous and bloody. From the air the Delta looked like huge rice fields. It was divided into acre squares and had dikes that allowed water to come and go. During the rainy season the squares were man-made lakes. Being from north Texas I knew nothing about growing rice but I would soon learn. The rice fields and dikes were the perfect place for booby traps and many lives were taken. There was no safe place on the ground or in the air in the Delta. The summer temperature was hot and when I say hot, it was 120 degrees in the shade. The humidity was high that it felt like a steam bath but the Huey flying at 100 knots kept us somewhat cool. The Huey approached the base camp and made a quick circle. Not a shot was fired at us, which surprised me. I saw no movement and everything was at peace.

There were a lot of Armored Personnel Carriers, APC, in the vicinity. An APC was the first modern "battle taxi"; developed to transport infantry forces on the mechanized battlefield. The main armament for this vehicle was a single .50 Cal heavy barrel machine gun, and the secondary armament is a single .30 Cal machine gun. The vehicle was capable of "swimming" bodies of water and I soon learned that was a real plus. It was not mission capable if any one track shoe was damaged. If the APC lost a track, broke a track shoe or threw a track, maintaining control was a bit hard. Land mines were a real threat to APC. I had great hopes of driving or at least riding on one. In the back of my mind I knew I was going walk. I was trained as an infantryman and the flag hanging from the flagpole was the Ninth Infantry Division. Along with the APC there was a short runway made into the jungle. At the end of the runway sat a small plane that looked like a Cessna 180. Later I would learn that those airplanes were the "Bird Dogs" of the Army.

The Huey made a quick circle as our altitude decreased finally touching down on a helicopter pad that apparently had been cleared out of the jungle. With the blades still turning, we grabbed our gear and jumped from the chopper. My eyes swept the area wondering how I could be here. There were several hutches made from sand bags and a few pieces of lumber dotting the camp. There were ammo crates creating the walls with screen nets covering the doors in an effort to keep the bugs out. That was a joke plus the rats and snakes had free rein of the hutches. The roofs were made of canvas tent material and with the sun and humidly it was a sweatbox. I sweat from the day I got to Nam until the day I left. Never would I complain about cold weather again. Soldiers were scattered through out the camp some sleeping and others reading, cleaning weapons and just talking. It seemed as peaceful as a tropical jungle could be with a few birds flying and making noises.

Loading my gear on my shoulder I turned to see a sergeant striding toward us. I did not know then but I would come to love this man like a brother. He was about 5'9" weighting about 160 pounds sporting a rough black beard. He looked a bit on the mean side or maybe he had been up all night. His eyes seem to stare through you and I knew immediately he was serious and took nothing from a private and most likely nothing from a lieutenant. He looked like a war machine. "People call me Cal cause I am from California," snapped the sergeant.

He started by reading our name from a list and asking us from what state we lived. If you were from Georgia, he called you George. My turn came and I proudly shouted out Texas. That meant he called me Tex from that point forward. Just because I had Taylor written on fatigue shirt meant nothing. I shortly picked up on the same lingo and to this day I never knew many of their real names. After naming us, Cal took us to our bunks and so we could stow our gear. We entered and there sat three men on cots cleaning their weapons. Weapon cleaning was done two or three times a day. A dirty weapon does not operate well and with no weapon a person would most likely get killed. Throwing stick really did not hurt the enemy. Cal opening remarks to the three men was, "We got new meat. They are really anxious to see a little action."

Without looking up the soldier on the right said, "Guess who's going on shit detail tomorrow?"

I had no idea what that meant but assumed it was bad. All three of their uniforms were full camouflage and having "new meat" did not seem to interest them in the least. The soldier's uniform that volunteered us for the shit detail had a patch identifying him as a member of the Big Red One and on top of that he was a scout. Well, that put me to silence knowing he and I were in the same outfit. The Big Red One usually got all the front line duty and had a reputation of being the best. This soldier was a scout and from what I had heard worked alone in front. They were the first one killed if seen or caught. They were also the ones that would go into what I called rat holes to flush out the V.C. The whole time the three never stood or acted like we were there.

Cal introduced me and told me to make myself at home. An empty bunk waited across the hutch so I walked to it and asked the soldier next to it, "Taken?"

"No, help yourself. He died two days ago."

A few low key questions came such as, "Where you from?"

15

I guess mainly they wanted to know any news from home if I happened to be from their home state. Not a smile was broken and there seemed to be wall between us at the start. I think they were really trying to say, "I don't give a damn!"

One of the men raised his head and said, "You're on your own Shithead. We are all short and not I or anyone else will lose his ass over you. You do as we tell you or die. Got it?"

Oh I got it alright these guys had made it through their time and they were not going to take any more chances to save my butt and anyone else. It was a long night with anticipation of a strike at any moment. I lay in my bunk with my eyes search every corner and my ears tuned to any movement. There was just no way to sleep thinking this was my life for the next year. Little did I know that it got a million times worse.

The next morning and it came not too soon, I found myself on a shit detail—literally. Because the country was so wet a 55-gallon drum was cut in half and sat on the ground with 2x4 board placed over the top. This was our latrine and every morning it was filled with coal oil and burned. Being the new guy on the block, it came my turn to handle that job first thing. Black smoke and a lovely smell came forth filling the camp with me watching it burn. The camp did have a semi-mess hall, basically a tent with a few tables and chairs. Breakfast was not that bad. There was no comparison to mama's kitchen but being in a jungle I saw no snakes or frogs on the menu. Conversation was short like usual and soldiers were in and out in minutes. I returned to my hutch and gave my bunk a going-over and finished unpacking my gear. Soldiers were lying in their bunks reading and seemed to be waiting for something to happen. I decided to join them and tried to finish my letter to mother and dad. By early afternoon Cal came by and told me to get to S-4, which was the supply, pick up gear and report for a meeting 1500 hours. S-4 was not a large place as the Sarge in charge, a little man with touches of gray hair, asked me if I was a scout. I said, "Yes."

How did he know? Did I have a stupid look on my face? He began issuing me camouflage fatigues, jungle boots, a steel pot for my head and a bulletproof vest. He stopped and looked me in the eye like he was going to ask me the most important question of my life. "What kind of handgun do you want?"

At home I owned an S&W .357 magnum and had learned to shoot it comfortably so I said, ".357 mag with a six-inch barrel."

He handed me a new S&W .357 magnum and loads of ammo. Next he asked, "How about a rifle or heavy gun?"

WAR FROM JUNGLE TO DESERT

I thought for a minute and gave him a solid answer, "M-60 with 1500 rounds."

"Holy shit, are you sure you want all that weight as a scout?"

The M-60 machine gun weighed twenty-three pounds of sore back and aching shoulders. The M-60 fired 450-550 rounds per minute of 7.62mm rounds. It provided a continuous stream of fire, unlike the M-16's that stopped when their magazine was empty. And it fired a heavier bullet, about the size of a 30-06. As he issued the M-60 I said, "I just feel better with it. I have my reasons."

"Hell, if that is what you want, you got it."

Returning to the hut with all the added gear Cal came by and looked in, "Get your stuff together. We are going out tonight."

The soldier sitting next to me came back at Cal, "What the hell are you doing sending this kid with us? You asshole! I'm due to go on R&R next week and I sure want to be alive to do it."

I found out later that R&R mean rest and retreat or a little vacation usually to Thailand. Cal replied, "He's got to learn sometime; might as well be now."

"Well, I ain't wiping his ass all night; you take him with you."

Cal nodded his head okay. Cal read off the names of the patrol for the night and the direction we were going. "For God's sakes, do things right tonight and stick to business. I want everyone back here in the morning."

We sat in the hut double-checking our weapons trying to kill the two or three hours of daylight. The weather had been good all day with patches of sun but the humidity was high making us sweat. Time slowly passed as I felt my nerves causing my stomach to go into knots. The others acted calm but they had to have a bit of the nerves. A black man in the corner played his radio as *I heard it through the Grapevine* was playing. I asked him if that was a new song and he asked, "You don't listen to music much, do you?"

"Not much recently. I have been in training. Good song."

At about an hour before dark I started putting camouflage grease all over my face. It was almost like a woman doing a makeup job. The camouflage techniques had been taught in training but this was the real thing. My hand shook a bit as I put the different colored strips on my face. I finished dressing with all the clothes and gear issued early. About the time I had finished one of the soldiers came by and took a look at me. He stopped and said, "Tex, you're not going to need all that gear. You will need to move fast at times and all that stuff will only slow you down. Take all your ammo, steel pot and a flash light but don't worry about the rest."

I gave him a look but assumed he knew what he was doing. He stayed with me a little longer and said, "Tex, do not fall asleep out there. It is a sure way to get killed or get us killed. A sleeping soldier is an easy target. Do not fall asleep! Another thing, if we run into V.C. try to get a number before opening fire. You want to know how many you are fighting. Don't try to be a hero. We all want to go home and a one—man hero is not the way."

The more he talked the more nervous I got. Quietly I asked, "Tell me something. What is the secret of staying alive out there?"

"Hell if I know but I watch Cal like he was a beautiful woman. He usual walks point and his every move is a key to us staying alive. Oh, he gets a bullet, your next in line so keep him alive."

I let my mind wonder trying to picture Cal as he worked his tricks.

Just then Cal stuck his head inside and motioned for me to come outside. It was not time to go so there must be something he needed to tell me in private. I got up and walked outside but Cal had not stopped. He walked and I took a few jogging steps to catch him. "Where are we going?"

He stopped and turned to me and I noticed his eyes were sad. My heart started beating harder as Cal said, "Tex, I have bad news."

My mind flashed in ten different directions at once. I waited for him to speak. "You are taking my place tonight. I leave in sixty days for home and this means you only have forty-five days to learn how to keep yourself and these men alive. I've been in this hellhole for ten month and somehow I stayed alive. I would give you all my experience in a pill if I could but it is just trial and error and a hell-of-a-lot of luck."

My shoulders fell limp and my eyes almost shut. "Cal, I don't think I can do this. I am not a leader or hero."

Cal's eyes opened wide and looked straight into me, "I guess you have to die in that fuck'in jungle. Private, you don't seem to understand, this is the U.S. Army and there is a war going on and you will do what you are told. This is not high school. You will do what you are told or I may just shoot your ass right now. Got it?"

"Yeah, got it!"

"Tonight will be your first night in class and the only way to stay alive is to stick to me. I walk, you walk, I lay in the mud, you lay in the mud or you can just take a bullet on your own. Do you understand that?"

I shook my head yes. "Private, DO YOU UNDERSTAND?"

"YES, SERGEANT!"

Cal continued, "Remember most of your fighting will be at night. That means you will be limited on your sight but use your other senses. Your ears and nose will pick up the slack. Listen to every sound no matter how small. The small sounds are the most dangerous. Goofing off and playing around has no place in the jungle at night. You will get a feel for the jungle and understand the signs and sounds. Never get into a hurry but at the same time move fast. Move like a cat, think like a predator. Look for the traps think about every step being a booby trap or a landmine. The traps are there and it is your job to find them without killing yourself or the men. Just remember, tonight stay close to me and watch. The squad has you and you alone to trust."

I found myself praying for wisdom and a little common sense. It was almost dark as Cal punched me in the chest, "Get mean, Tex, mean as hell. Grit is what we live on here."

I nodded my agreement as we walked back to the hutch. "Okay, get your gear so I can check you out before we go," Cal ordered.

I walked back into the hutch with my head down but with more self-confidence than I have ever had in my life. One of the soldiers looked up at me and said, "War is hell!"

"Yes, more than you know."

I gathered all my equipment and started to dress. I even put on my vest that was supposed to stop bullets. I had my .357 mag. on my belt and carried the M-60 as I walked out of the hutch looking for Cal. Cal met me and gave me a walk around. "That M-60 will get heavy as hell before we are finished tonight and if you drag ass I will leave you flat out."

"Okay, what should I carry?"

"M-16! It's light and you can move quicker and make less noise."

I went to supply and got an M-16. He was right it was a lot lighter and I could carry much more ammo strapped around me. I returned as Cal was gathering the others. I took a moment and sat down on a stack of sandbags wondering what would happen. I felt so tired and scared that I wondered if I could walk and staying up all night seemed impossible. Even with the sun going down the heat was still like a sauna and it sapped my energy. Sitting with the M-16 across my lap I thought about a girl back home. Tammy and I was an item and maybe she was worth all this, "So fight for her," I told myself. I sat there on the sandbags thinking of Tammy and watching the sun turn the sky a bright red.

CHAPTER 3

The sun was down and time to go to work. Cal called in a voice that meant all business, "Let's go. Do you have your compass?"

"Got it," I gave a quiet reply.

"Good! You might just need it. We might get separated and if that happens keep your mouth shut. I will find you. Just stay still and I will find you. Remember how to work a compass? Take a reading here at camp so you can use it to keep your bearings."

"Where are we headed?"

"Got an air report that Charlie was north of us. It's hilly and the jungle is dense and I mean thick."

Cal gave me a long look and said, "Hey private, you will do good. I have a strong feeling about you."

I gave him a nod and we started walking.

It was dark, I mean jungle dark but my eyes adjusted quickly. I counted twelve other soldiers headed toward our chopper pad. The Huey had its engines running and a soldier behind the mini-gatling gun mounted to the deck. This weapon could fire 6,000 .30 caliber rounds per minute and just made a roar when firing. Flairs were exploding in the distance and fear was all the way up to my throat. I wanted to throw up but did not. Cal motioned us aboard and as I came by he said, "Don't forget, shoot anything that moves and don't stop until it stops moving."

Those words need not be said because I was primed for anything. I was asking no questions. The Huey was only in the air for about fifteen or twenty minutes before it sat down. The pilot must have had night vision goggles. As soon as we hit the ground we scattered and sat up a perimeter as Cal talked to the base. He disconnected and told us that the area was crawling with

V.C. He turned to the men and said, "This area is hot so stay close to Tex and no dragging ass."

The men moved quickly into formation. I felt like a stranger in a foreign land with no one. There was no bond between the men and me but I had to lead them. The soldier behind me said, "I don't know you and you don't know me. You fuck up and I will blow you away. You hear me?"

"If I fuck up you or I will not live long enough to make any difference."

Cal turned to us and said quietly, "Shut up! We have more important things to think about than that bullshit."

Cal motioned for three of the soldiers to lag back and cover our rear. He told the remainder, "You know what to do. Do it and get it right. Tex, come with me!"

He took his map from his helmet, gave it a quick look and then started to walk. I followed his every step like I was his shadow. The jungle was thick, so thick that we had to push our way through it. The smell was more than bad almost like something dead. It would have been hard enough in the daylight but going through this in the dark was impossible. At times Cal would stop to communicate with the lieutenant that left me sitting in the wet. My head was like an owl turn from side to side waiting for something to move, nothing ever did.

A tap on the shoulder from Cal sent my heart right up to my throw, "Tex we are camping here tonight and see if Charlie will walk by us."

thought, "Camp? There is not even a dry spot to sit."

Sweat drenched my clothes like I was in a downpour. Staying dry was impossible and I kept hearing mosquitoes buzzing my head. I pulled out my repellent and covered as much of my body as possible. It only took Cal a second, "God damn private, are you trying to get all of us killed your first night? The V.C can smell that crap a mile away. If you ever do that again I will shoot you myself."

Cal grabbed a handful of mud and slapped it on my face, "You do the rest. I don't want the least amount of that smell in the air."

I picked up a handful of the stinking mud and smeared it on my back, neck and chest. I then knew how a pig felt and why they smelled so bad. We waited. It only took a few minutes before I felt a sting on my back, then several more on my face and chest. I had no idea what was going on until Cal came over and said, "Jungle ants, get them off."

I slapped myself quietly and pawed at my body. They kept stinging and I kept pawing. It was not long before their poison took effect. I began to feel sick and threw up, and then a fever started. I was shaking in the wet mud. Cal came by and poured water over my head, "They really hurt! I have been there myself." It was four or five hours before the poison and the fever left. By 3:30 it seemed that I had been there for three weeks. I just could not think about doing this every night. I sat there with my rifle across my lap waiting for the enemy trying not to think about the ant bites that were still burning. Cal was correct. It was lonely, dark and just seemed stupid to sit in jungle waiting for someone to come by and get killed.

The sky started to lighten in the east and I thought, "The sun, how wonderful."

Things around me took a different look. Trees became real and there was a river not far from us. Apparently, we had been waiting for a boat or raft to float by. The V.C had been used this river to transport weapons and supplies to a major offensive downriver. A quiet river flowing threw the jungle with birds singing and flying. The whole picture was not bad except for the ants. Again, Cal came by to check on me and said, "We are moving out shortly so if you are hungry now is the time to eat."

I dug through my pack and found my C-rations, "Yea!"

I soon learned the contents of these cans: one canned meat item; one canned fruit, bread or dessert item. There was also a B unit; an accessory packet containing cigarettes, matches, chewing gum, toilet paper, coffee, cream, sugar, and salt; a spoon, and can openers. Although the meat item can be eaten cold, it is more palatable when heated. I had no B unit and no can opener. Well, my hunting knife served as an opener and even cold meat I ate with pleasure. I even felt better with the 1200 calories. My parents had strict rules about dinner we always ate together and talked. Eating from this can made me think of home with what mother and dad would say if they could see me now. I bet mother would march up to Cal and demand that I get better food or she would take me home. My bothers came to mind and I prayed that they did not have to come here. Little did I know that one brother was in Hawaii and the other in Florida? We all three joined the service and it seemed I got the short straw. Being alone the girl I loved came to mind and how I missed her. We were just friends but I felt more than a friend to her. I carried a picture of her in my wallet and kept it wrapped in plastic so it would not get wet.

I was starting to open my wallet when Cal walked up, "Ready?"

"Sure, where are we going?"

"Never mind, if you get captured, not knowing might save your life. Pay very close attention to what I do and for God's sake watch for booby traps. You have to learn the signs. One mistake and you will take a leg off or die. We are into V.C. country and they do not like people surprising them. They are the masters of traps."

Cal called a medic and asked him to give me something for the swelling in my face and neck that occurred during my episode with the ants. The doc laughed and made some comment that most G.I.'s knew if they were sitting in an ant bed. He gave me a few pills and as he walked away he said quickly, "God soldier, just find a way to go home alive."

"Okay men, time to do a little hunting," Cal said. We waded into the river up to our chest. The water was cool and felt good but it had a muddy bottom with the smell of rotten eggs. I was up to my ankles in mud and as we crossed the stirred up mud when down stream. I thought, "All the mud is a dead give away that someone is in the water."

Cal was waiting on the other side of the river and told me, "Sit down and wait for the others to cross."

Even more mud went downstream. I was full alert expecting gunfire at any second. I waited. When the last man hit the bank everyone started to remove their clothes. "Tex, what are you waiting on, Christmas," Cal asked?

"Why? Why, are we stripping?"

"Don't ask, just do it."

I followed the other and soon we were all naked. One of the men said, "There are leeches in the river, dumb ass."

No one had to say another word. My clothes were off in seconds. I check every detail of my uniform. Cal came by again and said "Bend over."

We checked each other in the most private places. I found three of those little blood suckers on me but none had buried their heads into my flesh. I never felt them on me at all. They seem to attach themselves without anyone ever knowing.

We spent the next 3 or 4 hours walking in rice paddies. Rice was the mainstay of the Vietnamese people and even their social status depended on rice. Village solidarity was reinforced by shared beliefs, agricultural-oriented rituals, and cyclical ceremonies rooted in the agricultural cycle. Rice was tied to procreation, birth and death in human societies. Rice paddies served as graveyards preventing families from selling land. Water buffaloes were an essential part of rice farming plowing the fields and provide manure for fertilizer. Two to four crops per year were planted, depending on the area and water. Men did the work that requires strength, like plowing while women did the work that required skill, like transplanting and cutting.

We could not walk on the levees and dams due to booby traps. I guess the paddies were still used and were filled with water. Walking in the water meant wet feet and legs and soon my boots began to hurt my feet. About the time I was ready to call it quits, it got worse. We moved from the rice paddies to the jungle. I kept wondering how these people cleared the land to produce rice with only a buffaloes. The jungle was so thick and dense that we had to cut our way through it. The heat became even more extreme and insects thought we were lunch. Swarms covered us at times as we fought though the vines and trees. I was soaking wet with sweat swinging my machete. I had no idea what Tarzan had to go through to survive. No wonder he swung from trees and vines.

Cal and I were 300 meters in front of the platoon and I followed Cal's every step. A slight noise ahead caused us to freeze in our tracks. Again we heard voices and it sounded like Vietnamese. We both squatted followed by hitting the ground laying flat of our stomachs. At the same time I reached for my rifle and we started to crawl. I became aware of my senses being more alert than ever before in my life. I stopped breathing as every sound was as clear as a bell and my eyes were looking and seeing in every direction. I had a feeling of being very strong and scared out of my mind at the same time. I was terrified and I could fell my heart pounding so loud that I knew they could hear it also.

Cal stopped crawling and looked back at me. He shook his head downward at the ground. I had no idea what he meant. I hesitated trying to see what he was doing. He motioned with his head to come forward. Whap. His boot had kicked me on top of the head. Now, I was really confused. He shook his head no and then looked down between his legs and motioned me to climb on his back. I crawled along his body trying not to touch the ground. Finally we were head to head and with his hand he showed me what I could not see. There was a trip-wire across the trail and one false move could separate our bodies into many pieces. I managed to get off his back but I had no idea how to dismantle the bomb. Cal motioned for me to move to his side, I did. Cal whispered, "Move quick as hell until you get the V.C. in sight. I am going to blow this booby trap. When you hear noise, open fire. Remember they are there to kill you, so you had better kill them first. I will be there as fast as I can."

I thought about the men behind us and if we had not have been up front scouting they would be dead by now. This was my job and I knew I was saving American lives.

I did what I was told and started to crawl toward the sounds. I could hear them talking and knew there must be several of them, maybe ten or more. I was outgunned but I had surprise on my side unless I made a serious mistake. I was so scared that I was shaking and my teeth wanted to chatter. I held my mouth tight. I continued forward watching every limb and twig. One crack of a twig meant death for the others and me. My next obstacle was small pond. I stayed in the thicket and carefully and quietly parted the foliage just enough to see through it. I counted three V.C., so much for my estimate of ten. Questions flashed through my mind, were there more than the three? Had I heard ten? Worry covered me in a second and I was scared to take a guess of how many there were.

A noise to my left, I stopped breathing as the sound grew. There was someone walking and the person was right on top of me. Making a move was totally out of the question and I prayed he would not see me. He got to a point that I could identify him and sure enough he was on the opposite side. Charlie was almost standing on top of me. I did not know what to do. My first instinct was to open fire but maybe there were twenty more behind him. The three by the pond were still sitting and talking. He took a few more steps and we came face to face. I still lay there frozen but I know my eyes were like spotlights. Oh yes, he saw me. He made a move to get his rifle off his shoulder but mine was ready and I opened fire. Six shots fired and six shots hit his chest. I never stopped as I opened fire at the three by the pond. My finger never released the trigger until the magazine emptied the last cartridge into my M-16. The other three fell to the ground and there lay in front of me four dead men. I fell to my knees and prayed to God to forgive me. My whole body was numb as I sat there on the ground trying to breathe as quietly as possible. Another sound came from the rear and I swung my rifle but it was empty. I released the empty magazine and reached for another while never removing the M-16 from my shoulder.

Cal said softly, "Good job Tex, considering it is your first time out."

By this time the other men were approaching with great caution. Cal gave them a wave. They got to the bodies and began searching them for maps or any other useful items. One of the men took out his knife and cut one ear off all the V.C. I looked at Cal and asked, "What the hell is he doing?"

"Get use to it. They do the same to our dead. The V.C. believed that a person cannot go to heaven with a body part missing."

I just shook my head and thought to myself, "I am not worried about body parts, just the Sixth Commandment."

We continued to hunt but never saw another person for that day. Cal called for a pickup and we were back in camp alive.

CHAPTER 4

After my first night all I could think about was a shower and clean clothes. The shower came first and believe me a shower was not easy. A 55-gallon drum with holes in it, was hung, maybe by an ill tempered G.I., from a tree. The water flowed over me. It was cool and it felt like I was washing away the worries of the world. Even the mud came off, which allowed the water to flow over me. It was cool and it felt like I was washing away the worries of the world. Even the mud came off which made me feel almost human again. After being in the same clothes for a week, it was pure luxury to feel clean pants and shirt against my body. I had a dry pair of boot that felt like my Sunday-go-to-meeting shoes. Camp was a pleasure just thinking I had time to relax and talk to the men.

Back in the hut three men were listening to the radio as I entered. "Hey Tex, come on in for a smoke and beer. You have earned it. You are now one of us since you have a body count," said Country.

I never understood why we called him Country because he had a northern accent. I was not proud of the body count but I had no choice. "Sure I will have a beer but no smokes."

"Never hit pot before," asked Country?

"Naw never tried it. I can't say I ever had a need to try it."

"Where the hell are you from," asked another guy?

"Texas."

"Are you trying to tell me that Texas does not have pot?"

"Well, I am not saying that but I just never wanted to try drugs."

"Can you smell it?"

"Yeah and it smells a bit sweet. What does it do to you?"

"It will make you totally relax almost like two or three beers."

"Why not drink the beers?"

"Hell Tex, just try it."

Country held out a pipe but my attention turned to the other two men as they talked about home. They were talking about what they were going to do when they got back home. It hit me that I had been away from home a month, one hell of a month. I was not even sure I would be on this earth for another month and that hit me hard. I kept thinking about taking a bullet. My mind could not relax and I reached for Country's pipe. I took a long drag and started to cough. Country hit me on the back a few times like that was going to do me any good. "Okay?"

It took me a few seconds but answered, "I guess. What kind of stuff is this?"

"Don't worry it will relax you in a few minutes."

I kept sucking on the pipe and I did feel more relaxed. I sat on my bunk listening to music and forgot about the jungle. Evening came and after a meal in the chow hall I was in no pain. Cal informed us that we were not going out again. I lay on my bunk and wrote mother and dad until another soldier asked if I would turn off the light. The light was out but bombs and rockets could be heard from a distance. I just thanked God I was not in the middle of it. The hut seemed safe for now.

The morning came with Cal's voice, "Tex, you and Country fill sandbags."

Country mouthed back, "Cal, I am too tired and I need more sleep."

"Okay, you are off of sandbags and on latrine duty. That way you will not have to walk so far."

"Wait, I had rather fill sandbags."

"Too late, you had your chance. Now get moving."

Country and I stumbled from the hut. I gave him a look and said, "Sometimes you should keep your mouth shut. What are we suppose do?"

"You will learn soon enough."

We walked in silence and it took us about a minute to get to the woodshed latrines. The woodshed was a two-place outhouse and it came with toilet paper. The door even had a quarter moon cut into it. Country did not stop at the door but went to the back and raised a door that went all the way across it. There sat two oil drums. Country tied the door up so we could get to the drums. He and I pulled out the drums and dragged them about 50 meters into a clearing. We went back for a 5-gallon can of kerosene and poured it into both drums. Country threw a match into each drum and we watched it burn. Black smoke poured from each drum so we stayed upwind to avoid the smoke and smell. After the fire burned out, we got two new drums and positioned them in the woodshed. We were not going to look for another job so we sat on the side of a hill and talked. The conversation drifted to home and what kind of job we were going to do after we got back. The subject of girlfriends came to the top and I had to explain Tammy in detail. That killed a couple of hours so we headed back to the hut. Just before we got to the hut Country said, "I going to look for some beer."

"Sure, I am going to finish a letter to home."

Country must have found beer because I did not see him for the remainder of the day.

Another night came and the same noises and flashes of light were in the distance. A war was going on not far from us. I took catnaps as I kept one eye open expecting the worse to happen at any time. Nothing happen until Cal came by the hut and said, "Get your shit together. We are going out tonight. Get whatever you need and we will meet at 13:00. My heart sunk to my stomach again. I had rather clean the latrine. As Cal was leaving, Country asked, "Where are we going?"

"We are taking a ride."

I shrugged my shoulders at Country and asked, "What does that mean?"

"A ride with the mechanized unit. At times we go out on an A.P.C., not inside but riding on top. It carries 8 people inside but no one but the driver rides inside. That's okay with me because it is hot as hell in those things."

"Why do we ride on top?"

"Well, the roads or trails that the A.P.C. travels will most likely have a few land mines along the way. Oh, if you are inside and A.P.C. hits a mine the concussion will kill you. Riding on top gives you a better chance of staying alive. You might get a piece of shrapnel or broken bone but in most cases you will survive."

"Why are we not walking?"

"Hell if I know."

I started gathering my gear with a heavy load of ammo. Since I was not walking, the more gear I could carry. The A.P.C. was like a pack mule.

At 11:30 Cal came by and told us that the mess hall was open. "Chow down men, it will be a while before we get back."

I thought about the Last Supper. The food had not been bad. The cook usually did the best he could with what he had. There were no super markets down the street. As we walked to the mess hall Cal walked with us. He talked business most of the time, "Just because we are riding does not mean we can slack off. If we run into Charlie, Tex, you and I will be out front. Our real mission is to set up a perimeter around a well-traveled area and wait for Charlie to come to us. A.P.C.'s will be positioned a couple hundred meters away waiting for a call from us. When they come stay the hell out of the way and stay down. The gunners on the A.P.C.'s are not too particular about their targets. Any movement means a target to them. One other thing, remember it is night and when things get to popping people forget to watch where they are walking. The booby traps are still there. Watch where you are walking and stay calm. Also soldiers get trigger happy in a fight and shoot the wrong people, be careful."

Cal and I walked into the mess tent just as the lieutenant walked out. He gave us a half-smile and said, "You two just getting here? Hustle up we plan to leave in a few minutes."

"Yes, Six."

Six was what we called our lieutenant so if Charlie had ears around the base he would not know we were talking to an officer. Charlie was always around and knew more about us than we imagined. The mess hall had no fancy furnishings such as tables and chairs but crates arranged so men sit and eat. Everyone in the mess hall was wearing plain Army fatigues no camouflage was seen. I followed Cal as he turned to the right toward the food. I picked up a strange feeling and I noticed that no one would look at us. You would think that we had some kind of disease. I wanted to stop and ask, "What's wrong did I forget my pants?"

We got our food and walked to a crate. I asked Cal softly, "What is going on here? Something wrong with these G.I.?"

"It's your camouflage uniform. It is a dead giveaway that you are a scout. A scout is on the level of a green brae and some of the meanest G.I.'s in the Army. These people will not jack with you for a million dollars plus we have saved their ass so many times in the past. That patch on your hat tells them you are the first in and you know your shit."

They will give you the respect you deserve after you get them out of a hot spot a few times. We finished eating and left.

Cal and I loaded our gear and walked to the A.P.C. It was hot as usual and a few clouds dotted the sky. No rain in the forecast but our weathermen never hit 100 percent. We got to the A.P.C. and on top sat Country and two others. We climbed aboard and joined them. I gave Country a look and through, "This guy may be on the short side of a full deck. He always wanted to kill someone. If I could keep him away from me it would make me happy."

Cal carried an M-60 machine gun and he handled it like it was a baby. He knew every inch of that gun and if anyone was an expert of the M-60, it must have Country. Within minutes we had finished load and under way. The A.P.C. was smooth riding making me wonder why I ever walked. After a while Cal gave us our designation, the small town Tan An about twenty-miles from the base camp. Tan An was a port city on the South China Sea but the twenty miles was filled with dust. It always made me wonder how a country with so much rain could be dusty. The scenery was not bad with rice paddies and jungle on both side of the road. Tropical birds and oxen in the rice paddies were seen as we traveled. We were a bit noisy and twice we passed Vietnamese riding in ox drawn carts with a load of rice. They must have been going into the local market.

I was lucky enough to be on the lead A.P.C. that allow us not to eat the choking dust and see what was going to happen, if it did. The driver slowed and handed the lieutenant the headsets. The conversation continued for a couple of minutes and he then told the driver something. It was impossible for us to hear but Six had a smile on his face whether that was good or bad I had no idea. It must have been good because we got to Tan An without a problem.

Tan An was a disappointment with rundown hut along each side of the street. I did not expect to see a five-star hotel but this was poverty-stricken. We drove along the street and saw no one. Meat hung in front of some huts and how could these people kept from getting food poisoning. Not one person in the street and a bad feeling hit me, ambush. An occasional dog would come out to the A.P.C. as we passed but that was it.

Cal felt the same as he said, "Now is the time to pay attention. I think we are going to Saigon because I heard that North Vietnamese had penetrated parts of the city and we will run those bastards back into the jungle. Anyone speak French? In the mid 19th century, the French with the aid of the Spanish invaded Saigon. This event was the precursor to the long struggle between the people of Vietnam and France leading to the historical defeat of the French in 1954. In the years after the defeat of the French, Vietnam was divided into two separate countries and Saigon became the hub of resettlement for many as people from north and central Vietnam immigrated south. Already heavily influenced by the French in terms of culture and style, the city had an air of a French provincial town with a Vietnamese twist. Saigon was dubbed the *Pearl of the Orient*. With a population of over 5-millions people, Saigon is one of the densest urban area in the world. On many streets, it is common to see houses with the ground floor converted into a business front while several families share living areas on the upper levels."

Country turned to me and with a half smile said, "Where does he get all that shit?"

"He must have graduated from the sixth grade."

We made a few more turns and hit the pavement of Highway 12 to Saigon. To my surprise the highway was crowded with all kinds of military vehicles. Jeeps zoomed along the smooth road like it was an interstate. Soldiers waved as they passed but none had smiles.

I gave Cal a quick look and asked, "What's going to happen in Saigon?"

"Snipers! They love to take free shots at Americans."

"Okay, how do we get them?"

"Easy, we drive up and down the street with a bull's-eye on our chest and see if we can get someone to fire on us. If they do, then we kill them."

Cal leaned back to Country and said, "Who wants in?"

Everyone on the A.P.C. reached into their pockets and pulled out a $20 bills and handed it to Cal. Cal motioned to me, "You in?"

"In what?"

"Everyone puts twenty dollars into a hat and the one with the most body count wins the pot."

"What the hell."

I pulled a twenty out and gave it to Cal. Six gave us a bad look and said, "Knock that shit off and pay attention to business."

Thinking that Six knew something that we did not I turned my head straight ahead and watched every inch of the road.

Country raised his M-60 and said, "Hey, I need to see if this baby will fire."

He raised the barrel and let loose with a couple hundred rounds spraying dirt along side the road. "Alright Sweet Thing, you still have it."

Darkness was closing and the pit of my stomach was turning over with pure fright. Just like the Bible talked about evil loving darkness, the evil was about to begin. Charlie and his black pajamas would show at sundown. "Cal, how much further," I asked.

"Not long now. We'll come to a road guard, most likely one of ours so don't get trigger-happy and he will allow us to enter. After that, be ready. Does everyone have his vest and steel pots on?"

All gave a nod yes. Another fifteen or twenty minutes passed and the P.V.C. slowed for the checkpoint. There were four South Vietnamese soldiers and they gave us a salute as we passed. I stared at their faces and tried to remember every detail. Maybe they would save my life one day. The vehicle kept rolling and after we passed the checkpoint Country said, "I hear after we leave here our butts are going to Da Nang. Now, there is some bad shit going on there."

Six gave him a bad look, "Shut up and pay attention."

We moved into the edge of the city and the streets were much narrower and they were empty. "Where are the 5-million," asked Country?

I felt like a rocket would come down from a second story window and destroy us all. My stomach was getting tighter. We traveled along the narrow road and I let my mind wonder back to home. Somehow Cal knew and he slapped my shoulder, "Time to think about business."

The Gates of Saigon were in view and my eyes popped open as I saw a large city. It was white with lights shining against it buildings and all I could think was beautiful. I knew a city this large would be impossible to defend. There had to be snipers and booby traps throughout. The gated area had bunkers with machine guns surrounding it, almost spooky. The Vietnamese soldiers had fears written over their faces but showed respect by stand at attention as we passed. These people were scared to live and scared to die. We made two short passes through the Capital and nothing happened. We started on the third pass and I noticed that we were alone the other tanks had taken different streets. We continued until the driver stopped in front of a small white building. For some reason Six got off and motioned for Cal to follow. They walked about twenty meters and stopped. We all sat on the vehicle watching as they talked. Both turned and headed back in our direction. They climbed on the P.V.C. and Cal said, "Let's go."

"What's the plan," I asked?

"Our orders have been changed. You will see."

I sat back and took Cal's words as law. My finger moved to the trigger guard on my M-16. It was obvious that we were leaving and going back to Ta Ann. On the way out of Saigon we took a right turn and entered a housing area. I thought, "What the hell? Has Cal got a girlfriend that lives in this area?"

The driver drove through the housing district like it was a Sunday drive. We stopped in front of a house. Cal motioned for me to follow and we both climbed down. I knew Cal had some kind of information about this house that he was not sharing and that scared me. I slid my finger to the trigger of the M-16. Cal, however, walked up to the door and knocked with not much caution. Maybe this was the house of Cal's girlfriend but I knew he did not need me. I turned back to the A.P.C. and saw Country with M-60 in hand covering my back. Another knock and the door opened. A Mamasan, a woman of a well-worn 40 or 50 years old stood with the door half open. Cal took a quick look inside the house looking past her. She gave a smile and opened the door for us to come in. We entered and she gave us nods with her head. I returned the jester in a small way. I never took my eye off the room and my finger was tight on the trigger. "What were we doing here," I asked myself?

There were curtains and quilts' hanging across the room and it was not the most appealing of smells in the house. The curtains separated the house into small rooms and I was sure we were walking into a trap. The Mamasan waved her arms into the air and spoke. I was not sure what she said but from the curtains came ten women. Cal gave me a look and said, "Pick one."

It was a whore house! "Hey, what's this?"

"I said pick one and don't knock a good thing."

Well, we both selected one and Cal gave the Mamasan a twenty. We escorted the two ladies of the evening to the A.P.C. and all climbed on top. Country had a smile on his face about a mile wide as he said, "Way to go guys. Now you are thinking."

The women got inside the vehicle and we hit the road again. It was dark and I mean dark with no lights in any direction as we traveled for about two hours. We passed a few old hutches but they must have been vacant because there was no life anywhere around them. The drive finally stopped near a rice paddy and we got off and set up a perimeter around the A.P.C. There were three men on each side but the driver stayed inside. After a short period the back of the A.P.C. was lowered and we hung a blanket across the opening. One at a time we took turns inside with the women. That lasted a few hours because most of the men wanted seconds.

CHAPTER 5

It was almost daylight and we were on our way back to delivery the women. We dropped them off and Six barked, "Let's go men. We are going to hut V.C."

We rode in quietness for a couple of hours and Cal leaned over to me and said, "We are headed in the direction of the Plain of Reeds."

"I hate to ask but what is the Plain of Reeds?"

"A vast wetland depression of about 13,000 square km of acid-sulphate soils. The Plain lies in a flat lowland region subject to seasonal flooding. The Plain dries out during the dry season and is covered in dense vegetation with small natural streams and tall grasses."

"That sounds like a favorite vacation spot but what do I need to know to stay alive?"

"Well, how good are you at locating booby traps? Just keep your eyes and mind on business and hope you see them before they blow your legs or body apart. If we run into trouble don't be running or moving too fast without looking at every step. Snipers love to hide in the tall grass similar to a lion waiting for a deer."

I gave him a raised eyebrow thinking of a lion charging through grass and water after some poor little deer.

"Oh something else, you will see a lot of bunkers and you can be sure they will be filled with some type of booby trap. Something like a 'top popper'."

"What the hell is a 'top popper'?"

"A very cheap and effective way to kill you. Charlie digs a small hole and inserts a nail with the point in the up direction. Then he places a bullet on top of the nail so if you step on the bullet the nail will fire the bullet. The bullet is just below ground but when it fires it will go straight through your foot and maybe your body. Get the picture?"

"I think I got it."

A small village with huts came into view and I was expecting a sniper. I tensed and took a better hold of my rifle. Funny thing, the driver drove right over one of the huts and never even slowed down. I think that Six had the same bad feeling of an ambush and he gave us an okay that the area was a free fire zone. I gave Cal an up shoulder gesture and he said, "Anything that moves shoot the hell out of it."

The A.P.C. continued toward the rice paddies with jungle just behind them. The gunner on top of the A.P.C. opened fired with rounds spraying the jungle. That seemed to be an okay sign because we drove to the edge of the tree line. Before the vehicle stopped we jumped off making a formation at the rice paddy dike. It was quiet and no one returned fired of our machine gun. That was even more of a scare. Of course, that machinegun was loud as hell and as it tore bark off the trees. I was on my belly and crawled over the dike. I rose up enough to see Cal and asked, "Which way?"

"Follow your nose, Tex."

I had no idea what that meant but I continued. Maybe north was a good direction and about that time Six yelled, "North, go north."

North might be the direction to go but which way was north. I pulled out my compass and took a quick reading as I walked along the dike. I thought this is stupid walking out in the open and the dike could be booby-trapped anyway. I turned into the trees and noticed I was alone. I did not see anyone including Cal. The jungle was thick with vines and vegetation. The only way I could make any ground was to cut my way through with my knife. It was hot and the more I worked my way through the jungle sweat flowed over my body. Steam came from me as if I had a fire burning inside me. That was not good; anyone could see and hear me. I stopped frequently and listened but all I could hear was the men behind me chopping their way through the jungle. God it was hot! I listened with ears and all my senses became alert. I had a bad feeling that we were in for a surprise. A few more meters and I came to a clearing. It was small in area but it gave me a break so I stopped and took a few minutes to get my bearings. I notice that my bootlace was loose and when I bent over to tie it I noticed a piece of paper. I tied my boot and took a closer look at the paper. Was it a trap waiting for someone to pull it from the ground? It was not paper but canvas. Just before I decide to pull up the canvas Cal appeared. "What you got?"

"A piece of canvas, maybe a tunnel."

Call took a closer look and said, "I think you are right."

35

The clearing must be drawing a crowd because Six came from the rear and asked, "What's going on?"

"Take a look for yourself, Sir," Cal replied.

"Look at what?"

"It's a fuck'in tunnel, SIR!"

"You going down, Sir" asked Country?

I looked around and several other men had joined us.

"No way in hell," replied Six.

Call motioned to Country to check it out. Country circled the canvas a few times trying to determine if it was a tunnel. He took out his knife and poked around the canvas looking for a mine or any kind of metal, nothing. He looked at Cal and said, "This may be a hot hole."

"The only way to tell is to open it," Cal replied.

Country took one corner of the canvas and started to pull it up. We took a good look for wires or any other traps. Country continued to pull and I grabbed the other side to help him. It was a tunnel and the opening was small, only one man could get through.

Cal gave a look to Six and with his hands offered him the entrance. Six gave him a middle finger. Cal turned to me and said, "Ready for a lesson? You might as well learn now. You got a handgun?"

I nodded yes. Cal continued, "Not enough room for a rifle."

I stood in a daze and finally said, "I don't think I can do it."

"Hell Tex, you are not a chicken shit."

"Cal, I have heard about these tunnels all the way through basic training and it was not good."

"I don't give a shit what you heard, you are going to be a tunnel rat or die right here and now."

Cal cocked his pistol and aimed it at my head. "Go or die!"

Six interrupted, "Is this really necessary?"

"Sir, you want to go?"

I starred at Cal and checked my handgun to ensure it had a bullet in the chamber and a full clip. I never took my eyes off Cal and said, "Go to hell!"

I was so scarred that I was shaking as I got on my knees to take a closer look at the tunnel. "Remember, it's a free fire zone and shoot any thing that moves."

No one needed to remind me as I tighten my finger on the trigger. "Oh, one other thing, I am leaving in two weeks and you have a lot to learn. Don't worry I will be right behind you. You want a scout patch for hat don't you?"

"Hell no, I just want to live."

I turned my flashlight on and started down the hole. Before I got all the way into the opening Call pulled me back and said, "You want to live or die? You had better turn that light off. That flashlight makes a great target."

I threw the flashlight on the ground and for some reason asked, "Anyone else want to take my place?"

Not a word was said. I said a prayer and slide into the tunnel. I knew it would be my last time to see daylight. Maybe I would see a very bright light very soon and I could follow it. I got my body about half way into the hole and there was a step cut into the dirt. Inside it was dry with not a whisper of a noise. The men above were quiet as a mouse and that left nothing to hear. It was dark, oh it was dark! I felt like a target with a bulls-eye on my chest. I could see nothing and heard nothing and then my eyes started to adjust. A smell of dirt and bad water filled my noise as I noticed the walls were wet. All this did nothing for my bravery and I could feel myself taking deeper breaths. I could now see a chamber cut into the walls, very clean which had to be done with a knife or ax. My eyes were getting better with time so I began to crawl along the tunnel. I had my gun in one hand making sure I kept it out of the dirt. The tunnel continued and I had gone about fifty yards when I saw a faint light coming toward me. I could tell it was a candle and that was not good. I stopped and I could feel my heart pumping so hard that I knew my chest was moving. Like a fool I turned to see if Cal was behind me but no. I was there alone and never felt more abandoned. Okay, I had to do a John Wayne and attach. I slowly moved forward as quiet as death and came to another set of steps. It was six or seven steps that lead downward. At the bottom of the steps was a large opening, large enough to stand. So much for being a rat and I took a minute to look around. The walls were lined with ammo and weapons. I saw Russian made rifles, grenade launchers, and everything else that a person might engage in a war. I kept wondering about the candle. This place was a hotspot and used regularly. I was sweating maybe from nerves but I was ready for anyone. I took a few more steps around the room and found more steps. I looked up the stairs and saw a person. Instantly my .357 mag was on the person and fire came from the end of my barrel. The noise was deafening but I never took my eyes off the person. The person went down. Shadows came from every direction and I fired and I fired until my .357 clicked empty. I was dazed and my mind was in darkness to the point that I lost control as the noise and flashes of gunfire surrounded me in the tight chamber. My fear was my only guide. I tried to reload when I noticed a dead silence. I stood sweating and breathing so hard that I knew my heart would explode. "Was it over?" I scanned the darkness looking for more movement but nothing moved or made a sound. I finally got my weapon reloaded and started to look around. Three men had been sleeping on cots and they lay dead, bullets through their heads. One man lay dead at the bottom of the exit and a person lay bleeding as he was trying to escape through another tunnel. I walked to him and found he was a woman. I checked for a pulse but she was gone. When I turned, my eyes caught sight of a terrifying scene. There lay a small boy about 6 or 7 years old bleeding from his chest. I rushed to him, picked him up and held him in my arms. He was not breathing and his blood covered me as I held him tight. I screamed as I rocked him back and forth, "Why God?" I threw my gun on the ground as tears flowed down my face and I wept out loud. I did not know what to do. I just held the boy like he was my own. The woman must have been his mother but how could she leave him. He was just a child living in a war. The scene and my emotions were like a red-hot branding iron touching my brain. It was there and would remain forever. I laid the child in one of the beds and covered him.

I found my weapon and tried to locate the way out. There were tunnels leading in all directions so I picked one and started to crawl. I was lucky enough to pick one that lead to the outside or maybe they all did. I pulled myself through the opening and swallowed a mouth full of open-air. It might be my last I kept thinking V.C. would be waiting for me to pop-up like a rabbit. Just to get away from the smell of the tunnel was worth the moment of danger. I sat on the edge of the tunnel and put another clip into my pistol. I was still breathing hard and almost felt like a bull-in-a china-closet making so much noise. "Where was Cal? Where was anyone that cared about the Stars and Stripes?"

I must have been three or four hundred yards from the point that I entered but what direction. "Damn, I was lost."

The .357 Mag was not much of a weapon in a fire fight so my worse might mare was about to come true. I had to return the way I came. I took a few more breathing treatments and started back down into the hellhole. It took another few minutes for my eyes to adjust and I began crawling. I came into the room with the bodies and refused to stop or look. All I could think about was the squad waiting at the end of the tunnel. I poured on the speed and I could see the opening. I began to feel better and a smile came across my face and I gave myself a pat on the back as I emerged from the tunnel. I grabbed for more air and took a quick look and no one was there. I quietly gave out a long line of profanity. I was starting to panic and told myself, "Calm down those bastards can't have left me. Maybe so, they might have thought I was dead and no one was willing to take a look."

I was really on my own and no one would be looking for me. I had to get out of this alone. The jungle seemed to get darker after a look around and my .357 was no match for anyone. It came to me. There was all the firepower I needed underground. I jumped back into the tunnel and made my way back to the room. I want to carry everything but grabbed a Russian AK-47 and all the ammo I could carry. After all the AK-47 was the most widespread weapon in the world. It must be a damn good weapon. I stuck a few grenades in my pockets and started out. Before I left, I rigged a booby trap of my own and laid several grenades just underground with the pins removed. Anyone walking through the area would sure get a big bang out of it.

I had a compass, weapons, two good legs, and maybe a little common sense so I started walking. I remembered Six yelling to stay north so I started north. I knew those bastards had to be in the area if I could find tracks. The jungle floor was soft and it did not take me long before I found tracks from the A.P.C. and they lead north. I took every step as quiet as possible and watching every place that my foot touched the ground. I stopped every few yards taking a 360-degree glance. My time was running short and figured it was around two hours until dark. My plan was to walk until dark and then sit all night. Walking lost in the daylight was bad enough but walking through unknown jungle at night was committing suicide. Walking alone puts all kinds of thoughts into a person's mind such as how far is home from here and what is mother cooking for dinner. Being captured entered my mind and living in a POW camp would be worse than death. I just could not do it so I decide I would go down in a blasé of glory before I would let them capture me.

Dark came fast and I looked for a place to call it a night. At the edge of the jungle line was a cut out in one of the dikes. There I had a good view in all direction so I leaned against the dike with the AK-47 across my lap. I was so tired that I could have slept on a bed of nails. After all the sweating during the day it starting to get cooler, almost tolerable. That brought up another pain I was hungry. Mother's cooking flashed through my brain and I could smell the chicken frying. I tried to stay alert but my body kept telling me that I needed to rest so I leaned back against the dike and closed my eyes. It was dark and I was camouflaged enough that I felt safe, well as safe as I could in the middle of the jungle. With my eyes closed I noticed the sounds of birds as they found a nearby tree. They were a good alarm incase anyone came by. The night was beautiful as I went in and out of sleep. Suddenly I was awake, but not awake either. Was I dreaming but I heard voices in the distance. My right hand located the trigger of the AK-47 and now I could see three figures moving in my direction. The birds flew which ensured I was not dreaming. They were so close that I could smell them within a minute but I held my fire. Three men alone out on a walk at night were a bit fishy. There had to be more and if I killed these guys I might have a hundred breathing down my neck. They passed and that event kept me awake until dawn. I was so glad to see the sun and I continued with my plan to head north. It was almost noon when the jungle became so thick that I had to chop myself a trail. Sweat was pouring from me and I had no water.

An hour passed and I came to a clearing. I stopped and scanned it carefully hope to see my squad, nothing. I continued and next I came upon a hut along side of a rice paddy. I was a hundred yards from the hut when I saw a man standing in the doorway. I did not think he saw me so I found cover and waited. It could be a trap or maybe the man was a rice farmer home for lunch. His wife or a woman in the hut came out and he began to take her clothes off. Was he doing it for my benefit or his? The woman seemed to enjoy it and it was good to see someone making love and not war. I just had a bad feeling so I stayed there for a period without moving. No one else showed and the man and woman were in the hut. I was so hungry that I decided to go toward the hut. I visualized every step watching for booby traps. As I approached I could see the woman washing clothes at the back of the house. She saw me and gave me a hard look. I raised my arm that was not carrying the rifle and she bowed to me. I returned the greeting and she smiled. She was an older small woman with splashes of gray in her hair. She did have all of her teeth or what I could see and looked as if she had worked the rice paddies all her life. She offered me a place to sit and I took her proposal. She left me sitting and went into the hut. This I had a bad feeling thinking trouble was going to happen very shortly. She returned after a few minutes with a bowl of steaming hot rice. The bowl of rice could have been a two-inch prime rib and I took it without any doubts. She sat beside me as I ate but said nothing. I finished it quickly and she offered more but I said no thinking this was all that she had. I stood and gave her another bow and offered her a little change in my pocket. She refused to take it with a smile. I asked her in my version of Viennese, "Where G.I.'s?"

She pointed to the north so I assumed she and I were on the thought-waves. Again I bowed and she did the same.

As I walked away I said to myself, "Holy shit, I just carried on a conversation and ate food with a person and we never said a word."

CHAPTER 6

The morning continued to get hotter but after a short period of whacking through the jungle I came into another clearing. This one was large and I could see a long ways. I waited before starting but then I saw a welcome sight. The A.P.U.'s were moving north on the other side of the clearing. I wanted to scream with joy but decided to keep my mouth shut. I jogged across the clearing and Six saw me, "Tex."

Everyone turned to look and gave a cheer. Cal turned and walked toward me and as he got closer I could tell he was staring into my eyes. He grabbed me by my shoulders and said, "You lucky son-of-a-bitch, you got a good education last night."

"You just left me! You had better hope I did not learn too much."

He smiled and turned away. "Wait, why did you not wait for me," I asked?

"We got into one hell of a fire fight of our own. We lost a man. What happened underground?"

"I had just as soon not talk about it."

"I see you took a bullet or shrapnel to the head. Get it looked at. The medic is over there."

"Who did we lose?"

"I had just as soon not talk about it," replied Cal.

I walked to the A.P.C. and the other gave me a hand up. "God, I am glad to see you," Country said.

One of the men threw me a can of C-rations. The medic came to me and started clean my head as I ate. He then took a few stitches. "By the way, this little wound gives you a Purple Heart" the medic said.

I gave him a look and said, "Do you really think I care?"

The medic returned the look and never said another word. After he had finished I leaned back on the A.P.C. and fell asleep.

After another three days of riding the A.P.C. through the jungle and nothing eventful happening Six turned us to the base camp. I felt dirty and I know I smelled dirty because everyone else did. The base camp was like a vacation. I took a long shower and even shaved. My head was better but it still hurt like hell at times. Country came by and asked, "Want a beer?"

"Sure, you got some?"

"No but Illinois stole some last night and I would say we just take some of his."

We walked into a hut where several G.I. were smoking pot and drinking beer. Country walked in first and I followed. One of the men in the corner said quietly, "Look at the patch on that son-of-a-bitch's hat."

Country turned and looked at me and then the guy in the corner, "Yes, he is mean as hell so don't give him any shit."

"Don't worry I'm not fucking with him."

I looked at him and said, "Hey, I not looking for ant kind of trouble."

The G.I. in the corner said, "Come on over and have a smoke and a beer."

I took his advice and sat down opening a beer. He looked at my head, "You get hit?"

"Yeah."

"Bad?"

"Enough for stitches but that about it."

He made a semi-toast as he clinked his bottle against mine.

"Where are you from?"

"Texas," I replied.

"Damn, I have a brother that lives in Houston. I guess we are just ole country boys, hum, Tex. How did you ever get to be a Scout?"

"Just one of those things that happen. You don't ever volunteer for anything but they pick your name out of a hat."

"I know what you mean. I was lucky enough not to be Scout but I ended up here. What your name?"

"Pat, Pat Taylor and I have only been here a few weeks."

"Most everyone is talking about you around camp. You sure made a name for yourself in a very short period of time."

"I am just trying to stay alive."

"Huh, the word in other squads is that you are living on the edge. Some say you are mean as hell and others claim you are insane. Me, I think you are a little bit of it all. Mr., you scare me."

43

I gave him a grin and took a slug of beer. He stood up and said, "Yeah, I'll follow you into anything, any place and anytime. That is as long as you are in front of me."

"I would not follow me too close, trouble seem to follow me."

"Hey, you are the talk of the camp."

"Well, I guess they need someone to talk about. It really does not matter to me. What's your name?"

"Ark."

"I guess that means you are from Arkansas?"

"You got that right. Searcy to be exact."

Cal walked by the outside of the hut. Ark leaned in my direction and said, "You do know you are talking Cal's place? You will have to be one hell of a soldier because Cal is the best of the best. No one is better than saving G.I.'s than Cal. He should be a General."

I returned with a slow answer, "I didn't know I was competing with anyone?"

"You may not think so but everyone here is watching you. Cal has a body count of over 600. Think you can beat that?"

"I sure hope the hell I don't!"

Cal came back by carrying a M-79 grenade launcher and saw me talking to Ark. He stopped and entered the hut. The M-79 looked like a cutoff single barrel shotgun on steroids. He approached me and pointed the barrel of the M-79 at me and said, "Put your mouth over the end of the barrel and cover it with your hands."

As I did it Cal took a big drag off a joint and blew down the barrel. "Breathe in hard."

I did and it was quite a rush. I laid back and enjoyed the moment. Cal made a small giggling noise and walked out. I sat there trying to determine if Cal was a hero or asshole. At times he was the hardest man that I have ever known but then he had a streak of kindness. I did respect him and he was almost at the top of my list of heroes. He would be going home in two weeks and I would surely hate to see him go.

The war went on but I got to stay in camp for seven days without hacking my way through a jungle. I knew things were too good. Cal comes charging into my hut and screamed, "Get your shit together. We are leaving in five. There is another company in a jam and we are going to the rescue."

"Do we ride White Horses?"

Cal never answered but I knew he was serious. That could only mean that "A" Company had gotten themselves in trouble and it would be up to us to bale them out. I grabbed my gear, my new M-16 and all the ammo I could carry. I kept the AK-47 in the hut hoping to get it home somehow. Within minutes we were loaded into a Huey Helicopter and on our way.

The Huey flew for thirty minutes in the direction of the Delta. From that point I could see fighter jets making passes through the area. F-4's rained fire and hell down to earth and it was without a doubt going to be one hell of a battle. It was our drop-off spot and the Huey came to about tree level with a hover and moved to a small clearing. The helicopter gunner opened fire with the deck mounted 50 cal. machine gun giving us a bit of cover as the Huey got within five feet of the ground. My gut feeling was that the Huey was not the safest place to be since it was a very large target and carried weapons and fuel. I jumped hitting the ground and the others followed me. Cal screamed above the noise of the Huey for us to stay together. I took a quick look around counting heads as we formed a line walking in the direction of the trees. Six gave instructions over the radio, "They are dug in. Get those SOB's out."

Cal gave me a look and said, "That brave officer is leading us from the Huey."

Cal motioned for us to scatter and we moved in the direction of the tree line. We met fire almost instantly and I returned fire with everything I had. I threw grenades and bullets in every direction. I heard a grinding noise to my left and there was Country digging up dirty, tree, and bodies with his M-60. That machine was mean. Country stopped firing and spit. "Hey Tex, good day to die?"

"What are saying? This is not my day. I have a lot of living to do."

Two more steps and my eye caught a glimmer. I froze and looked down. My ankle was pressing against a trip-wire. I screamed as loud as I could, "Stop, freeze!"

The other did just that but kept firing without moving. I carefully bent down and gave the wire a closer inspection. Yep, a booby trap! Country walked around behind me and took a look. Country shook his head and asked, "You want me to do it or would you like the honor?"

"Damn, I will do it so stand back."

I gently took the line in my right hand and held it in place until I slid my boot from under the line. I kept the tension on the line and took a breath. I knew one false move and it would be my blood and guts all over Country. Country with a half smile said, "What are you going to do now?"

"I don't know! I am scare as hell."

"Damn Tex, I knew I should have helped. May I suggest that you keep tension on the line and walk the line one way or the other until you find the bomb?"

"You can suggest anything but stay back. No use in both of us getting killed."

I took a 50-50 chance and followed the line to my right. I moved slowly trying to think like a V.C. Are they mostly right or left handed entered my mind, would they put the explosive to the right. If it was left I was wasting a lot of time and it was hard on my nerves.

A few more feet and the line ended and it was attached to a grenade. A G.I. following behind caught up to me and saw the grenade. The G.I. bent down and wanted to pick it up but I grabbed his hand and screamed, "What the hell are you doing? That is a grenade and I mean a live grenade. Do not touch it!"

"Tex, I think it is a smoke grenade."

He reached for it again.

I touched him gently and said, "You touch that grenade and I will kill you personally, it the grenade does not."

Six had made his way from the helicopter and had joined us. "What's going on, Tex?"

"I am in a fix here with a grenade and this guy thinks it is a smoke grenade."

Six walked within a few inches of the G.I.'s face and said, "Move back, Private! Why do think Charlie would put a smoke bomb here in this battle area?"

I interrupted, "Damn people this is my life you are dealing with so I will handle it."

I gave the Private a hard look trying to think of what to do, "I don't know how long you have been in country but shut up and listen. Some V.C. grenades are designed to explode without delay and they look like our smoke bombs. There is no delay and I mean it blows instantly and you are dead. Understand?"

Between my words and Six the guy backed up about ten yards. I thought I was green but this guy was death waiting to happen. I asked quietly, "Where is Cal?"

Six turned and said, "I have no idea. You are on your own."

Six backed up with his arms in the air like he was surrendering. I had no idea what to do but it was time to do something. I reached down and gently picked it up making sure I held the handle. I was expecting it to blow any second but it did not. I just held it shacking inside and making sure I never moving my hand. I looked for a substitute pin to make it safe. I knew a small stick would not be strong enough to hold the handle. I still refused to move in any direction. Country came to me, "I have an idea. Put your arms around that tree holding the grenade on the opposite side and lay it on the ground. If it does blow, you will only loose a hand."

"Thanks a lot. Can't you think of something better?"

"Not really."

I motioned everyone back with my free hand and then wrapped my hand with the grenade around a tree. I went to my knees and laid the grenade and my hand on the ground. I said a pray, took a deep breath and opened my hand. The grenade just lay there and I could feel some V.C. laughing. I thanked God and backed away. We all made a circle around the area and when I was about fifty yards away I opened fire on the grenade. The damn thing blew up.

We had only gone about 50 yards into the jungle when I realized that we had delayed enough for the V.C. to be dug in. We had a feeling that the trees were full of snipers and the ground covering men in black pajamas. I spread the word to take it easy and slow. Companies A and B had taken a real beating and I could see why. Fighting people on their turf was a real disadvantage. I felt like a ant moving through the jungle looking for Goliath. We continued and we could see and hear jet aircraft dropping bomb ahead of us. We could feel the impact miles away. Also C-123's flew in all directions spraying Agent Orange. The C-123 flew low and slow taking all kinds of hits, some of the planes looking like patchwork quilts. Agent Orange was an herbicide that killed all vegetation that it touched. Even though we were not leaves or bushes we felt the results. Agent Orange had a chemical odor and our eyes burned with each pass of the aircraft. Any open wounds would burn like you had gasoline poured on them. It only took overnight to kill the vegetation. I kept wondering if that stuff would kill weeds at home but it kill everything including grasses. If the Government had planned eliminate Charlie from hiding in the vegetation, it worked.

Six walked near and said, "Cal has been hit, you are our point."

"How bad is Cal hit?"

"Bad enough that he will never use his right shoulder again."

My heart sank. He only had two weeks left. How could this happen? He was extra careful and knew the V.C. and jungle like his backyard.

"Are you sure it was Cal?"

"Hell yes! They are carrying him back to base camp."

I never saw Cal again. After I returned I looked for him several times but was never able to find him. I wanted to say good-by and tell him thanks for keeping me alive.

The fight continued all night and most of the next day. In my platoon we had Cal and two other hit. For the next three days the killing went on. We lost more men with four being killed. The V.C. took a lot more hits but no one surrendered. The fight seemed to last forever as Uncle Sam held the line and returned even more of what they received. There was no sleep and that caused errors. Encourage came from every man there and I felt proud. We were in a foreign country fighting for the freedom of a people we did not know but the word freedom was said by each. The people we were fighting must be brainwashed because every person I killed was younger than me, most were fifteen or sixteen. We were killing kids but kids that would kill you without hesitation. The kids were not soldier they were people that had no other option except to fight. God, I wish I had one shot at their leaders.

The mountains were rugged and when night came the temperature dropped and I sat shivering. I was tired and craved a good meal and just wanted to sleep. Those conditions were the formula of getting a person killed. No matter what happened I had to be clear of every decision and move. During the day the Air Force gave support trying the clear areas with 10,000-pound bombs. I was amazed after each bombing run to see the damage that the bombs did to the jungle. I pitted the person that might be in the range of the bombs. After the fifth day of jungle fighting wondering what it would take to push these people back to the north. They gave us the word that we were going back to base camp. I had lived through another battle and I thanks God every day.

CHAPTER 7

A shower and food was top priority as the Huey landed at the base camp. I lay in my bunk thinking about Cal and wondering how he was doing. I felt a need to say something to him. I got up and started asking questions and found out that he was already done. Damn, I hated that.

The next day I was sitting on a stack of sand bags with Country. We were drinking beer and Country was a little over the edge. When Country gets drunk he gets emotional and talked about home for hours. I laughed at time as he told about his life in the States. He had funny stories and the more he drank the more serious he because. The camp always thought of Country and I as being crazy. Well, maybe we did live on the edge but both of us were joined to a common thread, just being country boys.

Country did have a temper and fighting with other G.I was common. He was one of those mean drunks and after a few he just got wacky. One time he and a G.I. had a few words and Country jerked out his knife and cut the guy across his face. It was not a small cut and before the G.I. could respond I stepped between them. I pushed Country backwards and he fell. He jumped up and came after me but before he got there I had my .357 mag pointed at his head. "Get out of here and cool off. Someone is going to get hurt bad, understand?"

Country put the knife away and offered me his hand. He left with a beer in his hand. I could always depend on Country in a fight and he would be the man I would want beside me.

Back to the sandbags, Country and I spent a lot of time there. It seemed to be a place away from it all. We talked about home and girlfriends mostly. We talked and laughed about our first loves and used our imaginations to relive the desire of a woman. I had to tell him about Linda Grossbeck. She

49

was my first that heard the words, "I love you," from me. Our B.S. continued until we heard, "In coming, in coming," interrupted our evening. I jumped off the sandbags and pulled Country with me. The bunker was about 100-yards and we spared no time getting there. Those bastards would send a few mortar shells around dark into our camp just to keep us worrying all night. After the bombing stopped most crawled out of the bunker but I looked at Country and he was asleep. What the hell, I lay down and went to sleep beside him.

A few days later I was walking through camp when Country caught me, "Get to ammo dump and get all the ammo you can carry. We are moving up river in about fifteen minutes."

"Thanks for the warning. How bad is it?"

"Bad enough."

I ran for my hut and grabbed what I need from there. My rifle was clean and operational, boots were dry, knife was sharp, and I put a machete on my belt. I then ran for the ammo. I packed all I could carry and then headed for the helicopter pad. The Huey's blades were turning and I loaded all my stuff. It lifted off and we flew for 30 or 40 minutes along the river. Again we were flying low and easy pickings for ground fire but nothing happened. The Huey started along a large hill with trees and a lot of jungle. There we picked up 6 other choppers and formed a line looking for a place to land. Smoke came from the ground and I could hear the pilot scream, "Sam, Sam."

The missile came blazing by us and hit the Huey behind us. A huge ball of flame erupted to our rear and then the blast hit us. It tipped us to the side and then covered us with flaming pieces of aircraft. The G.I.'s never had a chance to do anything. They were dead instantly. Our pilot put the Huey in a dive and pulled the collective full up to stop us about ten feet from the ground. No one had to tell us to get out. We all jumped from the helicopter and rolled trying to keep from breaking any bones. I was lucky enough to keep myself in tact and after rolling I came up with rifle in hand. I took a quick scan around and did not see anyone or hear incoming fire. We made a perimeter around the chopper and waited. Six was on the radio trying to get the direction of the V.C. He was off in flash and came to me, "Tex, take the squad over that hill and you should meet with another company of G.I.'s. For God's sake, be careful it is a bit different here because these guys have big-boy weapons."

I started as the squad followed about fifty yards to the rear. Six stayed to the rear. I topped the hill and there was nothing so I kept moving in the same direction. Finally at the third hill I came to a company of G.I.'s dug in. They had dug themselves holes in the ground and looked like they plan to stay there for a while. I sat down and waited for the squad and Six to show.

Six finally got there and he radioed that we were coming in. As we entered the perimeter I could see these guy had been here for a long time and they looked exhausted. I stopped at one of the bunkers and asked, "How's going?"

"Damn we are glad to see you. Not worth a damn. Hey, I see your patch."

I was wearing the Ninth Infantry patch. I returned the gesture, "Hey Like your patch too. How long have you been here on the hill?"

"We have been here so long that I cannot even remember when we got here."

"What so important about this hill," I asked?

"Hell if I know. Say, what that patch on your hat? I know you're a scout but I have never seen a patch like that."

"Nothing really, It's a point patch."

"Say no more, I understand."

"Tell me why we are here and who are we fighting."

"Like I said before not sure why we are here but we are fighting the North Vietnamese Army."

"Oh shit, how often?"

"The last two nights, all night and half the day. The really have no certain time, they just shell us whenever."

Six came looking for me and said, "We're moving out."

The G.I. in the foxhole raised his arm, "Give'em hell and walk a soft point, soldier."

I gave him a smile, "Sure, try to get some sleep tonight because if they get through us you will be back in business."

Six called all sixteen of us together and gave a little speech, "If you want to die be sure and do two things, talk and fall asleep. You new men stay put and if you get lost, watch and listen to Tex. If he hits the dirt, you better be down also."

We spread out and as I walked off Six yelled, "Tex, let's go. This is not a picnic."

I returned his words with a middle finger and shouted back, "Up yours Six!"

The walk to the tree line was a short walk and from there it got thick. I cut my way through vines and bushes and came to river with tall elephant grass. It was so tall that an elephant could have hid and never be seen. The odor of the river was awful, like rioting or decaying flesh. I got a sign from Six saying not to cross the river. He came closer, "Let's dig in here in the grass and wait for Charlie to come down the river. We spread ourselves along one side of the bank and dug in. The river was about twenty yards across with gave us a good shooting distance. "Let take the advantage," Six said. "String several lines across the river and hang grenades just under the water. It might not kill those bastards but it will scare the hell out of them when they hit the lines. All we have to do is open fire."

About the time we started to get into the water we saw a boat being paddled along with two old men. The boat was filled with rice, either going to feed a lot of V.C. or covering something else. They did not see us and for some reason they came along our side of the river. Country raised his M-60 but I tapped him on the shoulder and pointed to my knife. He shock his head yes. We both unloaded all our extra equipment thinking swimming would be a lot easier without a pack. In the process of doing this I began to get a case of the nerves. I had never killed a man with my hands. Silently Country and I made our way through the elephant grass to the edge of the water. We still had cover so we waited for the boat. I heard the oars in the water and then the bow came into view. Country signed that he was taking the man in the rear. The boat continued and the first man was well in view. I started straight for him. I took him by surprise and wrapped my arm around his shoulder placing my knife against his neck. I whispered, "Dun lie, don't move."

The man went crazy fighting and screaming. I gave him a second warning but he continued. I tried to hold him but he was loud so I closed my eyes and pulled my knife across his throat. Blood squirted like a fountain and I could hear his airway taking blood. I was shaking but turned to see if Country had done his job. He had. He and I both were covered in blood, human blood.

On shore Six waved us in and we pulled the boat to the shore. We dug through the rice and found much more than rice. At the bottom of the rice were thirty rocket launchers and twenty rifles and ammo. We took the weapons and then sunk the boat in the middle of the river.

Later that night Six decided that the V.C. was not coming down the river. We moved about 50 yards away from the river to what we thought was a trail. We spread out and dug in again. Damn, we did a lot of digging. The mosquitoes and ants were eating us alive. How do they live in this jungle? I was busy trying to survive the mosquitoes when I heard shots at the other end of the trail. It was hard to tell how many shots but they were fast and loud in the jungle. I got as low to the ground as I could and froze. I scanned in every direction at once. I did not move expecting the worse but I sat there in the quiet for hours. I never saw or heard anyone or anything except birds, frogs and bugs. Daylight came and I still sat. I thought, "This is crazy. I am not seeing what is going on."

I looked for Six so we could start hunting instead of sitting. I walked in the direction of the shots and felt sure I would see Six on the way. I passed several G.I.'s and they kept asking me questions as to what was going on. I shock my head no. Finally, I saw Six. As I approached the area I could see Six was bent over the radio man and neither was moving. I thought they were a sleep at first but as I got close I could see bullet holes in Six's chest. I ran to him and saw that half his head was gone. The radioman was dead also. I rolled Six to his back and screamed. "Oh God, oh God."

I did not know what to do. A sniper had hit him early in the night and we just sat there. I gritted my teeth and hate filled my body. I slammed my fist into the ground, "Why? Why? We just did nothing!"

I walked away and called the medic. I hung my head knowing I was in charge. What do I do? The others had to know and even Country took it hard. The radio worked so I made a call to the base and talked to a major. He told me what I already knew, I was in charge and he would send help as soon as possible. Most likely that meant we would never see an officer.

We put the bodies into a body bag and waited for the chopper to pick them up. The chopper was there in about an hour and they took Six and the radioman. I appointed a new radioman but he had been in country for only two weeks. Country was sitting over by a large tree with his head down. I walked to him and sat down beside him after a long silence I said, "We have a job to do and I am going to need your help. Can you do it?"

He nodded his head yes. I gathered the platoon and gave them my version of a Six pep talk. Finally I said, "We cannot get through this alone so I need all of you for support. Hey, I am looking for a leader if anyone here what to take charge I will be more than glad to step aside."

No one said a word. "Okay, I'm all you have for now so I will give it hell."

The day was mostly gone so I decided to stay for the night. I looked for Six's maps and found them in his pack. I wish there were a woman here, they can always read maps or so they say. I found the river and what I thought our location but I was really not sure. I called for Country to do a quick reconnaissance check around the area. He took off but on his way out I told him, "Don't be gone longer than two or three hours."

The remainder of us divided into twos so one could sleep while the other stood guard. I warned them that if their buddy that stood guard fell asleep it could mean a bullet for both.

Country returned after two hours and had just wonderful news. He had found more V.C. "Tex, I found a heavily travel trail with a lagoon off the river and I am sure they are bringing in troop and equipment. The trail was wide and I could see vehicle tracks."

"Well, I guess we have to spend the night there."

I called everyone together which was nine of us. Told them the plan and we might be up against no telling how many V.C.

It was dark, really dark and a fog floated across the river into us. Maybe fog was good, more cover and sounds carried. We sat up with Country up front with his M-60 and a few claymore mines in front of him. A claymore was an antipersonnel mine when detonated, propelled small steel projectiles in a 60-degree fan shaped pattern to a maximum distance of 100 meters. My gut said they would come from the river and if they got by the claymores and Country they were damn good. Just in case I sat up a rear guard in case Charlie was coming to the river to pick up supplies. Everyone seemed to be on edge even Country. I knew I did not have to say anything about not falling to sleep. We were wound tight. I prayed, "Please let no one show."

We sat there for over an hour while the insects ate on us. I got to a point that I wanted them to come as I thought about Six. I got my wish. I heard voices coming from the river. I moved behind a tree and took the claymore triggers. I motioned to the others to get ready. A few minutes later I saw the first boat loaded with North Vietnamese Army personnel. Yes, we were in for a fight. The fog helped us to stay hidden. I got on the radio and told the base what was going down. They told me to sit tight that help would be on the way, yeah right!

The boat was within fifty yards of us and I could see it clearly. Damn, three more boats followed the first. We were in for one hell of a fight. I passed the word not to fire until they were close and I mean really close. The boats landed and were unloaded. There must have been fifteen or twenty men and they lined up in a row. They marched straight in our direction. At about thirty yards I could see their faces, old and young men dressed in war uniforms. They meant business and so did we. I thought that I could take the first six soldiers with the claymores. They seemed to feel us and they stopped about fifteen yards from me. I thought, "Now is the time."

I trigger the claymores one after the other until half were exploded. Country opened up with his M-60 followed by the M-16's of all the G.I.s.

I signed for one of the men to fire a flare and the night turned into day. The V.C. that was left took cover and spread from left to right trying to cover our flank. We had taken our share and we were holding our own. Then I noticed that more boats were arriving. I signaled for another flare and saw three more boats with another fifteen soldiers. I grabbed the radio again and said, "Now is the time. We are going to be run over very shortly. Try to send something."

The G.I.'s were firing, screaming, reloading and firing. We gave them one hell of a fight. Not one G.I. turned away. It looked like the Alamo. We were so outnumbered we all fought like hell. If help did not show, we would be a goner, nine bodies.

I saw Country melting the barrel of the M-60 but he was running low of ammo. I started toward him when a grenade blew in front of me. My face and neck were burning and I could feel blood running down my face and neck. I opened fire again but we were losing. We had V.C. around us in every direction. There were just too many of them.

"God, the cavalry is coming!"

I heard a chopper in the background. I waved for another flare. The chopper came in with its mini-gun firing 6,000 rounds a minute. Two rockets came blazing down at the boats. We took time to reload because we knew it was not over. A minute later the remainder of the company showed. I could have kissed every one of them. The remaining live V.C. disappeared and we stayed there until morning.

We began to police the area taking stock of the bodies and equipment. Country walked beside me and said, "Tex, you did a damn good job and I am proud to stand beside you anytime."

I smiled back at a man that had power burns all over him. "Country, glad you were here. I could not have done it without you."

More coppers arrived and one had a major on board. He walked around shaking his head. He came to me and said, "Excellent job, soldier, excellent job."

He kept thanking me over and over. A new lieutenant came rushing up demanding to know who was in charge.

"Take your pick," I took him pointing to the other eight.

"Is this the whole platoon," he asked?

"It's what is left."

"Well, you men did a hell of a job. We are guessing you were out numbered 15 to 1. I am here to replace Six."

Country and I looked at each other and laughed. Country looked straight at the lieutenant and said, "Fuck you!"

The lieutenant was standing in shock as Country and I walked off. A medic finally caught up to us and started to clean our wounds. I started to shake, maybe shock or just nerves.

I told Country, "God I hope we never have to go through that kind of battle again."

The medic continued as he asked, "I am going to put a few stitches in the wound on your back. You want a shot?"

"No, I can't feel anything anyway."

CHAPTER 8

Rest at last and the comfort of the base camp was more than welcome. I sat on my bunk writing a letter to home and took the time to reread some of the old ones. The urge came across me to get a store-bought haircut and maybe a shave. The village had a makeshift barbershop operated by one of the locals. Country was half a sleep and I asked "Want to go to the village?"

"Sure, why not."

I knew the only reason he would go is to spend a little time with a woman but what did I care.

We started walking to the village and when we arrived Country went one direction and I went the other. The barbershop was tent set up and there were three G.I.'s in front of me. There is one thing that I learned these people do not know the meaning of hurry. What the heck, I was in no hurry either. The weather was tolerable and I made myself comfortable. My time came and I sat down in the chair. The barber was old and a bit shaky. That did not worry me while he was cutting my hair but when he pulled out the razor, I lay my pistol across my lap. We understood each other. We exchanged a few words and he bragged of his skills as a barber. He liked my curly hair and talked about it as if it was a blessing. The old man finished the haircut and shave without a problem and I even gave him a tip. We bowed to each other several times before I left.

I found Country and about two hours before dark we started walking back to camp. Country had a smile on his face so he must have gotten what he wanted. We felt damn good about being alive and as we walked Country talked about hunting and fishing when he got home. He asked, "You hunt and fish?"

"I did a lot of both before I came here but now I think I am finished with both. When I get home it will be hard for me to kill a fly."

"Ah Tex, you don't mean that. You are just like me; it's in your blood."

"It may be in my blood but I don't care if I ever sleep under the stars again. I'm staying in a Holiday Inn."

We got back to camp and did nothing. We managed enough energy to clean our rifles while leaning against an A.P.C. A clean rifle was mandatory if you want to stay alive. I was scanning the tree line through my night-scope and I saw something I did not like. A V.C. flag flew from a pole along the tree line. I had never seen anything like that so I handed the rifle to Country to get his opinion. "Hey, take a look at this."

"Damn, that does not look good. I have a feeling that we are in for a little action. Why now?"

"We need to spread the word in case they try something."

We took a walk to the new lieutenant's hut and told him what we saw. "Tex, are you sure?"

"Hell yes!"

"I have to tell the major."

We walk back to out hut and Country started getting his equipment together. He was shaking. That was a bad sign. Both of us had a really bad feeling that all hell was going to break loose. Our lieutenant and Major came charging into our hut to tell us that we were going to sit here until they made a move. The major had called in an air strike and we were going to watch for once.

The noise of the F-4's could be heard in the distance. As they approached we watched as they let loose of all kinds of firepower, bombs, rockets and napalm. Country and I stood and watched and I said, "God that makes me proud. We have the power to win any war."

Flares were fired and the night became day. The Air Force continued to pour it on. Then we heard gunfire from the other side of the base camp. Country gave me a look and said, "We are in for a long night."

We sat by the A.P.C. listening to all the area being exploded. We even ducked our head when the round came too close.

Our relaxing mood turned to terror when the driver of the A.P.C. came running up and said, "We're going out."

What a way to destroy the mood of the night. Back at it again and my heart was pounding. We grabbed our weapons and joined the parade. By the time we reach the gate there was a major amount of gun firing and mostly at us. The A.P.C. continued off base and into the jungle. We fired at anything that moved but something was wrong. We did not see many of the enemy just a few here and there. That could mean only one thing they were on base. The driver turned the vehicle around and started back on base and all hell broke loose. The V.C. had dug in about one hundred yards out and men and weapons were pouring into camp. There must have been hundreds of them because they kept coming. I have never seen so many gooks as they came from every side and direction. We fought hard firing at every moving object. I had never seen so many dead bodies. They were screaming from their wounds but they keep coming in waves. God, I knew it was the end. They were determined to take the camp but we refused. Ammo was a premium but I fired as fast as I could. The fighting continued for five hours but we were not dying or giving up the camp.

By dawn we were still alive and the fighting had stopped. Staring at the camp we saw smoke rising from everywhere. The smell of burning flesh filled the air. Country had a huge cut running down his neck and I was covered in burns. I took care of Country and tried to stop the bleeding before the medic got there. We walked and looked for dead G.I.'s or maybe even some that might be alive. There were gooks laying death everywhere. I turned one over and saw it was the barber that had cut my hair just yesterday. That hit me hard. I carried him to an area that we had stacked the others. I wish I had time to bury him. I knew this old man and did not understand why he was here. God, I hate killing and war.

CHAPTER 9

Two months had passed and wounds were healed. I was feeling a bit perky because in two weeks I was due to go on R&R for a week. R&R was rest and recreation and we got to travel to a place that was peaceful with no bullets zooming around your head. I choose Thailand and I am not sure why. Talk of Thailand spread and the cost of everything was dirt cheap and all the Thai people loved the G/I or so I was told.

Six, our new lieutenant grabbed me in the mess and asked if I would drive him to Saigon. Six was a young guy, almost the same age as me. He was easy to get along and we had a few things in common. I told him sure and we packed a few things. "Six, what part of Saigon are you going?"

"I'll show you when we get there."

I thought, "Maybe it is confidential."

The trip was surprisingly uneventful, no bullets, booby traps or road rage. We arrived in Saigon and Six directed me through streets and side roads. He told me to stop; he got out and told me to wait in the jeep. There was a small store a few doors down so I made a quick trip for beer. I bought a couple bottles of rice beer, well, they called it beer and it was very strong. I sat there an hour with another trip to the store. Upon his arrival he directed me to a bar somewhere in the middle of town. The place was not only a bar but a message parlor. Six disappeared again and I join a couple of G.I.'s. The massage parlor was too much to resist so we got the full treatment. After the rice beer and the attention of two girls, I was exhausted so I waited in the jeep again.

Six returned and we started home. I could not hold back any longer and asked, "Six, what the hell are you doing?"

"I'm working on getting a massage parlor on our base."

I could not believe my ears and asked again, "Massage parlor? You have to be kidding?"

"No, this is the real thing. I have eight women ready to start."

"Wait, who's going to check them over?"

"Doc, every morning when the come through the gate their first stop will be the doc's office."

I knew Six was not doing this out of the goodness of his heart and money had to be made. I was just too stupid to get any of the action and I came home with nothing in my pockets. As I thought, the whorehouse was a howling success.

More time passed and I was on a routine mission into the jungle again. God only knew where but where riding on top of an A.P.C. We enjoyed the ride for about an hour and Six called a halt. We were back to being a foot soldiers and hunters. The intelligence report gave us information that V.C. was running supplies through this area. Before we had left, the major told us to watch for small gangs of kids that meant to kill every G.I. in sight. So far we had only come across a few small villages and encountered no resistance. I was on point as I walked a few hundred yards in front of the troops. It was getting dark when I came to small village so I waited for Six to catch up. He and I talked about the situation and he wanted to wait for visitors to show. I was in favor of taking the village and letting the visitors come to us. We waited.

I used this opportunity to sit and relax looking through my night scope. Everything was green but with a half a moon it was bright and sunny. I scanned the hut regularly and took in the trees around it. About an hour passed and I picked up movement near the hut. Three men were approaching the hut on the east side. I gave my rifle to Six so he could take a look and took us to sit tight. We could tell they were V.C. because they wore a uniform and carried a rifle over their shoulders. When I say uniform it was only a partial uniform but close enough. They entered the middle hut of the village and with a closer look we could see several large bunkers. The bunkers were very well constructed and looked similar to Eskimo igloos.

Those bunkers got the best of me so I told Six and Country that I was going to take a closer look. Plus, I wanted to take a closer look at three men in the hut. Six agreed and said, "Once you are in position do not move without signaling us."

I moved through the night not expecting any resistance but halfway there I came across a booby trap made from a C-rations can. There was a trip wire but I saw it in time. I dug around the C-rations can with my knife and found a land mine large enough to blow up a tank. Moving the can would have blown the mine and I count myself lucky once again. I gave a thankful prayer to God. I used the help of my God so much and He also came through for me. It seemed in every battle that people were praying and I knew that God was the only person that pulled me through at times.

About thirty yards from the hut I hear footsteps coming from behind me and Six came blazing by me. He opened fire. We joined in and kept pace with him. It was such a surprise to the three men it was easy to take them. Country approached Six and asked, "What the hell were you doing charging in like that?"

"We have to get this little escapade over. A chopper is coming to pick us up and I wanted to know about the bunkers."

Country and I made our way to the bunkers and each of us took a side and started digging. Usually weapons, ammo, maps and who knows what were found in these bunkers. As I dug I caught movement but I through it was a monkey. Monkeys were common and at times they would attach G.I.'s. They were not big monkey but they bit like hell. I turned and did not see anything so I keep digging. The movement came again and I swung my knife in that direction. I cut the monkey across the neck and blood sprayed me. It was not a monkey but a man. Country came up spinning with his knife in hand. "What the hell?"

I took a closer look and answered, "We were attached."

Country spun around again looking for more V.C. I was frozen making sure that the man was not going to get up. Country came around to my side of the bunker and slammed me on the shoulder. That brought me back to my senses and I walked a few feet and threw up. Country began to laugh but I took it dead serious. It entered my mind that a few seconds more and it could have been my blood spraying all over the ground. I offered another prayer.

Six showed a little later and we had to explain what had happened. The choppers were coming as we heard them in the distance. Again my mind wondered what we were getting into next. It had to be hot for chopper to pick up this soon.

Six keep his radio working and told us that "A" Company needed help. They were getting hit hard. I quietly told Country, "I sure hope that Six has a clue as to what we will do. It was night and flying into a fire fight at night was not the smartest thing to do."

The choppers were close enough that we fired smoke and they landed. We were on board within seconds and back into the air. We fly for a long while and I had no idea in what direction. I was totally lost and the flight lasted a long time.

The chopper landed in an open area and we made a formation around Six and the radio man. After the chopper left, I took point in the direction that Six pointed. "God, I hope he knew what he was doing," I said to myself.

I could hear firing in the distance. Maybe we were behind the V.C. and we had them in a crossfire. The jungle was not thick and rice paddies were on one side of me. We must be in the Delta. Again I heard shots being fired and I must have been at least 100-yards in front of the platoon. I could see tracer bullets being fired in the distance. A few steps more and a man came running from the tree line. I opened fire and cut him down. When I opened fire Six and the others hit the ground behind me. I waited to see if more were coming out. "A" Company must have been pushing them because five more came from the trees. The five V.C. were coming straight at me but apparently they did not know it. I opened fire again. It was too easy. Then I heard the platoon open fire and V.C. were coming in every direction. Bullets were flying over me coming from all sides. I was laid low but fired as fast as I could. Then I realized that I was in a crossfire myself. I dug a small hole thinking I needed to be as low as possible. My only hope now was that the platoon would keep the V.C. off me. My hole was not near deep enough as the bullets and firing was much closer. A chopper at treetop level fired rockets and a mini-machine gun aboard was blazing.

The V.C. dug in and we were there exchanging rounds for over nine hours. I lay in the middle with my head down thinking I was dead. I used hand signals to Six and we decided that we had to dig them out. Suddenly I heard firing from the rear of the V.C. and saw "A" Company blazing a trail. That got the V.C. moving in our direction and we finished them. The body count was over one-hundred that day.

Two weeks later back at the base camp, Six came by and said, "Get ready for a swim, an all night one."

I looked at Country and we both gave a grin. "What could he be talking about," I asked?

"Hell if I know."

We knew it was not for fun so we gathered our gear. We met Six and we drove to Saigon. On the way he explained we were taking an airboat ride. That did not sound bad and some of those things were fast. When we arrived in Saigon we drove straight to the docks. As we pulled up we could see the boats, well maybe a boat. They were about forty-feet long, loaded with all kinds of equipment aboard. They looked strange but they were well armed with plenty of ammo. We got on board and Six motioned for Country and I to get up front. "Make yourself at home, we are spending the night," Six said.

Things could have been a lot worse so we took advantage of the luxury and slept like a baby as someone else kept watch. The only thing that caused me to wake up was the sun. Six was awake and said, "How about chow?"

"Damn right," we both said.

The chow hall was not far and it was the first hot and decent meal we had in a long while. We went back several times and we all looked pregnant as we walked out. Back to the boat and it was time for a nap. I slept until noon without a worry. Life was good.

Country woke me up to say that he was going someplace to play poker. He offered me to tag along but I told him I was going back to the chow hall. The food was even better and I packed it away again. I should have been in the Navy just for the food. I was almost finished when Six sat down beside me and spread out a map. "Wait a minute Six; you are going to ruin my lunch."

We were mostly alone and he pointed to a place on the map, "Been there?"

"Not me."

I knew nothing about that part of this country. He changed the subject quickly, "You only have five months left. What are you going to do when you get home?"

"I don't really know. I have to use up five months and stay alive is all I know."

Six asked, "You have a girl waiting?"

I did not know what to say so I came out with a, "Sure."

At this point I began to feel a sinking feeling, "Six, what kind of mission is this?"

Six leaned back and ran his hand through his hair. Then he shuddered a bit and said, "They call it Number Ten."

"I've never heard of anything like that. What does that mean?"

"The damn place is covered with booby traps. Tex, you're the best we have and you will have to get us in and out in one piece. Oh yeah, we will be going at night."

I shook my head but never said a word.

The walk back to the boat seemed short so I took my position in the front of the boat; I think they call it the bow. I lay there trying to remember all the types of booby traps and what Cal had taught me. The little signs that keep you alive and what to do when you see or feel them came to mind. I remembered the times that I had been entangled in booby traps before and tried to use my mistakes and mind to relive them. Experience was my greatest ally. I knew that God had pulled me through the hard times and in most cases it was He that saved me.

I used what time I had to rest and finally I was able to sleep. I knew I would be up all night and being tired did not keep a person at the top of his attention span. Someone kicking my foot woke me. We knew touching or shaking a G.I. by his upper body might end up with a knife and a bullet in your body. Country was looking down at me. I came alive but lay there, "Did you win?"

"Yeah, over three hundred dollars."

"You're buying steaks when we get home."

I told him what Six had told me and his smile disappeared. I gave him a direct order, "Don't stay close to me tonight."

"Sure but why?"

"The area is filled with traps and no use both of us going together."

"I suggest you be careful and for God's sake watch where you are walking."

We sat but not many words passed between us.

About an hour after dark, Six came up front. We were moving and the engine was loud, really loud. The ride was smooth and for a large boat it was fast. The river was wide and after we left the dock we saw no traffic. For an hour and a half we passed villages along the river and saw campfires burning in the trees. We surely were not going to sneak up on anyone or anything with all the noise we were making. It was time as the boat pulled to the shore and stopped ten feet from the bank. We grabbed our gear and jumped over the side. The water was chest deep and we made our way to the tree line. We check for leeches and I took my position as point. Country followed just as I had told him. Six had the radioman in hand as they brought up the rear. Before we left the boat I had asked Six exactly what the target was. He gave a stupid answer, "Anything that does not look right."

I took a quick look at the map and started east. I found a trail and I paced myself about fifty yards in front Country. Every step was an eggshell and I never touched the ground without looking. The trail began to get narrower and the jungle got heavier. I check in all directions for possible snipers and listened for the three behind me. I could not hear them so maybe they were being careful also. It was hot so I decide to take a break and I sat down next to a tree. I rested for couple of minutes when I saw a G.I. with his back to me walking down the trail. The jerk was smoking a cigarette. I whispered to myself, "Damn Country, put that torch out. What's wrong with him?"

I walked back to him and as I approached I hissed, "What the hell is wrong with you? Put that cig out."

Two more steps and I saw an outline of an AK-47 slung across his shoulder. Not Country, I sling my rifle out my shoulder, and my finger was on the trigger for a three shot burst. The man fell. Carefully I walked toward him with my rifle still smoking. Something was wrong, why had he not tried to fire on me? Did I catch him off guard or maybe he was just a dope. I must have walked right by him and he never saw me. That taught me two things; one I was not paying attention, two I should be dead.

Country worked his way to me and each of his steps was as soft as a pillow. When he got close I shock my head and whispered, "Bad shit in here. There could be anything planted in here and that may be the reason this dumb ass is dead. He did not think anyone could walk this area and live."

"Let's get out of here. I don't like it at all."

I started on point again and the trail became a path. It was dark so I decided to get as low to the ground as possible and take a look using the stars as light. Nothing but my hand touched something solid that was buried. I slide my knife out and poked the area looking for a premier of the object. It was not big and I dug around it thinking it was a mine. After ten minutes of digging I determined it was a can. I got it to the surface and sure enough it was just a can. "Damn, I do not have time to dig up cans," I told myself.

Five steps later I felt a wire at my feet. It felt loose and that meant one thing, it was tripped. I hit the ground like a rock. Two seconds later an explosion blew behind me. Then a second and a third blew. Fire filled the air and pieces of shrapnel buzzed through the jungle like chain saw. These bastards did not want me they wanted the platoon. I jumped up when I heard someone scream in pain. Someone was hit and I ran back down the trail. I approached and saw Six bending over a man. The radioman had taken a face full of metal and it looked like it took his eyes out. I grabbed the radio checking if it was in working condition. It was and I called for a chopper. I walked to a clearing giving the chopper directions. The chopper found us and had the man in the air.

Country and I continued but not before we told Six what an shitty plan this turned out to be. I told Country to hang back and I took point again. After a short time I came to a pond with the heads of three G.I.'s stuck on poles in the middle of the water. My blood began to boil and I just wanted one shot at the person that did this. I was going into the water to retrieve the heads but I could see wires running in every direction. It was more than a trap it was suicide. I heard a noise in my area and I whirled only to see Country. "What is this, Tex?"

"The gooks did this and I will remember this as long as I live."

I took the M-60 from Country and opened fire on the heads until they were underwater. I turned the M-60 on the grass around the pond and explosion after explosion began blow. I must have hit fifteen or more mines. My finger never let off the trigger of the M-60 until it stopped firing. Then silence and Country said, "Great job, Tex. I have never seen so many traps in one place."

My blood was still hot and I felt revenge stuck in my throat. "I have an idea. Let's set here and wait for them to come back," I said quietly.

Country nodded yes. We sat there all night waiting but those bastards never came back. The sun gave us a new attitude and we finally gave in to resume with the mission. About the time we were going to leave four more G.I.s joined us. They had heard the shooting from the night before. Believe me they were welcome. I took point again and we hunted hard for signs and reason why this area was heavily traveled by the V.C.

I heard a trap explode behind me so I returned to check. We lost one of the men that had joined us. He was scheduled for a trip home in just twenty-two days. Six put a call into home base and within an hour the dead man and the other three were flying. Just a little late for one man.

I had a gut feeling that something was going to happen. I kept the feeling to myself but Country picked up on it also. We walked and hunted most of the afternoon but nothing except for more G.I.'s joining us. About an hour before dark we stopped and had dinner. Nothing like a can of cold food but C-rations was better than nothing. While we ate one of the guys sat down beside me. He had been in country for only a month and he was scared. When he sat down I brushed ants from his collar. He did not know what to ask but I knew what he wanted. He said, "Are we going to get out of this alive?"

All new men want to know that and I felt that way myself at times. "Hell yes! We are going to get out and put up one hell of a fight."

"Yeah, the fight is the unsure part. At times, I see me being killed and no one will give a damn."

"Soldier, don't give up. Never give up. Be a survivor and fight like hell. Think smart and don't panic."

"All I can think about is going home."

I turned to him and looked him in the eye similar to what Cal might do, "Going home is not an option so you have to grow up or die. There is no time for crying or homesickness. You pay attention in the jungle or death is a sure thing."

He gave me a look that I will never understand. I almost thought he was going to hug me. I changed the subject quickly. "What's happening at home? We never get news here."

"Okay, I guess there is a new age taking place—The Flower Child Age."

"I cannot even image what that is."

"You know—free love. Everyone loves everyone except for the military. It's really great. Surely you have seen it here?"

"I don't have a clue what the hell you are talking about. Okay tell me something else."

"Riots!"

"What kind of riots," I asked with a roll of my eyes?

"All kinds of protest against the war, marches in the streets and flag burning. I have seen G.I.'s returning home and people spitting on them. Oh yes, blacks are protesting for equal rights."

"Well, they can surely have my part of this shit. I have seen black in the Army fighting like hell. We have stood side by side."

"Yeah, but schools are segregated and it just does not seem right."

I lay back and told the soldier, "Get a little rest. A long night is about to happen. Oh yeah, keep your eyes on Country and me. We will be the first to get hit or start firing. Watch what we do and learn from it. You might get some of that free love."

I felt like Cal was inside of me saying all this.

He smiled and left. I hoped I had given him a little self-confidence. I would not see him until several days later. Night came and we dig in and waited. Waiting was almost as bad as fighting. The night passed in days not hours. A noise came from a distance. It was time and we prayed for a small platoon or even two or three but it was the North Vietnamese Army. It was impossible to tell how many because the jungle was thick and it was cloudy. Country spun and opened fire with his blazing M-60. I did the same but we were surrounded and lead was coming from every direction. I fired a few shots in all directions not knowing where to turn. Six was on the radio asking for choppers. It only took a few minutes before the choppers were firing rockets and unloading high-speed lead at the ground.

I dug in even more but there was not a hole deep enough. They were as close as thirty-yards. I was firing clip after clip, throwing grenades, and dodging bullets. My rifle clicked out of ammo for the last time and I had thrown my last grenade. I grabbed rocks and threw them as hard as I could. There was a few of us left and Country had been hit in the leg. I screamed for ammo but we all were empty. The choppers were trying to drop us more ammo but they were getting shot to pieces also. One chopper about a hundred yards away landed or maybe crashed. It was possible that the chopper carried ammo so I took off running. It was a miracle the chopper had ammo. We loaded everything and carried even more. Back to the fight and we seemed to be gaining a bit. Six gave me a shout, "Help is coming."

Why did the North Vietnamese Army want this damn area so badly? What was here that we did not know? Six came by again and said,"Get Country and let's get the hell out of here. We are getting our ass kicked."

I screamed back, "Just where do you think we are going to go?"

"I don't know."

Let's stay. Those bastards are everywhere. We better hold what we got. If we run we could run right into them. Get on the horn and get help!"

"The radio is gone! Run!"

"Six, no place to run in the middle of the night."

Six fell backwards and blood spirited from his neck. I caught him but he was bleeding from both sides of his neck. I let him go and opened fire again. I was mad as hell. The choppers were firing all around us but they were taking hits. We all were in a bad place and it looked like prayer was our only hope.

A moment of quiet came and the firing stopped for a minute. I grabbed Six, took my boot lace and tried to sew the wound in his neck. I just tried to stop him from swallowing his own blood and drowning. He was not dead and as I lay him flat on the ground he tried to say, "Don't let me die."

I told him not to worry that a medic was on the way. He did not know and neither did I if a medic was in a thousand miles. To my side Country was screaming and firing. I grabbed my rifle and joined his side. We did not see anyone but we wanted them to know we were alive and would give them hell if they came our way. We stopped and heard nothing. We dropped to our knees and took air into our lungs. Sweat was pouring down my face and I never felt so drained. Six was dead and Country was bleeding from a wound in his leg. That guy was tough as I did what I could for him. We calmed down and sat back in one of the holes that we had dug waiting for daybreak. We heard gunfire in the distance but none near us. The helicopters must have driven them back even more.

The sun came and tore away the nightmare of the darkness. My hands were burnt from all the firing and my arms were not any better. I was covered in dirt and gunpowder and all exposed skin was burning like hell. I looked for my canteen and took a drink thinking I needed water. I sat wondering what kept me alive. That had to be the worse firefight ever. The choppers had taken the wounded and dead including Country.

I heard a voice from behind and saw the G.I. that I had given the talk before the battle. He sat down beside me and said, "Tex, I have never been that scared."

The guy knew my name and I asked, "What's your name?"

"Tom."

"I'm glad you made it, Tom. One hell of a fight, how did you survive?"

"I took your advice and kept hope and watched you as long as I could."

"Tom, you might just make it to that free love."

We were picked up later that morning and carried to the base. Believe it or not there was new lieutenant waiting for us. He was gung ho but they all were at first. After a few firefights real life begins to take over.

CHAPTER 10

Three weeks later Country and I were back to normal. He came walking into the hut and said, "Let's get out of this place, Tex."

"Yeah sure, where are we going?"

"How about Saigon, get a shave, look for women, and drink a few more beers? I talked Six into giving us a three-day pass. Supply has trucks going to Saigon daily for supplies and they are looking for a front and rear guard. We could just do it for fun."

"You got it, let's go."

We mounted the next truck leaving for Saigon and I took the shotgun position in the cab. Riding was so much better than walking and the truck gave be thoughts of home. The countryside was quiet and beautiful.

No trouble getting to Saigon and the truck stopped at the supply base. Country and I were gone for another three days. No trouble picking up a ride to the nearest bar. We walked in and the whole bar turned in our direction. Maybe it was our long mustaches or our camouflage fatigues but no one looked at us in the eye. We sat drinking beer with a label that we could not read. It was bad! We kept drinking. Evening came and we got hungry. I told Country a great plate of Mexican food would hit the spot. He gave me a look and said, "Mexican food? There is no Mexican food here and surely not enough anti-acid. We are stuck with local food."

Two beautiful women approached us and for five-dollars they were available for the night. They were young and spoke a bit of English. We took them and forgot about dinner.

Later that night I lay beside the whore in a cheap hotel when I heard a noise. It sounded like Country. My hand was on my .357 as I got up and listened. I moved softly to the door and pressed my ear against it. About that time I had my ear pressed to the door for a second time a rifle was fired. I jumped back so quick that I fell. I jumped up and slung the door open. No one was there. Country came flying from around the corner and I almost shoot him. I released the hammer on the gun and asked, "What is going on?"

"I don't know but let's find out."

He walked to the bed and grabbed the whore by the hair, "Where are the V.C?"

She said nothing and he came across her face with his gun, "Where are the V.C."

She was bleeding from the last slap and this time he connected the handgun to her face again and she went out. She had to be dead or hurt bad.

Country took it personality and taking no chances he roared into the hallway and started knocking down doors. All he found was pissed off G.I.'s. I grabbed him by his shoulder and said, "Country, it is okay. Let it go."

His face was beet red and his eyes flashed up and down the hall. I shook him again. "Country, let's go to the bar."

I pulled him along and we stayed in the bar until sunup. We both were totally wasted and went back to our rooms and slept until noon. I woke up hunger and thirsty but more thirsty. I made my way to the bar and ordered water. I must have looked as bad as I felt because no one said a word to me. The bar had a few G.I.'s drinking beer but I paid them no attention. I was sitting on a wooden crate drinking water when one of the G.I.'s came over and stood by me. He stood there for a while and finally asked, "Where are you from?"

"Texas," I said without looking at him.

"Are you in the Big Red One?"

"Yeah."

"Scout?"

"Yeah."

"They call you Tex?"

I turned to him and asked, "What the hell do you want? They call me Tex, I'm in the Big Red One, I am a scout, and my mother did not breast feed me."

"Sorry, I keep hearing about a guy that can stay alive walking point and has the respect of the men that follow him."

"Is that all you hear?"

"Damn, I know you are the one."

He walked away.

I finished the water and went back to Country's room. I gave him a shake and said, "Let's go. We're going back to the base. This place is not for us."

"Tex, we have one more day."

"No thanks. I will meet you downstairs."

After a few minutes Country came down the stairs, gave me a wave, and headed for the bar. He came out with two beers and handed one to me. I took a pull and asked, "What now, no ride?"

"Let's walk."

"Man, what's eating you?"

God, I don't know but I am sick of this place and everything in it. Maybe I am just ready for home."

"Damn Tex, it sounds like you want to go home in a bag. That kind of talk will get you killed."

"Country, please keep me alive. I have a shity attitude."

"You got it."

We found a ride with a Jeep as far as Tan Ann so we stopped for a beer. With a beer in hand we were standing in the middle of the street and one of our A.P.C. came by. I waved it down and climbed aboard. I took the rear while Country took the front. After leaving town the driver said he had to make a quick recon and headed straight for the tree line. Country waved back at me and said, "Let's get off. This driver is using a well-used trail and anything could happen. I told Country, "Tell the driver to get off this trail."

Before another word was said the A.P.C. lifted off the ground with an explosion that could have rocked Texas. The A.P.C. had hit a mine dead center. I felt myself being propelled into the air from the blast. While in the air an ammo container buried into my chest followed by all kind of flying metal. There was no dodging as small and large pieces come my direction. I would guess I was fifteen feet above the A.P.C. and during that time my mind left my body. I seem to float seeing smoke and damage below me.

No doubt I was hurt this time. I came to the ground too soon and when I hit my back cracked and my breathing stopped. I took a few seconds putting my mind back in place and determined that I was lying in a rice paddy. I tried to move but nothing worked. I thought I was alive because I could see at times and I could smell smoke. I was not sure where I was hurt but moving was out of the question.

The next thing I remember I was fly in a chopper. I have no idea how they found us. On the way the medic kept me entertained by telling me that I was okay and I was going to be good as new. Even I knew better. As we landed

73

at the Saigon Hospital doctors were waiting and they rushed me to emergency. I do remember the docs taking x-rays and then I was out. They never told me how many others were killed. Country survived and was back in camp after a few days.

With help from God and the doctors I was back at base camp in three weeks. I watched every sunset, thought about home and God and told myself how lucky I was. I have always thought that a G.I. in battle has a God and he calls on Him at that time. I wondered why He spared my life and what He had planned for me in the future. I lay outside looking up at the clouds and fell asleep.

When I woke up a cup of coffee sounded good so I walked to the mess. On the way I passed a hut with G.I.'s and a local whore taking pictures. I just shook my head and kept going. The mess was out of coffee so I had to settle for tomato juice. The juice was not that bad after a little salt and pepper. I even had a second glass. We did not have juice at the mess very often. I took a different route back to my hut trying to avoid all the sex. I found paper and wrote a letter home but did not tell mom and dad that I had been hit and in the hospital. For once the camp was peaceful and I took full advantage and went to bed early.

The next morning Six came by and said that we were getting new men into camp. Six was number four that I had served but I'm not sure how many lieutenants we had. He told me to meet them on the pad. I saw the chopper land and made my way in that direction. There four of them and I carried them to the hut.

One of the soldiers asked, "Hey Sarge, where are we going?"

This soldier was about six-foot tall, thin, blonde hair, and like he had been outdoors working on a farm most of his life.

"Welcome to Nam, men."

"Thanks, is this as bad as they say?"

"Worse."

His question remained unanswered. He walked a little closer and said, "It's death out there, yes?"

"It will certainly be if you keep talking like that. Man, you got to think and think positive."

He said softly, "Point, you walk point right?"

"What about it?"

"Does everyone walk point?"

"Not unless you are unlucky and get to take my place."

"How long do you have left here?"

"Let me say this. Unless you are getting off the plane and touching U.S. soil, you have eternity here. That means you will be waiting for a bullet if you are not all business here. Where are you from?"

"Oklahoma."

Well Okie, if you are smart, you will stay by the people that have been here the longest. They can save your life. Another thing, did those Sooners beat Texas this year? I doubt it but don't tell me if they did."

He turned his back with a smile. "Damn!"

I showed them their bunks and told them chow was in about an hour.

I took my rifle and cleaning gears and found a place at the edge of camp. I had to clean my weapon at least once a day. I dirty rifle will get you killed for sure. I was about finished and decided to go to chow when a mortar round came whistling over my head. "Those dumb-ass gooks. I'm going to get even with them one day," I said out loud.

Everyone was running for the bunkers. As I slide into the bunker, I thought, "Damn, the new men."

I took off at full speed to the hut, no one there. I turned in the direction of the chow hall and almost took the door off as I blasted through it. Sure enough, four men sat on the floor covering their heads with their hands.

I screamed at them, "Get your asses in gear and follow me. This is not a drill."

We were running like scared rabbits for the bunker when a mortar shell hit behind us. The last soldier took a piece of metal in the back and went down. I pointed to the others to get in the bunker and they never slowed down. I returned for the wounded man, slung him over my shoulder, and started to run. Another shell came close and I was hit in the leg. We both went down. I could hear the men in the bunker screaming encouraging for me to get up. This was not a John Wayne movie and I was bleeding badly but the man I was carrying was hurt worse. I got up and I heard a cheer. I grabbed the soldier under his arms and pulled him to the bunker. A few feet away I got help from a couple others. A medic was waiting to take care of us both. My wound was only a cut and with a few stitches I was back in the jungle in three days. On the other hand, the wounded new man got a trip back to the U.S.A. He was only Nam for one day. I never understood how I kept getting hit and not one trip home.

CHAPTER 11

I worked with the new troops giving them all the words I could but both of us knew it meant nothing until we saw a little action. Three days later seven of us were sitting in his hut playing poker listening to the radio. Six came in and just stood. We tried to ignore him but finally I asked, "Are you waiting for someone to call attention? Well, it ain't going to happen."

He chuckled and said, "We are going out tonight so get your gear ready."

The new men took a deep breath. "Did you think we were here on vacation," I asked?

Country threw his poker hand down turning to look at Six and asked, "Where we going?"

"How about a boat ride?"

"Hell no! The last time Six was killed. I hate boat rides in the jungle."

I thought, "I bet we are going back to number ten hole and with new men."

Country shot me a look and shook his head. On his way out Six said, "Tex, you take Okie with you tonight. He is all yours; teach him well."

"Damn Six, a hot zone and I have to wet nurse a new man?"

"Just do it."

Six left and Country started in ragging my butt about telling Six that I was not doing a training mission in a hot zone. Country got madder and began to scream at me. I gave him a few words back, "Someone has to train these men. Did someone not train you?"

"I don't give a damn Tex you only have two months left and we have been through hell."

He kept on with his words so finally I told him to come outside. He followed me outside, "Country, what's wrong with you. These men are scared to death and with no experience. They will die without you and me watching out for them."

He began to calm down so I stuck my head back into the hut and told the new men to follow me. I took them to get ammo, knifes, and everything else that they could carry. I felt like a father of 20 years old showing his kids how to ride a bicycle.

We loaded our gear on an A.P.C. I gave the speech about how much safer it was to ride on top as to opposed to inside. They took my advice. I told Okie to sit by me so I could explain the facts of war to him one more time. The vehicle drove for Saigon and the waterfront. I leaned back and gave Okie instructions about every person that we passed. "Don't pass a person on the street or highway without trying to see what they are thinking. Look them in the eye and read if they are friend or foe. That especially goes for women and children. They will kill you faster than a soldier. In a battle keep your head up and look for an opening and take it. You hesitate, you die."

Okie listened but I knew he was scared and had no experience. I wanted so much to keep him alive and even more I did not want him to get me killed.

The harbor came too soon and we unloaded our gear. I took my spot up front and lay down on my gear to think. The captain came by and I asked, "We going to Number Ten Hole?"

He shook his head yes. I lay there thinking about home as usual with the sun pouring its ray on me. It was hot but for some reason it felt good. Three or four men were smoking pot. I hated to see that because I knew a clear head was a real plus. I washed my mine of it and told myself, "What the hell. It's their life, they can do what they want and why should I stop them."

The mess was not far so I decided to get coffee and food. I walked in the mess and they were cleaning up with no food left. A sarge sat at a table smoking and he asked, "You going on the boat tonight?"

"Yeah, second time and the first time was hell."

"Hang on a few minutes and I get you something to eat."

He was right, ten minutes passed and he came out with ham and turkey sandwiches, green salads, potato salad, and three desserts. I wanted to hug the guy but I just ate it all.

Back to the boat and waiting for dark was the next step. Everyone was checking his weapons and ammo. The sun was setting and the captain came aboard and started the engine. The huge windmills on the airboat were turning with a noise of a hurricane. I sat in my spot up front and Okie stuck to me like glue. He was a basket of nerves and talked non-stop. He wanted me to assure him that we would make it through the night with every detail of what might happen. Finally, I told him, "Okie just sit down and shut up. You will get us all killed with all the talk. Use your eyes and not your mouth."

Six whispered, "Not so loud."

I wanted to tell him that the airplane engine was so loud that we could not even talk. Okie gave me a look and said, "Funny, he is a lieutenant."

"Why do you say that?"

"He just does not look like an officer. Do we follow him?"

"Let me tell you that the only law in the jungle is staying alive. We lost our last Six in this same spot last time."

"Oh shit!"

Country added, "You had better stay out of my way. I mean business."

I looked at Okie and said, "He has a short temper and wants to make sure he get home. To tell the truth, he is the best at his job of killing. Watch him and learn."

Country began swearing, "Damn, we're going to the same damn hole. Tex, I hope your eyes are good tonight."

The boat swung to the shore and beached near the tree line. We were in the water carrying our gear to shore. After we got to shore we check for leeches. Six gave the word to move out. I hit the tree line at the same place as last time but this time I decide to come in from the rear. I walked about thirty yards up river. Okie was walking in my footsteps just like I told him. He was sticking close so I was sure I was not going to loose him. I was scared to death just like him but I was surely not going to tell him. It was quiet with the exception of frogs and other river creatures. We had turned into the trees and traveled about fifty yards when I found my first booby trap. I stopped and gave Okie a chance to see it. There was a trip wire attached to bamboo shaft connected to a bent tree. Tripping the wire would release the tree and the bamboo shaft would hit you in the chest. Most likely the end of the shaft would be covered in a poison so that if the shaft did not take our head off then the poison got you. The booby trap was outdated and it took a person a long time to rig it, that made me wonder. It was like they knew we were coming in this direction. We kept moving and I found two more trap with one attached to a flare. That was really a bad sign. They were close enough for the flare to light the area. I signaled Country and Okie to be ready. It was time to crawl slow and easy. I told Country and Okie to stay put as I made my way a few more yards. I thought, "Damn, if they were going to take us by surprise. I had to see them before they saw me."

No rush, just be careful and look.

In the distance I could see flares and hear firing in the area of the base camp. "God, where they getting drilled?"

Maybe the gooks were at our base area and all we would have was peace. I took no chances and stayed out of sight moving like a snake. I heard a noise and looked back and Okie was crawling behind me. I gave him the finger over the lips sign and he realized he was making too much noise. The guy had to learn but not at my expense. While turning back to business I noticed a flash of something shiny. I froze and never took my eye off the spot. I gazed at the area as if it was a beautiful woman and then it hit me, it was the barrel of a mortar tube. I pointed in the direction so that Country and Okie would pay attention also. Without doubt a mortar tube meant soldiers in the area. I eased my rifle to the shooting position and Okie did the same.

I scanned and waited for several minutes but my eyes caught nothing. "Those bastards are there, I just have not seen them yet," I told myself.

I moved forward with Okie almost on top of me and then I saw a semi-circle of grass and leaves. "What the hell," I thought.

I took another scan of the area but saw nothing. I gave Okie a sign to take a look at the leaves but he pointed to the mortar tube. I took his arm and pointed to the ground again and he still did not see it. I was not even sure what it was so I moved closer after telling Okie to cover me. I got close enough to the mortar tube to see it was an U.S. piece of equipment. It felt like a trap and I was going to be the bait so I slowed down making every step count. I took a couple of steps followed by a look around. Sure enough, the leaves and grass covered a manhole cover next to the mortar tube. I was scared and my gut felt like something was going to blow at any time. I motioned for Okie to come. When he arrived I got on my knees and started removing one leaf at a time from the cover. Okie was even more nervous with sweat running down his face. I got the leaves removed from the cover enough to see the outline so I backed Okie away and said, "Pull the pin from a grenade but hold it without releasing the trigger. He did. We went back to the cover. I looked at him and said, "You going to hold that thing all day or you going to drop it into the hole?"

He gave a look that said, "Who me."

Finally he raised the cover and dropped the grenade into the hole. We both hit the ground and the cover blew off the hole. I immediately started firing into the hole. In between trigger pulls I could hear people screaming and I dared anyone to try to come out of the hole. I stopped fire and told Okie, "Get into the hole."

He replied, "I can't, that's suicide."

I pointed my rifle at Okie's head and said, "Go or die your choice."

By this time Country had arrived and Okie gave him a look silently asking for help. Apparently, Country caught the gist of the conversation and to Okie's surprise Country raised his rifle to his head. "If Tex said to go you better be going or I will shoot you myself, no flashlight either. It will get you killed faster than a target on your chest. I added, "Leave the dead but bring back anyone that can talk."

He was in the tunnel with a little persuasion and he disappeared. "Reckon he will make it," I asked Country?

"I guess we will find out soon enough."

We sat up a perimeter and waited for something to happen. We waited but did not hear from Okie. Six came up with a radio in his hand and talking about a problem on a hill. He broke the connection and said, "Pack it up we are leaving."

"Six we have a man in this hole and we are waiting," I explained.

"I don't give a shit we are leaving, pack it up."

"Why don't they call in the choppers?"

"They did and they are still in trouble."

When I told the others there were all kinds of moaning and complaining. Finally, I lost my cool and shouted, "Get your gear together, we are moving out. I am tired of this bellyaching."

One soldier came to me and asked, "What about Okie?"

"Damn, he could be dead and if not he will get back one way or another."

I walked in silence to the front and took my position. It hurt bad to leave a man. Our walk was not long and within a few hundred yards I could see one hell of a fight. Tracer filled the sky and it sounded like the Fourth of July. I took a few minutes to get my bearings and looked for a way in without just charging into the middle. My mind kept flashing back to Okie when I told myself, "You are asking for a bullet if you don't pay attention." I was about to move again when I noticed three V.C. firing mortar rounds. I took a quiet look around for additional V.C. or armament. Seeing nothing else I opened fire and the three fell. Country moved in the direction of the V.C. I covered him for a few minutes and then followed. We were spread out walking through thick jungle and with all the flares being shot I could see most of what was happening. After a while smoke from the flares and rounds of explosives caused a vision problem. Maybe the smoke gave us more cover and I felt we had them in crossfire. We were at their backs and they were being driven into us. I found a place to dig in a little and waited. I could hear the enemy yelling like they were charging in victory but little did they know we were waiting. A gook came running to my left and two other G.I.'s took him down. Several more came straight at me as I leveled off to fire on one knee. Then I realized there was a lot more coming and we were in for a real fight. Grenades exploded taking lives and some of the V.C. were hit by their own booby traps. They were all around us but the smoke kept us hid until they were at pointblank range. I use most of my ammo when it seemed to get quiet. I never understood why there was so many V.C. in this area. The smoke even started to clear and we waited until sunrise. I was exhausted but did not even think of sleeping.

With daylight we could see some of the damage. God, bodies everywhere including G.I.'s. Some had limbs missing and there were some still alive. I walked and finally sat down and started talking to myself, "What a mess. Just a waste of human life and why? Was this jungle that important? Was it worth dying? Hell, most of the V.C. was kids."

We picked up the bodies and the wounded, used what first-aid we had, called for choppers and help load. I found Six, Give me your ammo. I'll be back when I can"

"Why?"

"I left a G.I. in a hole and I have to find him."

Six broke a smile and pointed to a G.I. about thirty yards away. There stood Okie. I walked to him, slapped him on the shoulder and said, "Did you miss all the fun?"

"Apparently I did because I was scared to death."

"Yeah, but did you learn anything?"

He smiled and shook his head yes. I was afraid to ask what.

"A few more of these trips and you will make a good live soldier."

CHAPTER 12

Back at the base camp a few days later I was sitting on a pile of sandbags talking to Okie. He had to take my place shortly and talking gave him more facts of what might happen. The sky was clear and nowhere did we hear gunfire. Country joined us holding three huge cigars. We sat there blowing smoke into the sky. "Country, how long before you leave?"

"Fifteen minutes."

I jumped up and said, "You son-of-a-bitch, you made it."

I felt a tender side of him as he said, "Tex, without you and Cal I might be lying in some rice paddy dead."

"You are the best damn gun I have ever seen and you saved my bacon several times. Just go home and love your family."

I grabbed him with a bear hug and he felt like a brother. I tried so hard not to let a tear show. He walked away.

"Okie, it is time to get down to business. Time is short and you still have a lot to learn."

Three days later we were on an A.P.C. headed in the direction of Tan An. As usual they never told us for how long but we had guard duty. That was okay because I needed to pick up some stuff and Okie needed to further his education. Riding on top of the A.P.C. I gave Okie points as to what to do and watch for as we motored along. Jeff the driver asked, "Are we stopping along the way?"

Six replied, "Sure, why not?"

Like clock work we pulled up in front of a whorehouse and everyone piled out of the A.P.C. We sat up a perimeter outside of Tan An. I lay on top of the A.P.C. looking at the stars wondering if they could see this many stars in Texas. On the side I could see flares in the distance and Viet Nam came alive. I guess that is why most of the V.C. wore black pajamas. They were night fighters. I took my night scope and scanned the trees. Yes, there were people moving but at least they were not firing at me. With only two months left, I just wanted peace.

Thinking of being home, people and places came to mind. If God would just help me make it through a few more weeks, I would know I was on earth for a purpose. I decided to go into the hut and as I entered the door the other end of the hut blew up. Smoke came pouring out of the hut as the blast blew me off my feet. G.I.'s were running in every direction but I covered my head and waited for things to come back to earth. I was not hurt but I knew it was those bastards that I had seen in the trees. I picked up my rifle and firing a magazine into the trees but I am sure I hit nothing. I went back into the hut and saw blood all over the back wall. My heart skipped a beat but then I saw that the mortar had hit a dog and it was his blood. I turned back to the A.P.C. to wash my face and eyes. My eyes were burned a bit and I needed to wash them. The fun was over and we managed to get moving again. At Tan An we pulled a few hours of guard and we were finished. We did not stop on the way back for anyone or anything.

The next day I was sitting on the dike about half asleep when I heard steps. I reach for my rifle but saw it was the medic from my squad. This guy was a short man, not much hair and looked to be about thirty-five years old. He did not go into the field anymore but did treatment at the base. I raised up a bit and said, "Hey doc, sit down and talk."

"What going on, Tex?"

"Same as usual waiting for some shit to start."

"Tex, I need to talk to you, you worry me. I have never seen such a loner as you. You have no personal friends and that damn M-16 is your best friend. You have lived longer than 90% of the men that have walked point. You do your job but you eat, sleep and live by yourself. Your state of mind is not right. Hell, everyone thinks you are kill-crazy. Did you know that? Tex, no one wants to be around you and you never talk to anyone unless you have too. Okay, my point may be going in the wrong direction but I need your help. Once a month we load a jeep with a movie screen, projector, and movies and take them to a small village. It is for the kids. The kids love the movies and most have never seen a movie before. Tex, I need you as a guard while the movie is showing. Will you help?"

I nodded yes and I felt a drop of water run down my face. The doc left to get the equipment.

Had this war destroyed me as a person? I just wanted to stay alive and they gave me a hard job to do. Could anyone understand? I wanted to love and be loved but everyday I was faced with killing. I wanted to throw my rifle but I wanted to live also. Did killing keep me alive? I thought out loud, "Kids, kids are special and a movie sounded great. Kids are here to make people happy and they don't mean to hurt anyone. I lay there on a sandbag with more water flowing down my cheeks.

About an hour later the Doc came with a jeep and I climbed aboard. We traveled about half a mile down a dirt road with an A.P.C. in tow. As we approached the village kids came from every hut. There were screaming in happiness and waving their arms. It did not take long to set up the screen and connect the projector to the A.P.C. for power. Two other G.I.'s and I sat in the jeep watching and a gunner was ready on top of the A.P.C. The movie started and it was Donald Duck. God, I loved Donald Duck. The kids were laughing and screaming all through the movie. It felt good to see kids have fun. Kids are the same in any country but some grow up sooner than others.

Three hours later we packed our gear and left. It was late and almost dark. The road home was rough and at time we passed through thick jungle, so thick that it was like going into a tunnel. The A.P.C. had no trouble and we bounced along. Ahead I saw a flash go off but it was already too late. A rocket hit the A.P.C. square on the nose. The driver never had a chance. I opened fire in the direction that the rocket was fired. We continued and I fired in every direction as we passed the point of the explosion.

The jeep came to a stop and I hit the dirt along the edge of the road. I kept firing and once I got some return fire. We had ourselves a small firefight. The Doc was crawling to the A.P.C. and gave me a yell that both driver and gunner were dead. I entered the jungle and was going to make my way to the rear of the gooks. I got into position but only found two dead V.C. with a rocket launcher nearby. Doc radioed for help and we carried the bodies back to camp. I lay on my bunk thinking could we not do anything without getting someone killed?

The days were dragging, as my time got short. I was reading old letters from home but it really did no matter. The thoughts were still good and it helped me to be sane. Okie stuck his head in the door and said, "Have you heard that we are going to the hill?"

I sat up straight; I'm too damn short to be going back to that place."

"That's what's in the air."

"Well, maybe the air is wrong. When are we leaving?"

84

"Tomorrow night from what I hear."

I got up and went outside to clear my head. I sat down on the dike and stared at the trees.

After a few minutes I heard someone to my left, Six was headed toward me. I stood and waited. I knew something was up and hoped it was not the hill.

"Tex, you're going on a re-con."

"Six, you know I am short"

He laughed and said, "You're still in the Army, Sarge."

"Just were the hell am I going?"

"The hill! There are all kinds of movement going on there and we need to know where they are headed. I am tired of going into that place blind. We always take hits. Two men can work their way in and out before we get there and maybe we could have the advantage. Pick a man, get saddled up and be at the chopper pad in thirty."

Six walked away. I sat down in a slump and thought to myself, "I must be a crazy son-of-a-bitch. I'm going to get my head blown off yet. Why am I chosen to do such things? I can't be the best they have."

I managed to get up and I walked to Okie's hut and gave him the lowdown. "Sorry, Okie but you have been voted to go. Get plenty of ammo and get your mind straight. It's just going to be you and me against the big bad wolf with no help. If we make a mistake, I bet no one will even know."

"Hey Tex, I don't want to go. There is no Indian blood in me."

"Indian or not your are going. Remember, you are in the Army and this is an order private. Try to image if a few years in the stockade would be better than a few bullets flying by your head. If you think I want to go, you are crazy but we are going."

Okie and I arrived at the chopper pad simultaneously and I gave him a once over. I grabbed his flashlight and threw it. "I don't ever want to see you with that damn thing again. Use your eyes."

I carried all the ammo I could carry plus half dozen grenades. The bulletproof vest was heavy plus it was hot so I tossed it. Once inside the chopper I got a case of nerves. Okie had the same and I noticed he was shaking all over. Flying at night was an easy target for some gook with a rocket launcher. Below the jungle was thick and suddenly an open spot appeared and the chopper headed down. Ten of fifteen feet from the ground the Huey hovered and we jumped out. My right leg gave way and I landed on my face. I came up cussing the pilot. I looked for Okie and he was behind me in good shape.

Okie looked at me and said, "Tex, I have never had to jump from that high before. Okay what now?"

"Get gear and let's get out of here. I sure there are a dozen rifles trained on us."

That made Okie move a little faster. I gathered my gear and started east. After about fifty yards, I sat down to try to figure our position. My mind raced, "The place was totally different; I recognize nothing."

The jungle was bad and it was raining. We had to get our bearings or we were worthless. I waved to Okie and whispered, "We need to get to a higher point and maybe we can see where we are."

We walked and came to a hill but even being on top gave us no advantage. I motioned for Okie to sit so we could watch and maybe pick up something. About a mile away flares were exploding. Nothing came our way and I had no idea of our location. Okie asked, "What are we going to do."

"We are going to sit here until daylight unless you have a better idea. Keep awake and watch for anything and for God's sake don't talk."

I thought, "I am going to teach this boy to talk with his hands."

We sat in dark with all the action happening in the distance. Without the flares the stars were bright and a person could count a million of them. Night creatures made noise and gave us company. A black snake came across my boot. It kept moving and I did not even show Okie. I surely did not want a scream or a panic. I kept checking our position thinking something would jump out at me but I had no landmarks or a GPS. Time passed slowly and I looked at Okie and noticed his head was against his chest. I pulled my knife and laid it across his throat. He woke up abruptly grabbing my hand. I whispered, "You bastard, if I had been a gook you and I would be dead. I do not want to die tonight."

Time again passed slowly but this time I heard someone walking in the jungle. I turned to see if Okie was awake and he was. I used hand motion to alert him of the noise and he shook his head yes. The noised turned into two V.C. coming directly into us. They were in hurry and apparently not paying attention. I decided to wait and see if there were more coming behind them. I motioned for Okie to be calm. I noticed Okie was shaking and prayed he did not make a noise. They passed and I tapped Okie on the knee to get his gear and we were following them. I thought they might even lead us to their main base. Following two men in the dark in strange territory was not easy. We tried to stay on the same trail knowing booby traps were scattered all over the area and they might know where they were located. We tried following them for over two hours when I discovered our Daniel Boone traits had failed and we were lost. We had gone through swamps and thickets with leaches, ants, and mosquitoes eating us alive. I knew we were in trouble and fear was beginning to show. No way were we just going to stop and sit in the swamp so we kept walking. Then a wonderful thing happened, the sun peaked at the horizon. I could see a hill in the distance so we made our way to it but it was not very high. I looked for a higher hill but the trees were too thick to get a view. Maybe it was time to call on the God. He had always got me out of these places before.

Nothing looked familiar and nothing looked right. I was totally lost. Okie sense that and asked, "Okay what the hell are we going to do now?"

"Not a clue. Okay let's think about where those two went last night."

Okie rolled his eyes and said, "Hey, I lost them really quick. I thought you saw them all the time."

I found a dry spot on the hill so I could see a good distance and sat down. "What are you doing, Tex?"

"I going to eat something and maybe take an hour nap. You want the first watch?"

"Tex, I can't hold my eyes open."

"Okay, you got the first nap."

Okie was out like a rock in a matter of seconds. I stood and stretched my legs taking a slow look around. "What went wrong last night," I asked myself?

I was lucky to be alive mainly due that I was not snake bitten in the swamp. I sat down and reminded myself that I had three more days to get back to Six with all the details of what was happening in this area. There had to be a major movement of the V.C. coming because Six had explained that five-hundred G.I.'s were depending on what I tell him. That's a lot of pressure and I did not have the least amount of info yet.

Sitting in the jungle was a humbling experience and I gave thanks to God for keeping me alive. Last night was one of the few times that felt alone with no one for help. Being alone makes a person religious. I knew we were still lost with no radio or communication and the jungle was thick. Could I use my basic instincts and find a way out of this? That is about all I had. If I would have had a woman instead of Okie, I am sure she would have pointed me in the right direction.

Okie woke up and we switched positions for an hour. I was so tired that I never heard a word that Okie was speaking. Too soon Okie was tapping me on the boot. I pulled myself to the sitting position and tried to wake up. My eyelids seemed weight a ton and they kept falling down.

Okie seemed to be fully awake and I asked, "Seen or heard anything?"

He shook his head no. I pulled out a can of fruit cocktail, opened it and slowly ate it. Okie pulled out a piece of C-4 plastic explosive and was going to light it for a fire. C-4 will burn at a high temperature and it did a great job at cooking a meal. It only became an explosive under pressure such as a blasting cap. Okie had planned on a hot turkey dinner. The fire was a bad idea and I shook my head at Okie and he put the C-4 back into his pack. "Okie, are you learning?"

"At times I think so then I make dumb mistakes. I seem to be screwing up all the time and you bail me out."

"Okie last night was a watch and listen night. What did you hear?"

"Mostly night animals and I did see snakes."

I leaned back and said, "This place is not good, no movement of anyone or anything. Just those damn mosquitoes."

Okie we are going back the way we came and see if we can get back into the traffic. "Sarge, I can't go back. That was a hell last night."

"Okie, your choice, same way, different way or stay here. Just remember the gooks will find you if you stay here and there are booby traps all over. At least we know there was none the way we came last night."

"Sorry I must be stupid. I never seem to think to the future."

"Okie, we are not here on vacation so think about staying alive."

"Two more things, make sure you are not seen by the V.C. If you are I am sure they will not hesitate to put a bullet in your brain. Second, kill anyone you see because they will spread the news in seconds."

We packed our gear and started walking. I held back and Okie turned and looked at me. I pointed ahead, "Guess who is walking point?"

"Thanks."

It was hot and sweat rolled off us and that drew flying bugs of every kind including mosquitoes. I have always heard that mosquitoes zero in on body heat. In the daylight we made better time and did not see a single person. Arriving back to our original spot I kept thinking it was near the river. If I could find the river, then I could get my bearings and find the sought after Number Ten Hill. I had a feeling the flares from last night were coming from this area. The ground was covered with tracks and shell cases. We took a good look around and Okie asked, "Which way?"

I pointed to a bend in the terrain hoping to get a view of the river. We were getting short of time with only one day and half left. If we missed our pick up at the hill, the chopper would not wait. Okie asked, "What happens if we miss the pick up?"

"We are here for a long time and we get back the best way we can."

"Sarge, being out here alone is hell and I don't like it a bit. How often do we do this?"

"Just do your job. We will be here whenever they tell us."

We walked for three or four hours before I gave Okie a signal to head for a nearby hill. We were due a break. Half way up the hill I found a place that we could rest out of sight. We sat there half asleep and I thought of hunting deer at home. I made a promise to myself that I was through hunting any animal or man forever. I was finished with killing and the past year seemed to have lasted my entire life. I had to get some kind of definition of the V.C. traffic before dark so I whispered, "Time to move out. I will take point."

"Thanks."

There I was with a gut feeling again that the hill we were looking was straight ahead. We walked for another couple of hours pressing through thick jungle. We came to an opening but soon found trip-wires of booby traps. I tensed and I came alive. We continued up the hill and if I were wrong this might be another hot spot. We continued but nothing, which was okay by me. I really did not want to be in a firefight. We walked into an open and there sat a pond. It seemed that ponds were the V.C.'s favorite place to set booby traps so we slowed down. It was so open that I decide to crawl using the tall grass for cover. It was not long before a trip-wire touched my hand. Damn, these guy have a thing for ponds. I followed the wire and found it attached to three forks of wood standing like an Indian tepee. I had seen this type of trap before so I told Okie, "Turn around and get the hell out of here.

We back tracked to the tree line and stopped. I steadied myself by getting on one knee and then scanning the trees. There it was, a trip-wire going into the trees. I could not see where it stopped so motioned to Okie. He shook his head yes to the wire but neither of us could see its designation. We crawled along the tree line and found the tree that the wire was attached. The wire ran down the back of the tree and along the ground. "What the hell is going on," I asked myself?

Tracing the wire another tepee, I motioned to Okie and said, "Stand still and do not go any further. I have never seen anything like this before so the whole area might blow with us in the middle.

Once again we back off and started the way we came. We had crawled about twenty yards when all hell broke loose. Okie had tripped a wire. Bombs were exploding in every direction. I took a blast to my front that it knocked be down but no blood. The explosions continued and with God's help I ran. The bombs were pushing me right and then left but I never stopped. The explosions finally stopped and so did I. I sat down for a quick rest and access the damage. Where was Okie? I took water from my canteen and washed some of the mud off my face so I could see. I looked for Okie and saw him sit on the ground with his hands between his legs crying like a baby.

That made me mad so I walked over to him and gave him a hard slap. "Are you hit?"

"No just scared as hell."

I began to laugh, "You son-of-a-bitch, you just saved a bunch of lives. If the squad had been here all of them would be dead. Hell, I would give you a medal."

"I don't want a medal, I want out."

I gave him another slap and said, "You are not out and I don't want you to spit without asking me first. We are damn lucky to be alive. I am too short for such as this and dying is not in my plan."

After my lecture Okie looked up at me and said, "Sarge, you are bleeding and looks like you need stitches. I don't have the first aid kit so maybe tape will work."

Okie pulls a piece of tape and closed the cut.

"Let's get out of here. Every gook in Nam must be on there way here after all that noise."

We ran as fast as we could watch for trip-wires and finally we had to stop for a breather. It was quiet so maybe we had escaped from all the traps. Okie took the first watch and I lay there with blood still running down my face. Okie seemed to be fully alert so worrying about him falling asleep was not a problem. My ears were ringing like I had been in a rock concert and my hearing was starting to return. I gave Okie a look and said, "Okie, you okay?"

"Yeah Sarge."

My head was hot and I had a fever. I was so tired that when I closed my eyes I was asleep. I guess an hour passed and I took a look at Okie. He was awake and going well. I closed my eyes again and this time I was out for almost two hours. When I woke my fever was down and I felt better. "Everything quiet, Okie?"

"Yeah, nothing going down."

I woke with a bad feeling flushing my gut. The feeling came over me in a flash that something bad was going to happen and happen soon. I wished I could have seen into the future or maybe not. The poor people that do see the future are always in pain thinking they have failed. All I wanted was to see over the next hill and find our way out of this hellhole. Okie was asleep after a couple of eye blinks. I let him sleep for a couple of hours while I studied the map. I discovered that a map is worthless unless you know where you are. Every map should have a "You are here."

I would have tossed the map but I was afraid the V.C. would find it.

I woke Okie after a couple of hours and told him to take point. He asked, "Where are we going?"

"Anyplace. Just walk."

"What if I see V.C. What do you want me to do?"

"Less than ten, shoot the hell out of them. Otherwise, stay out of sight."

For the next two and one-half hours we walked. Not easy and the flying creatures were eating us alive. Suddenly Okie froze in his tracks and I picked up on it. I froze. I slowly pulled a grenade from my belt and pulled the pins. With grenade in one hand and my rifle in the other I waited for Okie. He raised his rifle and opened fire. I threw the grenade in the direction he was firing and hit the ground. No return fire. I raised to one knee trying to see what Okie was shooting. I saw one man lying on the trail followed by two more behind him. All were dead. I came up to Okie and gave him a smile and whispered, "Good job."

We pulled the bodies off the trail and I motioned for Okie to move. He kept staring at the dead men. I pulled him by the arm, "Leave it. You are okay and nothing we can do."

We continued but I took point to give Okie a chance to clam down. "Tex, you ever get use to killing?"

"No but the time will come when you are mad enough that killing is not an issue. You have got to stay alive and that may be the only way to do it. Now, pick up your gear and get your butt moving."

About dark Okie said, "Tex, I about to starve to death."

I waved him on and said, "Top of the hill and we will make camp."

We opened our C-rations and ate from the can, no fires, and no lights. I gave Okie the first sleep while I took guard. Five hours later it was getting cold so I pulled my camouflage rain cover out of my pack. I was in the process of getting covered when I saw a dim light about three hundred yards away. The light disappeared and came back several times but I never took my eye off the area. The light meant one thing, motion of personnel or equipment. I thought, "Well, this is what we get paid for."

I woke Okie and told him about the light and that we were moving. Both of us checked our rifles for ammo and slid the bolt to make sure it was not jammed.

I started forward with Okie in tow straight at the light. I told Okie not to fire unless it was absolutely necessary. There were clearings and then back into the jungle several times. At about one hundred yards I saw the light again. We were close but I still had no idea as to what was happening. Were they setting traps? We moved slowly watching for trip-wires. I gave Okie a signal as to the light and he nodded. He was behind me as usual and I pointed for him to go left along the trees. As Okie started I noticed movement in the direction that I had pointed. I grabbed Okie's shoulder and pulled him down. I eased my rifle to the shooting position and Okie followed. I whispered to Okie, "Let them go."

I did not want to do any shooting unless we were discovered. We waited. Two figures came from the dark. I think I could see better in the dark than daylight and maybe that is why I was alive. We were frozen and the two V.C. walked right by us within ten feet. My blood was circulating through my heart so fast that I could feel it flowing. These two were young troops and both carried an AK-47 and a rice bag from their belts. Maybe they were taking a trip.

Okie never moved a muscle as sweat poured from his face like a river. They passed and we continued up the trail in the direction that our two friends had come. It did not take long before I had a feelings and it was not good. I stopped and waved Okie to do the same. About thirty yards to our right I caught the flash of a light.

I hit the ground and crawled with Okie beside me. We went a few yards and the smell of bad water came across my nose. I hated that smell and it meant that were near a creek or pond. I kept crawling but never saw the light again. Okie and I both froze when we heard voices. We worked our way to a small ravine hoping for cover. Then I saw a deep channel that had been dig cross the trail. It had a camouflage net over the trail part. My heart sunk when I heard voices all around us. My hands were shaking and I got tense. Okie started to back up and I grabbed him. I motioned for him to stay. He was so scared that I expected him to run but that was sure death. We lay in that ravine all night watching V.C. go in and out of the channel. It had to be large and most of it was underground. Was this the base camp we were sent here to find? Before the night was over there were hundreds of troops in and out and I counted everyone.

About an hour before daylight it was time to get out. From what I could tell a major uprising was coming and coming soon. I even thought that this was the spot that the Tet Offence started. Hell, I did not know but one thing I did know trouble was coming. I motioned for Okie to start crawling out. It was just as bad getting out as it had been getting in. We crawled a hundred yards before I felt we were safe enough to walk in the jungle. Walking in the jungle slowed us down and Okie worried about traps every second as he should. The guy was learning.

I took point and found our way back to the starting point. I backed up against a tree and pulled out the map. I still was not sure of our pickup point. The chopper was due tomorrow. "Okie, get some sleep while I work on getting us out of here."

Okie relaxed a bit and said, "Tex, you are the quietest man I have ever known."

"Just staying alive."

The night was clear and the stars and moon gave us all the light we wanted. V.C. moved into the area all night. There would be thousands by morning. From our view we counted over four hundred on the trail that passed us. Believe me we never moved a muscle all night.

We followed what I thought was the trail to our pickup point. We fought our way through jungle and we stopped for a break. "Tex, what did we watch last night. You think that is a major camp for the V.C.?"

"Anytime you see that many soldiers in one place they are planning a big hit. If we do not get this information to Six we could loose a lot on men. I figure we have to stop them now or they may take Saigon. Your are going to be in for a long year if that happens."

"What time is the chopper due at the pickup point?"

"Ten hundred hours."

"What time is it now?"

"08:40."

"Damn, it seems we have been walking for hours. God I need a shower and hot meal."

I found a couple of points that I recognized and we located the pickup spot. We waited. At 10.20 I could hear a chopper praying it was for us. The pilot picked us up. God, I love choppers. Once in the air, the pilot asked, "How long have you been in the bush?"

"Two or three days. Why?"

"Oh there have been some changes made."

"What kind."

"You will see."

I hate playing games but I kept my mouth shut. As we approached the base, my mouth fell open. "What the hell."

Most of the base was burned to the ground. The pilot gave me a look and asked, "We were overrun and caught hell."

I asked, "Did we win?"

"Well if you consider loosing one hundred and fifty a win, then we won."

"How many gooks?"

"I hear about six hundred."

We landed and I went straight to Six's hut. He was asleep but woke up when I entered. He rose up and said, God, I hope you have good news. We have to stop this before it gets started."

I sat on the opposite bunk and told him the whole story. He was excited and a smile broke across his face. "Let's get those bastards." I pulled out a map and showed him the exact location. He acted like he wanted to hug me. "Tex, you did a damn good job. Get to the chow hall and get soon sleep. I have a lot prep work to do."

"What about the attach here?"

"Never mind we are going to give them a taste of their own medicine."

CHAPTER 13

We ate, slept and showered almost every hour for three days. I toured the base and surveying all the damage trying to image the fight that must have taken place here. Every hut had damage and some completely destroyed. Late on the third day Six came into my hut with me lying on the bunk. I was trying to write home but Six sat down on my bunk. I could tell he wanted something. I was hoping for a surprise early out. "How do you feel, Tex?'

"Okay, ready to go home."

"Tex, I need you. We are making another trip to Number 10 Hill."

I interrupted, "Damn you Six!"

"Yes, I know you are short but you are the only one that knows your way around."

I knew there was no way to get out of it so I replied, "When do we leave?"

"Tonight at dark."

"God Six, why at night? The boat ride is bad enough in the daylight. You know there are trap and new traps being laid everyday there. Plus, all we have are new guys. I don't know any of them except for Okie. All the old troops are dead or gone. You had better have a damn good plan for this trip or a lot of men will be killed. I have seen how many V.C. are there and they mean business."

Choppers not boats took us to the Number 10 Hill. As they landed on base the air and fog was so thick that a knife could not cut it. The Huey blades were slinging water as they turned due to the moisture in the air. Why this night? It was bad in more ways than one. We fly in the direction of the hill and before we landed I could see nothing and hear nothing. The choppers were loud and moving fast. As we started down I could see fifteen or twenty choppers in the air behind us.

As usual, we had to jump ten or fifteen feet to the ground. I did not know if I should love or hate those chopper pilots. Okie was beside me again and he asked, "Tex, are we going to die?"

"Hell no! I am burning gun power today and if you say that again I will shoot you myself."

Our feet touched the ground and we were receiving fire. That only meant one thing we were in for an all night fight. I gave them all I had blazing my M-16 in all directions. I gave cover for the troops that were landing but lead was covering us up. The chopper lifted off and with a little altitude the gunner gave support. The sound of that 30 cal machine gun sounded good.

Six was on the radio behind me and I shouted for him to get help. He shouted back, "No help in the area."

My heart sunk and I shouted back, "Six, unless you get help we are all dead."

"We are on our own!"

Oncoming fire was coming harder and from every direction. They knew we were coming and had been waiting. They were dug in and it would take a 10,000-pound bomb to uproot them. I had never seen a firefight like this in my entire tour. Bombs, rockets, mortars and rifle fire came at us all at once. There was nothing to do except to dig in and take what they could dish out.

There seemed to be no hope. We sent several flares into the air giving us a little light. Several G.I.'s were killed during the landing. V.C. was pour out of the trees but seeing them was next to impossible due to the smoke and fog. We seemed to be sitting ducks waiting to be roasted and we were in the their frying pan. We held them most of the night but we were out of ammo. A chopper tried several times to get to us but was backed off. We were sitting there with no ammo and not very many rocks.

God must have been on our side because it was getting daylight. We could see. I had burns over my face, arms and hands but other than that I did not see any blood leaking out of my body. I could see bodies everywhere, G.I.'s and V.C. For some reason God wanted me to live and I am not sure why. I had never seen so much blood and torn bodies. I turned to my right and saw Okie with his head half blown off. I fell back and wondered why. I got to him and kissed him on the forehead. "Okie, you never had a chance, did you friend."

The fighting had stopped and I got up and walked. G.I.'s were lying dead that had only been here for a few weeks. They were new and did not know any better. I could smell burning flesh and the blood as I walked. I thought to myself that no one should have to go through this and remember it. God forgive us for what we had done. I hurt badly deep inside.

I kept walking and walking, not knowing where I was going. It hurt to bad to stop. I found Six against a tree with half his leg done. He was in shock and I applied a tourniquet to stop the bleed. I felt he had lost too much blood but he came around and asked, "Tex, we kicked their ass, didn't we?"

"You damn right."

"Tex, find a medic. I don't want to die here."

"Six." He faded out again but I kept working on him. He returned and I gave him all the encouragement I knew. "Six, there are no medics so you are looking at the doc. You are going to be fine so hang on. Help will come."

He gave me a sad look and said, "How many did we loose?"

"Not sure but a hell of a lot."

"Tex, take care of them. Make sure they go home. Are you hit?"

"No."

He closed his eyes and died in my arms. We tried so hard and fought so well.

I got up and began to walk again. I needed a radio to call for help. G.I.'s called to me as they screamed in pain. I offered as much help as I could but I had no medical equipment. I just did what I could and several more died in my arms. Help did come and we gathered the wounded and dead and carried them home.

A few days later back at the base I was sitting on the dike staring at the morning sunrise remembering what had happened on the hill. For the first time I felt that my mind was not right. I started praying for the dead, hoping there were angels to take them home where they belonged.

I heard a noise coming and I turned to see our new Six. He was short and a bit overweight with dark hair. He sat down beside me and kept silence for a while. He must have known I was hurting. Finally he said, "The Major wants to see you at headquarters."

After a few more minutes I got to my feet and turned to go. "Tex, I hear you're the best there is at point. The squad says you don't talk much and spend a lot of time alone. For what it is worth we could not do without your kind."

"Just what kind of person am I?"

"Tex, you are soldiers that puts his country first. There are not many of those around in this war."

I entered headquarters and the major told me to have a chair. I smiled to myself wondering where he got the chair. "Sarge, you've been here almost a year and I cannot tell you what a great job you have done. The United States Army and your Country thanks you. You are one hell of a soldier."

"Thanks. I just tried to stay alive."

"The men in your platoon say you have done more for them than anyone else."

"I was only doing my job the best way I knew."

"That's why we want you to stay here and help us. We need men like you. The Army could be your family."

"Sir, I'm tired and I really want to go home. I'm not even sure that my mind is working correctly. I feel I have been in the jungle too long."

"Do you need medical help?"

"No sir, just rest."

"Sergeant Taylor, what you need is a leave. I will send you home for thirty days and then come back and help us."

"Sir, I am really ready to go home for good."

"How about a big bonus? It's worth ten thousand dollars for another six months work. Just sign up for three more years. That includes two and half years of living in any country you choose."

"That sound good but Sir, I will pass. I am going home."

My mind was still dull and I could only see home. "Okay soldier, you got it. Here is a little something for you take with you. It is from the scouts."

It was a plaque and I held it like it was a treasure. It gave thanks for all that I had done.

I left Viet Num a changed person, maybe better, maybe worse.

PART 2 - 1969

CHAPTER 14

I boarded the chopper and I buckled myself to the seat. I had no desire to hang out the door or shoot any rounds into a green carpet of jungle. I just wanted a smooth ride to the airport. As we lifted off I felt heaviness in my chest like I was fighting grief. I had made friends and lost friends. Now I was going home to deal with the remainder of my life. Happiness was not overwhelming but I still had jungle mud on my boots. I did not understand but I should have been screaming with joy. My body was taking a few scars and pieces of metal as the chopper made a turn and headed in the direction of Saigon. There was no way I would ever forget the hours I had spent here and I was not sure how to forget. I wanted to wipe out the memories but wanted to keep the men that died serving by my side. I was riding a fence wanting to fall off on the easy side but I kept leaning to the bad side. I held my rifle like it had grown to me and I did not want to put it down. I was afraid in a way and I still felt alone. The chopper ride was not long and it put down next to a hangar.

I unloaded my gear throwing it on the ground and then I sat on top of it for awhile. Some guy kept telling me to go but I sat there. I had no idea who this guy was and I never even looked up. That same stale air that I smelled when I got off the plane was still in the air but it did not seem so bad. I gave thanks to God for keeping me alive. I let my mind wonder to the people in this country and wished them all a good life. They had to be fighting for something that was good. Most were good fighters but I knew we were not going to change these people to Americans not matter how many we killed. I thought of the kids and what a hard road some of them would have just to survive. The kids were warriors, sad.

The guy returned and said, "Sarge, you need to process out and if you do not hurry you will miss your plane."

"Thanks."

I picked up my gear and walked to headquarters. Just like the Army, it took over an hour to sign paperwork and get a ticket for the next flight out. They took my rifle and ammo and I felt naked. There were other soldiers processing and they were kicking butt getting out of there. I picked up my bag and walked outside and took a look around. They called us to load on a truck and carried us to the plane. Pan Am was there waiting and I found a seat near the front. The flight attendants were more than nice as they zoomed around getting drinks before we took off. I sat there forty-five minutes drinking a beer. No one sat beside me which did not bother me. I flipped through a magazine sipping the beer. After a few minutes the attendant came and collected the drinks and the plane started moving. It taxied to the end of the runway and poured the fuel to the engines. Seconds later we lifted off and the plane erupted in a cheer.

I laid my head back and thought of home. A year is not long but I had changed and I only hoped mom and dad were the same. Food came and it was not rice or anything that looked Asian. I would have been so happy for a hamburger. I ate and drank for hours. Again I looked through magazines seeing what I had missed in the last year. Bathing suits were small and most women did not wear a bra. I knew I could sleep without worry so I tried. Nothing worked I was waking up at the slightest noise or light that came on. I gave up sleeping and drank a few glasses of wine. Wine always put me to sleep. I asked for a ham sandwich and had it within seconds. I finished my wine and snack and decided to talk with a flight attendant. A cute blonde sat in the galley area reading so I began talking. She lived in Michigan and had worked for Pan Am for several years. My first question, "How did you get the Nam run? Is that some kind of punishment?"

"No, I just like a little adventure and I like soldiers."

We talked for over an hour and I closed our conversation by asking her to marry me. She just laughed but I was serious. Outside the plane I never saw her again. I felt better talking with someone that was not in the Army. I returned to my seat and went to sleep. I woke up with a blanket over me and I assume it was the flight attendant had provided a little extra comfort. We ate again and this time it was real eggs and bacon. God, I love eggs and bacon. The flight continued forever and a day but after a movie came the announcement that we were approaching New York. I had a three hour layover in New York before I boarded the plane to Dallas. When I walked into the airport it hit me that I was in the U.S.A. and a warm feeling ran through me. I wanted to give yell but I held back. No one looked at me and maybe all that I had heard about people hating soldiers was correct. I am a people watcher and an airport is great territory for such. Listening to the foreigners and the New York accents was a treat. For me New York would be a great place to visit but living there is another question. I walked to the bar and ordered a beer just to talk with a New Yorker. The beer came and I turned to see a woman in her 20's sitting next to me. She was drinking something clear, maybe vodka. I smiled and asked, "You live in New York?"

That was a mistake. She turned to me and laughed, "Where the hell are you from?"

"Wait, I asked you first."

"I live in Jersey and going to Florida."

"Okay, I from Texas."

"I should have guessed. No one talks like that except people from Texas."

"What can I say? Texas is God's country and we have our own language."

Of course, this was the first woman that I had conversation in a year except for those in uniform. I was a bit shy but she was fun. We finished our drinks and I bought another round. She asked, "Tell me about Viet Nam and what it was like."

I took a small drink and replied, "Just another war."

"Yeah, but what did you do there?"

"Usual, walked around."

"Okay you are not talking about it."

"Sorry."

We spent another thirty minutes talking and she left. I sat thinking about her and wondering if I could every talk about Nam. My plane was boarding and I found my seat.

Dallas was next along with mother and dad. For a three hour flight it seemed long. I read through magazines and newspapers but time still creep along. The wheels burned rubber as the plane touched down and after a short taxi the door opened at the terminal. I was up front so I was one of the first off the plane. As I walked into the terminal and a great cheer went up. There was mother and dad and about twenty of my friends with signs of welcome home. Mother could not hold back as she ran to me with tears of joy giving me hugs and kisses. Dad gave me a hug and said, "Welcome home son."

I felt water running down my face but I did not care. I had to greet all the others with hugs and a few words. It was such a happy time and one that I had been waiting for a long time. All of us walked to the car and no one ever stopped talking except for dad. To know dad is to know a man that has few words but never a doubt his love. I said good-by to all the friends and mother, dad and I left the airport for home.

Mother asked a million questions about my trip home while we were in the car. She had to know every detail about the flight. The word Viet Nam was never spoken and I was glad. I had a few weeks leave before I had to report back to the Army. I had two months left before my discharge.

As we pulled in front of the house and turned into the driveway, I saw Red in the back yard. Red was a large Irish Setter that loved to run. He and I had the best of times. I took my bag from the truck of the car and dad took it from me, "Save your strength."

Mother put her arm around me as we walked to the door and continued talking. While in Nam I remember every detail of the house and yard but now it seemed different. The front door was opened and all I could see was welcome home signs. Banners hung from the ceiling and walls. God, nothing had changed, same house with the same warm feeling like home. I smelled something cooking from the kitchen. Mother asked to be excused, "I need to check the roast."

Mother was the best pot roast cooker I knew. All that meat, potatoes, carrots, and onions in delicious gravy made me weak in the knees. She had homemade yeast rolls sitting on the kitchen counter waiting to be popped into the oven. Those babies were so light that they would float off your plate. Mother was a stay-at-home mom and cooking was her specialty. She worked hard and could have a meal ready in minutes for unexpected company. She had a knack in the kitchen that I have never seen before. No food was ever bought if you could make it from scratch at home.

My parents did not drink much alcohol and as a matter of fact I never saw mother drink a drop. Dad opened the frig and brought out two beers. He popped the tops, handed me one and we sat down in the living room. I never felt so good. We talked small talk about sports and TV shows. He gave me the lowdown on my brothers and their tour of duty. They were still serving their country but in the Air Force and Navy. Those two guys had painless jobs and my middle brother was stationed in Hawaii and the older in Florida. I went wrong somewhere along the line. Forty minutes later mother came in with an apron and called us to chow or should I say dinner. Mother had a thing about coming when called to dinner. I guess she worked so hard at cooking that she did not want it to get cold. We sat at the table with a feast in front of us and said the blessing. Of course, dad thanked God for me being home safe. I ate so much that I looked nine months pregnant. I helped mother with the dishes and we found lawn chairs and sat outside. Red would retrieve a ball a million times if someone would throw it. We talked for hours but never about Nam or the war.

The sun was going down and mother came out with a huge bowl of peach cobbler and ice cream. Red tried to get his share but I held him back. It took me an hour of pure slow enjoyment to finish the bowl. We laughed at times and that was the first time I had laughed in months. We returned to the house and sat watching TV. It was 11:30 and mother said she was going to bed. My room had been left just as I had left it except now the sheets were clean and it was dusted. Dad and I looked at each other and gave an agreement nod that we were going to bed also. I lay there in a bed that felt like heaven with the smell of outside dried sheet next to my nose. After all the eating it took me about a minute to fall asleep.

I heard gunfire followed by explosions and I was running. It was hot and I was pouring sweat and the bullets kept coming. I saw a man go down beside me with blood gushing from his head. I turned and fired and ran more. The grass was tall and I hit a trip-wire and my body went flying to the air. I woke up and my clean bed was soaking wet. I got up and went to the frig for a beer. I sat in the dark in the living room thinking this could not happen. I was home and safe. Sweat was still running down my face. Mother came in and asked, "Son, you okay?"

"Yes, just a bad dream."

"You want to talk about it?"

"No, I'm okay."

She gave me a hug and saw that I was wet with sweat. She turned for the bathroom and brought me a towel. She then went to the bedroom and changed my sheets. She knew the dream was about the war but she let me keep inside for now. How do mothers know about such?

The morning came with sounds and smells of bacon frying. Dad was home and we sat at the table drinking coffee. Mother filled the table with bacon, eggs, biscuits and gravy. It only took a short time for me to look pregnant again. After we finished I carried the dishes to the sink and there stood mother crying softly. I turned her to face me and she said, "Just glad to have you back home safe. I worried about you every minute. I have read your letters a thousand times and cried through all of them."

She gave me a long hug. I turned to dad and asked, "What are you doing today?"

105

"Whatever you are doing."

"How about looking at cars?"

"I can do that."

"Well, not new one but one that I might drive around here."

"Maybe we should check the paper."

We searched the paper and found several that might be worth going to see.

The excuse to look at a car was just to get me out of the house so I could talk to dad alone. We had driven a few miles and I asked, "Dad how is mother?"

He did not answer. "What? Is she okay?"

He gave no reply. I saw his eyes fill with tears. "Dad pull over, we need to talk."

He pulled into a grocery store parking lot and shut down the engine. "Son, your mother has a heart problem and it is serious."

"What kind of heart problem?"

"It is not beating correctly and they say she is due for a heart attach. Her blood pressure is low and the doctors have tried several things."

"What can we do?"

"I don't know. She is seeing a heart doctor and he seems to be doing all he can."

"Dad, I really do not want a car at this time. Let's go home."

He started the car and turned it in the direction of home. "Mother said you had a bad dream last night. Want to talk about it?"

"I'm okay. It was just a dream about the war. I had some bad experiences and they seem to be staying with me for awhile."

"Son, I'm sorry but I do not know what to say about that. I was farming and the Government would not take me. If you want, we can see a doctor."

"No, I will be okay."

The next few days were great and I talked to mother a lot but mainly ate good food. The dreams continued and got even worse. After the first week, I was staying up most of the night afraid to go to sleep. I would take naps during the day to survive. I tried to keep mother and dad from knowing but how could I hide staying up at night. I watched TV with the low volume at night but my hearing was not the best either. About every other day I would try to sleep at night but blood and jungle filled my mind. I would wake myself up screaming and with mother sitting next to me. She wanted to help by doing anything but even I did not know what to tell her.

Time passed fast and it was time to leave for Kansas. I drove to Fort Riley after buying a Ford. I was scheduled to stay for three weeks and then be discharged. The trip was uneventful and I checked in to the post. I was assigned to help with new recruit training but my attitude was not into being a real soldier. All I could see was these men being killed in some far off land. I wanted to teach them everything that I knew but that was not going to happen. They needed someone like Cal to hold their hand or threaten to blow their head off. All the training in the world could not prepare them for Nam.

I took a day and reported to sickbay telling the doc about my dreams. The doctor who was a major offered me a chair. I knew he was not going to give me an instant cure but I needed sleep. He was a man in his late thirties with a kind face. I felt I could trust him. He was quiet while I told him my problems and he took notes. He asked a few questions and he was easy going and seemed like he cared. My degree of confidence increased and I gave him a few of the details about Nam. He then made a statement that I really did not understand. He said, "Battle fatigue, you have a lot of symptoms of battle fatigue."

I had heard of it in the movies and joking around but what was it?

He continued, "Battle fatigue, is the World War II name for what is known today as post-traumatic stress, this is a psychological disorder that develops in some individuals who have had major traumatic experiences. The person is typically numb at first but later has symptoms including depression, excessive irritability, guilt (for having survived while others died), recurrent nightmares, flashbacks to the traumatic scene, and overreaction to sudden noises. From what you have told me this is partially the problem. One more thing, did you have any experience with Agent Orange?"

"Sure, we all did. They sprayed that stuff all the time. Why?"

"We are getting some more medical information about that stuff and it is not good."

"You mean kill me type of information?"

"No, but a lot of men are having problems after breathing that chemical."

The doc continued and said he would like to do a few test, physical and mental. He asked if I could report at 8:00 in the morning.

I was there at 8:00 and issued into an office by a private. The office did not look military but had soft colors and was well decorated. I was told to have a chair and the doctor would be with me shortly. Ten minutes later there were three men in the office and the highest-ranking officer was a colonel. I was a bit intimidated but all three were sociable and concerned. The colonel sat in a chair next to me and asked questions for about thirty minutes. I told him about Num, the dreams and how I felt about it all. He seemed really concerned when I told him that the other troops thought I was a killer and a loner. I stopped the conversation by raising my hand and said, "I am not a killer and I was just doing my job. I hate killing and watching my friends die. I am tired of watching for traps and waiting for someone to kill me."

The colonel replied, "Are you feeling threaten now?"

"I still cannot get it out of my mind."

An hour passed and then two and we kept talking. They kept trying to get me to re-experience the events and telling me that I was now in a safe, controlled environment. They told me that I needed to resolve strong feelings such as anger, shame, or guilt, which is common among survivors of trauma. The colonel told me that I would have to cope with the memories, reminders, reactions, and feelings without becoming overwhelmed or emotionally numb. Trauma memories usually do not go away entirely as a result of therapy but become manageable with the mastery of new coping skills. It was chow time and they told me to come back tomorrow.

The next day came without me getting much sleep. My butt was dragging and the dreams were still there. This time the doctors meet me and carried me to a testing room. They went through a complete physical exam. If they found anything except for scares, then they did not tell me. After that episode of embarrassment they took me to a quiet room and began to test me by asking question about my experiences. As I told them about some of the battles they asked for more details and they kept telling me that I was safe and had nothing to worry about. That lasted for three hours before they said I needed a break. They told me to take a nap if I liked. There was a large couch and it was comfortable. I tried and it only took me a minute before I was asleep. The next thing I remember was being on the floor. I had somehow rolled off the couch. I guess there was some noise and the doctors came in asking if I were hurt. I got up and told them, "I must have had another dream and I got a bit excited, sorry."

The colonel replied, "Not a problem, no damage."

We talked more and they gave me several books and more appointments. Before I left the colonel made me a list of things that I could do and be aware.

1. Learn skills for coping with anxiety such as breathing and negative thoughts.

2. Be aware and handling future trauma symptoms.

3. Preparing for stress reactions.

4. Address urges to use alcohol or drugs when trauma symptoms occur.

5. Communicate effectively with people to include social skills or marital therapy.

He told me that all the helps would be in the books that he provided. He also gave me medication. He said, "Medication can reduce the anxiety, depression, and insomnia. It may help relieve the distress and emotional numbness caused by trauma memories. It will help you sleep also."

I took the pills and left. I wondered if I was cured or they just did not know what to do. I talked to myself, "Did they expect me to read the books and cure myself? Maybe there was nothing wrong with me. Everyone has bad dreams and maybe they would stop. I took the paper out of my pocket and gave it another look. All those items seemed like the way a normal person should act but how did I act? The men in Num told me I was a bit strange but hell I was in Num killing people."

I paid the price and read the books but it was hard for me to judge. I still lay around thinking of the past and the dreams continued. Was I going over the edge? I had to get back home. I had only one week left so I went to talk with the colonel. He gave a Honorable Discharge along with my Purple Hearts and Silver Stars. I was going home for good.

CHAPTER 15

Mother and dad were just as happy to see me the second time and gave me all the luxuries of home. We had long talks but very little about Num. I was still out of sink with my sleeping I stayed awake all night. I was scared of the dreams.

Mother knew what I was going through and see was beginning to suffer also. After about a week she came to the living room and sat. She turned the TV down and said, "I am not leaving you until you tell me about your dreams and feelings."

I shock my head no but she sat there staring at me. She added, "This will go no further than this room."

"Mother, I cannot shake the war."

"I know and you need help. I have to know where to start."

"I am scared of the night. All our battles were at night and I see them over and over."

She moved to the couch and sat next to me. I could see tears running down her face. She had heart problems and I was afraid to give her all the details but she wanted me back as her little boy. Both of us leaned back shoulder-to-shoulder and she said, "Tell me more."

"Mother, this is not good."

"Tell me more."

I told her of the deaths and blood around me everyday. I told her that I had killed an unknown number of people and I could not live with it. I began to cry. She said, Baby, I am listening, go on."

I held my arms like I was holding a dying man and told her that I lost friends that were closer than bothers. They died in my arms. I did not want them to die but I had no say in the matter. "Mother, I was scared so many times that I was trigger happy and shot the enemy in cold blood. They told me I was good at my job but my job was killing. I called it staying alive. Kids were in the V.C. Army and if I got close enough to see their eyes, they were even more afraid than I."

Every sentence that I spoke was followed by encouragement and the words, "It's not your fault."

The exchange of emotions continued until morning. She went to the kitchen and started breakfast. Dad joined us and we sat at the kitchen table for about two hours. Dad talked at times and he knew mother had been up all night. He knew that mother would fill him in on the details later. While we sat there I asked, "Would y'all mind if I did not look for a job for a few weeks. I have money from the army so if it is okay I would like to hang out here for awhile?"

Mother gave me a hug and said, "As long as you want. Don't worry about anything."

Dad added with a laugh, "I need a yard person anyway."

I walked back to the living room and was asleep in ten minutes while watching TV.

The few weeks turned into a few months and the dreams continued. Mother begged me to see a doctor so I went. Another couple of bottle of pills and I was out of the office. I was hurting inside and no one seemed to have an answer. I was sleeping at night maybe three times a week. I kept telling myself it was time to get off my butt and do something. I looked for a job and a trained killed was not what I wanted on my resume. My car needed windshield wipers and I stopped at the local auto supply. I made conversation with the owner and he said he would hire me part-time. I thought part-time would be perfect and I did know a lot about cars. I worked weekends and two evenings.

After six months I was an old pro at the job. The dreams were only once or twice a week and I was sleeping at night. When the dreams came I was up all night and sometimes mother would be at my side. I did notice that my nerves were a bit on edge most of the time and it showed at work. I was getting more hours and making more money. Several times my boss told me to take the afternoon off and get some rest. One afternoon an older lady came into the store and as we talked I found out that she was retired Army of thirty years. Her name was Mildred Jones and she was so excited to hear that I had just got out of the Army. She asked, "Where you in Num?"

"Yes, for a year."

"What did you do there?"

"Scout."

"Holy shit, a real fighter."

"Yeah, several Purple Hearts and Silver Stars but I am have a hard time selling them for any real money."

"What's a matter the Army did not treat you right?"

"I just cannot get over what happened there."

"How about we talk? When is your next day or evening off?"

"How about Thursday?"

Okay, 8:00 at Joe's Coffee, that's 8:00 in the morning. I'll buy breakfast."

"Sounds good."

The meeting with Mildred was strange or should I say different from what I expected. She began by asking questions about my job in the Army and continued with details of my health, both physical and mental. I was not sure where she was going with all the questions but I knew she had a direction. The meeting lasted for about two hours and she wanted to schedule another after she had done some research. I asked her what kind of research and she replied, "The kind that might get you more benefits from Uncle Sam."

I had no idea what she was talking about but no reason to doubt her either.

I left for home and decided to take a nap. Gunfire and the sound of helicopters woke me. I was soaking wet with sweat and realized it was just another dream. Mother was cooking in the kitchen so I joined her. I pulled a beer out of the refrigerator and sat at the table. She was baking cream puffs. She was good at baking anything but I loved her cream puffs so much. She claimed they were better chilled but I was eating them warm. After a major amount of weight loss in the service I was gaining it back through mother's cooking. I told her about Mildred and she asked the most obvious question, "Why is she doing this for you? Does she plan to get paid?"

"I am not sure but she will have hard time getting money from me since I am mostly poor."

"Son, maybe she is just trying to help. If she does I will be hugging her neck."

Two weeks passed, Mildred called and asked for another meeting. This time she brought a check list. Her main concern was my hearing and mental state. She asked if I would be able to drive to Waco for a meeting with a VA doctor. I said sure and three days later she and I were driving to Waco. At the VA Hospital I was put through about a dozen tests and the most obvious problem was my hearing loss. After long conversations with several doctors about my dreams and emotional state, they told me nothing. One of the questions that caught my attention was, "Did you ever come in contact with Agent Orange?"

I explained to them that I was sprayed with Agent Orange many times and breathing was extremely hard during those times.

On the trip back home Mildred explained that she was working on getting me a disability from the Government. She explained, "There was no reason for the doctors not to say there is permanent damage after what you had been through. We will just have to stay after them to get anything done. In the mean time document everything that happens to you and all your feelings similar to a diary. We have to show you are having problems."

I was not sure if she meant metal problems or physical problem but maybe both. She was driving and turned to me and said, "We already know your hearing is damaged and that is worth a 25% disability. I just want what you deserve, no more and no less. After all you gave to your country the best you had and that caused you to pay a price. Loss of hearing, pieces of shrapnel still in your body and God only knows what else is a high price to pay. All those men running off to Canada or burning their draft cards don't deserve a free country."

The Government has never been known for its speedy processing of anything and the results of the testing was taking several weeks but Mildred kept in contact telling me to be patient.

Still more time passed and I was in the grocery store buying ice cream when a woman opened and slammed the freezer door into me. It knocked me back and I felt a bit light-headed. I stood there in a daze. The woman came rushing to my rescue and that is when I noticed she was not a woman but a beautiful woman about my age. She had long blonde hair worn in a ponytail, not much makeup, and she wore short-shorts that showed golden tanned legs. Still standing I heard a loud voice coming from that great body, "You okay? You hurt?"

I raised my hand in self-defense. She kept on talking, "I am so sorry. Oh my God, you have a huge knock on your head."

"Am I bleeding?"

"No, but I think we should go see a doctor."

"Why?"

"You are hurt."

"Oh, I am okay."

I took a few steps back and almost fell. "No, you are going to see a doctor and I am taking you."

She pulled me away from the freezer, grabbed a Popsicle, and walked me to her car. She told me to hold the Popsicle to my bump as she walked me to her car. She gave me support by putting her arm around me and that was not all bad. The doctor said I had a bump on my head and that I was okay. Back in the waiting room the woman waited and when I came out she jumped up and started asking questions. I stopped her and told her that I was okay. I really did feel okay and we walked to her car. We sat in the car and she said, "I have to make this up to you. Let me buy you a drink."

"First, I do not even know your name; second the doc said I should not drink alcohol"

"I can fix that my name is Sherry Lewis and we will stop for iced tea."

"Hi Sherry, my name Pat Taylor."

She pulled into a T.G.I.F. Friday's and we went into the bar. While drinking tea I could tell she was a bit athletic because she knew sports as we watched the TV in the bar. The woman was intelligent and beautiful and she had a nice smile. She did talk a bit too much but I listened with great interest occasionally staring at her boobs. Once, she took my chin and raised it with laughter, "My face is a bit higher."

"I am sorry but it has been a long time, if ever, since I have seen such a beautiful woman."

Sherry asked the waitress for a small bag of ice and she held it to my head for a while. We talked for about an hour and in that conversation it was determined that we both were single and never been married. She worked for a new computer company and did testing in a computer lab. That was way above my level and expectations but she was seemed fine that I was a war veteran. Before I left her we had another date or maybe our first date the next day.

First dates made me nervous and this was no exception. Being the middle of the week made it even more nail-biting. We had determined that she loved seafood so dinner and a movie were on the agenda. Mother seemed happy that I had a date and she offered me money but I refused. This was the days of dress up for a date and I dug out a suit and tie. It was the first one that I had worn in over a year. She lived in an apartment that I almost never found. The apartment complex was huge and it was like looking for a needle in a haystack. All the buildings in the complex were three stories and she had a bottom floor, thank God. I thought flowers would be a bit much so I rang the doorbell and stood. The door opened and I was in love. She was the most beautiful woman in the world. She wore a blue dress that covered about half of her thigh showing perfect legs. She also wore a big smile and said, "Come in. I am almost ready."

She disappeared in the bedroom. The apartment was decorated in good taste and a person could tell she was proud of what she had. Several paintings of Texas landscape hung in the living room. I heard a voice come from the bedroom, "Make yourself a drink. There is beer or cokes in the refrigerator or hard stuff in the cabinet."

"What are you drinking?"

"I like vodka and 7-Up."

Damn, one of my favorites also. I prepared two vodkas. Music was playing; candles were burning; drink in my hand; and a beautiful woman in the bedroom. What more could I want? I sat down on the couch and looked for two coasters. About a minute passed and she appeared. I stood trying to be a gentleman and she said, "How do I look, this okay for a first date?"

"Perfect!"

I offered her the vodka and we sat. We talked and it came so easy like we had known each other for years. I wanted to jump her bones but for some reason dinner came to mind and we left. Dinner was an event at a quiet seafood restaurant and we enjoyed each other's company. I kept holding my head and acting as if I was going to pass out. We laughed about the accident several times. We decided not to go to a movie and substitute a walk. We took each others hand as we walked in the velvet darkness. Our voices softly broke the silence of the night with a car passing on occasions.

We made plans for Saturday night and when I left her house I felt at peace with the world. The night was short and I slept without a dream. At work the next day my thoughts drifted to the night before on regular intervals. Customers would have to bring me back at times with a loud, "SIR!"

I really could not help myself. I kept asking myself why I asked for a date on Saturday and not Friday night. I might be able to have Friday and Saturday if I had asked.

Mildred called and wanted to meet with me. I told her tomorrow morning and we did breakfast again. She gave good news that my paper work was being processed for a 25% disability. That meant maybe I would get the disability. It had to go through a board of medical people. My hearing was not getting any better and my nerves were being tested everyday. She told me that she was applying for a 50% and we would keep going from there if I developed any more symptoms.

Weeks passed and Sherry and I kept dating. I was in love and we were together 3 or 4 times a week. I was so afraid that I would have a war dream at night that I refused to spend the complete night with her. She did not understand and I opened up my past life to her a bit. I could never tell her the bitter details but being in a war in a jungle was enough. She had a problem understanding the word jungle. She kept thinking that I had large animals to fight also. I did not want her to feel sorry for me but I also wanted her to respect the men and women that were there. She would ask me questions with real concern in her heart.

At home mother would have bad days with her heart and blood pressure. I worried about her so much that I took her to see the doctor several times. Her blood pressure was always low and she seemed drained of energy. She took pills but I am not sure they every helped. I think that was one of the reasons that dad decided to retire early. Mother and dad were like two people that I have never seen. Both were totally devoted to each other and neither would consider a life without the other. They would not show their emotions to each other in public but the bond between the two was so strong that it gave me a definition of marriage.

My feelings for Sherry continued to grow and she became the person of my life. We dated for a year before I got the courage to ask her to marry me. We had long talks about our future lives and that brought in other factors such as her family. I knew I could not take Sherry without taking her family. Her mother and father were divorced which gave me a sad feeling. I met both of them and both were very nice and outgoing. Sherry had an older brother that acted like a watchdog for her but he was okay.

Within four months Sherry and I were married and everyone was overjoyed with happiness. We moved into an apartment and our family gathered pieces of furniture to help furnish the place. Agreed that most of the décor did not match but we were young and in love and did not even notice. My job continued and so did my dreams and cold sweats. This only made Mildred more determined to get the benefits for me. My hearing got worse so I did another trip to the VA hospital and they awarded me a new hearing aid. I think I could hear less with it in my ear than out. The background noise was so bad that all I could say was, "WHAT?"

While at the hospital I asked to see a doctor about my nerves and dreams. That was a waste and they told me that I would need an appointment. I made an appointment.

Sherry made me talk when I was in one of my silence moods, which were often. She was a good person and loved me more than I loved myself. My feelings toward her were love but at times I would not be the best husband. My words kept getting in the way of showing my love. I was on edge all the time and I never felt calm. Maybe it was because sleeping at night was still impossible. I just had to be awake at night because the war came back into my mind. Sherry understood.

Within a year I received the news that we were going to have a baby. The excitement bounced around the family and we had all the things needed for a baby to arrive before she was born. God, she was beautiful taking after her mother. Now, I had two of Sherry and could not be happier.

Mildred came to me with a new study that Agent Orange was producing stress and nerve problems in G.I.s coming back from Nam. That really lit her fire and she sent in paperwork for a 100% disability. Another side effect of Agent Orange was the lost of teeth and my teeth began to loosen. The V.A. hospital took out four of my teeth to start and then all of them were gone within a few months. The Government awarded me a new set of false teeth. They were as bad as the hearing aid and it hurt so bad to eat with the new teeth that gumming my food felt better.

It was not long before my total social life was watching TV at night and taking care of the baby. I did not want to leave the apartment and I was getting worse. Sherry forced me to see a doctor. Week after week the doctor visits continued. The doc was nice enough but all we did was talk and I did not feel like it. He gave me more pills which put me in a state of "Who cares."

Another year passed and another baby came. I love kids and this was another blessing. Sherry was suffering with my illness worse than I. We talked for long periods and she helped me more than any doctor. The metal in my back caused me pain at times so I asked the doctor about taking it out. He said the danger of the operation would not be worth it unless the pain got worse.

Now, here I am with two kids and a wife, no teeth, can't hear well, and shrapnel in my back and unable to sleep at night, what a mess. Believe me I gave Sherry hugs and kisses everyday just for allowing me to stay in the apartment. I was time to move to a house so I could do some yard work. We applied for a G.I. bill to buy a house and within a few months we were ready to move into a three bedroom brick house. The kids had a room, we had a room and I had a yard to mow and flowers to plant. The first year was a bit shaky but we made adjustments to our lifestyle. I loved the yard and by the next summer it was a showplace. All the neighbors were talking to me about what did I do to make those plants so beautiful. I told them, "Bull shit."

Well, I really told them, "Cow Manure."

My grandmother had the most beautiful yard with every kind of flowers so I guess I got a little something in my family tree.

I felt better and my job became just a low paying place to stay during the day. I had to get going with my life and I thought of school. The G.I. Bill gave me money for school so after Sherry and I decided that I would try a semester. Not bad so I continued until I graduated. Night school took longer but both of us were proud. I thanked Sherry everyday for picking us the slack with the kids while I was away at night.

My job search was short and I left the auto supply business for forever. My degree was in geology and oil companies were in full production. I enjoyed every minute of work and was making a good impression. I did field work in Texas and Oklahoma looking for that next gusher for every customer.

I was at work and received a call from dad telling me to come by the house after I got off work. That usually meant he had something for me to lift or do. I called Sherry and told her that I was going by dad's so she would pick up the kids from daycare. She agreed and when I arrived I could see something was wrong. I sat on the couch and asked, "What? What's going on?"

Dad looked at me in the eye and said, "Your mother has cancer."

I just sat back with my mouth open and stared at mother. After a few minutes I asked, "Where? How bad?"

"Breast," mother replied.

"So what did the doctor say?"

"She is to start chemo tomorrow," dad added.

"What is Chemo," I asked?

"They pump radio active chemicals into your body to kill the cancer."

"Does it hurt?"

"Makes you loose all your hair, throw up all the time and saps all your strength to the point that you think you will die. It is a killer killing a killer," mother replied.

She began to cry. I gave her a long hug and she held me tight. We sat and talked about the procedure and the doctor did give her a good chance of recovery. I called Sherry and my brothers and broke the news to them. Both brothers were coming to the house as soon as possible. Soon Sherry, the babies and brothers were there and we were all in tears.

The next few months went badly. Mother continued with chemo and she was very sick and loosing weight everyday. Finally the doctor told mother that the chemo was not working and she would need a mastectomy. Both breasts had to be removed. Not being a woman maybe I did not understand but her breasts were part of her womanhood. She cried forever after the surgery and felt she should have died. We all were there for support but nothing helped. Her weight continued to decrease and I would guess she weighted about 100-pounds.

On a return visit to the doctor the news was even worse. The cancer was still alive in her body. This time she was in major pain most of the time. Nothing seemed to help. She suffered for over two years and then she got to the point that she was not mobile. She was now down to about 80-pounds and looked like a skeleton. I wanted to cry every time I was with her. No person should be in continuous pain for years but she never complained. The doctor told us there was no hope and our lives faded. She wanted to stay home with dad so she was allowed. Pain pills did not help and she lay in bed. It took her four years to pass and she did so at home. The sad part is that when a person dies of cancer they usual stare to death. She became unconscious for a week before she died and I was so glad for that.

Dad took mother's death very hard. It was not that he could not do for himself but he loved her and need a companion. The bad part in his life was that he thought all women were like mother. To him marriage was a total commitment that allowed no other outside people or things to be woven into the relationship. Mother gave him full attention as did he. Two people could never have been more mated to each other. Now that she was gone my dad had nothing. Looking for another wife was not easy and his standard was so high that no one measured up. That lead him to depression and from that point he married another person one year later. Dad choice this person on his own and we had only met the person once or twice. None of kids approved of her but maybe we were looking for another mother also. Within a few weeks dad tells us that he is moving to Baton Rough with his new wife. All was quiet for three month and dad returns without the woman. She had taken and spent most of his money and they were divorced. Apparently, the woman had another lover there and dad found her cheating.

Dad never acted so strange after he returned. We all knew he would never find another person like mother and we told him that. He had nothing to do and would not look for anything to keep his mind business. The only thing he did well was grieve.

CHAPTER 16

1978

Mildred continued to work on my disability and seemed to make progress. My job at the oil company was doing well. They did not care if I had teeth or not. I worked with good people and my attitude was on edge at times but it was okay. My boss called me into his office and began to ask me questions. I could tell he had something in mind but I could not tell what until he said, "Pat, how would like to work overseas and make a huge salary?"

That got my attention especially the last part. "When you say huge salary, what do you mean?"

"Six figures, tax free."

I took a deep breath and replied, "Six figures, tax free? Is murder included in the package?"

He answered with a laugh, "No but the location may not be the best. How about Iran?"

"Six figures, tax free and Iran. How about my family? Will they be able to go also?"

"Yes, we have a package that allows you to take your family and it includes schooling for the kids, housing, furniture allowances, and a rental car."

"You know I cannot turn you down but I will have to talk to the family."

"Surely no problem, take a whole week to decide. Oil is the life-blood of Iran and we need you there."

I could not wait to get home and tell Sherry. The girls were six and seven years old and surely would not mind if we went. Sherry was in shock that I would even ask that she and the kids go. She put her foot down and said, "No way!"

I explained the benefits to her including that we could pay off the house when we came back. She still was not convinced. I left it alone hoping to give her time to think. The next day I did research on Iran and talked with co-workers that had been there. Yes, it was hot and mostly desert but I like the desert. The people I talked gave me all kind of visions of how to shop and where to buy food. The only thing they said was not to buy clothing in Iran because it was bad. I got home that evening thinking I would have to do the big sale on Sherry but the first thing she said when I walked into the house, "When do we go?"

I gave her a hug and started planning. I love to plan trips and this was the going to be a like-changing experience. We made a list of items that we would need and what we would take. My company paid for storage of all our furniture and stuff we would not carry. Our projected departure was three weeks so I took several days off work during that time to gather all the requirements. I bought six very large metal re-enforced trunks for shipping our belongings. My company gave me a list of possible items to carry including bath oil for the dry weather. I was told that the humidly would never get over 5% and without lotions and oils that our skin would dry up and blow off our bones. The worse thing possible was getting overseas shots. The kids were terrified of all the injections and I should have been. I received the small pots vaccine and I was sick for three days.

Time to go was close and I carried our six trunks to the shipping department with most everything that we own inside. We carried our baby pictures and several other photo albums thing we could relive the past in pictures. We were told that the trunks were to be there in three weeks so we had to pack three large suitcases to carry on the airplane. We were to stay in a hotel until we found an apartment or house to live. We did a triple check of all the lists and could not find anything missing.

Our flight was scheduled to leave Dallas at 4:00 and stop at Frankfurt, Germany. We decided to stay in Frankfurt for three days and do some sightseeing. As we boarded Lufthansa 747, there were only a few people on board. What I did not know was that Lufthansa had a hi-jacking the week before and most people cancelled their fights. Well, it did not worry me in the least. There were more flight attendants on board than passengers. We got the royal treatment with anything we wanted even in coach. The Sherry and the kids really enjoyed the flight and we landed about 8:00 am in Frankfurt. We took a taxi to the Inter-Continental Hotel. The hotel was in the middle of town and but we were exhausted, maybe jetlag. After taking about a three-hour nap we were ready to do some walking.

We hit the streets and enjoyed the evening sun and air. The streets were clean I mean clean, no trash or dirt anywhere. The shops were exciting and we made it inside several. No one spoke English but after all we were in Germany. With a lot of hand-motion and the sight of currency we managed to buy several things for the kids. We got hungry so we decided to go back to the hotel and put our packages away before we ate. It was at that time we found that we were lost. We must have not been more than a few blocks from the hotel but which way? We asked several people on the street but they spoke no English. We found a policeman and thought we were saved. He spoke no English. I just wished I had made better grades in my German class. Then it came to me kids are taught English in school so all we needed was a kid. Now where was a kid when we needed one? We walked and we knew just standing might take hours. We also looked for a taxi. Forty-five minutes later the hotel appeared. Next time we knew to leave a breadcrumb trail. At the hotel we asked for a restaurant that the kids might like and the suggestion came back as McDonalds. We ate at the hotel restaurant and it was great.

The next morning we boarded a bus to take a boat ride along the Rhine River. The boat was large and flat-bottomed. It had an inside viewing area with seats but we had to stay outside even though it was a bit cold. We passed castles, vineyards, mountain and farms. I had never enjoyed anything more. The trip took four hours and when we land the same bus picked us up for more tours. We visited several wineries and did a lot tasting. We bought more German stuff including steins. They offered Cokes on the bus on the way home for two-dollars a bottle. What the hell, I was on a company expense account.

After arriving back to the hotel we took a quick shower and decided to stay in for the night. We ordered room service. Looking at the menu we all decided on a ham and cheese sandwich with French fries so I ordered four. That was a mistake! The order came and one order could have fed all of us. The sandwiches covered the whole plate and a separate plate for the fries. There was no way that we could eat it all and no way to store it. It was great food and we wrapped the leftovers but we knew they would not stay fresh.

The next morning we boarded a bus taking us through the Black Forest and on to Rothenburg. The forest and countryside were beautiful and as we passed through small towns we noticed again the cleanliness. At that point I decided to never throw trash out the car window again. Our tour guide gave us a detailed description of Rothenburg before we arrived. "Rothenburg ob der Tauber was one of Germany's grandest tourist attractions, a little city that had everything, fantastic Gothic and Baroque architecture, an almost-fully intact old city wall, and some of southern Germany's most colorful festivals. The setting was very picturesque. The old town was situated atop a sharp, steep bend in the Tauber River. The walls followed the cliffs on the inside of the bend, while on the opposite side there was an inner and an outer wall, separated in some places by a now-dry moat. Numerous tall towers dot both the inner and outer walls, many of them being decorated by a clock and beautiful archway. One of those towers, the Burgturm, opened to a beautiful Burggarten, a flowered park perched along a ridge jutting out over the beautiful, and undeveloped, valley. The city's two main streets—Herrgasse and Obere Schmiedgasse, formed an 'L' meeting at the central market square. This square was dominated by the town hall, and its 200-foot tall Imperial Tower. The bulk of the specialty shopping, eating, and activities fall along these streets. The city wall was a thirty-foot tall structure that encircled the entire old city. The wall had been largely reconstructed, with plaques on the inside honoring the many who contributed monetarily to its rebuild. There was a walkway that was easily high enough to provide an excellent view of the surroundings. Also, several of the outer towers are themselves full-blown fortresses that can be explored from the inside. For example, the Spitaltor in the east has a round tower manned with cannons."

The bus parked and we started walking the cobblestone street. It was more beautiful that I could have imaged. The sun was shining and we walked the streets like they did hundreds of years ago. We visited shops and hit a language barrier again but we did the hand motions again and got by.

It was night before we returned to the hotel and the next morning we were due for Iran. The flight was interesting or should I say boring. Looking out the windows a tan layer of landscape with mountains in the background lay before us. I had bought an English/Farsi dictionary thinking I could get by the language barrier but the letters of the alphabet did not match what I knew as English. We were in trouble when it came to communications. My company had planned for a man to meet us at the airport and carry us to the hotel. I would say we were easy to recognize since we were the only ones in the airport with blonde hair. We entered the terminal after going through customs and there must have been thousands of people grabbing and pushing. Later I found that it was an Iranian holiday. I know most of them had not had a bath in weeks. We worked our way to the baggage area expecting to pick up our suitcases but getting close was not an easy task. Keeping a wife and two children in tow through a sea of people was not pleasant. After about forty-five minutes our luggage appeared and I made the claim. That sounds simple but I soon realized that we needed a cart to transport the luggage. There was no way for us to carry the luggage by hand. "Where in the hell was my co-worker?"

All the carts were in use and people were fighting over them. This called for a family conference, "Okay, y'all can stay here with the luggage while I find a taxi or we can try dragging the luggage a few feet at a time."

Sherry gave me a really bad look and said, "I am not staying one minute alone here."

I drug the pieces of luggage about ten feet at a time making sure that the family or the luggage never left my sight. I was planning a murder for the guy that should have met us and dragging his body into the desert. It took about an hour to get everything to the curb. I gave a taxi driver the name of the hotel, Hotel Omid. He and I loaded the luggage into a very small car, not sure of the make. I asked him the price for the trip and he said, "800 rials."

It was late evening and I did not care how much it cost plus I did not know how much 800 rials were in dollars.

The driver pulled away from the airport like there was a fire. Within a few blocks we came to a huge white moment with four lanes of traffic spinning around it. There were only two lanes marked but little cars were buzzing around it full throttle. Our taxi driver never even slowed down as he entered the circle. He laid on his horn and waved his arm out the window. There was zero clearance between each car and I just closed my eyes thinking Vietnam was nothing. Our trip to downtown Tehran was more frightening than any horror movie.

The driver stopped in front of a large old hotel. The four of us walked into the lobby. It was a bit run-down but I am sure at one time it was a great hotel. I was praying that the desk clerk spoke English when I said, "I have a reservations for Taylor."

The desk clerk began looking through paperwork for our reservation and after fifteen minutes he said, "Sorry I do not have a reservation for Taylor."

My blood pressure was beginning to boil again because my co-worker was due to make the reservations.

I replied, "Okay I would like a room for four."

"Sorry sir, we are booked for the night."

It was about 7:30 and the sun was going down. I could feel myself beginning to loose my temper. I tried to speak in a calm tone but my voice came in great authority, "Let me speak to the manager."

"I am the manager until morning."

I leaned over the desk with my face about six inches from his and said, "Well, then let me explain. It is getting dark, I have two children, and have no place to take them. I WANT A ROOM FOR THE NIGHT!"

"Sir, we do have a room with one bed would you want it?"

"YES!"

We managed with the help of the desk clerk to get the luggage to the elevator. He gave us a room number that did not match any room on the third floor. We kept walking and it seemed that we passed into another century. The room numbers started to match and we found our room. I opened the door and sure enough we had gone back in time. A single light bulb hung from the ceiling that gave more light than what we wanted. We took a look around and saw one bed that looked like a hammock and two chairs. I prayed for running water as I entered the bathroom. Not only did I get running water but a bathtub and sink. Instead of a commode there was a round hole in the floor with places to position your feet while in use. There was a pitcher of water sitting beside the hole. Sherry looked shocked and asked, "What's that?"

"Same as a commode but it does not flush."

"No toilet paper."

"That is the reason for the pitcher of water. You wash yourself when finished. Oh, only use your left hand to wash."

"Why?"

"Not a clue."

With one bed we decided to let the kids take the bed and Sherry laid blankets on the floor for us. I had heard so many stories about Iranians coming into your room at night and stealing everything that the door lock worried me. I went to the door to give it a test. I pulled on it and it came open easily. I worked with the lock but nothing I did worked. Just like in the movies I positioned a chair under the doorknob. I knew and Sherry knew that the chair was just for show but the kids felt better. We got ready for bed and the light was off. We lay there in darkness and silence. After about ten minutes I hear sobbing. I quietly said, "What's wrong."

I heard a small voice reply, "I want to go home."

Our oldest child had the right idea but I needed to convince her and myself that we would stay. After a few thoughts I replied, "We will not stay in this room tomorrow. If we cannot find a better place to live then we will go home. Okay?"

"Okay."

The night was long and my nights in Nam came to mind. I knew there must be scorpions and snakes crawling around on the floor. I reached for my rifle several times during the night but only to find Sherry awake also. Morning came as we all dressed and made our way to the Hotel desk clerk. I told Sherry to entertain the kids while I handled the process of getting a room or checking out. I had fire in my eyes as I walked to the counter. My first statement in harsh tones "Let me speak to the manager of the hotel."

The man turned and went into the office area. A man dressed in a suit and tie came to me and asked if he could be of service. I told him the experience from last night and told him that I wanted a room suitable for guest not pigs. He replied, "You are not happy with your accommodations?"

"Hell no! No one would be happy with the room that you gave us. I want a room with two beds and a door that will lock."

"Certainly Sir. How long do you plan to stay with us?"

"Maybe a month if we like the room or I guess the Hilton will get our business."

He motioned to a man and told him to transfer our luggage to room 220. He handed me two electronic cards that served as keys. I thought to myself, "What the hell is going on here, electronic keys and last night we did not even have a door lock."

I found Sherry and the kids and we went to room 220. I opened the door to find a beautiful room with two queen beds, two chests, couch, dining table, and TV. The bathroom had marble walls and shower. The view from the window was the street below and those little cars were buzzing around like crazy. Our luggage came and we unpacked. The girls were happy.

We were hungry so we decided to go to the hotel restaurant for breakfast. It was very nice and they had an American breakfast. After breakfast I called my local company or the phone number that was given me. The phone rang and rang but no answer. I hung up. I just wanted to talk with Andy, the guy that had left us high and dry. I had visions of my hands around his throat or maybe him lost in the jungle in Num. With no contact to work and no one trying to contact me we decided to take a walking tour around the hotel.

One of the first things we noticed were small concrete ditches about 18-inches deep that ran along each side of the street. Water was flowing through them at times but mostly dry. Later I learned that these ditches were called jubes and melting snow from the mountains flowed through them provide all kinds of usage. From what I saw the water was used for washing cars or getting rid of some of the dust in the city in general.

This part of the city was old or maybe it just looked old. I saw new construction and it did not look any different from the existing. Small stores dotted the streets and those small cars and trucks were everywhere. I got close enough to read the manufacturer's name on the back, Paykan. The car must be a local manufactured car or the import salesman did a hell of a job. All the buildings and houses had flat roofs and We could see some type of air conditioning unit on top.

As we walked we came to a small grocery store about the size of a small 7-11 and went inside. They had a meat and cheese counter and snacking on cheese in the room sounded okay. The man behind the counter asked me what I wanted and I pointed to a huge round of white cheese. The next question was critical, "How much do you want?"

"A pound"

The man gave me a funny look and shrugged his shoulders. It hit me that I needed to tell him something in a metric format. I turned to Sherry and said, "How much is a kilo?"

"I don't know, maybe a half pound or less."

I turned to the man and ordered three kilos. He cut a huge amount of cheese, wrapped it, and hanged it to me. I was in shock. There must have been six or seven pounds of cheese. After walking away I flung open my Iranian/American book and found that a kilo was 2.2 pounds. Well, we had cheese for a while. The store had pistachios really cheap and I bought one kilo. We also picked up cookies and chips but we did not recognize any of the brand names.

The trip back to the hotel was not easy carrying all the food and cheese. Walking, we passed women begging and we tossed them a few Iranian coins. Our main goal for the evening was to learn the currency and a few words of Farsi.

CHAPTER 17

The next morning the phone was pressed against my ear as a busy signal sounded. I began to wonder if there was only one phone line connecting my company to the world. I tried for another thirty minutes with no success. I had no idea as to what I should do, maybe catch a taxi to the place but there were several places at different locations. I interrupted the kids from watching the one American TV station and said, "Let's eat breakfast."

All agreed and we had our usual at the hotel restaurant. For the next few hours all I heard was a busy signal when I called the office number. About 11:00 I got the phone to ring on the other end and I was overjoyed. The next word I heard was "Salam"

I returned Salam meaning hello, goodbye, or just a greeting. "Do you speak English?"

A soft female voice said, "Some."

"May I speak to Andy Jordon?"

"He does not work here anymore. He went to the United States last week."

That statement hit me hard and a silence fell across the line. "Does he have a replacement," I asked"

"No Sir."

"May I speak to a manager?"

"Yes Sir."

The phone line was quiet for a few minutes but I was surely not going to hang up. Next a harsh voice said, "Meyers."

"Hello, this is Pat Taylor. I am due to start to work here and to meet with Andy Jordon but I understand he is not here anymore. I have no other name or person to call or contact."

The voice smoothed a bit and said, "Hello Pat we were expecting you next week. Where are you staying?"

I gave him the hotel and the address. Meyers replied, "Do you have lunch plans?"

"I will pick you up at noon. See you then."

The phone went dead and I sat in quiet. I conveyed the conversation to Sherry and her only response was, "Weird!"

At 11:45 I went to the lobby of the hotel and took a seat waiting for someone that sounded like an American on the phone. Five-minutes later a man about six-feet tall with dark hair came powering through the hotel door. That had to be him. I stood and he came straight to me, "Pete Meyers, VP of Iran Oil. You must be Taylor?"

"Yes."

"Great to have you. You are the man we have needed for a long time. I hear we left you and your family hanging when you arrived and I sincerely regret that. Andy left the company without notice and took information like your arrival date. We will make it up to you, I promise."

"No harm done except to the family. They were ready to return to the States as soon as we arrived."

We walked to the street and got into a car that had Chevrolet markings but I had never seen one before. "What kind of Chevy is this," I asked?

"Something they manufacture here in Iran along with millions of Paykans. This car is the top of the line for Iran."

The conversation continued through lunch as he told me the details of my job and a bit about Iran. He told me to take the next couple of days to get settled and maybe look for an apartment. The company would pay for 30 days in the hotel including meals and all other expenses. He would send a person to pick me up the next morning to show me around the city and the company.

The next morning I left Sherry and the girls and met my co-worker in the lobby. He introduced himself as James Owens and had been in Iran for two years. We started in what seemed like rush hour traffic but James said this was about normal for any hour. At times I was afraid to look because there were on an inch between us and the next idiotic driver. Once the guy in front of us dodged an oncoming car and went into the jube. We stopped and three of us lifted the car out of the ditch and he was back on the road again. It took about an hour to get to the office but we got there alive. James showed me my office, nothing fancy but it had a desk and chair. I noticed that there was no telephone. "James, why no phones here?"

Well, we could give you a phone but there are only two telephone lines for the whole company. The really plus of living in a third-world country."

The tour continued for most of the morning and we ended in the chart room. There were charts covering every inch of Iran. Oil was the objective and they needed to punch more holes in the ground. It was my job to tell them where to start.

We ate lunch and James and I moved to the next step. I had to have a car and a rental car was his only answer. We arrived at Avis and completed all the paperwork. The manager said he would deliver the car to the hotel after it was cleaned. They gave me a Chevy Iran with automatic and air. James carried me back to the hotel and said to take a couple of days to adjust and be at work on Saturday. This was Tuesday. What he failed to tell me was that Thursday and Friday were the weekend. Well, that was different but two off is two days off no matter what you call them. Fridays were the Moslem Holy Day similar to our Sunday.

That night the general opinion for dinner was pizza so we asked around the hotel and got directions to an Italian restaurant. It was only about five blocks away so we walked. I guess I was shocked to find out that the Iranians treat foreigners rudely. Sherry has reddish-blonde hair and the both girls have blonde. Cars passed as we walked and men would be leaning out the car windows screaming words and whistling. It was not until later that I found out that a woman with blonde hair, mostly Americans were thought of as whores. We would see Iranian women walking the streets with no covering for their hair so we determined it was okay for us. The Iranian women at work kept their hair covered all the time so I thought it was not mandatory. The Italian restaurant was great for a change and I paid the correct amount. We were learning the currency.

We returned to the hotel and watched our one channel for a while before bed. We planned a day of shopping for tomorrow and turned out the lights. I did not seem to be stressed but the dreams came back. Sherry came to full alert when I started to swear and kick. I woke up and I was soaking wet with sweat. I thought I was passed the war but it kept coming back time after time and I had no control over what I did. Sherry held me tight and we both got up. I paced the floor for a while as she whispered words of comfort. I opened the door to our balcony and stood in the night air telling myself that this is not Nam and all is at peace. Tehran's lights were in every direction and the dry air helped clear my head. Sherry had tears in her eyes as she held me tight.

We had breakfast in the hotel and the car was delivered as promised. I retrieved the keys from the desk clerk and stepped into the parking lot. Driving had always been a natural for me but never had I driven with every other driver trying to kill me. I turned to the family with a smile and said, "Ready for shopping trip?"

I received 'yes' all around and we got into the car. I made sure everyone was buckled and back out of the parking space. I moved to the street and a line of cars were coming at me as far as I could see. I waited for an opening. It did not happen. Finally, I said, "Hang on, we are going."

Sherry yelled, "No, there are too many cars."

I hung my arm out the window waving it like I was seeing Mr. President and shot into traffic. Horns honked and I kept waving. I was in and Sherry had the map. I made a right turn at the next corner and some guy in a Paykan made the same turn from the opposite direction and our fenders touched. Damn, two blocks and I had my first accident. I stopped and the so did the other guy. Of course, he claimed it was my fault and I argued the point. I was told that never call the police in an accident because if you are an American with insurance it will be your fault. The Paykan was in such bad condition that it belonged in a junkyard but I gave the guy $20. He was happy and left. From that point on I drove with one foot on the brake and the other on the gas and one hand on the horn and the other ready for waving. This was on-the-job-training for a defensive driving course. I never took my eye off the road or the car beside me. I had to have a navigator telling when to turn and giving directions.

Shopping in Iran was not easy. A person was expected to bargain for every item. Sherry and I had to develop a skill of saying no for every sale. After much debate over a single price allowed you to end the argument with a camel kiss. If the seller would not come down on his price and you thought it was unfair then you kissed the end of your fingers, threw the kiss at him and walked off—no sale.

The Iranians love children and at every place people would talk with the kids and touch their blonde hair. It was good luck for the Iranians to touch golden hair.

We found several good books for day trips around Tehran and being the weekend we decided to take a tour. Tehran is built on the side of a 14,000 foot mountain with the Caspian Sea on the other side. The old city of Tehran was called Rey and it was down in the valley. Smog was always so bad that a person could never see the old city from the mountain side. The King of Iran's palace was built about half way up the mountain. We decided to go to the Caspian Sea and we gathered our bathing suits. We zoomed along a single lane road going up the mountain. People passed each other like there was a pot of gold at the top of the mountain. I tried to remain calm and drove in peace. The road was winding and a sports car driver could have a lot of fun. Nothing but rocks and sand on the Tehran side of the mountain but as we got closer to the top there was greenery. The guide book told of a jungle equipped with tigers, bears and all kinds of jungle animals. There were rice paddies and huge fields of fruit trees. God, this brought back memories.

We passed through several very small cities and came to the Caspian. The sand was dark but the water was not bad. In the water were Iranian men and women swimming. The men were swimming in their underwear and the women were swimming fully clothed including their hair. A bit strange but the kids did not care as they hit the waves. We gathered seashells walking the beach. I did not want to drive that winding road at night so we did not stay much longer. Passing through one of small towns we decided to stop for a snack. I stopped at a small grocery and we stocked up on chips, cookies, and drinks. I noticed in the drink refrigerator containers of beluga caviar. I had never had caviar but the world claims it is wonderful or maybe it is just the high cost of the fish eggs. We were at the Caspian Sea the source of the finest caviar, so I pick up two containers and carried them to the counter. There was an Iranian five on the top but I was not sure if that meant 5 or 5000 rials. I asked the price. He gave me a price in rials equivalent to $3. To make the guy feel better I paid what he asked. Back in the car I could not wait to open one of the containers and try world class beluga caviar. When I opened the container a fishy smell filled the car and there lay black fish eggs. I took a chip from the package and dipped it into the caviar. "Who wants to try it first?"

No one spoke. Sherry gave me a bad look and said, "You alone are going to eat that stuff."

I stuff the chip into my mouth. I wanted to spit it out but pride kept me chewing. I put the lid on the caviar and grabbed another chip and a drink of Coke. "We will save this for guests."

Saturday came and back to work. I drove and was feeling like I could handle the traffic but certainly not over confident. I spend the morning talking with people and after lunch I was given a location to meet an Iranian official for more talk. I studied the map and felt I could find the area. Being on my best driving behavior I started. About twenty minutes later I was sitting between two trucks at a signal light when I heard a loud crash followed by my car being crushed between the two trucks. A woman going at least fifty miles per hour plowed into the truck behind me which caused a four-car accident. I was not hurt at the time but both the front and back the Chevy were destroyed. The woman in car was bleeding but walking. People from the street came rushing with bandages for the woman and help for the truck drivers and myself. My car was not going anywhere and I was told that the police was called. This was bad. We waited for two hours for the police and in the meantime people I did not know or could speak brought me food and drink. Another hour passed and the police came. They took the woman with bandages wrapped around her head and me to the police station. I had all my papers including my passport and drivers license. The woman agreed it was her fault so they let me go. I called Avis and they brought me another car and I assumed hauled the Chevy away. This time I was driving a Paykan. It only took five hours to finish all the details of the accident. I got to the hotel at 6:00 pm.

The next morning I felt like I was paralyzed, whiplash. I returned to work and gave everyone a blow-by-blow description of the accident. I was at my desk when my boss came in and said, "President wants to talk with you."

"President of what?

"This company and let me give you a few pointers. He is a really nice guy until you cross him or you get caught screwing around. He will do whatever it takes to make this company the best and throwing you out the door is not a problem for him."

I picked up my notebook and marched to his office. The woman guarding his door asked, "You must be Mr. Taylor? Welcome to Iran."

"Thanks, it has been exciting so far."

"Mr. Finley will be with you in a minute, please have a seat."

Thirty seconds later she told me Mr. Finley is waiting. I got up and entered his office that was nothing special but well decorated. There stood a tall thin man in his mid fifties. He stood with his hand out and I returned the gesture. I sat down. "Pat, I heard you had a rough start here in Iran but surely things will smooth out. Anyway I am here to help you anyway I can and we will do anything necessary to ease the pain of this place."

"Thank you Sir, that is good to hear."

"I understand your background and education but I am mostly interested in your Army experience. Pat, I want this talk to be between you and me and no one else. Understand?"

"Yes Sir."

"We are here to pump oil and make money for the Iranians. This is the situation; the President of the United States called and gave me a job and that is why I hired you. I need your help on a top secret project. You have been cleared and the President gave me all authority for the go ahead. Before I tell you more does working undercover hit you the wrong way?"

"No Sir."

"If I tell you the information about the job then there is no turning back or quitting. Is that understood?"

"Yes Sir."

"Okay, if you are in then let's get it done. In August 1974, the Shah envisioned a time when the world's oil supply would run out, and declared, "Petroleum is a noble material, much too valuable to burn...We envision producing, as soon as possible, 23,000 megawatts of electricity using nuclear plants. Bushehr would be the first plant, and would supply energy to the inland city of Shiraz. In 1975, the Bonn firm Kraftwerk Union AG, a joint venture of Siemens AG and AEG Telefunken, signed a contract worth $4 to $6 billion to build the pressurized water reactor nuclear power plant. Construction of the two 1,196 MWe nuclear generating units was subcontracted to ThyssenKrupp, and was to have been completed in 1981.

By 1975, The U.S. Secretary of State Henry Kissinger, had signed *National Security Decision Memorandum 292*, titled **U.S.-Iran Nuclear Cooperation**, which laid out the details of the sale of nuclear energy equipment to Iran projected to bring U.S. corporations more than $6 billion in revenue. At the time, Iran was pumping as much as 6 million barrels of oil a day. President Gerald Ford even signed a directive in 1976 offering Tehran the chance to buy and operate a U.S.-built reprocessing facility for extracting plutonium from nuclear reactor fuel. The deal was for a complete 'nuclear fuel cycle', with all the dangerous consequences that would entail including the possibility of this plutonium being used sooner or later to make weapons. The Ford strategy paper said, 'Introduction of nuclear power will both provide for the growing needs of Iran's economy and free remaining oil reserves for export or conversion to petrochemicals.'

President Ford's team endorsed Iranian plans to build a massive nuclear energy industry, but also worked hard to complete a multibillion-dollar deal that would have given Tehran control of large quantities of plutonium and enriched uranium—the two pathways to a nuclear bomb. Iran has deep pockets and close ties to Washington. U.S. companies, including Westinghouse and General Electric, scrambled to do business here.

A number of declassified documents were found on the website of the President Ford Library and Museum. Two documents in particular, dated April 22, 1975 and April 20, 1976, show that the United States and Iran held negotiations for cooperation in the use of nuclear energy and the United States was willing to help Iran by setting up uranium enrichment and fuel reprocessing facilities.

Accordingly, the Vice-President and Secretary of Defense were all involved in backing Iran's Nuclear Program designed to extract plutonium from nuclear reactor fuel.

The President's concern is that we are helping Iran build a nuclear power plant for other purposes than electricity. That is a no-no per the agreement. We have very few people monitoring the construction or what is going down. This is where you come into the game."

"Sir, I have no nuclear power experience and would not know an atomic warhead if I were sitting on it."

"That okay Pat, we want a man to get in and out and gather information. At times you might need to take in an engineer or physicist. We need someone undercover to do the research as to what they might be building on the side. We have U.S. people monitoring the construction of the power plant but the President feels we need to keep a closer watch on them. Your record in Vietnam was outstanding and we need your help. One other thing, I will double your salary if we do not get caught by the Iranians."

I heard the words double your salary and my ears began to tingle and this job did not require killing anyone. Mr. Finley, "If I take this job would everyone here know what I am doing?"

"Absolutely not! No one will know. This is a top secret project that will between you, me and the President of the United States."

"Sir, I love adventure but killing people are another side of me that I want left in Nam."

"Pat, you can have any weapon you prefer and carry it for self-protection only. None of my people are going to get hurt and that is why I want you. You are the best at finding booby traps and getting in and out without being seen."

"When do I start?"

"Today."

Mr. Finley reached into his pocket for some type of control. He pressed a button and the wall behind him began to move. Behind the wall was steel door with several coding devices attached. He turned around and rested his chin on a curved bar. A greenish light came on and did a scan. Another red light flashed "Accepted." He then spoke a few words and the best I could determine this machine was checking for a voice code. Another red light flashed "Accepted." Next he punched in numbers on a key pad. The door opened. He turned to me and said, "Just playing it safe."

Inside were blueprints and all types of other drawings and papers but no money. At the back of safe was another door and behind it was a large table and desk. "This will be your work area until you know every inch of the nuclear plant. All the building information is contained in the other room," Finley said.

"How long do I have?"

"As long as it takes for you to feel comfortable with the job. You will never work here unless I am here. The safe combination is set for only two people, me and one other American."

"When do I start?"

"Tomorrow. I have all your clearances arranged so you will not have any trouble getting into my office. Remember never take any paper out of this safe. You have to have it all in your brain."

Three weeks later we had found an apartment to lease. Basically the apartment was the up stairs floor of a large house. The apartment was very large and I would guess about 2500 square feet. We took it. It had marble flooring throughout with large rooms and air conditioning. It had central air with a water cooler air conditioning unit on the roof pumping wet air through the house. The humidity was about 2% and any moisture made the air feel cool. We spent time looking for furniture and soon had the house furnished. It came with a washer, dryer, refrigerator and cooking stove. There were several balconies on each side of the house and we could see a long ways on clear days. Our landlord lived below us and he was always bring us Iranian food to eat. We returned the gesture after settling down and the wife always found a headscarf before answering the door. That was okay with us. The house had a concrete fence around the street side with cut glass embedded along the top of the fence. Not much of a security system but it might slow a person down a bit. During the past three weeks I had three more car accidents but was not moving in any of them. I just called the rental company and they handled all the problems. I kept the same car with dents on every side. It was beginning to look like an Iranian car.

Driving was getting better or should I say I was not lost most of the time. We were invited to dinner by one of the VPs at work and found ourselves on time which was a miracle. While having drinks after dinner we heard a loud crash. We all go running outside and see a new Mercedes Bends smoking. A little kid maybe 10 years old jumps out of the driver's seat and starts crying. His mother came to the rescue. A few more steps toward the Mercedes and I could see that he had plowed into another car. The other car looked bad with the whole side bashed in. After a closer inspection I could see that the other car was mine. It was totaled. We took a taxi home and I called the rental the next morning. Avis had another car there after a long explanation. This was my third car in five weeks and all the man could say when he arrived was, "Please be careful."

CHAPTER 18

Work was almost like a James Bond movie as I studied every detail of the buildings. I began making plans for entrance and escape routes. Air shafts, power supplies, waterways, doors, windows, and every possible means of getting in and out were drawn. The only thing I could not determine from the drawings was people schedules and guards. I would have to be there to see what kind of schedule they ran.

After a few more days of plotting and planning I told Mr. Finley that I needed some time in the area of the buildings to judge the number people and security. The man seemed to know everything about Iran and gave me information about Bushehr, the location of the nuclear power plant. We sat in his office drinking tea as he spoke, "Bushehr has a population of 165,000 and located on the southwestern coast of Iran, on the Persian Gulf about 400 km south of Tehran. It is the chief seaport of this country which makes the local climate hot and humid. It has a long history and was founded in 1736. In previous centuries, many Africans settled in Bushehr. Although there is no discernible linguistic influence from Africa in Bushehr, there are cultural and genetic influences. Bushehr is 12 km from the site of a nuclear power plant. We estimate that one reactor is 50% complete, and the other reactor 85% complete. The Russians signed a contract to supply a light water reactor for the plant. Although the agreement calls for the spent fuel rods to be sent back to Russia for reprocessing, the we has expressed concern to Russia that Iran would reprocess the rods itself, in order to obtain plutonium for atomic bombs."

He stopped talking and stared at his desk. I did not know what to say but finally I spoke softly, "Who am I going to get in and out of the building?"

"A Russian scientist to start. Do you speak any Russian?"

"No Sir, none at all and not very good English to boot."

"That's okay he speaks some English. What kind of equipment will you need?"

"I could make a list but such things as vehicle, spotting equipment for daylight and night, flash grenades, rope, handgun, and clothing."

"Okay, finish the list by tomorrow morning and I will have the equipment by tomorrow."

The next morning I handed Mr. Finely the list and he gave it a quick once over and said, "This afternoon."

The equipment arrived in a large box as promised. My words to Mr. Finley before I left were, "If I do not come back I want you to get my wife and kids back to the States. Also if I do not come back I will be dead not captured. I am not staying in any jail."

"Don't worry about you wife and kids. They will be well taken care of without a doubt. Pat, I have all the confidence in the world in you so you will come back. You are the best. Remember, I want you in the building first for a quick look around and then you and the Russian in next."

"I will have to do some surveillance for several days before I try to enter so I need the name of the Russian and where I can meet him when I need him."

Sherry and I arranged to start the girls into an American school and a school bus came by the door so driving was not necessary. We also joined the Iranian Country Club. The words country club may be misleading but there were clay tennis courts a large swimming pool and they did serve alcoholic drinks. The club was not far from our house so a short taxi ride was all that was needed. Sherry played tennis but the clay courts took practice. She and the kids stayed around the pool mostly. The club members were from all over the world and customs were a bit different. One of the first things we noticed was that women were sunning topless. Also a poor woman that must have been nine months pregnant sunned only in her bikini bottoms. The kids did a few stares but kept the pool water splashing.

Getting Sherry situated to the idea that she would have to stay alone for a few days was hard. I made sure she had cash for taxies and shopping. I also made it clear for her not to go to the open market for any reason. We had small stores close to the house. One such street store was a half a block away and the owner was very friendly. He carried our groceries to the house and I always gave him a tip. These street stores were very small but they carried such things as Cokes, ice cream, cheese, chips and a lot of other snack food.

It was time to make the trip. My latest vehicle was a Toyota and it had a standard transmission which gave me another pedal to operate in traffic. I plotted my way to Bushehr trying to avoid any large cities. That was easy as I traveled through mountains and desert. I never saw a tree except for those along a river or some water source. I stopped twice to stretch and get something to drink. At the second stop I noticed the air had moisture and it was hot. The target was the Persian Gulf so the moisture must be coming from there. I took all the information, directions and maps that were available but I had every building located in my mine. The Bushehr Nuclear Power Facility is located 17 kilometers south of the city of Bushehr between the fishing villages of Halileh and Bandargeh along the Persian Gulf.

The words of Shah Mohammad Reza Pahlavi kept me thinking there must be a bad apple in the barrel, "Petroleum is a noble material, much too valuable to burn…We envision producing, as soon as possible, 23 000 megawatts of electricity using nuclear plants."

A German company signed a contract with the Shad for $6 billion to build this reactor. Six billion dollars is several barrels of oil or maybe that was pocket change for the Shah.

I arrived in Bushehr and trusted my map to find the hotel that Mr. Finley had given me. I was told that it was a 3-star hotel but when I arrived at the Reza Hotel I knew someone had too many stars. It did have a restaurant so after checking in and seeing that the TV had no English stations I went to eat. It was getting late and it seemed that people were leaving the hotel in there work clothes. I made a few inquiries and found that during summer outside work on the power plant was almost suspended during the excessive heat of day but continued unabated through the cool of the night. That sure put a different light on the subject.

I decided to spend my night touring the city checking for police and military. As suspected there were people with guns and military equipment in abundance. I made a drive in the direction of the power plant but was stopped short by seriously armed guards. That was okay I was not going the front door anyway. From the guard gate I could see the place was lit like a Christmas tree and it seemed brighter than day. Huge structures could be seen with hundreds of people working over the area like ants. It was after midnight so I returned to the hotel for sleep.

Morning came and after what the Iranians called breakfast I took another drive. The city was filled with foreigners or should I say people that were not Iranian. That was great giving me a chance to blend in even more.

I wanted to contact the Iranian Nuclear Regulatory Authority but these people would be like talking to the fox that guarded the hen house. They were responsible for the operation of nuclear power plants, nuclear installations, equipments and instruments using different radiation levels in the fields of industry, medicine and agriculture may have dangerous consequences. I could not see any benefit of alerting them that I was interested in the project. I drove to the project and made several attempts to circle the area. I was being watched or I felt that the security was more than met the eye. I could see two areas that construction was being preformed and assumed that these were the core for each plant. I did not want to be taken for questions so I decided that there were questions to be asked in town.

People with loose lips were always found in a bar but this was Iran and bars were no where. All those Germans had to drink beer someplace so maybe the hotel was a start. I returned to the hotel and as I entered the restaurant it was obvious I was in the correct spot. There was a several tables pulled together and eight German men were loud and drinking beer. I found a table nearby and listened. I bought a round for the table and I got an invite to join them and they changed to English for my benefit. Now, if I were in Texas I would say that these guys were good old boys. We laughed and joked about the U.S. and Germany. More beer came and I started asking about the power plant. They all worked there and had a dislike for the Iranians. One huge blonde man asked, "What are you doing here?"

"Looking for oil."

That brought a big laugh and one man said, "Try looking down and digging ten meters anywhere you like. The stuff is everywhere. Those rich bastards must control all the oil in the world"

"That's strange! Why do they need a nuclear power plant if they have all that oil?"

"Oil hell, they want a nuclear bomb so they can control the planet," one man said next to me.

I asked, "Can they build a bomb from what you are building?"

"Hell yes" came from the other side of the table.

"A bomb big enough to wipe out millions of people," said another man.

"Wait a minute this is an electrical power plant so how can they make bombs," I said.

"The waste! It would be a dirty bomb but it is possible. Plus, with a little more time and they could develop heavy water to make their own nuclear warheads" shouted one man.

"So how much time do we have before the plant is operational, I asked?

The table broke into laughter. "Most likely never because one rector is about 75% complete and the other about 50%. When the money stops we stop and the rectors will just be pieces of junk," one man said through the laughter.

"Why would the money stop," I asked?

"How long have you been in country," asked one man?

"About a month."

"Take a look around and you can see movement in the direction of a revolution. The Shad is living on thin ice and he had better do something quickly. All his oil is underground and it might just stay there for awhile. That means this power plant will be shut down also."

"What about a revolution? What makes you think there is one coming? Tehran seems to be at peace," I asked?

"Revolutions come from the bottom and I see people everyday with hatred for the Shad and his rule. This country is based on religion and the Shad is going to the West. Take my word he will fall because of his Western attitude. There is no middle class here and that is a problem that will hit the Shad between the eyes."

The guy was making a good sense. I wondered how he saw it and the U.S. failed. I am sure the U.S. Government knows what is going to happen but all those billions of dollars that the Shad is spending go right into U.S. companies' pockets.

We talked for a couple more hours and put down several more beers. I left for my room and tried to put the facts and the conversation with the Germans into rank. What I did not understand was why Mr. Finley would want me to take a top level scientist into a place that the information was readily available from any of the workers. Did the German know more than they were telling? Maybe something was being developed that the Germans did not know. Hell, the Germans were building every inch of the place so they would know.

There were hundreds of foreigners working the project so all I needed was two ID badges and we could walk in the front door. It took me three days and a lot of beer to lift two badges from the Germans. I called Mr. Finley to send Raymond Sawyer, the scientist, to the hotel and we managed to get pictures of each of us. Raymond was much younger than I was thinking and looked about 35 years old. He had dark hair and skin and sported a mustache. He was a person that looked like he spent as much time in the gym as he did the lab. I changed the pictures on the badges but kept the same name. To my surprise Raymond spoke German. We talked about what was required the next morning but I seemed to be a stooge because I understood nothing. I told him I was not a scientist and he agreed that I was there as an assistance to keep him out of trouble.

The night shift gathered at the hotel and we mixed in with the workers. I wore clothing so that I would not be recognized or as least I hoped. I had a hat that I kept pulled over my face as much as possible. I never said a word to anyone. Raymond told them that we were new to the company. Small talk continued and a bus came and we boarded along with the others. Entering the gate was easy as we flashed our badges. The guard took a quick look and waved us through. The .357 in my back hostler was never noticed and no one was being searched. I followed Raymond into a large building. Several other men entered also and they went to their stations. We just walked with Raymond taking notice of every piece of equipment and person working. We nodded at workers but kept walking. As far as they knew we were the president of the company taking a tour. The next building was smaller but hot as hell. Within two hours we had made our rounds of the complex and Raymond was satisfied he had seen it all. We were back to the gate and two guards stood in our path. Words were exchanged in German and Raymond turned to me and said, "No one leaves until the shift is over."

"What did you tell him?"

"We are inspectors and we are finished. He said no one leaves."

"I guess we do this the hard way."

Raymond started around the guard and both guards pulled their rifles to the shooting position. I reached for the .357 but Raymond had the two on the ground in a second. I could not believe my eyes. The two stayed down and we walked around them. "What the hell was that," I asked?

"Nothing just a little gym work. Those guys have never seen the inside of a gym."

"Damn, glad you are on my side."

"How are we getting back to town," Raymond asked?

"I would say we take one of those cars in the parking lot."

We only had a few seconds before the gate guards would be up and sounding the alarm.

"How about a BMW," I asked?

"Perfect!"

A white BMW sat at the end of the row of cars and I pulled out a wire from my jacket pocket and popped the locks. Within a few seconds I had the car hotwired and running. "Damn, glad you are on my side," Raymond laughed.

Within a few seconds the Beamer was pushing 120 mph. The roads were on the sandy side but the car handled well. "Okay Raymond, tell me what we do now."

"I have to make a report to the Oval Office which means that I need to do that in person."

"What do you think about this place? Is it a bomb ready to explode?"

"Not for awhile, maybe three to five years but it will happen. The platinum process is slow and takes a little help from the Russians. One plant is about 60% complete while the other is about 40%."

A Paykan came from a side street and made no effect to stop as he entered the highway. I slammed on the brakes but it was no hope so I put Beamer into a side-side trying to slow it down. That did not work either so I tapped the brakes and hit the throttle. The car straightens for a second and I slung it to the opposite shoulder. In passing we clipped the front of the piece of shit. I never stopped but I could see the driver of the Paykan standing in the road in my rear view mirror. "Where the hell did you learn to drive like that," Raymond asked?

"Must be a natural talent," I laughed.

The journey to Bushehr was short and we were sure we had police to avoid so we stopped at a local market place. We gave the parking lot a quick glance and saw an almost new Toyota. We waited for a few minutes for Iranian shoppers to clear the area and unlocked the car. We drove out of the parking lot without any disturbance and supposedly unnoticed. "Back to our hotel or what direction would you like to go," I asked?

"Not the hotel. How about Shiraz? There is an airport there that might get us out of this country. Oh sorry, get me out of this country."

The map in my coat came in handy as we found the highway to Shiraz. I carried Raymond to the airport and he boarded an Iran Air flight. I wish him good luck because I knew Iran Air was not Southwest Airlines. I went to the rental car area and rented a car. The Toyota was left at the airport. Twenty minutes later I arrived at the Shiraz Eram Hotel. I had never seen this place but it was a hotel and I needed a place. To my surprise it was not bad.

I took advantage of the credit card and called Mr. Finley and gave him a report. He offered me anything I wanted and told me I did a great job. It was nothing on my scale of heroic happenings but he seemed to think it was a great job. He seemed to know all the details of what had happened. I was in some kind of operation that I did not understand. He gave me the option of returning to Tehran or taking another job. I told him I had to see Sherry and the kids and maybe after that we would talk.

My next call was to Sherry and she had a million tales, some funny and some not so funny. We talked for about two hours and I told her I would see her tomorrow. She started to cry and it was so hard to hang up. The hotel had a restaurant and I was hungry. I sat at a table near the wall and watched people.

After thirty-minutes, I noticed a man watching me. He was blonde, blue eyes, and most likely in his early thirties. He looked German and maybe a touch of Russian. He was alone and moved away from his table. He came in my direction and stood in front of my table. "Mr. Taylor, may I join you," he asked with a foreign accent?

I reached for my .357 mag. in the direction of my back. "No need for that Mr. Taylor. I mean you no harm."

I stood and he held out his hand, "John Doe, Mr. Taylor, may I sit down?"

We shook hands and both sat down. He turned and waved to the waiter. "Two of your best cognacs."

"Do you expect me to believe that your name is John Doe," I asked?

"No, but what does a name matter?"

I leaned in his direction and looked him square in the eye, "Hell yes, a name matter and how do you know me and how did you know I was here at this hotel?"

"No matter, we have business to conduct and I have a special project for you. My country needs a person such as you for several reasons."

I reached to my back again and saw three more men rise from their table with their eyes glued on me. I moved my hands back to the table and they sat down. John Doe smiled and said, "No need to worry about those guys. They are harmless."

"Okay, what is your name and what's your country. Maybe we can talk after you explain a bit."

"Mr. Taylor, may we move to another location that is not so public?"

I offered my hand and he led the way out of the restaurant. His three people followed and once outside I stopped and stated, "These three will have to empty their pockets before I go any further."

One of the guys pulled out a handgun with the barrel in my direction. I slapped the gun from his hand and sweep his feet. He lay on concrete while another reached for gun. My elbow landed square on his nose and that brought blood squiring. My left hand buried into side ribs and he fell. I looked at the third guy and he raised his hands. "Please Mr. Taylor, just talk."

"Okay just you and I."

We walked along the street in the night.

"Now, who are you and what do you want," I asked?

"I am from the USSR and I live in a small town near St. Petersburg. Believe me I want the same as you."

"And that is?"

"I need your services and I am willing to pay very well."

"My services are not for sale to the Russians."

"Wait, hear me out. Both our countries will profit. Within the next few months Iran will be in a revolution."

"Are you crazy? There is no sign of a revolution. These people are happy."

"Yes, mark what I say. The U.S. has forced fed the Iranians into a Western culture that their religious leaders do not agree. Just take a look at the women wearing western dress on the streets of Tehran. These people will not change from the ways of their religion and they will prove it. A revolution is coming and very soon."

"Okay, let's say there is a revolution. What does that have to do with you and me," I asked?

"Mr. Taylor, You and your friend has just seen a taste of what might happen if Iran develops a nuclear weapon."

"Wait a minute the USSR is an ally to Iran."

"Not near as much as the United States."

"You just said that a revolution is coming so the Shah and the U.S. will be out. The USSR will be selling arms and weapons to Iran. What a surprise!"

"Mr. Taylor, I am talking nuclear weapons and if Iran develops those rectors then the world is not safe. Iran will have no allies with that much power."

"So what do you want with me? I am one person and certainly not any political figure."

"We believe that Iran will have this weapon in five years if nothing is done. The German company will certainly not slow the progress but you can."

"Hey, I am just a county boy from Texas and stopping nuclear wars is not within my dominance."

"You are wrong. You have been inside the plant and you have the experience."

"Okay, if what you say is true then I have to get my family out of country first."

"Yes, we have time but not much time. I will contact you."

CHAPTER 19

The drive back to Tehran was quick mainly because I had the pedal-to-the-metal. It seemed like I had been gone for months and seeing Sherry and the kids was like a breath of fresh air. I had called Sherry when I was close and she had a great home-cooked dinner waiting. She had chicken fried steak and mashed potatoes and that were not easy in this country. The night was great and I could not bear to tell Sherry the news of what I had learned until the morning.

The kids had gone to school and we sat in the quiet of each other. I felt so bad about telling her that we were going to be in trouble very shortly. I tried to start slowly but it seemed to unravel quickly. She did not go to pieces but calmly asked what we were going to do. The closest she came to excitement was riding a Jeep up a mountain. I gave her my suggestions and we agreed that she and the kids should leave Iran. As we talked we heard a very loud explosion in the distance. We ran to the flat roof and saw a huge cloud of smoke coming from the area near Tehran. As we watched another explosion clouded the sky even closer. Then a familiar sound of a bullet zoomed by my ear and then again. I grabbed Sherry and pulled her down below the ledge of the roof. We worked our way back to the door to the house. "Damn, what the hell is going on," I asked?

Then the words of the Russian hit me like a load of brick, "Revolution."

So quick? We never stopped in the house but out the front door headed for the car and the school. We charged into the school and went straight to the kid's room. We never said a word except, "We are taking the children."

Both children were in the car as we made our way to the apartment. In the process we drove through burning cars and crowds shouting. "Kill America!"

I pushed the kids to the floor of the car and told Sherry to get into the back seat with them. The street became blocked with screaming people, front and rear. I started to get out of the car with my .357 mag but I was not going to leave my family. The crowd closed in fast and they saw that we were foreigners and they assumed we were Americans. They began to beat on the car and shake it from side to side. Then I decide that it was them or us so I pulled the shift knob to low gear and slammed the gas pedal to the floor. I ducked my head as I saw bodies and rocks coming to the windshield. I heard them hit the car but I never let up. The car's tires were spinning as they tried to stop us. My windshield was broken but no glass inside as we passed the last of the crowd.

Sherry peaked up from the backseat and said, "Iran is our ally, correct?"

"Not any more. I have a feeling that the Shah is quickly loosing control."

Sherry asked, "Who are these people and why are they so mad at Americans?"

"Religion, Honey, religion. These people are not ready for democracy or Western ways. American is Satan to them."

"What should we do?"

"We are going to the apartment and lock the doors, and then I am going to get some answers."

We were at the apartment within fifteen minutes and I gave Sherry and the kids direct orders to stay away from windows and doors.

I called Mr. Finley, "Sir, what is happening?"

"Four of the leading Generals for the Shad were killed this morning if you have not read the paper. These men stood for America so now we are paddling without a paddle. I expect the Shah to leave the country very soon."

"Sir, do these people have a leader?"

"Oh yes, some museum priest by the name of Ayatollah Khamenei but he is not in country as yet."

"How can a man rule when he is not in the country?"

"He will be here."

"So what do you want me to do?"

"Stick tight for a few days and do not leave your home. Keep your family as low key as possible. I will be working on a way to get them out."

I gave Sherry what news I knew and she just sat in a trance while I talked. I felt that she would explode at any second but I kept talking trying to ensure her that we would be okay. She stood and said, "Food, we will need food if we are stuck here for several days."

"Good idea. I will go to the corner store and buy what I can."

I slowly peaked out the front door remembering the roof episode. I took a quick look in every direction and started along the sidewalk. It was only about 50-yards to the grocery store and as I opened the door the owner met me. "Sorry, I cannot let you inside. Men are watching my store and if I let you inside they will destroy my store. I am so sorry. I enjoy you and your family especially your children."

I backed out a bit and said, "I understand and I wish you the best during all of this."

I jogged back and unlocked the door to the apartment. Sherry was waiting with a terrified look on her face. "What," she said in a stern voice?

"The owner will not let me into his store."

"That son-of-a-bitch, why not?"

"Honey, it is not his fault. People are watching his store and if he lets me inside they will burn it."

Tears began to roll down Sherry's face. "What do we do now," she asked?

We walked back into the living room avoiding windows and sat on the couch. "That little store is not the only place in town to buy food. There is a place on the base similar to a grocery store if I can get there. I bet the security is tight."

We sat together making a list of food that we could store or take with us if we had to leave by car. It was getting late so I decided that I would make the trip first thing in the morning. We looked through the kitchen for something quick and started dinner. About half way through the cooking process the power went off. I took a looked at the wall clock and it was 6:00. I told Sherry and the children to stay as they were and I walked to the window. Every light in neighborhood was out. "What the hell is going on," I asked myself?

I turned back to the kitchen and almost ran into the kids and Sherry. "What happened," Sherry asked?

"Not sure but the power is off through the whole neighbor. See if you can get anything on TV."

'That might be hard to do with no power."

"Oh yeah! Do we have candles?"

"Somewhere, I will have to find them."

Within a few minutes we had candle light. We checked dinner but only half cooked. "How about a sandwich," Sherry asked?

The kids screamed peanut butter and jelly and I agreed. Sherry asked,

"Do you think they turned the power off or did something blow up?"

"Well, I am not sure but I would bet we are under some kind of curfew."

The next morning the lights came on at 6:00 am. "Six o'clock to six o'clock so I think someone is turning off the switch," I said lying in bed. It was not long before the kids came to our bed. We had a few giggles and then cooked breakfast.

By mid-morning I drove toward the air force base hoping to find food. At the gate huge barriers were in the road and when I was stopped the guard had words I did not want to hear. The grocery store and the commissary were closed and no one was allowed on base. I asked him about the power problem last night and he agreed it was the Iranian Government. Within two days there would be a curfew from 6:00 pm to 6:00 am. No one would be allowed on the streets during these periods. I turned the car around and started looking for a place to buy food. The streets were quiet and traffic was light. I drove slowly searching every building. I passed stores that had been burnt and remembered what the man had said at out corner store. I drove a little faster and soon came to another area and found one of the larger grocery stores in town. I found a parking place and walked in like I owned the place and no one said a word. I grabbed a basket and filled it with everything I saw on the list or not. I just knew it had to be in a can and require no refrigeration. I got in line at the check out with my basket filled to the top. I never look at anyone or said a word. I handled the person the money and was gone with the goods.

I was so happy when I reached home with sacks of groceries. Sherry met me at the door with a big smile when she saw the sacks. "Got on base," she asked?

"No, and it is a long story."

It was mid-afternoon so I prepared everyone for the power to go down at 6:00. We got candles and games and snack food ready for the blackout. Right on time the power was off at 6:00. We had so much fun play table games that it seemed like a blessing. In the middle of it all the phone rang. That could be only one person, Mr. Finley. "Hello," I said quietly.

"Pat, we need your services again. Can we meet in the morning?"

"What kind of services?"

"We will have to talk in the morning and not over this phone."

"Okay where?"

"Your old hotel lobby, 10:00."

"Okay."

151

Sherry gave me a really bad look and said, "No, don't go."

"It's okay I will stay out of trouble. Remember the money?"

"I don't care about the money."

"You will when we get back to the States. The kids need college money."

"Yeah but without a husband or father. Okay, but don't tell me anything until you get back."

The next morning I was at the hotel by 9:00 thinking that the traffic would be heavy but not many cars moving. That gave me a bad feeling. Mr. Finley showed at 9:45 and we went into the restaurant and found a table in a quiet place. We ordered coffee and sat in the quietness without a word. We drank a few sips and he began with his proposal, "Pat, I need you to take a little trip to the north and meet with several of my associates. They have a package to delivery and they are hesitant to come to Tehran."

"I am assuming when you say north you mean northern Iran. I told you I was not leaving Iran without my family."

"But of course, just a road trip to Astara on the coast of the Caspian Sea. It is about 200 miles and you will be in the mountains some. I have you a room reserved at the Speniyas Hotel and it is a 4-star hotel."

"What kinds of package are we talking about, no guns, no drugs?"

"Certainly not, just papers. If I told you what kind of papers it would just mean you are more involved and I am sure you do not want that."

"Okay no killing, remember."

"Believe me; I do certainly not want trouble. These papers are very valuable so I am choosing you as the best person to return with them."

"When do I start?"

"In the morning and I registered you as Jimmy Stewart. Your contact will find you and the password is 'movie'."

I took more sips of coffee and said, "See you when I get back."

I made the trip back to the house with ease and that worried me. I told Sherry that I would be gone for a couple of days and we made plans of things that she would need. I was not sure about the water supply being turned off so we filled several containers with water. The food supply was good for at least two weeks.

The next morning I gave everyone what seemed like a thousand kisses and hugs and left. I was not sure about the distance but I carried a map in hope of finding Astara. The car had over a half tank of gasoline but I decided to fill it up before I left town. The service station that I normally use had a line of cars waiting for gas. I wondered is there a price cut on gas or does everyone need gas. I stopped and soon found out that there was going to be a shortage and that was the reason for the line of cars. I waited and filled up. The drive over the mountain to the Caspian Sea was winding and everyone seemed to think it was a Formula 1 racetrack. The curves meant that some fool driving down the mountain would be going 100mph in my lane. It took full attention to the highway just as usual. It was afternoon and I was getting a bit hungry. I stopped at a small store to get nuts hoping I would not have a problem. I opened the door and took two steps and a man started waving his hands in the air and screaming. Not sure what he said but I turned around and walked out. If the hotel had the same reception, I did not have a plan as to how to pick up the package. I passed through several more small towns and soon arrived at Astara. To my surprise it was larger than I expected, maybe 50,000 people. My Iranian tourist book gave a brief history and told me that this city had been here for centuries and was used as a trade port. It was hard finding the hotel since I saw no English for street signs but I lucked out and located it after about 30-minutes. Believe it or not it was a nice place and I wished Sherry and the kids could have been with me. Things were going smooth as I checked in as Jimmy Stewart. It was late afternoon and I still had not eaten lunch so I went to the restaurant for a snack and a beer. I showed my room key and they gave me anything I ordered including beer. Snacks in Iran were not pizza, chips, or ice cream but flat bread with dips of eggplant or things I did not recognize. It tasted good if you washed it down with beer. I went back to the room and waited for someone to show that knew the password. I kept my trusty .357 mag. tucked in my belt for no reason except it made me feel better.

Six hours had passed; it was dark and very near to 9:00. I had watched the one channel of English speaking TV for that time period. There were just old re-runs of "I love Lucy" and all the show from the 50's. Finally a knock at the door and in broken English the word "movie" came forth. I reached for the .357 but left it in my belt. I slowly opened the door and there stood a young Iranian boy, maybe 15 years old. He smiled and said, "Movie."

I returned the smile and saw that he was alone and waved him into the room. He carried a large envelope that was over stuffed and he handed it to me. I gave him a friendly look and asked, "Is this the complete package?"

I should had been talking to the wall because all he did was smile and nod his head yes. I was not sure what to do next so I offered him a large tip. He took it and said thank you several times. He walked toward the door and I gave him a farewell smile and I closed the door.

The package lay on the bed as I stared at it from a chair thinking could this package of paper be worth anyone's life? Why would anyone need me to transport a piece of paper? After about 30-minutes, my curiosity burned and I flipped open the envelope. I pulled out the papers and began to sift through them. Most of them were written in Farsi but one series of papers were written in English. I took my time reading. It was a day-by-day schedule of what was going to happen during the revolution. My mind flashed in all directions as to whom had written this and where was it going. I studied the maps and dates and what seemed to me the important events. It would happen fast if this schedule was correct.

A knock came at the door. "What the hell," I said to myself?

I did not say a word but stuffed the papers back into the envelope. Another knock came and then the window on the other side of the room exploded as a teargas bomb fell to the floor. At the same time bullets burst through the door from an automatic weapon. "Maybe Sherry was correct, she would be a widow," I said out loud.

I lay flat on the floor and replaced the .357 mag. with the envelope in back belt. I snake-crawled to the wall and through the shredded door I could see two men to preparing to burst through the door. I jumped to my feet and waited for them to come through. It was only a couple of seconds before the first guy came running hard after he had given the door a hard kick. As he entered I grabbed his arm and flipped him to his back. His weapon flew across the room. The second man came through the door like he was on fire and I grabbed his weapon as he passed and slung him in the direction of the first. The tear gas was filling the room and my vision was starting to fail. I made a quick look outside the door in case there was more and fired a few shots into the floor to get their attention. Neither spoke English as both jabbered in Farsi. The teargas had taken both into another land of dreams as they gasped for air. I stood in the door and decided it was a good time to get fresher air. I fired several more rounds into the floor and headed down the hallway in a run. About halfway down the hall I met two more men running in my direction. They carried automatic weapons and waved the business end in my direction. I heard shots coming from my backside and fell to the floor. The sound of bullets whizzing by my head gave me dark memories. I rolled to the wall of the hallway with one of the men in front of me staggering and fell to the floor. "Damn, they had killed one of their own men," I said to myself.

It was my turn to do something when a door open and a woman screamed as I made my way passed her and closed the door. Oh, she never stopped that unbelievable loud noise so I opened the doors to her balcony. I made a quick jump over the rail and landed on my feet about ten feet below. It was as bad as jumping from a helicopter and it hurt my knees when I hit the ground. I looked back at the window and waved at the woman. My car was close and I was driving in a few seconds. No more gunfire but questions flew through my brain like a covey of Quail. "Who were those guys and how did they know I was there? I'm sure they were after the papers but why wait until I had them. That little delivery man should have been their target."

On the drive back through the mountains I had plenty of time to think. Was Finley really the person he claimed or was he just another player? I had only met him twice but he sure knew a lot about me. He must have contacts with the government or maybe he really is the government. I had no way of knowing but maybe I should do a little research before I handled him the papers. I had time. By 6:00 am I was back in Tehran and the curfew was over. Home had been on my mind for hours and there was not a minute that passed without thoughts of Sherry and the kids. I prayed that they were okay and safe.

CHAPTER 20

I drove up the street and parked in front of the house and as I got out of the car both kids were waving from the window. I bounced up the stairs and slung open the door with Sherry and two smiling children grabbing for me. Again hugs and kisses made the rounds and we moved to the living room. "Everyone okay," I asked softly?

"Sure daddy."

Sherry gave her okay with a head nod. I had one each girl sitting on each knee holding them like never before. "Daddy, can we go to the park?"

"Not right now but maybe later, how about some breakfast?"

"Pancakes?"

"Well, we'll see what mother can whip up."

Sherry gave me a punch and said, "This is not a restaurant but I will what I can do."

During breakfast, I told about the trip but saved the part about the hotel. It was then that I thought of the serious problems that could have taken place if Sherry and the kids had been there.

The children finished and wondered into the living room. A board game kept their interest for a couple of hours. Sherry and I washed the dishes as we talked. "Okay, what really happened," asked Sherry with a serious tone?

"I drove up north and enjoyed the scenery of the Caspian Sea, stayed in a nice hotel, and worried about you a lot."

"No bullets or guns?"

"Now, I did not say that."

"You bastard, you tried to get yourself killed again."

I gave her a hug and whispered in her ear, "I am too mean to get killed or you would have killed me long ago. Honey, we do have to make some changes."

"What do you mean? We have made a lot changes."

"No, I mean major changes such as how to get out of here."

"Is it going to get worse?"

"Most definitely."

"How do you know?"

"I took a peek at the papers that I picked up and it is a schedule for someone, written by someone concerning the upcoming revolution."

"Wait, can't the King and all the U.S. equipment in this country put down a few sheepherders?"

"All I know is what I see and read. It does not take much for the Iranian military and the herders to turn against the government. This is a religious revolution and the King and the U.S. will have their hands full."

"That makes it easy for us. We are leaving tomorrow."

"That sounds easy but it may not be possible."

"What do you mean, not possible."

"First, we have the kids to think about. It is not all safe out there in a car. Second, the airport is closing at times and flights are not on any kind of schedule. I will spend time tomorrow nosing around and maybe come up with a plan."

Sherry's face dropped and I held her close. "Honey, we will be okay."

A sob was heard in my ear as she laid her head on my shoulder. I pulled her closer and whispered, "Let's check on the kids."

The curfew came at 6:00 as usually and we played games using candles. It was fun and we were a really close family. I am not sure if the trials we endured brought us closer but we were together and happy. It was bedtime and the girls were tucked in. Sherry and I went to the roof and listened to darkness as it shown in every direction. We told each other soft words and kissed. Our love had grown and we knew each other's feelings better than ever before.

The dawn and kids came to our room about the same time so we all went to the kitchen for breakfast. No milk. no bread, and no meat, so we had homemade biscuits. He had to use dry milk and there was not much of that left. The biscuits were good with jelly and I even tried peanut butter. We all scored breakfast an 87%.

My next thought came to business and what I was going to do with the papers I had collected. Should I call Finley or do a little research first? Research seemed to be the logical answer but being in Iran made it a bit more difficult. I gave Sherry a stare and told her that I needed to make a trip into the base. I was driving within twenty minutes with the papers lying on the seat beside me. Traffic was bad but I managed to keep the car moving as I snaked my way through several side streets. I was getting better at driving with total concretion of other drivers. I entered the base without a problem after the guards searching every inch of the car. I had the papers stuffed in my belt. As I passed the first copy machine I stopped and copied the papers. Making sure no one was around I hid the copy behind the copy machine.

I walked up stairs and entered the office of the highest-ranking American officer that I could find. It happened that he was the Commander of the Base and a full-bird Colonel. There was a Capitan sitting at an outside desk and I approached asking to see the Colonel. I gave my name and she asked my business. I told her I had very important information concerning the problems in the country. She went into the Colonel's office and returned. She waved me in the direction of the door but stopped me for a search with a wane metal detector before I went into the office. I entered the office and the Colonel was gazing out his window. I waited for him to speak and that took several minutes. He turned and asked, "What can I do for you Mr. Taylor?"

Not forgetting my military training I stood at attention. "Sir, in my possession is papers concerning the upcoming revolution."

"Revolution, what revolution?"

"The one in progress. Sir, I need to be perfectly frank with you and you me. I come to you because I have no one else that I can trust at the moment."

The Colonel turned to his chair and sat down. He pointed to a guess chair and said, "Have a seat Mr. Taylor. What do you really want?"

"Sir, you know a Mr. Finley from the CIA?"

The Colonel remained quiet for over a minute which seemed like a year. He leaded forward in my direction and said, "Finley, how are you involved with him?"

"I work for him at times."

"Okay, what do you do?"

"My family and I came about three months ago. I was brought here on the pretense of finding oil but after I arrived I was told that they or Mr. Finley had different plans for me.

Since I have been here I have be doing special favors including spying and getting beat up with bullets flying around my body. My last job was to travel to the Caspian Sea and pick up a package. Well, one man was killed and I left in a big hurry. I did get the papers and that is what I want to show you. First, you have to consider this information secret and our meeting has not taken place. I tell you that people are getting killed for this package and they certainly would not mine killing you or me."

"Okay, okay, what do you have?"

I handed him the package and he spread the papers out. He took a quick glace and called the Captain, "Get me an interrupter."

Two minutes later an Iranian walked into the office and I grabbed the papers. The Colonel gave me a go-to-hell- look and said, "What the hell are you doing?"

"These are only for you to see."

"This man has a top-secret U.S. clearance and he works for me as an interrupter. If you want to know the truth as to what they say then you had better lay them back down."

I took another look at the Iranian and he gave me a nod. I handed the Colonel the papers and he spread them out again. He took the ones that were in English and handed the other to the Iranian. The Colonel scanned the papers and raised his head looking me straight into my eyes, 'Where did you get this?"

"A long story but I had an assignment to meet a person at the Caspian Sea and he would delivery me a package. Well, I opened the package and this was the continence. Just like you I could only read the English version with my limited Farsi but I could not believe that written plans for a revolution were before me."

"Okay one more time, who sent you to pick up this package?"

"A Mr. Finley that works for the CIA."

The Colonel screamed, "Captain!"

The door open within two seconds and the Captain were standing at attention. "God damn it Captain, get me verification that a person by the name of Finley is in country working for the CIA."

"Yes sir."

The Colonel continued reading the papers and within three minutes the Captain entered the room again. "Well?"

"No sir, no one working for the CIA by the name of Finley is here in Iran."

I fell back in my chair and whispered, "Shit."

"Well, Mr. Taylor who is your man?"

My words came slowly, "I don't know."

No one said a word for at least a minute as the Colonel continued to sift through the papers. "Where in the hell did you met this person," asked the Colonel?

"He came to me with a CIA ID and he knew my job and every detail of my past life and experience. He claimed that I was brought into Iran to do work for him. There seemed to be no question that he was with the CIA until I received these papers and they provide more questions than I had answers."

"Okay, tell me every meeting and what you did for this guy."

I went through every detail that I knew about Finley and the Captain took down each word. I was near completion when the Iranian shouted out, "Very bad! Very bad!"

The Colonel took a look at him and said, "What? What the hell are you saying?"

"These words! This comes from France and means much trouble."

The Iranian began to read, "There was much opposition against the Mohammad Reza Shah, and how he used the secret police, the Savak, to control the country. Strong Shi'i opposition against the Shah, and the country is close to a situation of civil war. The opposition will be lead by Ayatollah Khomeini, founder of Islamic Republic who lives in exile in Iraq and later in France. His message will be distributed through music cassettes, which will be smuggled into Iran in small numbers, and then duplicated, and spread all around the country. This will be the beginning of Iranian revolution. We will begin today."

"Who wrote that shit," asked the Colonel?

The Iranian gave him a blank look and shook his head, no. "No signature but written to a Mr. Finley."

"Damn, this guy has to be Russian or some other communist," said the Colonel.

"I don't think he has to be a communist but for sure a member of some Muslim sects such as the Shi'i.

I sat there with my mind racing wondering what a country boy from Texas was doing in such a mess as this. I was just here to work not be a spy. I stood and walked to the Colonel and started to pick up the papers. "What are you doing? You are not getting these back."

"Colonel, my deal with Finley was to deliver this package and if I don't we will never find out who this guy really is."

The Colonel motioned for the Iranian to give the papers to me. The Captain offered to make copies and she took them. Five minutes later she was back and handled me the papers. The Colonel stood and said, "What are doing to do now?"

"Easy call him and set up a meeting."

The Colonel gave me a stare and said, "We will be there with you so make it a public place. This guy must have contacts with all the underground Shiit people waiting for the word to start a revolution."

I walked from the office and stopped on the way out to pick up my copy of the papers. I managed to find a phone and called Finley. He seemed pleasant and happy that I had retrieved the package and we set up a time to meet at the hotel as usual. I called the Colonel and gave him the time and location. I had three hours to kill before the meeting so I gave Sherry a call and told her I would be a bit late returning and then looked for a place to get a beer. The only places that sold beer in these times were large hotels and mainly chain hotels. I found the Hilton and went to the bar. There were two other men walked in just after me and sat at a table so that I was in view. Okay, were these guys some of Finley's friends or Government. It did not make mush difference because all I wanted was a beer and to kill some time. After three beers I decided to take a walk and see if my friends would follow. I gave them a nod as I left the bar and they returned the gesture. I walked through the lobby and my tail was right there. These guys were not very good at tailing people or they did not care if I knew.

It was time for my meeting and I drove to the hotel and found a table in the restaurant. The restaurant was a bit crowded but most could have been the Colonel's people. Within minutes Finley showed and he sat down at my table. He was a bit jumpy or nervous. I sat a briefcase which contained the package near his chair. The waitress brought tea and we had a few words but nothing concerning the package. Finally, he asked if I had any problems and I said quietly, "Hell yes, one man was killed and I was lucky it was not me. Is the package worth getting killed?"

"It is a very valuable package and that is why I am giving you a bonus."

He handed me a small envelope. I took a quick look and it was filled with thousand dollar bills. "To save you from counting it, there are one-hundred of those bills," Finley said.

I stuck the envelope in my coat pocket and said, "Must be a very valuable package. Can I ask you one question?"

"Sure."

"What country do you have an interest that is worth all this risk?"

"U.S. of course! I am CIA."

I stood and that must have been a signal because four men rushed to the table and took hold of Finley. I assumed they were the Colonel's people because one said, "Finley you are coming with us" as he whipped out handcuffs. That did not last long as a loud gunfire echoed through the room and the man holding Finley fell to the floor. Yes, bleeding from his chest and looked mostly dead. That was not the end but the beginning. It seemed everyone but me had their handgun out and bullets crisscrossed the room making it hard to determine which way to go. I decided the floor was best. I had gained weight since Vietnam but I lay so flat that I left my imprint on the marble floor. Two more of the Colonel's men fell bleeding and Finley and his gunmen walked out the front door. I was slightly outnumbered to be a hero and try to stop them so I attended the dead and wounded. I heard the sirens from the police cars so I decide to vanish through the back exit.

A few blocks away I called the Colonel, "What the hell are you trying to do? All your men are dead and Finley walked free as a bird. You cannot take this guy for granted and he is one step ahead of you and I both. Why in the hell did you not tell me you had men there to pick up Finley?"

"One fucking minute, I had no one assigned to your little reunion. What happened?"

"A major amount of shooting with several people dead. Apparently, Finley suspected confutation and had his own people standing by. The other team acted like cops with handcuffs and weapons but they are all dead now."

"Well, why did you not help?"

"I did help. I stayed on the floor while a hell of a lot of lead flew across the room."

"Get back to my office. We need to talk."

"Sorry General, I mean Colonel you will have to come to my house because I have to check on my family. Oh, if you come bring beer. I talk better with a couple of beers."

I hung the phone up and got back into the car and drove home. I did not want to talk to anyone except Sherry and the kids. I checked for the envelope on my way into the house and it was still there. Sherry met me at the door with two little ones hanging on each leg. I held Sherry for a long time and whispered, "You have a good day?"

"No, how about you?"

"Better than you think."

I pulled out the envelope and handed it to her. "What is it?"

"Open it."

She looked inside and I could see her go limp so I put my arm around her waist. "How much and who's are these?"

"I have not counted them but I was told there is one-hundred and they are all yours."

"No way! Where did you get this money?"

"Just doing my job and dodging a few bullets."

"Damn you Pat, I knew whatever you are involved is dangerous and the money is not worth it."

"Maybe you did not hear me. There are one hundred of those bills in that envelope."

"Oh I heard you but me spend them alone is my worry."

The night came and we sat in the living room with two candles watching the girls have fun with their non-stop giggling. We had fun with games and stories and happiness consumed the house. Bedtime came for the girls and that left Sherry and I alone on the couch with the flickering candles. It was not hard to love a beautiful woman that cared so much for me. It was after 11:00 when a quiet knock was heard at the front door. Sherry jumped off the couch with her mouth open and pointing to the door. I found my .357 and walked slowly to the door. I waited. Another knock came and I asked, "What?"

The person returned with, "Pat, I need to talk with you."

The voice was a whisper and it was hard to determine if it was an American. I asked again, "What do you want?"

"Pat please let me in. It is Finley."

I looked at Sherry and she shook her head no. I raised the handgun and opened the door slightly. Yes, there stood Finley and he was alone. "Damn you! You have your nerve coming here after the gun war that you got me involved. I guess you want your money back?"

"Pat, every bullet was direct in some other person besides you. I gave my people direct orders that you were not to get hurt and they abided. It was not my fault that the shooting started. May I come in?"

I opened the door a little wider and he walked in. He stood looking at Sherry and said, "Hello I am very sorry for this late hour but I have very important business that needs taken care of as soon as possible. May I have a word with your husband?"

Sherry gave him a hard stare and said, "Would it make a difference if I said no?"

I raised my hand and walked between them. "Honey, it will be okay."

We made our way to the living room and sat down. Finley began, "Pat, I feel you and your family need to be removed from this country before it gets nasty. I am willing to pay for you and your family to take a long vacation until the Shah gets things back into control."

"What do you mean by a long vacation?"

"How about Thailand for three or four weeks until some of the problems are resolved?"

I looked at Sherry and she broke a half-smile. "Okay how soon?"

"Can you be packed by tomorrow?"

"Sure."

"Pat, I am going to give you a little spending money for the trip."

Finley pulled out an envelope and handed it to me. I looked inside and more thousand dollar bills. "The last time I counted them there was one-hundred."

"I suppose this little gift mean another pickup?"

"No Pat, I have a package for you to deliver. No guns or any kind of violence. A person will contact you the first day that you are there so you will not even have to worry about it while you are on vacation."

"I should know better by now, no free lunches."

Finley handed me the package and walked toward the door. I opened the door and at the same instant the sound of a rifle record was heard and a bullet hit the door missing Finley by an inch. I slammed the door shut and Finley made a run for the balcony. He jumped to the ground and was gone in the night.

Sherry began to cry and I held her and gave her words of comfort, like one hundred thousand dollars worth. Not much sleep that night and we were packed and leaving by 9:00 am. Our flight to Bangkok was on Air France which did nothing for my moral.

It was almost Christmas and the kids were excited about getting out of the house. As matter of fact, Sherry and I were excited also. The flight gave me bad memories as I sat in my seat with the engines making a slight roar, "Was Thailand like Vietnam. I could see jungle and smoke coming from bombs as I flew over the tree tops firing the machine gun from the Huey. I could smell the death of years past."

I was sweating when Sherry asked, "What's wrong? You sick?"

"No I'm fine."

I just could not tell her my thoughts. The plane landed and as we left the door the heat and humidly hit us like a brick. We boarded a bus with air conditioning thank God and it started for Pattaya Beach. The people looked the same as the Vietnamese, the heat was the same and if I had to eat rice I would throw up. The drive to the beach was about two hours but the driver was in no hurry. The trip passed through jungle and small town and we made a stop at one town so we could shop. The shop owner must have been the driver's brother-in-law because he kept telling us what great deals this shop could offer. Upon arrival at the Royal Wing Resort, I was shocked. The whole family just stood in the lobby and gazed around. It truly was a 5-star hotel. A twenty foot Christmas tree made of bamboo stood with all kinds of presents. It was fun just to see such a tree. I went to the desk and told the gentleman my name and he acted like I was his long lost brother. The presidential suite was reserved for us. The service personnel took charge of us and marched us to the suite. It was a mini-apartment with a private butler. There were three bedrooms, three bathrooms, three lounges as well as a central dining area and guest cloakrooms. Within a few minutes after the tour the butler arrived with fruit and Champaign. He poured the bubbly liquid and explained that he was our servant and he was available for any request. Well, this was a little much for a country boy and I had no idea what to do except tip him with a fifty dollar bill. That brought a smile to his face and he bowed several times with his hands together and in front of his face. I soon found out that the bowing was a common gesture of most Thai people. The butler left and Sherry looked at me and said, "You think that tip was a little much?"

"Hell if I know. I have never been to a place like this.

Let's unpack later and take a tour of this place."

Sherry grabbed her purse and the kids and we were out the door. The butler was waiting outside the door. I bowed and said, "We are going for a tour of the hotel."

He smiled and bowed. We found the lobby again and in the process we passed a restaurant called the Le Benjarong and apparently it was for dinner. A reservation was required and they had a dress code. Sherry said, "Looks great to me for dinner but I am not sure I have anything to wear."

"There is a whole country out there for shopping and they specialize in clothing."

We kept walking and soon came to the pool area. This was no ordinarily pool. It had a restaurant in the middle of the pool. It had a French name also but it translated Island Oasis. It advertised serving light snacks, lunch and afternoon tea and a candlelit 5-course dinner under the stars. Again Sherry spoke, "We will try that place."

The swim-up bar looked wonderful so I stopped a waiter and ordered drinks. We sat down in the shade of a palm tree and waited for the waiter to return. About half the women sunning around the pool was topless or completely naked. No one complained about that except for Sherry. "Why do they do that with children present?"

"I would say that their children are acclimated to it."

165

"Our children are not!"

"Tell them not to look and I am sure they will look that much harder."

The drinks came in coconut shells and I made sure that the kid's drinks had no alcohol.

We continued the tour and at every turn the beauty resumed. What a hotel and what I did not understand is why Finley gave us this trip. We walked back to the room and there stood the butler and we gave him another bow. We opened the door and found all our clothes hanging in closets and neatly folded in drawers. Sherry turned and said, "I am not leaving."

I went to the mini-frig and took out a beer, "Anyone want anything from the frig?'

Of course, the kids had to have a Coke. It was mid-afternoon and Sherry suggested that we go shopping for clothes. I pointed to the door and within ten minutes she and the girls were on their way.

The room had a balcony and with beer in hand I join the leisure of the world. There was a good view of the pool but I must have had jetlag because I was asleep in minutes. Sometime later a man woke me up calling my name. It was our butler and he announced that there was a man here to see me. I removed myself from the chair and walked into the room. The butler opened the door to the hallway and there stood Finley. I gave him a half smile and said, "What the hell are you doing here?"

"Just checking on you to make sure all is well."

"Come in."

We sat down and he began to talk about Iran, "Pat, we have a problem in Iran in that the revolution is moving too fast."

"Wait! You said we have a problem."

"Yes, I know what I said but you are involved in this also. You know more than the Shah and the U.S Government about what is being planned."

"Why did you really send me here? There is no package or person is there?"

"No, I just needed to get your family out of the country so we could work. The Tehran airport is closed and no one is getting in or out now. I would suggest that you send your family to the U.S. from here."

"I will but where does that leave me?"

"Pat, I need you in Iran. The money will continue in the same amounts as before."

"What can I possibly do in Iran?"

"The nuclear power plant has to be disabled before the Shah leaves the country."

"The Shah is leaving?'

"Yes, with all the U.S. people and equipment."

"Finley, can I trust you? No one else seems to think you are for real, just a terrorist from another country."

"I don't give a damn what other people think but you can trust me with your life."

"Well, if I go with you what exactly will I be doing? Okay, what is the plan?"

"In two weeks I will be here to pick you in a private jet and we fly to Iran. In the meantime you and your family will have a wonderful time here in this hotel. Get your family to the U.S. a couple of days before that. I will see you in two weeks."

He walked to the door and Finley made his exit with the help of the butler.

That conversation called for vodka and the mini-frig handled that request. At 5:30 the door opened and in walked one lady and two young girls carrying as many packages as they could with two other hotel personnel carrying packages on a cart. "Oh my God, is there anything left in Thailand?"

Smiles broke across their faces and Sherry said, "We left plenty for tomorrow."

The next two week passed very fast as we shopped and spent a lot of hours at the beach. We adjusted to Thai food and ate lobster and shrimp almost everyday. I still left the rice on my plate. I broke the news slowly to Sherry that she had to return to the States without me and that was another tearful episode. Everyday we made love and acted like lovers but the time came for her and the kids to leave. We had to buy more suitcases for all that we had bought and she even hand-carried some of the breakable items. We had spent a lot of time in jewelry stores and her fingers were sparkling. With many tears I left my family as they lifted off the ground for the U.S.A.

Boy, was I stupid for staying in Thailand while the people I love had gone home? Something inside of me kept telling me to stay and that I required the excitement of bullets flying by me. Had I gone pass the saneness of a normal human being? Was I addicted to danger? So many times I had told myself that I would never pick up a gun again and there I was with a handgun in my belt most of the time. What was I doing? I surely did not want the dreams back in my life on a daily account. They were still there once or twice a week but I was living with that. God, I hated war and killing!

Finley was due tomorrow and I had to make a decision. Of course, his idea of battle was nothing like the hell that I had seen. I stopped for a beer and before I sat down there were two whores by my side. I gave them a wave to leave and they did. I kept drinking and tried to piece the entire puzzle together. My gut feeling was that Finley was not CIA but what was he, KGB? Our military had no record of the guy but that did not mean anything either. If the CIA did not want a person known, then he did not exist. Yet, how could this guy know so much about me? He predicted my every choice and why I would make those decisions. Surely he knew I had a lot to loose and was not willing to depart from family. The fourth beer went down easy so I made my way to the hotel. I lay on the bed and one of Vietnam dreams woke me up in a cold sweat. I got up and began to pace telling myself I wanted out. All I wanted was to stop dreaming and live in peace. I went to the mini-frig and pulled out vodka. I found a Coke and poured both into a glass. I went to the balcony and sat sipping the drink. It was hot and humid and I sat there with drops of sweat rolling down my face. A feeling came over me that the heat was my punishment and being hot was forcing me to remember Nam. The pool looked cool but there were several women without tops sunbathing and I wanted no part of that. Sherry had been by me every moment and I was not going to betray her now. Night came and I ordered room service.

Without much sleep I checked out of the hotel and took a taxi to the airport again. I asked about a hangar for private jets and was guided to another area. I made a few more inquiries and no one knew Finley or his airplane. That worried me. I found a waiting lounge and sat down for Finley to find me. I was almost a sleep when a hell of a loud jet came taxiing to the hangar. I got up and looked outside and saw a Gulfstream IV business jet with no markings. The door opened and out stepped Finley. "Damn, a Gulfstream," I said in a quiet voice.

He came charging into the hangar like he knew exactly where I was. He waved from a distance and continued walking toward me. "Pat, how are you?"

"Good."

"Ready to go?"

"Sure, let me get my bag."

He followed me to the lounge and he picked up one of my bags. He then gave it to a man waiting near the door of the Gulfstream. We continued into the plane. I had never been inside a business jet and did I have a shock. Every detail was leather or fine wood through out the interior. It was so nice that I really did not want to take a seat but Finley offered several times so I did. Within minutes the engines were started and we were taxiing. The wheels lifted and we left Thailand. A flight attendant came with drinks and tray of cheeses and fruits. Not much was said as we drank. Our seats swiveled around a table and Finley placed his arms on the table, "Pat, let me give you more information about what I would like for you to do."

I turned and looked him in the eye and gave my opening statement, "Tell me again what agency you are with."

"Does that really matter now? We have a mission to accomplish and you are best tool that your government has."

"My government? Are you sure we are working for my government?"

"Absolutely! Pat, you are the key to world peace."

Finley opened a briefcase and pulled out a folder. While the case was open I saw a document with a Russian flag in the heading. I switched my eyes to the folder as he opened the contents. The documents were in a language that I did not recognize. Finley spoke softly, "How is your Korean?"

"Not good. I have never spoken it and I don't want to speak it."

"That's okay because I am going to give you a quick lesson in Korean."

Finley gave me a small book with what I assumed was a Korean dictionary and said, "It is very simple, just look for any markings that match the ones in the dictionary."

"Are you crazy? I am to go through Iran looking for marking that match anything in this book?"

"No, no just look around the nuclear power plant and a warehouse that I will give you the address. You will be looking for crates or paperwork showing that it came from Korea. All we need are pictures of what in the crates if you find any."

"Should I ask for help to open the crates?"

"Well, you could but it might cause a bit of a stir. Oh yes, we will need a small explosion at the power plant to slow things down a bit."

"Explosion, how small is small?"

"Just enough plastic explosives to stop the building for ten years or so."

"Damn, I will need an Air Force Bomber to do that."

"I will give you a map as to where you should set off the charges and that should halt operations for a while."

"Okay where do I get all the equipment?"

"I have it with me and you can start tomorrow. I need it done within three days."

"I need a car and not a Paykan."

"Not a problem you have one sitting outside the hangar, Range Rover that is and the boot is packed with all the equipment you will need."

Finley handed me another envelope filled with Iranian money. "Keep what you do not use because it will not be worth much in the very near future. "

"How much is in here so I will not come up short?"

"In dollars, about $50K."

"That should do it for a trip south."

"Let me warn you, it will not be as easy as last time."

The plane landed without a problem.

I walked to the four-wheel drive vehicle and unlocked it. I did catch Finley using the term boot and usually only Europeans used that term. This guy was not an American and he was going to get me killed. I took a quick inventory of the car and found clothing, detail maps, weapons, and explosives. There were no markings on the clothing and even the labels were torn out. There were no markings on anything. At least someone was thinking ahead.

I drove away thinking that I must be some kind of fool. Money flowing like water and this guy thinking that I can save the world, that's a joke. The good thing is that I did not have Sherry and the kids to worry about or at least here in this hellhole.

The highway was the same but I made several turns that might cause a little confusion if someone was following me. I stopped four times to check the skies looking for helicopters and taking a hard look at approaching cars. No military, U.S. or Iranian, vehicles passed while I waited. At the first stop I took a concentrated look throughout the car searching for bugs or tracking devises. I searched carefully through the explosives looking for a live timer. There were plenty of timers but none live. I found nothing but that did not mean that they were not there. Remembering the schedule for the revolution it was time for things to start moving in full throttle. Then it hit me as I screamed to myself, "I have no plan for escape and that fuck'in Finley said nothing about getting out of the country."

I banged the steering wheel. I felt like I was in whirlpool being suck down the drain by money. My mine kept digging taking a hard look at Iran's neighbors thinking I might drive out. There seemed to be only two choices, USSR or Turkey and Turkey sounded better. I arrived at Dezful and to my surprise the city was large so I looked for a hotel. I drove through the streets like a tourist knowing no one spoke English but my Farsi was getting better. After thirty minutes of burning gasoline, I decided to stop and ask about a hotel. I pulled to the side of the street and entered a clothing store. I shopped around and found a couple of shirts and pants and took them to the cashier. I tried English first and the word hotel did not compute. I had no idea the Farsi word for hotel so I did a game of charades. The man enjoyed my acting but we failed to communicate. I paid and as I was walking out a heard a voice, "Sir, I know English."

It was a teenage boy. I asked him the location of a nice hotel and he gave me a long list of directions. He was pleasant so I asked him if he would ride with me to the hotel. I held out a rial bill that was worth about fifty dollars. A big smile broke across his face and we walked to the car. I would have never found the hotel without the help of the young man so I gave him another fifty dollars. He grabbed a taxi and was gone.

I entered the lobby stood and looked around. This place was no dump and might be a three-star hotel. I was thankful for any place that had a bed without fleas in this country. After unloading my clothes in the room I made my way back downstairs finding a place for a beer. Two beers later I was walking along the streets getting a few stares from passing people. My clothes must have been the keys for everyone noticing that I was a foreigner but most likely my blonde hair. In the middle of the next block a tall man with the appearance of an American came from a store selling brass and copper. We bumped each other and a couple more steps and I felt lightheaded. Things began turning and I went down. I was conscience but my body was not functioning and my ability to raise my arm was gone. I tried to speak but my tongue would not move. My thoughts came to one conclusion, this must be the end. The man was joined by another and they carried me into the shop. My muscles were paralyzed when they landed me in a chair. There was no way I could sit there and I rolled to the floor, facedown. They went through my clothing apparently looking for weapons. I had none. After about thirty seconds I began to feel my body coming back to life and was able to turn my head. I grasped for air as my lungs began to pump oxygen.

One of the men asked, "Going shopping?"

I said nothing as he rolled me to my back. The one man looked into my face as he bent down and grabbed my hair pulling me to a sitting position. He let go and my head banged the floor. "Oh, did that hurt?"

The other man gave a chuckle and said, "I guess we are going to have a little conversation. I know you want to talk about how you are enjoying this wonderful country."

Both men were well dressed and could have been Americans except for their accents. They could have been Russians but I was not sure. By now my body was recovered enough to raise my arms. One of the men pulled me to the chair again and started to backhand me. I caught his hand before it made its way to my face and turned his wrist sharply. The sound of bones snapping was not a happy sound especially with him screaming. "Oh, did that hurt?"

My legs were weak but I got to my feet. The other guy reached for a handgun inside his coat. I slung the guy with the bad wrist into the other guy. Both men were on the floor and I lifted the gun from the screamer. He did not care anyway. "Who the hell are you guys?"

A silence filled the room except for the whimpering from the guy holding his wrist. I pointed the handgun in the direction of the two and pulled the trigger. A bullet buried itself into the counter next to them but got their full attention. I took a step closer and pointed the gun directly and at the forehead of the man with the gun still in his coat. "Very slowly remove the gun and lay it on the floor. Then slide it to me."

He did as told without hesitation. Still no words came from either guy. I picked up the gun from the floor and held one in each hand. "It seems I hand all the toys and now I want some answers. What do you morons want with me?"

I fired another shot and Mr. Broken Wrist replied, "We are to stop you."
"From what?"
"Going to the power plant."
"How do you know I am going to the power plant?"
"Where else would you be going?"
"I am on holiday and touring Iran."
"I don't think so."
"Are you guys Russian? I want to see some ID."
"No ID"
"Maybe a bullet through your left earlobe might help and I am not a very good shot."

I fired another shot in the direction of his head. "I told you I was not a very good shot so I will be aiming a little closer to your head this time."

"Okay, Russians working for the German government. Apparently, the Germans have a lot invested in the project and want it operating."

"The Germans are proud workers but hiring Russians for protection was their biggest mistake. Get up!"

The two struggled to their feet and I motioned them to the back of the store. "There is only one person that knew I was going to the power plant so he must be your boss. Does Finley know how stupid you are?"

"We do not know Finley."

"Oh, I think you do to keep you quiet I am going to kill you."

"No please, we are just men doing a job and we have no regards to Finley."

"You will have even less regards with holes blown through your body. Is Finley Russian?"

I fired another shot and they raised their hands. "Wait, yes Finley is Russian and working for the Germans."

I said to myself, "God that had to be a lie, the Russians working for the Germans."

I had to think about what to do with these two guys kill them or let them go. Finley was the one I needed to have a conversation but I felt that I needed to blow the power plant for the U.S.A. It would slow the Iranians down a few years until the Russians or Koreans brought in new equipment.

I pointed my gun to the door and said, "Get out! If I see or hear from you again, bullets will not be bouncing around the room unless they go all the way through your body first."

The two left without looking back.

CHAPTER 21

The remainder of the night in the hotel was quiet and the next morning I was driving again. I drove in peace thinking about Sherry and enjoying the Rover ride. I was hoping that I would not need the four-wheel drive but I was glad I had it. I was about twenty miles from the power plant construction when I noticed the plant security in my rearview mirror. They followed me for another five miles and I found a place to stop. I was going to let them pass but they pulled along side of me. There was no way they were going to search the car so I got out and stood with my arms crossed. In very bad English one of the men said, "What are you doing here? I will need to see papers."

I handed him my passport and he spent time studying it. "What are you going here? This is Government property."

"Oh, I did not know. I did not see any signs. I have never been on this road before. I am here looking for the construction of the power plant. I sell equipment that is being used for the construction and it is time to reorder."

"What kind of equipment?"

"Steel tanks for cooling. Can you give me directions to the plant?"

"No, you are not allowed in this area."

"But Sir, I have a job to do."

"Not here. You must turn around, now. You must have a government pass to enter and your name is not on my list."

The security man pulled a handgun and pointed it in my direction, "You must leave."

I held up my arms and said, "Sure okay, whatever you say."

The two men would be an easy takedown but I decided not to cause problems.

I returned to the driver's seat and started the Rover. I made a u-turn and kept the security car in my rearview mirror. They kept driving the opposite direction. When they were out of sight I stopped and dig out the maps of the power plant. I found my location on the map and scanned the area for an outer fence. There was nothing in sight for miles that I could see. I need a better view point so I decided to give the Rover a test and head for a peak about two miles in the desert. The Rover did as well in the sand as the pavement and I was at the hill within five minutes. I parked the vehicle so it could not be seen from the road and went on foot. I had found a pair of binoculars in the back of the Rover and made good use of them. I could see the construction and better yet I could see a fence. I decided to wait until sundown so I made myself comfortable and took a nap.

I was not sure how long I had been a sleep but my awakening came by a wet tongue licking my face. My eyes popped open to see a very large dog. I gave my face a wipe but the dog kept licking. I pushed him away but he came back and lay beside me. In a quiet voice I asked the dog, "Where did you come from? You need to go home, boy."

He did not answer but he raised his head and his tail stirred up dust. He really needed a bath. It was getting dark so I walked to the Rover and pondered what to carry. The dog followed. I gave him a bad look but he stayed with me. Now what was I going to do with a dog. I had a mission to accomplish and a dog was no part of it. Maybe he was hunger or thirsty so I gave him a candy bar and shared a little water with him. That was a mistake. He wanted more.

It was late and it was as dark as it was going to get so I load everything that I was going to carry and started walking. The dog followed so I gave him a rough talking but he seemed to think I was playing. I finally got to the fence and it must have been ten feet high. I did a few tests to make sure there was no electricity and started to dig under the fence. I heard a noise and looked up and the dog was on the other side of the fence. Apparently he had his own entrance and exit. I walked a few yards along the fence and found a hole that I could easily slide under the fence. What a great dog. He was not barking but I heard a low growl coming from his throat. I took a quick look around and saw three men coming in my direction. There was nothing to hide behind so I lay flat and motioned for the dog to go to them. He trotted off in their direction and I heard a lot of Farsi. They stopped and turned in the opposite direction. One of the men whistled for the dog but the dog gave him no mind. I said to myself, "That dog just saved three lives."

The men were out of sight but the dog was back lying beside me. I gave another candy bar. I had walked about a mile and the power plant was in plain view. Another low growl came from the dog. This time I had a small building for cover and waited. Two men came within a hundred meters but kept walking. I gave the dog another candy bar, my next to last one. I worked my way into one of the large buildings. The noise was loud as men were working across the building. I had left the dog outside but somehow he had got in the building and was walking down the center aisle. The workers did not give him a second look so he must have been a regular. He saw me and headed in my direction. I moved back out of sight and he followed. "What the hell am I going to do with this dog," I whispered?

I stayed within the crates and boxes and that is when I noticed that some of them did have Korean words on them. Of course, crates with Russian written on them were common. I decide to open one of the Russian crates but it was hard with my limited tool supply. I looked around the floor and found a large screwdriver, perfect. The crate was about five feet tall and I managed to pry one end up enough to see inside. It was dark so I dig through my pack looking for a flashlight. The building was so noisy that no one could hear me so my only worry was for someone to see me or the dog. To my surprise the dog stayed hidden with me. I had my head and the light inside the crate seeing a shit-load of rifles and weapons when I heard the dog bark. The dog was in the aisle barking at two men that were coming in my direction. That dog seemed to be on my side of the fence. I pushed the crate top down and moved so I could not be seen. The men kept walking to an exit door and were gone.

The dog came back to me. I wanted to give him a name but surely he would be gone shortly. I gave him my last candy bar. I made my way to the Korean crate or what I thought was Korean and copied the writing on the crate. I had to open it just to cure my curiosity. This crate was bigger and better sealed using steel bands and the screwdriver did nothing to help open it. My survival knife was the tool as I snapped the bands. The dog jumped back as one of the bands came off like a spring. I gave him a pat and he returned with a lick. I worked my way into the crate with the screwdriver but there was another aluminum wrapping of whatever it was in the crate. I was half inside the crate working my knife through the aluminum when the dog grabbed my leg and started pulling. I said in a low voice, "What the hell is going on now?"

The dog kept pulling so I worked my way back out of the crate and yes

176

the dog had my pants leg pulling hard. I gave him a look and heard a voice in what I thought was Russian. I turned and next to me was a very large man dressed in a uniform, what kind of uniform I did not know. He wore a handgun and his hand rested on it. When he saw the knife in my hand he unsnapped the holster and started to draw the gun. I raised my arms trying to get control of the situation. I could not say I was an inspector dressed in black so I took a swipe at his legs and he fell to the floor. I planted my knife handle to the back of his head and he went to sleep for a while. The dog came and licked his face. I pulled the man out of sight and went back to the crate.

It only took a few more minutes to get the object exposed but that did not help. I had no idea what it was or for what it was used. I took a couple of pictures hoping someone would know what is. I had done all the spying I wanted so the only thing left was to set off charges. I was not sure if blowing up this place was worth the effort. These people were sheep herders and why they thought they could build a nuclear bomb was beyond me. The power plant covered so large of area that is would take Air Force bombers to do any real damage. The few charges of plastic would only make security tighter. It would take a bus-load to do any real damage. All building would stop shortly anyway. The Germans and Russians wanted no part of a revolution in Iran. The USSR had their sights set on Afghanistan not Iran. Why anyone would want this pile of rocks was beyond me—damn oil.

The dog and I walked outside and started for the main building that contained the reactor. The dog was begin to be an old friend and why not? He had saved my butt several times. There was not much activity and I was able to walk into the building without a problem. There was no use at looking around so I unloaded all the plastic and the caps. I set the times for one hour and pushed them under a table. This small amount of C-4 would most likely damage the table only. We walked to the door and the dog began to growl— trouble. I pulled my knife and waited for the door to open. I heard two people talking but the door never opened. I waited a couple of minutes and opened the door slowly. The dog trotted out. Poking my head around the door I saw nothing so I continued.

The trip back to the Rover passed quickly so we sat and waited for a small explosion. The dog kept licking my face and I kept pushing him away. Twenty minutes later I saw a flash in the sky and then heard a blast. A smile broke across my face and I gave the dog a pat on the head. Fifteen or twenty seconds later all hell broke loose. There was a huge flash of light followed by a shock wave that rocked the Rover back and forth. The noise followed and was so loud that that the dog howled. A frighten feeling came to me as I said, "What have I done?"

There was certainly something more in the building than plastic. Three more explosions followed so it was time that I made a retreat.

Okay I knew this would happen, no escape plan. I was sure that I was on my own. That damn Finley was most likely in the USSR or someplace save in a far away country. I never considered the USA as his far away place. The maps were damn good and gave detailed roads around the power plant. I was sure that all major roads were totally barricaded so that left the dirt roads. The Rover would get a good workout along with the dog and me. I decided to go north and try to make Kuwait. They had oil and might be willing to give an American a ride home. I drove with the lights off and that was not a good idea. I hit high-center once and had to winch my way out of a ditch. I found what might be called a road after the sun was starting to rise. I am sure it was used by camels but it was more than a trail. I would smell sea air at times but never saw any water.

About noon I could see a town so I found the main road. The dog and I were hungry and tired. It was more like a village than a town but they had a market with fruits, veggies and meat. I bought a sack of apples and tomatoes and a large hunk of lamb for the dog. We found a place to park and the dog made good use of the meat. I chewed on an apple while I studied the map. A military police car with sirens blasting come speeding through the town but we were off the main street and not noticed. While the dog was making short work of the lamb I changed clothes so I looked more like an Iranian. After two apples and three tomatoes, I leaned the seat back for a nap. I heard noises but just normal city noises and the dog did not mind. My eyes were closed and did not open for a couple of hours. It was hard to get into a heavy sleep after Vietnam so the slightest movement of the dog made me uneasy. It got hot with the windows up and with them down the dog would go on alert at the slightest noise. I gave up sleeping and decide to drive. Before I left town, I stopped for cookies, nuts and cheese at the local market.

I drove through small town and stopped for drinks and food several times, mainly to keep me awake. I stopped for fuel thinking I needed a full tank just in case. The dog lay in the passenger seat most of the time and we took potty breaks on occasions. I took several stops for map reading trying to determine if the dirt and sometimes paved roads were going the direction of escape. I had to travel through Iraq so why was I driving to Kuwait. There was an International airport at Al Basrah, Iraq so why go through another border crossing. The road that I was driving was small and very lonely but I did not want to go through the border inspection. I was sure the police had information on me and getting across the border would not be easy. I reviewed the maps and found a way that I thought might be passable without going through the check points. I drove as far as I felt was safe before I got to Iraq and then the road turned to dirt. The Rover did its job as well as any camel, plus I did not get fleas except from the dog.

Things were not going bad until I came to a river. I was not sure but I did not thing the Rover would float for very long. Anyway, floating down a river in a car was not my idea of a fun adventure. The dog and I got out of the car and walked to the river's edge. The dog kept going and was swimming like a fish. He loved it so I joined him. To my surprise the water was only chest deep. Could the Rover make it through four feet of water? If not, it was a long walk. The river was not running fast so I looked for the best looking place to cross. I waded into the water upstream and it was a bit shallower. I checked the sand and rocks in the area and it seemed okay. A wet stinking dog sat beside me as I eased the Rover into the river. I made sure it was in four-wheel drive and gave it a little gas. I tried to keep the motor at high rpm's thinking the water would kill the engine. What the hell, I floored the accelerator and the Rover bounced its way to the other side. I climbed out of the riverbed with ease. "Damn, I am going to buy one of these things," I told the dog.

I rolled the windows down and turned on the a/c fan at full power trying to dry the dog. The smell was killing me.

I followed the map knowing I had to be in Iraq and drive north. I came to a paved road and said, "Thank you Lord."

Road signs in English were extinct and I was not even sure what language they spoke in Iraq. It really did not mater because there were no sign anyway. I kept the Rover moving toward Al Basrah, or at least in a northerly direction. I could see a town in the distance so I knew there was hope. Another small town and I had no idea the name of it. No English to be seen so I used the map and best guessed the town was Bebahan. If it was Bebahan, I was on track but I really did not have a choice. I kept driving.

Traffic got worse and several times I was reminded of Tehran. Truck and cars took their half of the road in the middle and the Rover stirred up dust as I drove on the shoulder. Al Basrah was near as houses and building could be seen. Finding the airport was going to be a problem but the dog did not seem to be worried. He was letting gas and snoring in the passenger seat. I had a bit of luck as I saw an airplane taking off so I went in that direction. Another small plane came in for a landing about a mile away. The planes were just like a beacon guiding me as I dodged traffic. I pulled into the parking lot of the airport when it hit me, what was I going to do with the dog? I did not even have a leash or crate. I could not just leave the dog in the parking lot. He was my best buddy. I locked the dog in the car with the windows half down and went into the airport lobby. I bought a ticket to the USA with several stops in between. My passport did not show entry in Iraq but they did not seem to care, well, with a very large tip. I asked about a crate for the dog and the ticket person said they were very expensive. I gave the man $300 for a crate that looked like an apple box. It was time to give the dog a name and the only thing that fit him was "Bad to the Bone," maybe Bone for short. I even got the dog shots before the airline would allow him a ride. After his swim he was not as dirty but still had a peculiar smell.

CHAPTER 22

The plane stopped in Athens and London which gave me opportunity to check the dog making sure Bone had food and water. I made a call from Athens telling Sherry I was on my way home. The woman went crazy knowing I was alive and out of Iran. "Oh honey, I heard about the explosion at the power plant and I knew you were in trouble," she explained.

"What explosion? I have been out of contact for the last few days."

"The power plant in Iran had an explosion and destroyed a lot of critical areas."

"That's too bad."

Changing the subject quickly I said, "I am bringing home a friend that has been by me the whole time in Iran. I hope you do not mind."

"Of course not, I am looking forward to meeting him."

"Oh, he is mostly quiet so he will not be any problems."

"It does not matter just get home."

I read a London newspaper while in Athens and it seemed that the revolution in Iran was going full blast and I mean a blast. On the plane ride home I gave serious thought to our adventure in Iran and I was waiting for Finley to pop around the corner at anytime. I tried to sleep but my Nam dream came back and I woke up in a sweat. I had thoughts that I was finished with those nightmares but there it was. I tried to wake up slow, checking what the guy next to me was thinking. He was asleep, thank God. The flight attendant came by and offered me anything I wanted to eat or drink. I told her vodka and she brought me two, compliments of the American Airlines. She must have been watching me while I was asleep or should I say dreaming? We had a stop in New York and I called Sherry again. She was even more excited. The last leg to Dallas was only three hours away. Sitting in an airplane seat for hours and hours killed my back and legs. I should have made the Government take the shrapnel out. Anyway the shrapnel made the metal detectors go off and slowed me down even more. Two more vodkas on this leg and I was ready to get off this beast. At the airport Sherry had huge signs with "Welcome Home Pat" and the crowd gave me a cheer. That was more than I got coming from Nam. It was over and I was home. I covered everyone with kisses and hugs made my way to pick up Bones. Damn, I saw Finley but he never acted like he saw me so I kept walking. I had his money and I was alive and I did not want any part of him ever again. I told Sherry and the kids that I had to pick up my friend. I think Sherry was beginning to see the picture since we were at the customer service desk. After a bit, that brought out Bones in his huge cage. The kids saw him and that he belonged to me and they went crazy. I guess I should have gotten them a dog before now. I let Bones out of the cage and snapped a leash on him. I gave the cage to American and we all walked to the exit. Bones was clam and the kids had their hands on him all the way. Sherry just smiled and asked, "Where is Bones sleeping?"

"On the couch."

The kids joined in with, "Can we sleep on the couch with Bones?"

I gave Sherry and the kids the story of how I picked up Bones in the desert and how he saved me. Sherry reached for him and gave him a quick rub on the head, "Good dog."

Home was a welcome sight and Sherry had the place cleaned and shining. The yard was not great but Sherry was never a yard-person anyway. She had a great meal cooking and we had roast and potatoes that was almost as good as mother would make.

FOUR MONTHS LATER

Spring was here and the yard was looking much better. I had not found a job and thought that we could survive on my disability and the money we had received from Finley. The kids had a hard time in school and mostly due to the Iranian schools. I felt bad for them but they worked like dogs making up for lost knowledge. We had put the money from Finley into a college fund and were making sure they had a chance at college.

ONE YEAR LATER

My nerves were on edge a lot and I could not sleep at night again. My back hurt almost continuously. I took pills but they never helped. I watched TV at night like before and the fear of dreams was always there. Sherry never understood my feeling and she was drifting away from me. She found a job and I think it was just to get out of the house. She worked more and more hours while I took care of the kids. That part was not bad but I missed Sherry. I made several trips to the VA Hospital and talked with a shrink but he offered me nothing that I could use. I did not even understand what to do. Sherry had insurance at her job so I decide to see a doctor about my back. It was getting that I could not bend over. The doctor sent me to a specialist. This guy did x-rays and MRI's and I seemed to be his test rat. After several weeks he made a decision. He called me in the office. He sat me down and began, "The shrapnel was very close to your spine and we have found small pieces inside your spinal cord. An operation is very risky and it could mean you may never walk again or even die."

"What are my other choices besides an operation?"

"Live with the pain and you will get worse and worse."

"What about the shrapnel in my leg?"

"Sorry, I do not do legs, just spinal operations. I could have another doctor take the metal out of your leg but I cannot do it. It would mean more time in the operating room."

"Would that mater?"

"No, just wanted you to know."

"Tell me more about the back surgery."

The surgeon went into great details of what it would take to remove the metal. He gave me 75% chance of recovery but the other 25% was the problem. I agreed to the operation after I had talked with Sherry. The operation and the recovery period would be expensive. I left the doctor's office and stopped for a beer. I drank in silence thinking that my life would only get worse without getting cut. Then it hit me, living in a wheel chair would be worse than dying. Sherry did not desire a man in a chair. I kept the self-pity going for a few more hours and decide to go home and talk with Bones.

Bones was there and we sat on the porch with him lying by my side. We talked for a long while and I heard Sherry arrive. I should have had dinner started but just wanted a hug from Sherry. It seemed like a long time since we had hugged or even kissed and when I held her tight she asked, "What's the matter?"

"I am thinking we need to talk so can I fix you a drink?"

"That bad?"

"No, but you will need to relax a bit?"

I poured us vodka and we sat together in a swing in the backyard. I really did not know where to start but our relationship seemed to be as good as place as any. I did not rush into anything but let her guide me through the conversation. At times I wanted to say no but kept my mouth closed and listened for once. Somehow we had lost our feelings toward each other without me being aware of it. I knew and she knew it. I guess we were headed in the direction of a divorce and we talked about that. My mother always said to never stay a few words and divorce was one of them. The word was not to be used as a bluff but was very serious. I asked Sherry if she wanted a divorce and she said, "No."

She wanted a marriage with love and respect but we did not have that. We tried to stay away from each other rather than growing closer. She moved a bit closer to me and asked, "What can we do?"

Tears were falling down her cheek as I looked her in the eyes, "Honey, I don't know but I am willing to try harder to make us one again. What do you want me to do for you?"

She was quiet and it was hard for her to talk as she said, "Love me and sleep with me. I feel so alone at night. I need your touch without reservations. I need you to give and I will give you more. I know you have stress but I have feelings that require love and kindness and you have the ability to heal me. I don't want another person. I don't want another life. We have it all but we don't use it for each other. Can you understand that?"

I took a few more sips of the vodka and answered, "Sherry, I see our marriage as an oak tree that blows and bends but never breaks. I know I am the one that is causing the wind but you are our foundation. I try hard at times but I seem to fail. I just can't be at peace and I am not sure why."

"I know I have seen many doctors with no results but I want you to give me a chance. My healing is a process that only you can help. You have to tell me your feelings everyday so I can know. I can give you more love than you can handle and maybe the dreams and bad thoughts will disappear."

She continued to encourage me and I her. We both repented and promised to do better.

I continued, "Now that we are building a new life for us and the kids I have to tell you something. I saw a spinal surgeon today about the shrapnel in my back. Honey, I live in pain and I am getting numbness in my shoulders and arms. The doctor said it would get worse and I am not sure I can handle worse. He wants to operate and remove the metal."

"Why? Why did you not tell me and I would have gone with you?"

"I was not sure you cared enough."

She gave me a hug and held me for a long time and finally said, "I love you more than life and I care so much. What did you tell the doctor?"

"I wanted to talk to you. You see, I may never walk again or maybe totally paralyzed. Hell, there is a 50/50 chance of dying. He gave me a year without the surgery before I was in such bad shape that I could not move."

She released me and put her hands to my face and began to cry. "Why is it getting worse?"

"Apparently, the metal has worked its way into my spinal cord and starting to put pressure on the spine and nerves."

"No, no, this cannot happen to us. You are all that I have and I will not let you go."

"Sherry, we have a year possibly with no operation."

"Are you crazy? You cannot live in pain. You must have it done."

"What if I come out in a wheelchair and never get out?"

"Can a wheelchair destroy our love? Absolutely not!"

"We may never make love again and I could not stand for you to be without that part of us."

Again she kissed and hugged me and whispered in my ear, "We will be okay and I know you will be a lover, wheelchair or not."

We continued to talk and make plans for the remainder of the evening and when night came we made love. I gave up my nightmares for at least one night and we snuggled all the night. I felt like a new man in the morning as we made love again.

Two days later we walked into the hospital with our hearts in our hands and ready for the future. It was Monday at 5:00 a.m. and I had not eaten since Saturday. The coffee from the lobby smelled so good but I passed it directing myself to the check-in desk. The lady was very friendly and I wondered if she was on drugs being overly nice at this time of the morning. I completed a small amount of paperwork and was shown to a room to get dressed or maybe undressed. One of those hospital gowns does not cover much. Sherry stayed right by me every second as I lay in the bed waiting for the next event. I had two doctors come by and ask questions but nothing that seemed important to me. The next person was the anesthetist asking my weight and verifying facts I had given before. It was a real parade of people dropping by. The last person to drop in was a nurse that gave me a shot of something that made me float. She called it a "Don't give a damn shot." The time came and Sherry and I said good-by with no tears. We had made a promise that neither would be crying when we left each other. Two nurses slid me to a bed with wheels and we rolled down the hallway and into the operating room. By this time I was so sleepy that I was in and out and really did not care what they did to me.

Sherry met her parents and my brothers and family in the waiting room and the wait began. They talked and drank coffee and had the greatest of hopes for a full recovery. Sherry checked with the nurse's station on regular intervals and they kept telling her that she would be the first to know when the operation was over. Three hours passed and the whole family was in a restless mode that kept them walking. Two more hours dissolved and Sherry was at the nurse's station every fifteen minutes. The doctor came through the waiting room door and Sherry jumped to her feet. The doctor came closer and put his arm around her and pulled her to a chair. "Pat is sleeping but he did well. He is a strong fighter and without that will he might not have made it. I took the metal from his spine but I am not sure how much damage was caused. We are not sure until he wakes up and we can do some test. I just wanted you to know he is doing well. You may go into to see him in about an hour."

"Can he walk?"

"Not sure until a bit later. It was a very delicate operation that required Pat to do his part and he did."

Tears began to fall from Sherry's face and the doctor gave her a hug, "Nothing to worry about yet. There is nothing to cry about. He is doing much better than I thought. You can see him in about an hour."

The doctor walked away and Sherry's parents and Pat's brothers gather for support. The hour passed like a day and finally the nurse allowed her to go to the ICU. Six other beds were around the room and Sherry scanned the room looking for Pat. She saw him and walked slow to his side. Tube and monitors were attached all over his body and bandages and tape holding everything in place. He was asleep and peaceful as she held his hand. The nurse came up and said, "He should be waking up in about an hour so maybe then you can talk with him. I am so sorry but you are only allowed ten minutes with him."

Sherry reached down and kissed him and walked back to the waiting room. She gave a report to the family. The decision was made to get something to eat while they waited another hour. The cafeteria was usual hospital food but no one ate much anyway. With twenty minutes to spare they were back in the waiting room. The nurse saw them and asked if two of them would like to go in now. Sherry jumped up and gave a quick look at the family, "Who?"

Her mother said, "Let one of his brothers."

Sherry took my oldest brother's hand and they walked into the ICU. I was smiling and as they approached. Sherry walked faster to me and gave me a kiss. She was afraid to hug or put any pressure on him. They talked with the usual questions and answers and I almost went to sleep. The ten minutes was gone quickly and Sherry gave me a silent kiss and they left. Before they left the nurse told them that I would be transferred to the recovery room and they could spend more time with me there. Again back to the waiting room and they told the story to the others.

For the next few days the hospital was home for all except the kids which were taken to their grandparents every night. The doctor came and did test after test expecting Pat to walk. It was his legs that were not moving and the nurses wheeled him around in a wheelchair. There were words of encouragement from everyone. Sherry and I had long talks with the doctor and nothing was known but the test continued. Another specialist was call in for consultation and he continued the test. Two more days passed and the physical therapist and I had hours of pain. Sherry and I prayed to God daily as I felt no better. The doctors were expecting more and I worked as hard I as could doing the exercises but I still sat in that chair. I lay in bed after midnight on the fifth day when I could only see and feel the war again like it was happening for the first time. It was a dream or a vision that was happening while I was awake. I saw men and blood and heard the sounds of gunfire and helicopters. I gave a loud scream and woke Sherry. She ran to my side with terror on her face, "What? What is the matter?"

"Not sure but I was in a firefight in Nam."

She held me tight as she said, "That might be it. Your sub-conscience is telling you that if you walk you will be back in the war."

"No, surely not, I know I am not in Nam."

"Maybe not, Honey, you are still having dreams. I am going to say this very bluntly. You may not be walking because you may think you will have to go back to war."

"How could that be?"

187

"I do not how but strange things happen. You need to tell me over and over that the war is over and you are finished."

Never had I thought about what she said. My mind cleared and I became aware of what was happening. I knew I was with the person I love and I swung my legs to the floor and stood. No pain and I took two steps and Sherry held my arm. She began to cry and tears began to fall down my face.

I was released from the hospital three days later without a wheelchair. Home was a welcome sight.

PART 3 - 1981

CHAPTER 23

I was walking and going about what I wanted when I made a promise to build a live that would make our family proud. Pain in my back caused me to walk with a limp at times and standing for a long time was even harder. I felt I had to push myself to complete recovery but at least I was not in a wheelchair. I knew I was one of the lucky ones. I made friends with people while in the hospital and the recovery sections and some of them were still sitting. I made visits to some of these people and we talked about how lucky we both were.

I wanted to find a job but I was not sure I could stand the stress or any physical labor. I gave myself to physical exercise and built my strength in my back. Sherry kept her job and worked supporting us. The money we received from Finley was in the bank drawing interest and we were determined not to end up broke. The dreams still occurred but I was surviving without telling Sherry. There was time I knew she would know with me in a cold sweat at night. I decided to make a war room and took a lot of my metals and equipment from Nam and started to display them. As I dug through what I had packed away I came across my survival knife that I had tucked away for all these years. I thought of a way to frame it or at least display it. Without that knife I would have been dead several times. I gave it a rub and started to the garage to find a cleaner when I dropped it. The end of the handle dropped off as I said, "Damn how could break it now?"

I found the loose end and when I tried to see how to repair it I notice something inside the knife handle. A piece of paper rolled tight is all that I could see. I got a pair of twisters and worked on pulling the paper out. I was afraid of tearing the paper but it came out after carefully working it from side to side. I took my time and when I removed it from the handle there was a smell that I recognized. It was Nam, the smell of death. I unrolled the paper and a small rod with markings that I had never seen fell out. The paper had writings and not Viennese. I had no idea what language. The rod had engravings and was the same as the paper. I found a magnifying glass and took a better look. No doubt the rod had some of the same markings as the paper. Touching the paper I was not even sure it was paper. It felt like paper but it certainly did not look like paper. What had I found and why was it in my knife handle? Being as careful as I could I put both items in an envelope? I made my way to the library thinking someone there should know this writings. I was wrong. I spend four hours asking questions and searching but nothing. It was time for Sherry to get home and I was at the library. I made a dash for the house and looked for something to cook. I found the vodka and made Sherry a drink. The school bus stopped about that time and the kids came running asking for a snack. I gave them a hand full of grapes and they were off for TV. Fifteen minutes later Sherry arrived with a kiss and I offered my gift. I offered the drink and a smile came across her face. I continued with dinner and we ate thirty minutes later.

I was anxious to tell Sherry about the paper and rod but I thought that I would wait until the kids had their homework done and in bed. Sherry and I sat watching a boring TV show when I turned the TV off. Sherry gave me a look and said, "What, we going to bed?"

"No, I have something to show you."

I told her about the knife and then unrolled the paper or what I thought was paper. The rod was next. She never said a word. She took the paper very carefully and studied it and the rod. She acted like she knew what it was. She was silent. "Okay, tell me, what is it?"

"Damn, I was hoping you would know. I do not even know if this is paper."

"Certainly not, this is not paper and the markings are nothing I have seen. It is not Chinese or any Asian language, well, any modern language. Who do you think put this in the knife handle?"

"No idea."

"It has to be someone you know or had access to your knife."

"Don't know."

Sherry got up and looked for a magnifying glass. It took a few minutes but she came back with a large round glass. We turned all the lights in the living room on and found a desk lamp to add to the illumination. Sherry studied both objects with the glass for thirty minutes. I was working up a sweat under the lamp and she said nothing. I kept asking her what she saw but she kept looking and waved me off. She got up again and went to the kitchen and brought back a sharp knife. She picked at the edge of the paper with the knife while looking through the glass. Finally she said, "This is not paper or any kind of animal skin."

"Okay but what is it?"

"Hell if I know."

She took the rod and gave it a long look through the glass. She kept making moaning sounds. "Will you stop making those sounds, we are not having sex."

She gave me an elbow to the ribs and kept looking. "This rod is not bone or wood or any kind of metal that I have seen. You take a look."

I held the rod close to the glass and raised it to the light. My hand touched the light bulb and I jerked away. Sherry smiled, "Hot?"

I gave her a look and then back to business. I could see it was very smooth with no fibers. The color was ivory white but it was not bone or ivory. I was afraid to tap it against anything hard thinking it would break. I looked at Sherry, "I am going to tap it very gently against a piece of metal and see what kind of sound it makes."

"Are you crazy?"

"Well, it does not look like it will break."

I took the knife that Sherry had brought from the kitchen and carefully tapped it against the side of the knife. The sound that came from the rod was loud and high pitched. It almost hurt my ears. "Okay we know it makes a noise," I whispered.

Sherry took the rod and wrapped it in the paper. "Now let's talk about where your knife has been to pick up such a trinket."

"Hey, U.S. Army issue."

"Yes, I guessed as much but where has it been since Vietnam?"

"I took it with me to Iran. It is like an old friend that you depend on every day."

"I was in Iran with you and never saw it."

"I never carry a weapon so other might see it. That usually means someone looking for trouble."

Sherry hesitated and said, "Now Pat, I want to know where you kept it in Iran that I never saw it."

"Usually in my underwear drawer but I carried it at times."

"The maid had full access to all your drawers including your underwear. Did you carry it after the kids and I came back to the States?"

"Certainly, I needed it at times. Have you ever thought about becoming a lawyer?"

193

"Just trying to determine who might have had access to it other than you. Does the knife have a serial number on it?"

"No."

"Could someone have modified the handle in Nam?"

"I guess it could have been anyplace and by anyone."

"You are correct. We just need to find more information about the markings."

We both decide bed was the answer and the morning might provide a few answers. That sounded good but I still lay in bed with my eyes open and had no intension of going to sleep.

Two hours passed and my brain had thought of every possibility so I tried to get out of bed without waking Sherry and headed for the computer. The damn thing was so slow that it took me forever to find the simplest subject. An hour later I went to bed.

Sherry was up and getting ready for work when I drug my butt out of bed. We ate together and she was gone. I packed the package and was almost out the door when the door bell rung. Bones made a small barking noise with a growl thrown in between barks. Maybe he knew more than I but I opened the door anyway. My heart started pounding as I saw Finley. I wanted to welcome him with a crosscut to the jaw but he was smiling and said, "Hello Pat, long tine."

He held out his hand and I returned the shake for some reason. I stepped back and he came in. Bones stood his ground. "I can't believe you still have that dog."

"He's a member of the family and stays as long as he wants."

Finley reaches to pet him but Bones back up. "What do you need now," I asked?

"Oh, just stopped by for a visit. I heard you have been asking about a foreign language."

"How did you know?"

"It came through the grapevine. I might be able to give a little help in that area."

"What area?"

"Translating the markings you have."

"What do you know about markings?"

"I have a similar piece that has the same markings but we need both to know what they are saying. Where did you find the rod and paper?"

"In my Nam knife handle. You know something about it?"

"Enough to know I need you and you need me to make any type of translation."

"Let me see what you have before we continue with any more words."

Finley walked to the living room and sat down and I followed. He gently took a small envelope from his coat pocket and laid it on the coffee table. He opened the envelope and slid out the paper or what might have been paper. He unrolled it and there was a rod with marking similar to mine. I reached for it and he moved his hand to stop me. "I want to see what you have before you start touching. I walked to the bedroom and took the rod and paper from a dresser drawer. I laid them on the coffee table and Finley began to smile. "Okay what do we have," I asked?

"I am not 100% sure but I have been looking for the second items for years. I have tried for years to get the markings translated but people tell me that it is impossible without what you have. I have had sources alerted for anyone that might have something similar and there you came up with the second items. I could not believe it."

"Knowing you, there must be a value price on these items."

"Not really but what they say is very important."

"How do you know all this shit?"

"I deal with people that know. This could be the find of the century. Who do you think stored this in your knife handle?"

"Don't ask me. How would I know? If I had known it was in the handle I would have taken it out years ago. Okay, tell me what you know and we might work a deal. This piece is not leaving my house without me."

Finley rolled his findings and put them in a bag. I did the same. Finley said, "Let's go. We have questions to ask."

"Where are we going?"

"New York so you might want to call your wife."

"What the hell is in New York?"

"A person who knows a lot more about this than you and I."

"What about a change of clothes?"

"We are not staying overnight. A two hour conversation will do it."

I took the kids to Sherry's mothers and thirty minutes later we were entering the airport. We bought a round-trip ticket and boarded. We were in New York by 1:00 pm looking for a rental car. I had promised myself never to fly again or drive in hellish traffic but there I was doing both. Finley was driving and the ride was bad but nothing compared to Iran. Fifty minutes later we stopped in front of a small apartment building. It was not in the best of neighborhoods, as a matter of fact, it was damn scary. Finley motioned for me to get out and we walked to the entrance. He rang a buzzer and what sounded like a very old man answered. We got the okay to enter the building. The outside of the building was better than I thought because as we walked into the hallway I stepped in a hole in the floor and fell. Finley looked around but said nothing. I composed myself and we stopped at apartment 156. Finley knocked. The door opened and the smell of something cooking flowed into the hallway. It smelled not half bad and after I got into the room I put a name to the smell, pinto beans. The man that met us at the door was at least 80 years old and looked like an almost used up American Indian. Now, he did not have war-paint or anything like that but his features pointed to a man that had sat by a camp fire for a long time. He was about five-feet tall and that may have been because he walked bent over. His weathered skin told me that he had been outdoors most of his life. There was nothing speedy about his movements so I felt a bit sorry for him. He turned and walked back to the kitchen without saying a word and we followed.

The apartment was dressed in the simplest décor so it was plain to see he lived alone and made these rooms his home. He took the bean pot off the stove, sat it on the table and searched for three bowls. He opened a large package of flour tortillas and placed them beside the pot of beans. Again let me say the man had not said a word as yet. He motioned for us to sit and we did. He took three large helpings of beans and passed the large spoon to me. I love pinto beans so I took about a half bowl and passed the spoon to Finley. He took about a half of spoon and smiled. I found my spoon and took a bite. I could feel smoke pouring out my ears and my face had to be beet-red. The heat from the stove was nothing but the man had the beans so spicy that they would make a Mexican pay attention. There was nothing to drink so I grabbed a tortilla. The little man smiled at me and shook his head yes. Finley ate one bean and put his spoon down. The little man and I kept eating and after a few bites my mouth was numb so I continued. Sweat began to run down my face so I took my sleeve and wiped my face.

I finished the beans and sat wishing I had a cold beer. I scanned the room and a large painting in the other room caught my eye. Damn, it had the same type illustrations as the paper and rod. The painting was done in what looked like watercolor from the kitchen. I almost got up thinking I would take a closer look when the old man finally spoke. "What do you want?"

He was not Indian but sounded Arab. Finley had been sitting quietly and jumped at the chance to speak, "We have several things we would like for you to see and give us information."

Finley began to pull the rod from the bag and the Arab raised his hand. He rose from the table and went into the living room. He sat in an old chair that looked older than he and began to light a pipe. The smoke smelled strong but it was not weed. He took Finley's rod and gave it a brief look. He then pointed to the painting and began to talk.

"This writing is very old and used by my people before Mohammad. The symbols displayed exact meanings, such as the name of a place, the name of a leader or a date. This only allowed to display small information, and was used when whole sentences or thoughts did not need to be said. To completely understand the entire meaning, one had to understand the relationships between the symbols and have a basic understanding of the story it shows. The writings in this system are used for religious and historical writings in AD 500.

The first recorded text in the Arabic alphabet was written in AD 512. It is a trilingual dedication in Greek, Syriac and Arabic found at Zabad in Syria. This version of the Arabic alphabet used includes only 22 letters, of which only 15 are different, being used to note 28 phonemes.

Pre-Islamic Arabic inscriptions in the Arabic alphabet are very few; only 5 are known for certain. These mostly do not use dots, making them sometimes difficult to interpret, as many letters are the same shape as other letters."

That conversation must have taken an hour because he was in no hurry and his pipe kept going out. He stopped talking and we sat for a few minutes in silence waiting for the next subject to come from his mouth but it remained quiet. I smiled a bit and looked at Finley. He shrugged his shoulders. The silence remained so Finley asked, "Can you read this?"

"Yes."

"Okay, can you tell what it says?"

The old man refilled his pipe and puffs of smoke filled the room. If that was the tobacco the Persians used in their pipes, then no wonder they fought all the time. It had a powerful smell that hung in the room. He rose to his feet and walked to the kitchen. He took a pad of paper and a pencil from a drawer and walked back to his chair. He stared at the rods and seemed in no hurry as must have been his way. He wrote something on the paper and we both strained to see but his handwriting was so bad that we could not make out what he wrote. He switched from one rod to the other several times. He kept writing as we watch in silence. I picked up the paper and asked, "What material is this?"

He replied with a head nod.

Finley looked at me and asked, "What did he say?"

"Not a clue."

Finley gave me a bad look and I shrugged my shoulders. The old man kept writing. He stopped and smoked.

Finley could not wait and asked, "Are you finished?"

"Yes."

"What does it say?"

He started with slow words similar to a real story teller.

"In early times my forefathers read the word of God and found that a Savior was coming. They began to store valuables and materials to build a temple for his arrival. The words of God and all the valuables are stored in a location described on this tool."

Finley interrupted, "What kind of valuables?"

I gave him a frown and the old man answered, "Mostly gold but the writings of God are more important. They have been there for many years."

"Again Finley, "What country would they be stored?"

The old man took his time and read the rods even closer. He waited and smoked. Then he spoke, "I am not supposed to smoke and I hope God will forgive me."

I replied, "I am sure he will."

The old man smiled at me and went back to the papers and the rods. He rose and went to the painting on the wall and held the rods close to the markings. He turned the rods in several directions and then spun them slowly in his hand. Finley was getting impatient and asked, "What country?"

"Trucial States"

"I'm sorry but I do not understand, Trucial States."

"On the Persian Gulf, a country of sand."

My heart sunk at the thought of going back to that part of the world. Was he speaking of Iran? I had never heard of Iran called such. Maybe Saudi was the sand country? Of course there are several small countries that are on the Persian Gulf. Thinking hard I came up with the United Arab Emirates and it had plenty of sand. Iran was just a across the gulf.

The old man continued, "The story is old and my grandfather passed it to me. During the time of Moses and the forefathers a great gathering came about and gold and jewels were placed on an island in the Trucial States. There are over two hundred islands that have been searched looking for the treasure. I believe it never existed or they gold was divided and disappeared. The writings tell the location and which island but I am sure it is of no value."

"Why do you say that," Finley asked?

"Many people live there now and people are always looking."

"But we have the exact location, right."

"Maybe so, there are words that guide you across the sand. Maybe the water location is the most valuable thing of the desert."

Finley and I sat back with our mouths open as the words came from the old man's mouth. His speaking stopped and we waited but nothing except silence was in the room. The old man sat like he was exhausted but Finley kept popping questions. The answers were coming slowly, if at all. I punched Finley on the shoulder and shook my head no. He got the message. I walked to the old man and said, "Sir, we need to leave and let you get rest. We will return tomorrow, if that is okay?"

The old man shook his head yes and we took our rods and walked to the car. On the way back to the hotel we began talking about the old man and if he was real. It seemed that we both had the same idea at the same time, what about the translation of the rods. The old man still had it. Finley made a U-turn and we were back at the old man's apartment within twenty minutes. We made several knocks on the door and decided to go in. We turned the knob and called for the old man but no answer. We split up, Finley going into the bedroom and I took the kitchen. I gave Finley a call, "In here."

There lay the old man with a knife in his chest and blood still pouring onto the floor. I reached for his neck and check for a pulse but nothing. Finley walked in and screamed, "Oh shit. Is he alive?"

"Not that I can determine. Call the police."

He grabbed the phone and made the call. The police were there in about twenty minutes with an ambulance. They checked several times to see if he was alive but he was gone. Before the police came Finley started looking for the sheet of paper with the translations but it seemed to have disappeared. All Finley could say was, "Son of a bitch." I started to help look for the paper but it were gone. Between the two of us we searched every corner of the small apartment before the cops arrived. We had no idea how to remove all the finger prints from the apartment so we told the cops that we had visited with the old man for a couple of days. A million questions followed and we were taken to the police station. Three hours of more questions and we were told not to leave town. We never told them about the rods or the real reason we were there. We claimed we were historians and doing an interview, sounded good to me. We knew whoever killed the old man had the translations and we seemed to be on the short end.

I opened the conversation with, "Finley, you have been researching this

199

for years now who else is involved? Hell, I bet the killer is your partner."

"What is wrong with you? I came straight to you as soon as I knew you had the other rod. I just want to know one thing, whose knife do you have and who put the rod in the handle?"

"That's easy; I do not have a clue. You are the one spreading the news all over the world."

"If we are ever allowed to leave New York, we are giving that damn knife of you're a very close inspection."

"Okay smart ass where did you really get your rod?"

"I bought it for one million dollars with a guarantee."

"That is the most stupid thing I have ever heard, a guarantee? What kind of guarantee? If you do not like it, you get your money back? You're a sucker. I have some beach-front property in Arizona, if you are interested."

Finley gave me an obscene gesture.

We found a taxi at the police station that carried us to our car. The drive back to the hotel and the ride was a bit sluggish compared to our past experience. We stopped by the hotel bar and found a table. After a couple of beers and some quiet conversation as to what we might do, we decided to go to bed. I gave the elevator button a punch and we made plans for breakfast in the morning. The room was lonely so I made a call to Sherry giving her a briefing. She was really mad. I agreed with her and told her that she should be mad. I tried to tell her why I went to New York and the lost gold story but she would not believe I was sincere. I gave her more details of the old man and what had happened. That made her even madder and this time scared. An hour and half later I hung the phone up with Sherry in a semi-clam stage.

The clock radio in the room went off at 8:00 and I made my way to the bathroom for a shower. Dressing I decided to call Finley and make sure he was up and moving. No one answered. I called the desk and made sure I had the correct room and I did. I kept dressing thinking he must be in restaurant drinking coffee. Fifteen minutes later I entered the restaurant but no Finley. I sat and the waitress brought coffee. Three cups later I decide to call again, still no answer. I was getting mad thinking he must be out walking so I ordered bacon and eggs. Finely was forty-five minutes late when my breakfast came so I ate it. Never let your eggs get cold was my theory. Another half hour passed and I am thinking bad things about Finley like he has left town and flying to the UAE without me. Two more cups of coffee and I left the restaurant for his room. I knocked hard thinking he might be asleep but no answered. I grabbed the clean woman and asked her to open the door. She said no at first but a twenty dollar bill brought her key from her pocket.

I had decided that if all his things were gone I was calling the police. She opened the door and took a few steps into the room and stopped. The next thing that happened became a blur as she started screaming. She turned and ran into me as she took a quick exit. She screamed all the way down the hallway and into the elevator. I went back to the room and walked in slowly. There lay Finley in a pool of blood on the bed, his neck was lying open. All his clothes were thrown in the floor so I searched for the small bag with the rod. It was not in the room. The hotel security came into the room and for some reasons they were holding guns pointed at me. Yes, back to the police station and this time they stored me in a cell. You meet some of the nicest people in jail. One of them that really impressed me was a guy about 20 years old with tattoos head to toe and weighted about 300 pounds and most of that was muscle. He kept asking, "What are you in for, man?"

"Nothing, I did nothing."

"Then why are you here?"

"I don't know."

"Oh sure we are all in here for nothing. The guy that made fun of my MOTHER tattoo is bleeding some place but it was not my fault."

I gave him a smile and a head shake as he walked my direction. "You like this tattoo?"

He bent down and stuck his arm in my face. "Sure, looks great."

He smelled like he was dead but I said nothing. He walked back to his side of the cell. I lay back thinking I might get a nap but the guy in the next cell kept a conversation going with my tattoo friend.

Eight hours later the guard came and unlocked the cell as my tattoo friend jumped to the door. The guard pushed him back and said, "I want you" and pointed to me. We took a walk to a room with mirror similar to the room you see on TV and I was handcuffed to the table. I sat for another hour and a man wearing a suit and tie came in with a guard, "Unlock him."

The guard did as he was told and the suit sat down with me at the table. "Why are you always around when there are people being killed? Who are you?"

I gave him my name and sat in the quiet. "We have done a little checking and we see you are from Texas so what are you doing here?"

"Finley and I came here to see an old friend that we knew in the war."

"Bullshit, you and the dead guy are here looking for something that someone else wants more than you. You know why these two guys were murdered and you are not leaving here until you tell me."

"Are you crazy, I have nothing to say because I have no idea about what is going on?"

The suit leaned across the table into my face and said, "What the hell is this?"

He threw the rod and paper onto the table. He continued, "Is this worth two murders. Is this the answer for two deaths?"

I wanted to take the rod and run but about 30 feet was as far as I would go. I did not know what to say so I gave him a song and dance story telling him that the rod came from the old man as a gift. I told him it was a family gift that my father owned and somehow the old man ended up with it and that was one of the reasons we came. "So what is it?"

"I don't know but my deceased father kept it for years so I thought I should continue the family tradition."

"What are those marking?"

"Not a clue. I think it is some kind of fertility rod."

"You planning to get pregnant," he asked laughing?

"Maybe!"

"I am sending you to Texas because I don't want any more murders and you seem to be attracting them. Don't think we are finished with you because you will be back here in a second if we find anymore evidence in your favour. Get the hell out of here and take your whatever this is with you."

The rod and I were on the first plane back to Texas. All the way I kept wondering what to do now but came up black. I called Sherry to meet me at the airport and I gave her the story on the way home. She was almost crying but I assured her we were not in any danger. Then she gave me the bad news, her mother is staying with us to watch the children. I just could not image her mother watching over any kids as she was a man-chaser and spent so much time look for a rich man.

CHAPTER 24

Hours of conversation continued as Sherry became my closest and only ally. I gave as much information as I thought would not start her crying again but knowing that she was in danger also pushed me forward. How in hell could I get involved in such a mess? If I had a chance, I would just give the rod to whoever wanted it. It almost seemed like a TV adventure or some cheap movie but we were involved and we had kids to protect. Sherry and I decided to have her mother take the kids to her house. I did not know which would be better, dodging bullets or dodging men, so we decide men. Sherry packed their clothes and the kids were happy to spend time with grandmother. We decided to take the kids amd Sherry's mother home the next morning.

Putting what we knew together we decided that the bad guys or maybe they were good guys was unknown. Anyway they did not find the other rod at the old man's house or the paper that he did the translation. They would not have killed Finley if they had found what they wanted so all was up for grabs and I suppose they were coming to me next. I thought about tying the rod to the outside door with a note. "Take it." The money or the supposed treasure did not belong to us so even if we found it what would could we do with it? My brain kept bouncing around as I thought, "Why would I risk anyone's life for more money? We have money and more would only be problems."

I asked Sherry, "Do we need to go looking for a pot of gold?"

She would not answer so I repeated the question. "I don't know. Think of all the good we could do. How would like to go to breakfast and tip the waitress a thousand dollar bill."

"Is that what rich people do? So what are you telling me? Should we head for the desert?"

"Wait, I did not say that but having a few coins in the bank might be nice."

I waited for a bit and said, "Forget the money and decide what we have to do to get rid of our friends that are killing people."

"Do we need the other rod to find the gold?"

"Not sure if the rod I have tells the location or the story. I guess we have a 50/50 chance. We need to get it translated."

We decided to go to bed and work this out in the morning. It only took about an hour before my Nam dreams were back and I was kicking and fighting in bed. I grabbed my pillow and went into the living room. I was sweating and out of breath so I flipped the TV on and found myself a beer. I landed on the History Channel and there was the Romans building an empire as they marched through Europe. I had enough fighting for one night so I changed the channel to travel and Mexico City was the topic.

I took the rod from the end table and gave it a twirl. I really wanted to throw it in the trash but I kept looking at the marking and when I turned the rod I noticed for the first time that the markings made a symbol that I could see and understand. It was like watching a movie in slow motion. I had always thought that the markings were to be read from top to bottom and maybe right to left but they were going around the rod. I reached for the magnifying glass and gave the rod a slow turn and it was like a map. I said in a whisper, "Wait until Sherry sees this."

The next sound I heard was Sherry saying, "See what?"

"Oh something I discovered by accident."

"Okay what?"

"Take the rod and the magnifying glass. Now, turn the rod slowly counter clockwise while looking through the glass."

Her eyes opened wide as she viewed the map, "Holy shit!"

"Is this a map for the gold?"

"I don't know. It could be a map of New York City but I doubt it."

"What do you think is on the other rod, more directions," she said softly?

"I don't think so but who knows. I am beginning to get mixed emotions about the whole thing. I do not understand how this rod got in my knife handle and what does it all mean. It all seems a bit on the crazy side or made up."

"Hey, two people killed already and I have a feeling we are on the list. My main concern is who would kill people. So what should we do?"

"Not sure but we cannot stay here and that includes the kids. We have to get the kids to mother's house first thing in the morning. We will leave them there for awhile, mother will not mind. Sherry got up and started for the closet to find our luggage when a bullet came blasting through the window

204

and missed sherry by fractions. I made a run for her and threw her to the floor, "Stay Here!"

I crawled to the kid's room and rolled them out of bed. Sherry mother's walked into the room and asked, "What's all the noise?"

I motioned her to the floor but she was a little slow getting there and another bullet came threw the wall and stopped in her leg. She fell to the floor and started screaming in pain. Her leg was bleeding badly so I grabbed a T-shirt from the drawer and applied it tight to the wound. She screamed louder so I covered her mouth which followed by a bite to my hand. "We are getting shot at and you caught a bullet. Stay with me and we will get you to the hospital but now we have to take care of whoever is doing the shooting. Call the police! Kids, you stay here and keep on the floor."

I made a run for our bedroom and pulled out the .357 from the draw. I gave a quick check for bullets and went looking for Sherry. She was still in the closet and I pulled her to the kid's room to take care of her mother. I crawled to the kitchen and opened the back door. A shot was fired and breakage in the kitchen was next. That was a for sure sign that the garage was my next position. I slowly raised one the garage windows and made my way into the night. I gave my eyes a bit time to adjust and started around the house. There was car sitting at the curb and a person with a rifle positioned behind it. The person apparently did not see me so I worked my way across the street and in position for a shot. I slowly walked toward the person and stopped with the 357 close enough for a clean shot, "That's enough, drop the rifle!"

The person slung the rifle in my direction and I pulled the trigger of the 357 and the person fell backwards. I walked carefulyl toward the shooter and saw that the hit was in the shoulder. I kicked the rifle away and then I noticed the shooter was a woman. She laid there without saying a word but I knew she had to carry another weapon so I never took my eyes off her and told her to stand. "Who are you?"

Nothing from her and I gave her a quick search and found a survival knife and a communication device. "I am not going to ask you again. Who are you?"

Still nothing, I punched the talk button on the communication unit and a reply came, "What?"

I softly answered, "Your partner is dead and you are next. I take no prisoners."

A click on the unit came next followed by the police.

I pulled the woman to her feet and tighten my hand on her coat. She winched from the pain of her shoulder and my face pressed closer to her, "Last time, who are you?"

She managed to whisper, "Holy is Mohammad"

She pulled my arm with the 357 to her chest and somehow the gun fired and she fell to the ground.

An ambulance arrived and took Sherry's mother to the hospital. We stayed with her for most of the night. Finally, Sherry and I took the kids to a hotel and we checked in under a different name. After a few hours sleep, Sherry and I decided to call my brother and ask if the kids could stay with him for a period. There were not problems there and we drove to his house after making several stops and turns checking if we were being tailed. No one gave an indication of following us so we continued. About three blocks from my brother's house I stopped the car. If by some means they had put a tracking device on the car the short walk might delay them a bit.

We were met at the door by my brother and his wife and he had a handgun tucked behind his back. I had given him a brief explanation of the situation and I was glad to see the gun and his precautions. We enter his house and made our goodbyes to the kids. Sherry and I went back to the hotel and what a surprise the room had been ransacked and that was enough that we left. We did not even take time to find our clothes and pack. Sherry was a nervous wreck so we got in the car and drove. I was about fed up with all this cloak and dagger and was ready to make a stand. First I had to deposit Sherry in a safe spot but there seemed to be no safe spots. I decided to keep her with me. I thought Nam was tense but having Sherry to protect was making me on edge that I kept the .357 in my lap all the time. My eyes kept flashing from side to side and the rear view mirror. I was trained to work alone and in a jungle and I am not a James Bond. Sherry's head was like an owl panning every car that passed.

I pulled to the side of the road and turned the key off. Sherry went into a panic, "What? What do you see?"

"Nothing and this is crazy. We have no idea what to do and we see shadows everywhere. We are stopping and for the night."

"Not here."

"No."

I started the car and drove the nearest hotel. It happened to be a Hilton and we got a suite. I was thinking we might be there for a few days. We were exhausted and the bed felt like a hug from an old friend. The bed was good but we lay there with eyes that refused to close. I had the handgun beside me under the blanket and Sherry could not stop talking. She wound down after about an hour and silence filled the rooms. She had a slight snore which ensure me she was there and still breathing. I was out of bed and watching TV on mute. The suite had a work station with a computer so I pulled up the internet. I got a beer from the mini-refrigerator and looked for an opener.

I did a search for a map of Saudi Arabia and looked at all the desert. I thought, "How could anything be found in all that sand?"

I remembered it was not Saudi but a neighbouring country on the Persian Gulf. I found a new country called United Arab Emirates and it did not look any better than Saudi.

I turned my train of thought to the rod and the markings. It seemed that we had focused on the rod and left the paper. There had to be a reason for the paper and it definitely had some of the same markings. I tried rolling the rod over the paper to see if they would match but nothing aligned. I wrapped the rod with the paper and pulled it fast to see if there was another motion endued image. Nothing seemed to match or gave a clue to anything that I could see. I laid the paper on the desk and by mistake the sweat from the beer bottle was absorbed by the paper. The paper started to change color, a dark blue appeared in places. I was afraid to touch it but I had to see what was happening. Only places that the water had touched the paper were changing. I said to myself, "Okay, if water makes it changes then how about more water."

I went to the sink and found a glass and after making sure it was clean I filled it with bottle water. I lay a paper towel on the coffee table and placed the paper on the towel. I gave it a small pour of water, nothing. Then I gave it a bath and waited. Sure enough, blue areas began to appear and it looked like a map. I made a dash for the bedroom and found the camera and by the time I returned the blue areas were starting to disappear. I took a quick picture and then more water. I thought my eyes were doing tricks but another image appeared. All this noise woke Sherry and she stood looking over my shoulder, "What are you doing?"

I did not answer but shot another picture of the second image. Again the image started to disappear. Sherry question got louder, "What the hell are you doing?"

I stopped and gave her a few details and she grabbed the glass of water and gave the paper another soaking. Almost immediately another image began to turn the paper blue. This time I was ready with the camera and got a clear shot of the shapes. We let it dry and as usual the image disappeared. Sherry was excited and talked the whole time but I gave a deaf ear as I studied the paper. Sherry had the bottle in her hand ready for another soaking but I held her back. "Let wait for a few minutes."

We waited. All the blue was gone when a small dark red dot appeared and then faded. I clicked another picture of the red dot before it was gone. We waited for a longer time and the markings came back.

We took a break and tried to put some of the pieces together. I asked, "What do you think?"

"Do you think the blue is a map of something?"

"It could be but I do not recognize the shape."

"Maybe if we put all the different area together, like a puzzle, it would mean something."

I gave her a look as if she had a solution and said, "I don't think we are finished. We need more water."

She refilled the bottle in seconds and with water flowing over the coffee table and paper it began to turn blue again. We were back to the first image and I took another quick picture. I told Sherry to take notes. We let it dry a little and another red dot appeared at a different location. The process continued showing six different blue areas followed by red dots.

In the early morning we sat with film in hand waiting for some place to open to get it developed. There had to be a connection of the blue areas and the dots. Sherry went to the kitchen and brewed a pot of coffee and then started breakfast. There was no sleeping. We sat at the table eating bacon and eggs without saying much. Then Sherry began to talk like a broken record. She had question after question and I had no answers. Then she started to answer her own questions and I kept the coffee cup up to my face so she would not see me smiling. Finally, I took a napkin and waved it in the air as if I was surrendering. She gave me a bad look and said, "What? What is wrong with you?"

She started to smile and we both burst into laughter.

The local pharmacy photo department opened at 8:00 and we were there waiting. They claimed that it would take an hour so we did a little shopping. We did not buy anything but did a lot of looking. It was a long hour and we showed back at the counter fifteen minutes early. The pictures were ready. We flipped through them at the counter and all had something on them so I paid and we headed to the car. Sherry kept looking at them all the way back to the hotel but they made no connection to her. As we arrive I took charge of the pictures and spread them out on the coffee table. It was like a jigsaw puzzle and I was not good at those things. Sherry sat beside me and pushed a picture around about the time I thought I might have something. I grabbed her hand and said, "Let me try first."

I continued for about twenty minutes and said, "Any ideas?"

She reached to the table and picked up the pictures. She took them to the bedroom and came back with a pair of scissors cutting them into pieces. "What the hell are you doing?"

"Cutting the blue parts out."

I threw up my hands and said, "Back to the photo place."

"Wait a minute I think this will work."

She continued cutting and laid each blue area on the table. After a little shuffling I could not believe my eye, there on the table was the State of Texas. Sherry found tape and connected the pieces. I gave her an "A++" for using her brain and imagination. Texas meant nothing so there had to be another clue and the red dots had to be the answer. Connecting the dots was nothing and the shape that they were arranged was no help or at least to us. The dots were in somewhat of a circle but one was out of alignment and was in the upper panhandle. There had to be a reason for this one to be out of the circle. Sherry took over and I watched as she drew lines from the one dot to all the others. She erased the lines and then started drawing lines from red dot to red dot. This got a little confusing but then to my second surprise all the lines crossed at one point. We dug out a Texas map and the point looked very close to Fredericksburg. Fredericksburg is a small German town in central Texas but what could this little town and the Arabs have in common?

One bad apple was the red dot in the panhandle. That red dot was near Dumas, another small town. I asked, "Are you sure these blue pieces are taped together correctly?"

"Well, it does look like Texas and all the corner match so unless you have another idea this is it."

"What about the dot in the Panhandle?"

"It has to mean something or maybe it is a pointer or tool we use from outside the circle."

Sherry started to draw more lines connecting the lone dot to anything and everything. Nothing seemed to fit or connect so she took a compass and made a circle going through the point that the other dots made or should I say Fredericksburg. That did nothing to improve the situation. I took over the line drawing and drew a line though Dumas and Fredericksburg all the way to the Gulf of Mexico. I hit the water at Indianola. I looked at Sherry and asked, "Have you ever heard of Indianola?"

"Never."

"Do you think the Internet would have anything?"

I grabbed Sherry by the arm and said, "Let's go home we have a book about Texas towns."

"Are you crazy? They are most likely watching the house."

"I don't think so since they shot it up before. They would not think we would come back. Anyway, the police are in the area."

We arrived at the house thirty minutes later and all was quiet. We entered through the garage and took flashlights. Sherry was not excited about turning on the lights.

We found the book and took it to a closet. Sherry held the light as I flipped pages looking for Indianola. My mouth must have flown open when I found it. I started reading, "**INDIANOLA, TEXAS**. Indianola is Texas' Queen of ghost towns. The port of Indianola, on Matagorda Bay in Calhoun County, was founded in August 1846 as Indian Point by Sam Addison White and William M. Cook. In 1844 a stretch of beach near the point had been selected by Carl, Prince of Solms Braunfels, commissioner general of the Adelsverein, as the landing place for German immigrants bound for western Texas. One immigrant, Johann Schwartz, built the first house in the area in 1845. Indian Point became firmly established as a deep-water port during the Mexican War. For thirty years its army depot supplied frontier forts in western Texas. In February 1849 the name of the growing town was changed to Indianola. The town grew rapidly, expanding three miles down the beach to Powderhorn Bayou, following its selection by Charles Morgan as the Matagorda Bay terminus for his New York-based steamship line. In a short time, Indianola achieved the rank of the second port of Texas, a position it held until the catastrophic hurricane of September 16, 1875, devastated the low-lying city and caused great loss of life."

CHAPTER 25

We both sat in the closet thinking about what I had just read. I said softly, "Damn, I have lived in Texas most of my life and did not know about Indianola. I really do not understand what Indianola has to do with the map. Why would this ghost town be of any importance?"Sherry gave me a blank stare and said, "No idea."

We gave up the idea of Indianola and decided to make our way to the car. We got into the car and opened the garage door and a bullet came through the back windshield and out the front windshield. A second bullet hit the trunk and not sure what stopped it. A third hit the gas tank and a very large explosion followed. I grabbed Sherry dragging her across the seat making my way to the house. It was getting really hot in the garage and the back door of the house seemed a better exit. Sherry was limp and I gave a quick look for blood but nothing but glass in her hair. Inside I stopped and picked Sherry up and looked her in the eye, "You okay?"She gave a small nod yes and she stood. "Close huh!"

She gave me a bad look but she was walking. We spared no time getting to the back door and I pulled my .357. I pushed Sherry to the side and slowly opened the door. A huge piece of wood flew from the door followed by another loud rifle record. I pushed Sherry back into the house and said, "Stay there, I will be back in a minute."I dashed out the door and wondered why the people were such bad shots. They had hit everything but us. Then I though, "Maybe they are not trying to kill us."

The bullets were real and I had a .357 slug waiting for each of them. I stopped behind a tree and got a flash from something the guy was wearing. This guy must be an amateur and I pulled the trigger on the .357 twice. I hear a loud scream and decided it was time to retrieve Sherry. I ran back to the door and there stood Sherry with a gun to her head. The guy was large and acted like he meant business as he said, "Drop it or your sweet honey will have her brains on the floor."I slowly lowered my weapon to the floor. Before I released the gun Sherry makes a whining elbow to the guy's ribs and he let her go. I had two shoots into him while he was reaching for Sherry. He fell to the floor and Sherry and I were out the back door in seconds. No car; so we ran. We continued to run for five or six block before I was breathing so hard that I had to stop. Sherry stopped and asked, "You okay?"

She was hardly breathing hard. "Hell yes, it is all that fatty foods you fed me.""Excuse me, the fatty foods I eat?"

We got to a 7-11 and called the police. We waited for them to pick us up and back to City Hall. There must have been ten police cars along with fire trucks. They took my .357 and one of the local policeman said, "We will keep this for safety.""Safety of whom?"

"Do we have to explain, your safety of course?"Four hours later they called a taxi for us.

Sherry called my brother and checked on the kids and they were doing great. "So should we take a drive south and get a little ocean air," I asked? "Sure but we need to pack a few clothes. I need a shower anyway. The bad part is that we do not even know for what we are looking, gold, silver or what."

"You're right but asking the right questions to the right people will produce something and maybe stir the pot a bit more."

We asked the taxi to take us to a rental car and we rented the fastest car they had which was a Mustang. We drove back to my brother's house with several detours again. We explained all the details to my brother and family and asked if they could keep the kids for a day of so. My brother pulled me aside and I gave him the bad details and he gave me assurance that he would protect the kids with his life. I hated so much to get him involved but I had no choice, bullets and kids do not mix. Sherry was a bucket of nerves about the kids so I told her what Jeff had said about protection. It took us a little over an hour before the car was moving in a southward direction. We had no other clues as to what to do so maybe Indianola would give a start. Apparently, the bad guys had not seen the map or they wanted the map and the rods. I wished I had some idea of what was happening and why and who were these guys. People getting killed for what reason was my mystery. I drove while Sherry gave directions and a detail synopsis of my drive ability. Two hours passed and a quiet enter the car and I took a look at Sherry and she was asleep. I made an exit from I35 and took a tour of the back roads. I watched my rear view mirror thinking that there may be a slight chance of us being followed but nothing out of the ordinary. There was an old pickup truck that turned onto the road as I passed but the driver seemed to be just a farmer. I drove a little faster and the pickup disappeared. Driving in peace for a couple of hours gave me a chance to review the pass couple of days. The pieces did not fit but I continued to force pieces into the puzzle. It was hard to come to any real decisions due to no facts but we were getting chased and shot at for some reason.

Sherry came alive and to her surprise she had fallen asleep as she said, "How could you let me fall asleep?""No problem, you were tired and I needed the quiet."

She gave me a punch to the shoulder and said, "What did I miss?""Cows and an old yellow dog"

"How many?""Cows or Dogs?"

"Either, where are we?""South of Waco on highway 6. We are taking the scenic route. We get to see more cows."

"I don't want to see cow or dogs. I want to see the Gulf of Mexico.""You will, just a matter of time before we smell that salt air."

She took the map and began plotting every mile. It took her mind off our real problems of bullets flying by our heads and the kids. We came to Hearne, a small town and before my eyes appeared a Diary Queen and I pulled in. "How long has it been since you have eaten at Diary Queen?""Not long enough."

"Let's try it."We walked into the place and it reminded me when I was a kid and could get ice cream cones for a nickel, they were sixty-nine cents for a small now. I ordered a Belt-Buster hamburger with fries and strawberry malt. Sherry just looked at me and grinned. She ordered a salad.

From that quick stop down memory lane we drove to Austin by way of several other small towns spotting more Dairy Queens but we push on. My navigator did not have much to go on except for Port Lavaca but we were driving in that direction as if we were on a mission. I guess we were. My driving instructor told me to go south from Port Lavaca so I did. We did a few turns and ended up on highway 316 going to nowhere but I kept driving. I drove a few more miles when we got there. In front of us stood a sign that read, "Indianola - Pop. 100."

We stopped in amazement as there were only a few house and they looked as if they were going to fall down. We drove slowly looking for the remainder of the town and as we continued we came to the La Salle Monument. I stopped the car and decided to take a closer look. It was a great monument of marble and we both wondered why a statue of La Salle might be here. We continued to walk hoping to find an older person that might give a clue as to what happened here in the past. Surely something important took place in this area. We walked by several old houses on stilts but not a sign of a person. We looked for business that could have been there for a while and they all looked old. Yes, this was a ghost town. The main street gave us hope as we saw two old men sitting on a bench in front of what might have been a grocery at one time.

I gave Sherry a hand as we stepped onto the porch. I gave a smile and said, "Howdy, a bit warm today." Both looked up at Sherry and then to me. One gave a half grin and said, "Sure enough is. Summer must be getting close."

I introduced us and they returned with their names, Jake and Frank. We shook hands and I sat Sherry on the bench next to them as I said, "Y'all lived here long?"Jake answered, "All my life except for a spell I server in the war."

I thought we had struck pay dirt and continued the small talk. Both men wore overalls while Jake was as thin as a fence post and Frank could have lost a few pounds. Jake did most of the talking and would spit on occasions due to the chew of tobacco in the jaw. He would always look at Sherry and say excess me after each spit. Both men wore straw hats that must have been as half as old as they.

The word "war" kept coming back to my mind so I asked, "Tell me about what happened here during the war.""Now, what war are you talking about I or II?"

"Either.""Let me give a bit of a history lesson. Camp Hulen, formerly known as Camp Palacios, was on Turtle and Tres Palacios bays just west of Palacios in southwestern Matagorda County. Gone now. It was one hell of a United States Army training center during World War II. It was originally established as a summer training camp for the Thirty-sixth Infantry Division of the Texas National Guard. Some 6,500 men came to the first training session in the summer of 1926."

He stopped talking as if he could not remember any more but he just took another spit. He continued, "Civil contractors and the WPA, you know about the WPA?" I shock my head no. It was something the Government set up after the depression to keep families from going hungry. WPA stands for

Work Projects Administration. They constructed additions to the camp, which eventually included some 400 semi-permanent buildings and almost 3,000 floored, framed, and screened tents, as well as a tent theater, fire station, bakery, weather station, library, dental clinic, post office, and 500-bed hospital. At its height the installation's troop capacity was 14,000. Along with Camp Hulen were the Indianola Battalion Camp, the Wells Point rifle range and antiaircraft firing range, the Olivia projectile area, and the Civilian War Housing Project."

He stopped talking again and pointed to the store across the street. "Y'all thirsty?""I replied, "Sure, let me buy. What do you like?"

Both men answered, "RC Cola."

I walked across the street to the store and it seemed I went back in time fifty years. I bought four RC Colas and back across the street. The talk continued. This time Frank joined in the conversation, "In January 1944 Camp Hulen was converted to a prisoner of war camp; the Germans housed there were farmed out to help with agricultural work in the county. In 1946, the War Department declared Camp Hulen surplus and returned it to the Texas National Guard." Jake stopped the conversation by raising his hand, "Just a minute Frank. These young folks might be interested to see your German Bowie knife that came from one of those prisoners."

I said, "Sure, you have a knife from one of the prisoners?""Yes, there were all kinds of war surplus stuff we took from those Germans. I am not sure how he got to this camp with a knife but it was found."

Frank slowly got up and went inside the building. Ten minutes later he came out with the knife in hand. I almost fell of the bench when I saw what he had. It was a survival knife exactly like the one I had carried in Nam. I just starred at the knife in disbelief. Frank walked toward me and handled the knife to me. Sherry saw the knife and her mouth came open along with a starting of a sentence. I held my hand up to Sherry and she stopped talking. I took the knife carefully from Frank as he smiled and said, "Looks in good shape for a sixty year old German war souvenir.""Yea, it sure does. How long have you had this knife?"

"Oh I would say close to forty years."I gave the knife a closer look and there was a Nazi swastika engraved on the blade near the handle. I could feel my insides starting to shake. I knew there had to be a connection between my knife and this knife but this knife came from WWII. Apparently this knife was made in Germany and I had no idea where my knife was made. I always thought it was made in America. I asked, "Frank, you ever do any research on this knife?"

"What kind of research?"

"Well, who it belonged to or how it got here?"

"No, not really my father took it from a German in the prison camp is all that I know.""Frank, my wife and I are looking for such artifacts for a museum we are going to open about Texas history. Would this knife be for sale?"

"No, I guess I will keep it.""Frank, would you take $1000 for it?"

Frank's ears perked up and he smiled, "You just bought yourself a knife."Sherry stood in amazement at my offer as she said, "Honey, do you think the museum will have a place for that knife?"

"Oh sure. We will even put Frank's name on a placard next to the knife."Frank's face broke into a big smile and handled me the knife. I wrote a check for $1000 and everyone seemed happy except for Sherry. I knew I would catch hell from her as soon as we were alone. We paid our respects by talking for another fifteen minutes and I told them we had better get gone for home.

As we walked back to the car Sherry gave me the works. "You could have offered that guy $100?" "I wanted the knife and I had to make an offer that he could not refuse before he had time to think."

Sherry began to laugh, "I know the museum will be so proud of you.""Well, did you have a better idea?"

"I guess that was a good one because he sure fell for it."We got to the car and started driving north. After about twenty miles I stopped the car and did a little investigation of the knife. I tried to loosen the tip of the handle but it was tight. There were other markings on the blade but we needed more than our naked eyes to read it. So I started to drive again looking for some store that might have a magnifying glass. We did not pass through any large towns until we got to Austin. I found a Wal-Mart and bought the most powerful magnifying glass they had.

The glass was powerful enough that I could see the markings but I had no idea what was said or the meaning. I do know that the markings looked the same as on the paper that came from my knife. I took paper and a pen from the glove compartment and started copying what was on the knife. I made sure that I got every detail including the swastika. The angle or direction might be a clue to whatever was written on the knife. I finished copying and Sherry and I sat looking at each other. She asked, "What now?""I am not sure. It seems that we have been lead to this knife by someone so there must be a message here somewhere."

Sherry fell back in the car seat and said, "Honey, I have a feeling that this has nothing to do with the knives but a person, maybe the dead German that owned this knife. I think the knife is a tool to get you to this person.""I know. I have the same feeling. Hey, we are in Austin and they have a great Texas library here. Let's do a little reading."

We drove to the University of Texas Library and spent the next 6 hours flipping pages. We searched through every book that had German prisoners of war located in Texas. I started making a list of all the men thinking their name was the clue. Finally I told Sherry to stop bringing me books and sit down. "Sherry, we are missing something. Maybe we cannot see the trees for the forest. Let make a list of all the facts that we know."She pushed the books to the side and said, "Tell me what you know."

She wrote what I gave her without saying a word.

The list became longer than I expected and after I had stopped talking Sherry started to draw lines as if she was connecting some of the topics. "What are you doing?" "Get ready to make a flow chart."

"Why?""We have to know if any of your statements are cause and effect."

Maybe I was two steps behind her but I had not a clue what she was doing. She drew squares and circles and then she lean back in her chair and Said, "I got it."I hated to ask what she had but she broke a smile and that was my hint to ask. "Okay what have you got?"

She pushed the list of names in my direction. "See if you can find a name that does not belong on the list.""Hey, I wrote the names and they all seemed okay."

"She flipped the top sheet to the side and there was a sheet of paper that she had copied. "Pat, take a look the sixth name in the second row. Does that look German?"My finger passed down the page until I came to Al-Nahayan. My brain stopped and so did my finger. Sherry's smile turned into a giggle and my face turned to her with a smile also. "What kind of German has a name as Al-Nahayan."

Sherry continued with information and reminded me that the old man in New York was Arab.

The library had several computers so I took Zaid ibn Al-Nahayan to the Internet. It responded with information that was unbelievable. The guy is the present King of the United Arab Emirates. Sherry said quietly, "Okay but where is United Arab Emirates?""I don't know but I bet it is somewhere near Iran."

I did a search for United Arab Emirates and found it on the Persian Gulf and there was Iran on the other side of the Gulf. I kept reading, "Sheikh Zaid ibn Sultan al-Nahayan, the ruler of Abu Dhabi, has been the President of the UAE from the founding of the Federation." Sherry was reading over my shoulder, "Oh look, he was born in 1923 which would make him about the right age for WW II."

CHAPTER 26

As we drove home our conversation continued putting what facts we knew together. I could not believe that we had tracked what we thought would be treasure to some Arab in the desert. Maybe we were on the wrong track but every thing just popped out at us like someone was giving us the answers. In my heart I knew there was no gold at the end of this rainbow but there was something or someone that wanted us to keep going. The rod and paper was the key and I would guess we needed the other rod to make the story complete. Getting the other rod meant dealing with our friends at home. I thought in silence for a moment and then asked Sherry, "Honey, we need the other rod so could you stay with the kids until I persuade our friend to give it to me?" "Hell no, I am with you and we will get back the rod together."

"Well, you could have been a little more direct with your answer. Honey, you know there will be trouble and you could get hurt.""Why are you calling me honey at a time like this? You will be the one to get hurt and I will have to save your ass."

"Okay lover, when have you ever saved my ass? You are turning me on. I am stopping the car so get in the back seat.""Are you crazy? We are not having sex in the back seat."

"Why not?""Take a look at the back seat, this is a Mustang and your back is not going to survive. We are not teenagers."

"Can we try?""No."

We arrived at our house late and it was still in a mess. Bullet holes in all the walls and broken glass sprayed like a coating of paint. I walked in amazement through each room wondering how we survived. I checked the electrical power by flipping on a light and it was still working. Sherry gave me a funny look and asked, "What are you doing turning on the lights?""Well, we have to let everyone know we are back and ready to be captured."

"Are you having a death again?""I have an idea. Let's make a forgery of the paper and make some changes to the writings that way we will have the only true whatever it is."

"Okay but how will we duplicate the paper or as you say whatever it is?""I am thinking maybe some kind of soft plastic might service as whatever this stuff is.

The lights in the house did not take long to draw the snake to the fire. A voice came from behind us saying, "Glad you returned. We have missed you."We turn to see three men holding handguns pointed in our direction. I gave Sherry a nudge and said, "I told you this would work."

One of the men motioned for us walk to the front door, "Try not to run because I have not had dinner yet and the sight of blood would spoil my appetite." Sherry replied, "What is wrong with you people? Does killing mean nothing to you? What have we ever done to you?"

"Damn, a lot of questions for a woman with red hair," replied one of the other men."Oh sure, my hair color has everything to do with it."

The man behind me gave me a push out the door and said, "Quiet, both of you."We walked a half block away and made a turn into the driveway of one of our neighbors. There stood a Lincoln Town Car and we all got in. The drive was short and we entered a warehouse through a side door. We could see a room near the back with a light on. I looked at Sherry and said, "I told you we would get to see the headman if we waited."

The door opened and there stood two more men in suits, apparently business men. Both were tall with dark skin and had an Arabic flavor to their appearance. "Please sit down."We took a chair that looked like it belonged in a warehouse. Sherry started to talk but I stopped her. We waited for the businessmen to open the conversation. The first one to say a completed sentence wore a dark suit with an outstanding red and gray tie, "We believe that you have in your person something that belongs to us."

"Sorry, we have nothing that belongs to you.""Okay, let me kill them now," came from the other suit.

"Wait we are businessmen and there has to be a price," came from the guy directly in front of us. "How about $25K for the rod that belongs to us?"

"What rod," I answered?"Okay, I am tired of playing game and I will start with a bullet into the brain of your wife. Will that refresh your memory?"

He pointed his gun at Sherry's head. I knew he was bluffing but I don't think Sherry did. She screamed, "You bastards, we will give it to you after we see yours to make sure they are a pair." I thought, "Good job Sherry, at least we will know if they have the other rod."

The guy motioned to the other suit and he walked forward, "Show the bitch the whatever it is."

The man pulled a small cloth bag from his coat and carefully opened it. He acted if the rod was a pot of gold and gently handed it to the man with the gun. The gun was still at Sherry's head but when he reached for the rod the gun moved and that was my cue to take it. I did a slight twist of his wrist and the gun fell into my hand. I softly said, "My turn to asked, who are you guys." The man in the rear pulled his gun and I shot the man in front of me in the arm. "Anyone else want this poor screaming man to die?"

Sherry moved closer to me and watched the men like a cat watching a mouse. The wounded man pulled himself together enough to say, "What is wrong with you bastards, can't you see he is serious."

"Damn serious, now if I remember I had a question that needed an answer.""The other man in a suit said, "Say nothing!"

I shot him in the leg and he fell to the floor, "That's not the answer. Oh by the way, please give the other item you took from me to my wife. I just hope this gun has a full clip because it seems no one is listening to what I say. I sure want to share all these bullets."Sherry took the rod from the guy on the floor and I softly said, "Now, do I call 911 or maybe just the police. I hate that you are bleeding on the carpet and it will cost you. Now, back to my question, you represent whom?"

The guy on the floor answered, "What difference does it make, you would not know anyone I said and you will be dead before the end of the week anyway?"I fired another shot but missed on purpose, "Okay, okay, it is an Israeli person with full backing from the Mustafa."

"Thank you now please deposit all your weapons on the couch." An armory began to be deposited and I pointed to Sherry to gather them. It was a load but she managed. "Gentlemen, please stay indoors until we have left or I will not miss or even take a cheap shot."

We walked out the door and to the car. Funny, no one followed us.

We drove away without a problem. Sherry began to shake and I stopped and gave her a long hug. Quietly tears ran down her cheeks and I kissed them off. She asked, "Why do we do things like that, we do not need the money?"I left a bit silence while trying to think of an answer, "Honey, money is not worth your life or mine but something or someone is guiding us and whatever it is it has a strong power on me. Think what has happened and no harm to us."

"Pat, I am not a strong person when it comes to guns, car chases, and escapes so I want you to know that I will not leave your side until we find out what is happening to our lives. I may be shaking and crying but I will be there."I held her for a long time as we melted together. I started the car and we headed in the direction of my brother's house.

Our reunion with the kids was a joyous one with everyone talking at the same time. Even a few days seemed like a year being away from the kids. We gave a long hug to Jeff and Marge telling them what a great family they were to take such good care of the kids. Jeff threw several steaks on the grill and Marge put baking potatoes in the oven and started a salad. The kids never stopped talking telling us how much fun Uncle Jeff and Aunt Marge had provided them. I wanted to tell Jeff and Marge about what we had planned but decided to wait for the kids to go to bed. There was no way to get them to bed before 10:00 and we tucked them in at 10:20. The four of us sat drinking coffee making small talk in the living room. I know Jeff was dying to hear what had happened and Marge keep Sherry talking.

Finally, I opened my next sentence with, "How would you like an all expense paid vacation to United Arab Emirates, that's the UAE for short?"Marge and Jeff both gave us funny looks and Jeff said, "Where in the hell is the UAE?"

"In the desert of the Middle-East.""Do they have swimming pools there or just sand and camels?"

Marge added, "What about bullets and fighting? There is nothing but war in the Middle-East now."Sherry replied, "Not there. It is one of the riches places in the world. All is at peace there."

"So what is there that we would want," Jeff asked? I showed Jeff the Marge the rods and paper and told them the complete story. At first they sat with their mouths open and then came the questions. Two hours later the conversation slowed to a point that I could ask them if they would really like to go to the UAE. Jeff looked at Marge and said, "I guess we had better sleep on it."

"Oh sure I understand," I replied.

I leaned back in my chair and said, "Jeff if you do not mind may we sleep here tonight? Our house is a mess and I am not sure we could take the kids there."Marge jumped up and said, "By all means stay here."

She went to the second spare bedroom and began to prepare the bed. We followed her trying to help. There was not much conversation in the bedroom so I gave her a hug and said, "I love you, Marge, you are the best."She left Sherry and me in the bedroom as we said goodnight. I left a crack in the bedroom door hoping to get some feedback from Jeff and Marge but they were quiet. I guess the shock of all this was too much for them. My back was killing me so I went straight to bed followed by Sherry. I turned and twisted and Sherry got up and looked through her purse for pain pills. "Back pain is the only thing that would keep you awake."

"Damn, you are good."It took about thirty minutes for the pills to take effect and I was gone.

Morning came with the smell of coffee and bacon. I rushed through a shower and met Sherry in her bra and panties going to the shower. I opened the door and there was Marge with a robe for Sherry. They were about the same size and she handed me a clean shirt and jean for her also. I made my way to the kitchen and Jeff was sitting at the table drinking coffee and reading a large book. "I see here that the UAE has found oil under all that sand and it looks like it will be a gusher. They even thinking that there is a major supply in the Persian Gulf. Would the rods and paper have anything to do with the oil?"I hesitated before I said, "I am not sure. I would say oil or religion. That is two words that sums up the Middle-East."

Jeff kept reading and final said, "You know the UEA is not a very old country. The Brits gave them there country back or should I say freedom? I bet the Brits are sorry they did that after they found oil.""Well, the Brits did not have any rights maybe I should say mineral rights anyway. The King of the UAE is kicking butt and he is no dummy."

We drank coffee and talked until Sherry appeared. She looked good in borrowed clothes and I pushed out a chair for her. Marge took our breakfast orders as I said, "Whatever is available is fine, nothing fancy. Ten minutes later we all sat at the table with eggs, bacon, and potatoes. It seemed we all were hungry because our plates emptied quickly. Two more cups of coffee and I got enough nerve to ask the question. "Any decisions made last night?"Marge turned to Jeff with a glancing look and said, "We want to go if you are sure it is okay with y'all."

I let out a yell and answered "You damn right it is more than okay. We need all the family comfort we can get.""When are you planning to leave," asked Jeff?

"Just as soon as you two can get packed and a passport. We can drive to Houston and get your passport in one day. I will start making plans for all of us today."

All our faces were covered with smiles and I guess the extra noise woke the kids and they appeared. Marge jumped up and offered pancakes. I have never known the kids to turn down pancakes with bacon. I got on the phone and made reservations for the trip to Houston thinking driving would take too long then booked passages on American for Business Class to Abu Dhabi. I had never heard of Abu Dhabi before a few weeks ago and did not even ask the cost. I knew we were all going even if I had to sell the house. Of course, the house was not in the best of conditions. Our bank accounts was in good condition but there had to be an end to our short lived wealth that we had received in the past few months. We were adjusted to living a much more frugal life without any frills. The money we had received in the past year was like a bonus that we did not deserve well maybe we did. Being shot at and having our house destroyed must be worth something.

After breakfast, I gathered the group to the living room and we discussed about the location of all our birth certificates. Sherry knew the locations of hers and the kids but Marge was not 100% sure of hers and Jeff's. The search began. Folders, boxes, and safes were opened with no results when Marge began to pout. She plopped down in a chair with her head resting on her hand. I could see she needed a little encouragement so I started naming places that we had not looked. When I hit bank deposit vault her eyes perked up and she yelled, "That's it!"Jeff said in amazement, "I did not know we had a bank vault."

"You remember about six years ago we decided to rent one in case the house burned.""No but I will take your word for it. Do we have any money or valuables in it?"

"Yes, our marriage license. I was planning to put the deed to the house in it as soon as it was paid off.""Oh boy, another twenty years and we get to open the vault again."

At the bank we blew the dust off the deposit box and removed the birth certificates. We had all the documents we needed to apply for a passport and our flight left at 7:00am the next day. Jeff, Marge, Sherry and I spent the remainder of the day guessing how we might get an audience to the King of the UAE. Surely they would not let just anyone be received by the King. A phone call would be worthless so we decided to write an introduction letter asking for an interview with the King. We had no experience at such documents so we just started writing as if we were applying for a job. Sherry came up with the best idea and that was to attach a picture of the rods. At least someone could see we were on the level. We opened our letter of introduction by giving a brief history of how we came in ownership of the rods. We gave what we knew as the history of the rods and how we determined that they belonged to the UAE. The letter ended up being about two pages and Sherry typed it. We took pictures and dropped them off for one day service. We did not have a second plan so we assumed that if this did not work we would develop the second plan after the first failed. Marge had another great idea, "We need to know the customs and procedures of the country just in case we do get an appointment to see the King.""Okay, how do you suggest that," I asked?

"How about the library or embassy," Jeff replied?I replied, "Great, let's cover both areas and divide up. Women and kids take the library and Jeff and I will cover the embassy."

There was some grumbling about who carried the kids but I explained there were things in the library that the kids could do while the research went on. Finally, all was in agreement. Then it hit me, which embassy, US or UAE. We did not have time to visit both today so we decided to try the USA Embassy first and maybe we would have some time after we got back from Houston to cover the UAE Embassy.

The women and the kids left for the library and we pulled out of the driveway shortly thereafter. As Jeff and I pulled onto the street a dark sedan followed us from a distance. Maybe it was my brain being over-alert of what had happened in the last few weeks. Anyway I told Jeff not to look back but take a turn at the next street and circle back to the house. The damn car did the same so I walked back into the house, found my .357 and went out the back door. I circled a couple houses and came up on the car from the opposite side of the street. There were two men sitting in the front seat and for some stupid reason they had the car window down. Maybe they were listening for me to return but it was hard to hear anything with the barrel of my .357 firmly placed into the ear of the driver. I pulled the hammer back on the gun and said, "Did you hear the hammer of this .357 mag go to the firing position?"The driver slowing said, "Yes."

"That means if my finger moves then so does your brains. If I were you, I would tell your partner not to make any moves unless he wants a dead partner."The man in the passenger seat reaches inside his coat and I press a little harder with the gun barrel. I driver raised his hand and said, "Wait! What do you want?"

"Are you crazy? What do you want," I asked?"We are CIA sent to watch you."

"Now, why should I believe that?""Let me get my ID and I will show you."

I reached to his coat and gave it a pat. There felt like a shoulder holster full of hard steel. "Maybe I should take weapon before you show me anything." Jeff arrived and I told him to slowly remove the weapon from the man sitting in the passenger seat. Jeff gave me funny look but went to retrieve the weapon. I was afraid for Jeff so I told the man to remove his weapon using two fingers after opening his coat wide. Amazing, the guy did as he was told and Jeff took the hardware. I continued, "Sir would you like to remove your weapon in the same matter or a very large hole through your brain?"

The guy slowly removed the weapon but there must have been some kind of alarm attached to the hostler because four more dark sedans arrived within seconds. Even if I pulled the trigger there would be so many bullets in the air that Jeff and/or I would surely be dead within seconds. I removed the .357 from the driver's ear and said, "Oh, we have other people joining the party." The driver repeated his first statement and said, "We are CIA and we plan no harm."

I told Jeff to throw the gun on the ground and I did the same. Seven men came from all directions with weapons drawn and not a smile on any face except for mine. "I raised my hands and said, "Gentlemen, there must be a misunderstanding. We mean no harm and we surely do not need any help from the CIA." No words were spoken but what seemed to be the leader took my .357 and pushed me to the car and gave me a quick search. Jeff got the same treatment. They brought Jeff to my side of the car and again the leader started, "Pat, I wish you were working in our department because you seem to be getting into all kinds of situations and that cause me to fill out a lot of paperwork. If you worked for us you could fill out your own damn paperwork. We are just trying to give you a little protection and for some reason you are refusing. Now what is wrong with you?"

"Are you CIA?"

"Yes."

He flipped open his badge and it looked like a CIA badge but a person could buy them at the grocery store if they really wanted one. "Okay but what do you want with us?"

"Nothing! We are just keeping an eye on you before you leave the country. You are always in a dilemma but somehow you manage to get out of all the trouble without our help." "I have never asked for your help. Why should I ask for help?"

"I am beginning to think the same thing but you are playing with some heavy hitters and they play for keeps."

"Who are these people and what do they want?" asked Jeff.

"These people have no names but a hell of a lot of money and they will do anything to keep their pockets filled. Killing you or anyone else would mean nothing to them."I walked to pick up my gun and said, "Hey, don't worry about us we are just going on a vacation."

"Don't turn you back on anyone."

We returned to the car with great amazement wondering what are we doing involved with the CIA and some mob group. Jeff had a dry mouth and when he spoke he was a bit scratchy. We shot questions back and forth to each other all the way to the embassy but not many answers came forth.

We decided to try the UAE Embassy first and save the USA for last because we would most likely be in jail. We managed to get into the UAE Embassy after filling out paperwork, going through a security check, and giving detail information as to our business. The people doing the interview kept asking the same questions over and over. I assumed they were hoping that we would change our story along the way. At some point during our conversation we must have convinced them we were not crazy.

As we entered the office of what I thought must be someone important we were seated and offered tea. I took the tea and nodded for Jeff to take the cup. One thing that I had learned from what little bit of travel is that you do not refused any offerings from a person that you plan to do business. We drank tea for another fifteen minutes and the door opened with a man dressed in white came in. His dress was one of what one might see in the Middle East including a long white dress and a black headband. Jeff whispered, "You think his flying carpet is outside?"I never answered. The man spoke broken but good English and offered us more tea. I accepted.

The Arab took papers from a file that was given him and began to ask us questions. We told him that we were planning a trip to the UAE and needed procedures to see the King. At that point he smiled and said, "Why would you need to see our beloved King?"I continued with my story about the rods and then showed him pictures of the rods. His smile went away. He studies the pictures and then asked one of the men near him to bring him a magnifying glass. I assumed that what he said because he spoke in Arabic and the man returned with the glass. Again he studied the pictures and then laid them down. He rose from his chair and came to my side of his desk and with a hard look on his face he asked, "Who are you and what do you want?"

Again I repeated my name and told him I wanted to see the King of the United Arab Emirates. This time there was no smile and maybe a sneer on the man's face. There was a silence and finally the man asked, "Do you have what's in the picture?"

"Yes."

"Where did you get them?"

"It is a long story that I prefer to tell your King only."

More silence and it lasted for several minutes. The man walked around his office like a cat on the prowl and then stopped facing me. He walked to me and with his face very close to mine said, "Show me what you have.""Sorry, no one sees them except for your King."

He waited with silence again, "How much do you want for them?""Wait a minute I did not say they are for sale. If they belong to your King I will give them to him. I just want the real owner to have them and I think your King is the man."

"How soon can you be ready to go?""Just a minute, I am taking my family and brother along and we are ready. We just need an audience before your King."

"Be at the airport at noon tomorrow, everyone. You will be flying in my private jet.""Your jet?"

"Yes, my King provides a large business jet for transportation."He handed me a card with the address of the plane hanger and told me to use the card for entrance. Apparently, that was our exit cue because two men came to us and pointed us to the door.

We drove back to the house and there were our friends parked a few blocks away but we ignored them. The wives and kids were home and as soon as we walked in they began to talk without taking a breath. I finally had to wave them down and that slowed the conversation. I raised my voice a bit and said, "Hold everything. We have a new plan. We are taking a private jet to Abu Dhabi for an audience before the King of the United Arab Emirates."Sherry gave a blank look and asked, "What do you mean?"

"The UAE Embassy is flying us there on their airplane," I replied."Oh no, it is not safe. Why would they do that anyway?"

I sat the group down and told the story. Questions began to pour from both the women but then a bit of excitement came into their voices. "Private plane and it is free," Sherry quietly said.She stood and started to walk away when she said, "I'm for it. Let's go"

All gave a nod of agreement.

CHAPTER 27

The morning finally came as Sherry and I tossed most of the night. We woke up talking about the kids and if taking them was the right thing to do. I was determined to take them because my life without them had been long enough. I knew Sherry wanted the best for them and I was going to do my best to watch them every minute of the trip. We were about half packed and without breakfast Sherry began neatly folding clothes and placing them in one of three large suitcases. I fell in suit and grabbed what clothes I had laying around and threw them into the suitcase. Sherry stopped me and waved me away, "I will do the packing. You will never be able to wear those clothes without pressing them." I gave a smile and went into the kitchen. Marge was sitting at the table drinking coffee and she got up to pour me a cup. I took her hand and asked, "You okay with all of this?"

"Sure but can we trust these people?" "Marge, we have nothing invested. The rods mean nothing to me and they must mean something to the King. The guy at the embassy had a look that I have never seen before. He acted like someone had took him he had cancer. The rods have a meaning that we do not know. We will be okay, don't worry."

She handed me the coffee and my bother walked in with a grin. "What time are we leaving?" "What did he said noon or so?"

"What should we take?" "I am taking the nicest suit and tie that I own. Meeting the King of any country has to be a formal affair."

"What color?" "A dark one and you do the same. The ladies will need long dresses."

We finished breakfast and started the packing process. Sherry had her suitcase out and was packing like she was going to stay a month. I tried to slow her down but she kept arranging clothes and shoes. Another suitcase came out and the kid's clothes were folded and packed. Another hour passed and clothes were still being packed. I gave up and flipped on the TV. I looked for a news channel thinking there must be something happening that I do not know about.

Sherry came bouncing into the room and said, "We are ready." My heart almost stopped when I saw the TV flash a breaking story about two CIA agents being killed in our area. Again Sherry said, "Okay we are ready."

I never said a word to her and the news story but said, "Check with Marge and let's get out of here." I took the luggage to the car and told a good look in every direction. There was the black car two blocks away but it looked empty. My brother came out of the house with more luggage and we stuffed it into the trunk. I said quiet, "I just saw on the news that two CIA agents were killed in this area."

His head popped to the direction of the black car, "Must not have been our friend because there is their car." "True but do you see anyone in the cat?"

"No." "Let's move a little faster."

Within ten minutes we had everyone in the car and pulling out of the driveway. That was a miracle in its self. I made a few turns and apparently we had not picked up a tail. Forty minutes later we were pulling into the airport. We asked for directions twice, well I mean Sherry asked for directions. We found the hanger and there sat a 747 with armed guards surrounding the plane. The marking on the tail were in Arabic and that was all except for a red and green strip along the side. We found a parking place and unloaded our bags. We were approached by two men and they were carrying rifles. They spoke English and asked to see our passports. It took several minutes but we passed the security check. They took our luggage and we were escorted to the stairway that entered the cabin.

Sherry gave me a lost look and I felt what she was saying. I offered her a hug and we started up the stairs. We were met by several women flight attendants and as we entered the cabin. We all stopped in amazement. This was not an airplane but a luxury hotel. The room that we entered was covered with leather lounge chairs that swiveled with beautiful carpet and paintings on the cabin walls. Each chair had a table made of birds-eye maple with gold trim along the edge. Every place we looked was gold trim and I had a really good feeling. I knew all the trim was real gold and it shined as if it were new. There was soft music playing and we all wanted to see the next room in the plane but we sat. The plane was still in the hanger and as soon as we sat the doors were closed and we could feel it moving. A tug pushed us onto the pad and turned us to the direction of the runway. A door opened and the man from the embassy joined us sitting in one of the chairs. One of the flight attendants brought drinks and cheeses and sat it on each table. The trays were silver and the cheeses were great. We had wine while the kids drank orange juice. The man from the embassy welcomed us and we heard the aircraft engines start. He made small talk about the weather and ensured us we would enjoy the flight. We taxied for another twenty minutes and we rolled down the runway. The huge plane lifted off like a kite and it turned to the east. The man excused himself and disappeared through a door at the rear. We felt more at ease so the conversation started. Marge and Sherry talked about clothes and what they had planned to wear. The kids were excited and at flying and looked out the windows talking about everything they saw. The chair reclined and I was ready for a nap. Well, my nap was interrupted by a flight attendant handing me a menu for dinner. The menu was four pages long and gave the name of the chef at the top of the page. I was a bit in shock just by reading each item. It was a French restaurant in the air and every bite of food was explained in great detail. My first choice was the lobster in a cream sauce and Sherry took the swordfish. The kids wanted a burger and fries. Fruits, hot roasted nuts, cheeses and some kind of fancy looking bread were offered. Sherry gave Marge a smile and we sampled it all. There was no way that I was going to fill up before the lobster came so I stopped eating and drank my wine. The kids still looking out the windows continued to talk about everything on the ground.

The attendants kept our glasses filled to the point that I had to go to the lavatory. I asked the attendant to point me in the general direction and she walked me to an unmarked door. I entered and thought I made a mistake. The room was large with gold sinks and fixtures accented with marble. The mirror ran the length of the room with gold trim that surrounded every side and indirect lighting filled the room. The navy-blue walls were dotted with gold emblems and pictures. I was almost afraid to use the facility. Heated towels were draped over racks in several places. There were two showers at the end of the room complete with gold and blue marble tiles. The commode was gold and I almost walked out but I had to go so I did. I hated to leave the sink with water spots but when I turned the water off a blast of air came from around the sink and blew away the water. I took a towel from the stack. I made my exit with a grin on my face and Sherry picked up on it. "What? Why are you smiling?" "It's time for you and Marge to go to the restroom."

"Why?" "Just go."

The two disappeared for thirty minutes and both came out smiling. Sherry came close to my seat and said, "Can you believe that? I hope you did not use the facilities.""I certainly did and even washed my hands."

I just shook my head.

The attendant brought hot wet clothes thinking we needed to clean up a bit. Shortly afterwards the food started to coming and did not stop for two hours. Oh my gosh my lobster was more than wonderful and they brought out desserts that no one turned down. I ate so much that I thought it was Thanksgiving and I waited for the football game to come TV. It was dark outside and the kids watched movies on their own TV that rose from the table in front of them. The attendant came by and offered to show us the bedroom. I had no idea there was a bedroom but we all followed the woman through another door. There were four small rooms with a queen bed in each room. In keeping with the décor the bedrooms were just as gorgeous. The surprising part was the presents of night attire for everyone. The kids finished their movies and we took them to bed. We returned to our seats and had a nightcap. We talked about the plane and tried to picture the palace. We finally agree that sleep would be next on our agenda.

Six and half hours later the lights came on dim with soft music. The smell of coffee came through the cabin and my eyes opened. Sherry and I got to the showers first and new clean clothes were hanging in the closet. A suit of clothes was not a suit of clothes in this case, there hung designer clothes. They all fit like they were tailor-made. Sherry and I came out of the laboratory looking like we just walked off Fifth Ave. Marge's mouth flew open and said, "Where did you get the clothes?""Part of the package," replied Sherry.

"You need a shower and new clothes will be waiting," I added.Both Jeff and Marge jumped up and disappeared in the lavatory. We sat talking with the kids telling them that they were getting new clothes and how much fun they would have in Abu Dhabi. An hour and half later Jeff and Marge came out looking beautiful. Sherry took the kids next after the attendant made a quick cleaning of the lavatory.

We were all dressed and more fruit, cheeses, and drinks came. Sherry made sure the kids got nothing on their clothes. The man in charge of the UAE Embassy joined us with compliments of our dress. He asked if we would mind if he gave us a bit of history of the UAE. I answered, "Please do."He started with some information about the King. "Zayed is about forty years old, handsome, with humorous and intelligent eyes, of fine presence and bearing, simply dressed, and clearly a man of action and resolution. As a younger man he had only been formally in charge of the Abu Dhabi sector of the oasis and its surrounding deserts for some two years, he was experienced in the politics of the region, and was already by far the most prominent personality in the area. He had a sure touch with the Bedouin. Zayed had an opportunity to learn the practice of Government and also, during the Buraimi dispute of the late nineteen forties and early nineteen fifties, gave him experience of the wider world. Tribes from throughout the desert region of the Emirate, and from far away deep into Inner Oman, grew to trust Sheikh Zayed as a conciliator and as a mediator in disputes, a man whose even-handed justice earned respect from all. The same patient and painstaking efforts to resolve arguments between brothers teamed in Al Ain can still be seen today in Sheikh Zayed's equally patient and painstaking efforts to solve the disputes between brotherly Arab countries. Sheikh Zayed also had the task of guiding the development of Al Ain itself. Putting the scanty resources at his disposal to work, he ensured that the 'falajes' were cleaned out, and built a new one, helping to stimulate agriculture in the area. The process was aided by a decision from the Al Nahyan family that their own private shares of the water supply should be turned over to the public, setting an example that others were swift to follow. This growth in agriculture in turn encouraged Al Ain to develop its traditional position as market centre for the whole region, bringing new business and prosperity - even if on a small scale. And, in a foretaste of the massive station program that has today changed the very face of the Emirate, Sheikh Zayed began the planting of ornamental and decorative trees that are today grown to maturity. Working with scanty resources, but generating a new optimism among the people of the area, Sheikh Zayed was able to move ahead with the development of the Al Ain area faster than anyone, except perhaps himself, would have expected."

He stopped and seemed to test us if we were listening. Sherry leaned forward waiting for him to continue. He broke a small smile and continued. "In 1953, accompanying his brother, Sheikh Zayed made his first trip to Europe, visiting Paris for legal hearings on an oil dispute, and being impressed by the Eiffel Tower, and going on to Britain. In interviews years later, he recalled how his first impressions had included the schools and the hospitals enjoyed by the people. When Sheikh Zayed had money, he decided, such facilities should be provided for his own people. The Paris legal hearings, where judgment was in favor of Sheikh Zayed, were a sign of the change that was shortly to begin to sweep across the Emirate as oil exploration got under way. The first exploration well in Abu Dhabi had been drilled at Ras Sadr in 1950, to be followed by others in what is now the Western Region, and then with other wells offshore. By 1958, the first commercial oil-fields were discovered, first onshore, in the Bab field, and then offshore, at Umm Shaif. The first export cargo of oil left Abu Dhabi in 1962. With the oil revenues beginning to flow, the people of Abu Dhabi were eager to share in the development that they could see already taking place in other oil-producing emirates further up the Gulf. With the record of his achievements as Ruler's Representative in Al Ain, Sheikh Zayed was the natural choice to preside over this process, and, in August 1966, he succeeded as Ruler of the Emirate of Abu Dhabi. He was a man in a hurry. The oil revenues were swelling year by year as new fields were discovered and, while, at the same time, the rising expectations of the people meant that the development program had to get under way equally fast. Moving quickly to establish the first formal Government structure for the Emirate, Sheikh Zayed embarked upon a large-scale construction program, building roads and schools, housing and hospitals, not just in the capital of the Emirate, Abu Dhabi, and in Al Ain, but extending out to the Bedouin settlements in the desert, to ensure that the benefits of the new wealth taken out to the people. At the same time, Sheikh Zayed also saw clearly that Britain would not forever maintain her presence in the Gulf, and that the Emirates of the region would need to come together in co-operation and partnership if they were to enjoy a stable and prosperous future."

The attendant brought tea so he stopped again. He was like a story-teller bringing detail that we had not known until now. The King seemed to be a hero among his people.

He continued again, "Less than eighteen months after he became Ruler, in January 1968, Sheikh Zayed was visited by a British Minister who had come to inform him, and the other Sheikhs of the Trucial Coast, that the British military and political presence in the Arabian Gulf would cease at the end of 1971.

Sheikh Zayed was ready to react. In early February, Sheikh Zayed met at As Sameeh, half way between Abu Dhabi and Dubai, with the Ruler of Dubai, His Highness Sheikh Rashid bin Saeed al Maktoum now the UAE's Vice President and Prime Minister. The two men agreed to establish a federation between their two emirates, and invited the other five Trucial States, as well as Qatar and Bahrain, to join them. The wisdom of the move was widely recognized, although it took nearly four years, and some hard bargaining, before the seven Trucial States agreed to form a federation. Qatar and Bahrain chose to proceed to a separate independence, but are now closely linked with the UAE through the Gulf Co-Operation Council. Sheikh Zayed's own determination, powers of conciliation, and willingness to compromise for the common good were crucial in the eventual success of the negotiations, and when the federation of the United Arab Emirates was officially formed in 1971, Sheikh Zayed was the logical choice as the President of the new state. After decades or centuries of a separate existence, the individual emirates moved into a new period of their history when the flag of the new state was raised on December 2nd 1971, facing the future as one. 'It is Islam that asks every Moslem to respect every person,' Sheikh Zayed believes. 'Not, I emphasize, special people, but every person, In short, to treat every person, no matter what his race or creed, as a special soul is a mark of Islam. It is just such a point, embodied in Islam's tenets, that makes us proud of Islam. To be together, to trust each other as human beings, to behave as equals.'

That faith is the key to the man, and to an understanding of why he has succeeded so well."

He stopped and again so I assumed that he was finished so I asked, "So what do the rods mean to the King?"

He gave me a hard look and slowly said, "The rods belonged to his famous grandfather, Zayed bin Khalifa Al Nahyan, who ruled the emirate from 1855 to 1909. I will let Sheikh Zayed tell the remainder."

The plane started its decent and butterflies hit my stomach. I was not sure why because I held all the cards but meeting with a king is a bit scary. We landed and the aircraft taxied to a hanger. We all gathered our carry-on's and I made a quick check for the rods making sure I still had them in my bag. They were there.

It was late afternoon as the aircraft door opened and it only took two steps down the stairs before Jeff said, "Damn, it is hot."

By the time we got to the bottom of the stairs Sherry was breathing hard. She turned to me and asked, "Do people live in this heat on purpose?"

"Seems like Nam without the trees."

The humidly was high because we were on a small island. "How hot does it get here when the sun is out," I asked one of the men in the hanger?

"Oh, maybe 120 to 125 degrees."

Sherry replied, "Is there air conditioning here?"

"Oh, sure."

A white Rolls-Royce pulled near the plane followed by another one. The drivers jumped out and opened the doors of both cars. Sherry, the kids and I got into one and Jeff and Marge got into the other. The smell of fine leather filled the car and Sherry smiled as she ran her hand over the seat. We drove for a long ways but I guess it was only 25 or 30 miles. We were afraid to touch anything in the Rolls so we just rode and looked at what we could see since it was dark. There were trees planted along the highway and that was about as far as we could see.

The driver made his way through the city with taxis and wild drivers cutting in front of him. He acted as if it was everyday driving and never gave any other crazy drivers an obscene gesture. We made several more turns and came to a stop at a high wall with an iron gate.

An armed guard opened the gate and both Rolls passed. We traveled a bit more into the complex and stopped in front of what must have been the palace. Doors were opened and we were ushered into the building or what might be called a palace. I called it a building but it was surely made for a king. Every direction we looked was gold, costly paintings, sculptures, carpets, and thing I had never seen before. Sherry took the children's hands to make sure they did not wonder off and break something. We were met by several servants that took us to a large room prepared with food and drinks. We sat and were offered all kinds of food and some I had never seen before. I tried it all. It seems that I must have led a sheltered life because this place had all kinds' stuff that I had never seen. It was late and we were offered a bedroom. The kids were given a room adjacent to ours and even had a connecting door. Marge and Jeff took the room on the other side of us. Our room was like heaven with all a person would need for any occasion. Our night clothes were there and the closet contained an assortment of clothes including a tux and evening dress. The servants showed us all the features of the room and I offered a tip before they leave. They acted a bit insulted that I offered and one said, "You are our guess."

I returned the money to my pocket with a warm friendly fuzzy flowing over my body. We changed clothes and made our way to the silk sheets. "Sherry, how come we do not have silk sheets at home?"

"Same reason we do not have a Rolls Royce at home."

After that I decided to sleep.

Morning came and the kids were shaking our bed. I looked at the clock and it was 8:40. I gave Sherry a nudge and she said, "What?"

"It's late and the kids are here."

"I don't think so."

"Kids, go wake your mother up."

They flew to the other side of the bed and started shaking her. "Okay, okay, I will get up."

Hot coffee, juices, milk, and pastries were on a tray in the room with a note that said, "Breakfast will be served at 10:00."

Sherry took the kids to the tray and divided a roll with milk. "This should hold you until we get something more."

We were all dressed in what clothes we brought thinking we would not meet with anyone important at breakfast. We join Marge and Jeff and started walking. We fell in line with two of the servants and followed them to the dining table. On the way one of the men explained that we would be eating in small or private dining room. When we arrived there was a table set for 12 people. The buffet next to the table was covered with gold serving containers. One of the men offered his hand and said, "Please help yourself."

He handed each of us a small plate and we began to fill it with fruits, cheeses and cold meats. After we had started eating the serving dishes were taken and then large gold trim dishes were brought to the buffet. Seeing some of the dishes we all slowed down on the fruits and cheeses. I stopped eat for a second and a man rushed to me and asked, "Finished?"

I nodded my head yes and he took my plate. He then offered me a larger plate and again said, "Help yourself."

Before I could get up a man enter the room. He was dressed in white Arab dress with a black headband. All the servants stopped and took a small bow. Jeff and I stood trying to be polite for another guess to join us. He motion for us to be seated. He stood at the head of the table with a wide smile and said, "I am Sheikh Zayed bin Sultan Al Nahyan President of the United Arab Emirates."

My heart stopped and hit my stomach and I tried to get my lips to move. Finally, I managed to introduce all of us. The Sheikh walked to kids and bent down and gave them a hug and a kiss. "You have beautiful children, please continue with your eating. We try not to be formal here."

He returned to the head of the table, took a seat, and servants brought him plates filed with food. He began with small take about our flight and we told him we were treated like royalty. He continued to laugh and talk about some of his experiences in the States. He was just a regular guy and he made us feel so at ease. He invited us to a formal dinner in the evening with other head people of the country and we gladly accepted. Then he brought up the subject of our visit and wanted to meet with Jeff and me after we ate. The Sheikh finished eating and excused himself but only after he had kissed the children one more time.

I sat with my mouth open and finally said, "What a great guy. He has the demeanor of a Texan."

Sherry replied, "Yeah right. I have never seen a Texan that nice."

One of the servants took Jeff and I to another room while the women and kids went on a tour of the palace. Jeff and I sat in leather chairs of what could have been a library or office. A beautiful huge wooden desk sat in the corner of the room. Only a few minutes passed before the Sheikh came through the door. He had a big smile again and made his way to the desk. "Sorry for the delay but I am so excited about what you have brought."

"Sir, I hope you are not disappointed and I hope these belong to you. I just feel in my heart that they are yours and they are valuable to you and your country."

I removed the rods from my pocket, unwrapped them and handed them to the King. His touch was very careful and he gazed at them with deep concentration. His smile was gone and his eyes were narrowed. He turned them slowly viewing every detail. No words were spoken by anyone. At least two or three minutes passed while he examined the rods. He held them to his chest and sat back in his chair. A single tear flowed down his face and he wiped it quickly. I was afraid to speak but I asked, "Do they belong to you?"

The Sheikh hesitated but finally said, "No, my grandfather, Sheikh Zayed bin Khalifa."

He turned to me and asked, "May I ask how they came to you?"

"It is a long story but I was in the Viet Nam War and I carried a combat knife during the period I was there. I managed to keep it after I got out of the service. One day I dropped it and the end of the handle came off and the rods or what you have were inside the handle. I have been trying to determine their value and usage for over a year. People have been killed trying to get them from me and my house was mostly destroyed by the same people. I do not even know who these people are and I am not even sure why they want the rods. From my research and a deep feeling I knew they must be value to you but they mean nothing to me. I wanted you and you alone to have them."

Another tear flowed down his face. I stopped talking and waited for his reply.

"My grandfather was a great man among his countrymen and was most trusted for his leadership. My countrymen in the days of my grandfather were nomads in the desert and they looked to him for a leader. Between him and my father I owe all my knowledge and wisdom. He picked me as a leader to follow in his steps to lead the countrymen to a better life. He spoke to me daily providing an education in all things. These tools were his most prized possession."

"What are they," asked Jeff?

"They will afford a traveler passage through the desert."

"How?"

"The markings are symbols that will show a person the required direction for travel."

"What language are they written," I asked?

"My grandfather made up symbols that represent paths and points in the desert that a person would need to follow for water and such."

"I have been almost killed and several other people were killed because of the tools. What makes them so valuable in today's world," I continued?

"My grandfather buried gold along the paths so that travelers could take and replace gold as needed. Apparently, there was more replacing than taking and the sum of gold scattered along the paths is in the tons."

"How could anyone read the tools if it is an unknown language?"

"Oh, it was known to certain people that my grandfather trusted."

Jeff had to asked, "Can you read the symbols?"

"Yes."

Jeff continued, "Then the tools are a treasure map."

"Yes but the gold will remain in the desert. The tools mean more than gold to me because of the memory of my grandfather."

"Still I would keep them in a safe spot."

"They will be safe here. What do you require as a reward for bringing them to me?"

I looked at Jeff and then back to the Sheikh, "Nothing. We just wanted the right person to have them and we knew the guys in the United States were not the right people."

"You will be a trusted friend for life and whatever you need it will be supplied. Your service is beyond my belief and you are welcome to live here with my family."

"Sir, we did not come for money and a friend such as you is more valuable. We wanted you to have the tools because you should have them. I have such great memories of my father and grandfather and gold means nothing compared to their memories."

The Sheikh replied, "Love and loyalty to family shows great human traits. I respect you and give you honor."

The Sheikh rose from his desk and gave us both a hug and a kiss on both cheeks. He reminded us of the dinner and told us that we would be his honored guest.

Jeff and I started back to the room and we talked along the way. "That man is a leader of men and his tender side is so exposed when it comes to family," Jeff said.

"God, I feel good about returning the tools to him. I am sure we did the right thing. He seemed to feel a part of him had been returned to his life," I added.

"Pat, we do not have the same respect to our fathers as he and we should make it a lesson learned for us."

"I know."

"Mother and dad had a family respect and tried to teach us but I feel we failed," Jeff said quietly.

"Maybe so. Maybe we have more love to our parent and family than we know."

Jeff gave me a look, "Think so? That man in the room had tears in his eyes and was deeply moved by seeing something that his grandfather had lost. I know the tools meant a lot to him and his grandfather but I could see so much love in their relationship."

"We have the same, Jeff."

CHAPTER 28

Sherry and Marge were bouncing off the walls waiting for us to return with the news. "Okay, okay, what were the rods," Sherry asked?

"A map of the desert."

"Come on what was so important about the rods?"

"Well, the tools marked paths in the desert including water supplies and gold deposits."

"Gold? How much gold?"

"Tons, per the Sheikh."

"Are we going to dig it up?"

"No, we are letting the desert keep it."

"Why?"

"It does not belong to us but to the people of the desert. Hey, we have a party to attend tonight."

Sherry and Marge seemed disappointed so we went into more details of our conversation with the Sheikh. We decided to go shopping before the party and asked one of the men to carry us to a shopping area. Within an hour we were shopping at a great mall. One man stayed with us maybe as a bodyguard. Sherry went crazy and wanted everything she saw. The prices were much cheaper than the States. We loaded dresses, shoes, jewelry, and perfumes to the cashier and it totaled over a thousand dollars. Before I could get my credit card out, the man had it paid by nodding his head. I wondered why that did no work for me.

Back at the palace the kids were hungry so I asked one of servants about a pizza place and he waved me off and said, "Fifteen minute, Sir."

We took time to admire some of the furnishings around the suite and to our astonishment we did not have anything similar in our house since most of

241

the items were gold. A knock at the door brought us four pizzas with different toppings on each. Another tray came with drinks. It was outstanding pizza and I think the kids would have been happy with frozen. After we ate we all took a walk around the palace appreciating the work done to the greenery and all the waterfalls and fountains. It was hard to believe that we were in the middle of a desert. It was getting close to 6:00 so we decided to start our preparation for the formal dinner. Sherry and Marge would take at least an hour and one-half and wearing a tux for the first time in many years I was not sure how long I would take. It was kind of fun getting all dressed up with some place to go. We were due at 8:00 and the clock said 7:30 with Sherry not dressed. She was still doing hair. I prepared her a drink and she took a big swallow and said, "Thanks."

The kids and I were ready but I did not say a word to Sherry, after all she was the most beautiful woman in the world. She kept an eye in the kids making sure they did not get wrinkled as I flipped through one of the many books in the suite. Like an alarm clock she came from the bedroom on time. She was a beautiful creature with a turquoise evening gown that fit her perfect. I will never know how I married such a beautiful woman. She made several compliments as to my attire and we all felt like a million dollars. We stopped by to pick up Marge and Jeff and I was shocked to see how well Jeff cleaned up. Marge was outstanding in a black formal. Again we were escorted and this time to the formal dining room. We were offered drinks before we sat as soft music played in the background. We stood drinking wine when three Arab men with what I guessed were their wives walked into the room. The men were dressed in their traditional white dress while the women wore gorgeous evening gowns. They came straight to us and introduced themselves and all I understood was the word Sheikh. They spoke good English and they began small talk asking us about the States and where we lived. The women never said a word and stayed in the background. Again the room became quiet when Sheikh Zayed entered the room. The woman behind him was his wife we guessed. The man seemed to put cheer in the room with his smile and a most friendly voice. I would say he was next to being a "good ole country boy." He came to us and asked, "Have you met my brothers?"

It hit me that the three men must have been family and rulers of divisions of the UAE. That gave me an uneasy feeling but all were more than friendly and made a great effort to make us feel at home. Apparently, Sheikh Zayed had told them why I was in country because they thanked me several times for what we had done for their family and country.

We were offered seats at the table and dinner began. Before we started the Sheikh offered a toast to his American friends and for a long and happy life. Waiters began bringing food of every description starting with appetizers and finishing with desserts. It was not your basic steak and potatoes but gourmet that most people would not know how to pronounce. Most of the time I had no idea what I was eating but it was delicious. Sherry kept giving me an elbow asking, "What is this?"

"Eat it, it's good."

The conversation was very interesting as they including us in most subjects. We had to tell about the tools and how we obtained them for everyone to hear and great laughter and happiness was had by all. Dinner continued for almost 4 hours as per the custom of the Arabs. The kids were really tired and before we finished a woman came and offered to take them to bed. Sherry agreed and the kids left after a few kisses. We stayed having drinks and were entertained by dancers and music. The evening came to an end too soon and we made our way back to the room. We checked on the kids and both were asleep while the same woman watched after them.

We lay on the bed stuffed like a Thanksgiving turkey moaning because we were so full. I asked, "Having fun?"

"Sure. I could do that every night if I did not have to eat so much."

I gave her a long hug with my mouth next to her ear and asked "Feel like fooling around?"

"I feel like it but my body is having hard time breathing because of all that food."

We decided to stay one more day and tour the city and ended up in Dubai. Both cities were beyond words. We had never seen so much construction and the buildings that were completed were like never we had seen before. They were so modern with unusual architecture making us wonder if we were in a storybook land. We did more shopping and as usual our guide/driver paid it all. We returned to the palace and wondered how we were going to get all our new stuff back to the States. We ate again and started packing for home.

I walked to the library hoping to see the Sheikh one more time. He was sitting at his desk reading. I entered softly and said, "Excess me, Sir, do you have another minute?"

He stood and said, "Most certainly, come in and have a seat."

"I just have one more question. What type of material are the tools made? They seem to be nothing that I know."

PAT SCHNEIDER

The Sheikh smiled and answered, "That is a very good question. There is a long story that goes with that question and I am no sure it is true. When my grandfather was a boy he saw a rock fall from heaven. He kept it for years but he had no way of cutting or shaping the rock. He tried all kinds of cutting tools but nothing worked until he met a stranger from the desert. This man knew about the material and made the map on the rods. He helped my grandfather to develop the symbols and language used on the tools. How this man made the tools or the map is not known but it was the most accurate tool for traveling the desert and finding water that we know. The reason for two rods was so that my grandfather would be in charge and one rod would not provide any information without the other. The tools were stolen several times but they were returned to my family by someone like you. I do not think they have any kind of power or magic but they have saved many lives. The gold that is buried in the desert may even be rumor but I am willing to say that there is more gold buried out there than trucks could carry. My grandfather allowed other travelers to carry the map and maybe that is the reason they always return to my family. The desert is a holy place and an oasis is life giving. Without the water or ways to find the water so many people would die. Does that help with your question?"

"Sure, that is such a great story. I am so glad that I was a part of it. Thank you again for your hospitality and we have so much respect for you and your country. We plan to leave for the United States in the morning if you are willing to provide us a trip back."

"I will fly you anywhere to like. You and your family are my trusted friends that I will remember forever."

The Sheikh took and came to my chair so I stood. He kissed me on both cheeks and said, "May God be with you."

Back in Texas it seemed like a bit boring and I wondered why we did not stay in the UAE longer. We were back in our house with construction going on and the noise was continuous. Life seemed so plain and boring after the trip to the UAE. Sherry sat at the table balancing the check book when she started screaming. I made a jump in her direction and asked, "What?"

"Someone deposited $100,000,000 in our checking account."

"No way."

"Look, you see all those zeros?"

"Well, that means nothing. It must be a mistake. Call the bank."

She was shaking as she dialed the number. Five minutes later she was dancing around the room screaming, "Yes, it's real"

244

I fell back to my chair with my mouth open, "It came from the UAE?"

"Yes, the Sheikh."

"Bless his heart. What a great guy."

After a bit more screaming Sherry got on the phone and called Marge, "Have you check your bank account lately?"

The conversation continued but Sherry never mentioned the big money. She hung up. "Why did you not tell her about the money," I asked?

"I wanted her to check her account first and if they did not get money then we would share ours."

"Boy, you are generous with our money."

"We cannot spend a $100 million in a life-time. The bank said that the taxes have been paid on the money also."

The phone rang and I could hear Marge screaming from my chair. Sherry held the phone away from her mouth and said, "They got money also."

"How much?"

Sherry asked, "How much did you get?"

Sherry waved at me and said, "Same as us."

My heart pumped even faster just thinking about what to do with that much money.

More conversation followed between Sherry and me and finally we decided to go out for dinner. "How about a steak?"

The kids answered with an all around yes so we drove to the best steak house in town. Our waitress was over whiningly nice and a fun person that treated us like customers. We even had dessert and that brought our check to $329. I handed her my credit card and she returned with the copy to sign. I winked at Sherry and said, "Watch this."

I put a $1000 tip on the bill. I closed the folder with the bill and we sat there for a five more minutes. We gathered the kids and started out the door when we heard, "Excess me, Sir."

We stopped and our waitress stood with the check in her hand, "Sir, there must be some mistake the tip is for $1000."

"I know you did a good job."

"Oh my gosh I have never had this happen. I am so grateful. Thanks you so much. You are a life saver and you saved my car from being taken."

"Wait a minute."

I took the check and made it a $2000 tip, "You need some money for yourself also."

She gave me a hug with tears running down her face. Sherry smiled as we walked to the car, "You are such a nice husband."

PART 4 - 2006

CHAPTER 29

Our ranch is about 1000 acres in the Texas Hill Country with the house setting on top of a hill providing a view that the Sheikh would have died to own. We read in the paper and heard on TV that Sheikh Zayed had died and his son was now the President of the United Arab Emirates. We sent flowers along with half the other people in the world.

Over the passed years we have built a house on the ranch that was not huge but it was Texas style. We have barns for the horses and cows but I was getting to the point that I am too old to really enjoy all that we have accomplished. My back hurt a lot and no doctor could perform any miracle to heal it.

Both kids have graduated from the University of Texas and one is practicing law in Austin. The other is working her way through medical school. I felt at ease with what they have accomplished and know in my heart that they will be okay. My lawyer is married but no child on the way as yet. Kids have stopped having babies early in life.

Last year Sherry had a tumor that turned out to be cancerous and it scared the hell out of us. She has been great after all the treatments. We both had long hours of talk with each other that sobered our way of life.

We have five saddle horses that we love and cherish daily. Our girls ride with us on the weekend and we usually cook on the grill in the afternoon. About sundown the deer and other animals come out for corn. I keep several corn feeders full year round. We never allowed hunting and some of the deer are tame enough to eat from your hand. The girls are great about coming for visits which give us a chance for updates of their lives.

We have a bunkhouse that houses two Mexicans. They helped with the ranch and we work side by side so many times. It is to the point that I trusted them with everything that goes on at the ranch and pay them well. Maybe I pay them too well because they would do anything to stay on the ranch. They are just plain good people. I bought them a pickup truck to drive around the ranch and they used it daily for everything.

Jeff and Marge lived down the road about ten miles with about 700 acres. They went all out on their house with swimming pool, gardens, waterfalls and all kinds of other rich things. Their house was totally different from ours but to each his own. He has a couple of horses and about 100 head of cattle. I am not sure he cares for animals personal but he is always there for Sherry and me. Both Marge and Jeff give us a lot of their time and lives. We always have a good time being around them.

I guess my favorite time of day is early morning sitting on the porch drink coffee. The air is fresh and the birds and animals come by to say hello. Sometimes Sherry joins me and we talk about everything. The times I am alone I let my mind drift back to the war reliving a few moments. God must have been with me so many times that I must not be finished with my life as yet. I am sure God expects me to do something great before I die. I am just not sure what. I pray a lot asking that question and sometimes I even throw in to ease my back pain. We seem to be having military and political problems in the Middle East but my friends in the UAE are keeping clean. Our soldiers fighting in the sand and heat must be hell. Maybe God plans for me to take some kind of action in the desert but I think I am too old, plus I am tired of sweating in 120 degree heat. I think the deer would miss me also.

CHAPTER 30

It was late October and I was sitting on the porch watching the deer when the phone rang. Sherry answered it and then called for me. The voice on the other end was foreign and I strained to understand what was being said. I asked if he could repeat and he said, "This is Sheikh Khalifah of the United Arab Emirates. I would like to meet with you."

I finally made out what he was saying and was a bit in shock. Why would the Ruler of the UAE be calling me but I clear my throat and answered, "Sure, I will be glad to meet with you."

"I will send my plane for you if you can come to my country."

"Sure, I would be happy to visit your country again."

"A driver will pick you up at noon tomorrow. Thanks you so much."

I told Sherry that we had another trip to the UAE for tomorrow and she was nothing but smiles. I called Jeff and told him about the phone call and asked him to watch the ranch if he would. I knew my worker would tend to everything but Jeff was my backup. Sherry and I dug out our suitcases and wondered what to take. I threw in my Nam knife as always. Last time we needed nothing but who knows about this trip.

The next morning at 11:40 a limo entered our driveway and stopped in front of the house. A well dressed man got out and rang the bell. Sherry grabbed the door and said, "Just a minute. Please come in."

The man entered and took our luggage to the car. Sherry was running around as usual looking for things that she had over looked. Finally, she came to the limo and got in. The limo took us to the Austin airport while we were looking for the 747. The limo stopped in front of an Airbus 340. The aircraft was a block long with no markings except for a tail number. It dawned on me that maybe any kind of markings especially in Arabic would draw a lot of attention. We entered the plane and it was even more beautiful than the 747. Leather seats and tables made of glass and wood with gold trim on walls, lights and every other piece of furniture or furnishings. Sitting in one of the chairs was like sitting on a cloud. Again attendants began serving drinks and appetizers. We heard the engines start and soon we were in the air. More wonderful food came in waves. Hours later it was bedtime and the bedroom was equipped with a kind size bed including night clothes. Sherry and I talked for a long while wondering what we were doing on the plane going to the Middle East again. "Do you think he wants his money back," Sherry asked?

"Not a chance but what makes it worse I have no idea what he wants. It's a nice trip and much better than first class."

The morning came with more food and after a shower and clean clothes we were almost on the ground. I sat in the huge leather chair thinking that maybe this was my answer from God as to why I survived the war. Was it that important for me to be here? Well, I guess I would know soon.

A Rolls Royce picked us up as usual and I was thinking that I could get accustom to the service. The drive from the airport looked different with trees on both sides of the road and a forest of trees in several areas. The city had change so much that I could not recognize anything that I saw. There were new buildings, parks, flowers, expensive cars in every direction causing both of us to rubber-neck. What had happened to this place in the past years? The city belonged to the rich and architects. Never have I seen such buildings. Each was a master piece of architecture. We drove along the Persian Gulf with beautiful white sand beaches and turquoise water. Parks and gardens were continuous along the way and a person would never know they were in the desert.

The driver stopped at the gate of the Emirates Palace. He gave us a short description of the palace and told us we were staying there. He said that it is the most expensive hotel ever built and that we would meet with the Sheikh at the hotel. At the front of the Palace we were taken though the entrance and there was no way that we could believe our eyes. It was the most beautiful thing we had ever seen. We were greeted by several of the staff that took us to a suite. The suite was about the size of a football field with the most gorgeous décor in the world. There was more gold accenting the rooms than in Black Beard's pirates ships. Gold sinks and fixtures with a sunken Jacuzzi tub cover a small part of the huge bathroom. I loved the paintings of falcons and the UAE desert. The king poster bed was covered with a designer bedspread and pillows and a wet bar was along one wall. It was time for a drink. I opened the cabinet and it was fully furnished with all the best spirits. A few minutes later a knock at the door with a man carrying a tray with a letter. The man said, "For you, Sir."

I took the letter and fumbled for a tip. The man held out his hand saying no so I said, "Thanks you very much."

The envelope had a seal on it and I carefully opened it without tearing the paper. It was a letter from the Sheikh thanking me for coming and asking if I could meet with him in the morning at 10:00. I opened the door and the same man was standing there. I told him to tell the Sheikh I would be glad to meet with him in the morning. He nodded and left.

I made us both another drink and we walked to the room's balcony overlooking the gulf and white sand. We talked about the hotel and the suite and possible reasons why the Sheikh would want to see us. Sherry seemed to think it was the money that we had received. "Honey, the money was given to us years ago by his father so that cannot be the reason."

"Then what else could it be?"

"Maybe something to do with the tools. Maybe someone stole them again."

"Are you crazy? If someone stole them, he would have the armed forces to find them."

"I guess you are right."

"Let's go for a swim in the gulf."

"Great idea."

We finished our drinks and went in to change. I opened the door and asked the staff person, "We would like to take a swim in the gulf. Can you arrange that?"

"Most certainly."

One of the staff lead us to the sand and then to a cabana with towels, drinks, lotions and a fan. The cabana also had two beds and a massage table. We left our bathing suit covers and headed to the water. The water was warm and so clear that we could see fish swimming around us at times. Sherry kept worrying about sharks and maybe she had good reason because we were the only people in the water. We stayed in the water for almost an hour and I noticed we were getting red. The cabana seemed like a great idea.

Sherry wanted a massage and she lay there moaning as the woman gave her the works. I flipped through one of the magazines looking at pictures mostly. After Sherry had finished she kept telling me that I had to try a massage. Finally I gave in and a man walked in with muscles in all the right places. Sherry said, "Boy, I got the wrong person."

"You got the right person! I have the wrong person."

I thought he would kill me at times but when he finished I felt like a new man. We went back to the room and tried the tub. It was large enough for two and that was certainly fun.

We were getting hungry and there were a lot of fruits and nuts in the room so we snacked. Again I opened the door and asked the staff person about dinner. He said it would be at 9:00 and that we could visit the bar before dinner if we liked. It was 7:00 now so that gave us time to dress and Sherry to apply makeup. She had gotten better with age and she could apply all the necessary paints in about an hour. Again clothes were provided but we decided to wear what we had packed. Sherry wore a stunning red evening gown that gave her a glow that I had never seen before. Maybe it was the massage but she looked incredibly beautiful and I told her so. I got a kiss for paying attention as I finished with my tux.

It was 8:15 and a drink at the bar was our goal. We were lead in that direction and sat at a table with stunning leather chairs. They felt like a glove. Service was great and we finished two glasses of Chateau Pavie Saint-Emilion 2003 each. We were escorted to dinner and seated at a table that that gave us a view of the restaurant and the live music. The dinner music was quiet and we could talk with ease. The waiter came and we ordered the same wine. It was the best that I have ever had. Menus came after about thirty minutes and I could tell it would be an eventful dinner. Dinner would be a 4-hour event I was sure. Well, there was nothing else to do that would be better than this exquisite dinner. The waiter returned and took our orders. We both ordered the lobster. Another half hour passed and appetizers came so many that they covered the table. I warned Sherry not to eat too much because I had a feeling that the lobster would be great. Soups and salads followed and we ate with elegance using the fine china and silver. We slowed our eating remembering we were not in the States. I wished the meal would never end with Sherry sitting beside me in the red evening dress that made her the most beautiful woman in the world. The lobsters arrived and I was right because each lobster must have been four pounds. They were huge and served with a sauce to die for. It was more than butter and every bit of lobster had to be dipped. Grilled veggies came with the lobster and there was a light cheese sauce that was poured over them sparely. Oh my gosh, the food was wonderful. Mama never prepared anything like this. Dessert came and we just picked at it.

The next morning we could not even think about eating again so we dressed for the meeting while drinking coffee.

At 9:45 we were escorted to a large conference room and there were more pastries and coffee waiting. The room was filled with nine men dressed in white that gave me the impression that they were important. As we entered they all rose and greeted me. Sherry was smart enough to not sit at the table and took a chair along the wall. I gave her a wink. I was offered the chair at the end of the table like I was someone important. I sat and the men started with small talk about the States and the UAE. Ten minutes later the Sheikh entered and all rose again and bowed. I did the same in respect. The Sheikh waved his hand and all took their seats. The man had a half smile as he introduced himself. He talked directly at me as he said, "We are so privileged to have you here and we want to make you as comfortable as possible."

"Thank you, your hospitality has been wonderful."

"I know you must be concerned as to why I have asked you here. The men at this table are the leaders of the seven countries that make the United Arab Emirates. We are here on your behalf to ask you a great favor. My father told the story of a great man that returned the tools that we had used by our forefathers for guidance through out desert. He said that this man was of great bravery and honesty. This man was a leader of his people and was not a politician. This man could be a leader of all men because he loved men more than money. You are this man."

He stopped for a drink of tea and then continued, "My countrymen that live in the desert and they have great influence with me have requested to met you. The navigation tools that you returned to them are life to these people. They do not understand why an American would be so unwavering to return what did not belong to him. The stories of the tools have been circulated around the country and even into Saudi. You are a hero to them and me."

I stood and offered great thanks for all the kind words and told him that I would be very happy to meet with these people. I never knew I could feel so good by words that were spoken. It made me proud that I did the right thing. The Sheikh continued, "We will meet in the desert in three day. Until then you are my guest and whatever you want will be given to you."

I thanked him again and he came to me and kissed me on both cheeks. It was such an honor for him to do that. Sherry and I left the room after another hour of conversation with the men at the table. All were heaping praise on me. They talked with me about being a soldier in Nam and it surprised me that they knew so much about me. Of course fighting a war in a jungle was a mystery to them so I used the desert as a case in point while talking. They seemed to understand and a history of war was familiar as they spoke of their forefathers. These people were honest and sincere and I wondered what they could want with me. Surely they knew I did not need money and my experience of war in a desert was limited. Time passed quickly for me anyway and we made plan to talk again tomorrow.

Back at the suite I made Sherry and I a drink and we both sat down. "You know Sherry I do not understand people of this world. I did such a small thing and get such a great reward. I am not talking about money but respect of my fellowman."

"Honey, you did the right thing and it may only seem small to you. These people are deep in family tradition and customs so you gave them back part of their lives. The tools meant nothing to us but they mean so much to these people."

"I feel closeness to them and I have never met them. I am almost thinking the tools have some kind of power."

"What do you mean, power?"

"Maybe something that draw people to an inter peace with each other."

"Maybe. The people here seem so friendly that I feel the same."

For the next two days we shopped and did sightseeing. Sherry spent a lot of time at the Marina Mall that was unbelievable in itself. I spent time talking with people in and around the palace. I took walks along the beach stopping to get to know a bit about the people. Mostly simple people but their attitudes were happy and content. I wonder why the US had gone in a different direction of stress and moving fast in every direction. Were we in the US more socially acceptable than the people here? Questions popped into my head with no answers.

Sherry and I sat on the balcony looking at the sun going down and seeing the peace of the evening. "This is almost as nice as the feeding the deer on the ranch," I quietly said.

"Can we stay longer after the meeting tomorrow?"

"I would say we could do whatever we want."

A knock at the door and we opened it to see three men standing with clothing. "Sir, these clothes are acceptable for the meeting tomorrow."

He brought the clothes into the suite and hung them in the closet. Sherry and I stood in amazement as we stared at the clothing. It was typical Arab desert dress. Again a knock at the door and one of the men said, "I am very sorry but if you need help with proper dress we will be here."

"Thank you and I am sure I will call you in the morning."

Sherry looked through the garments and said, "I have not idea if some of these items are yours or mine. There are things here I have never seen before. I am not sure if you wear them on the outside or inside."

I gave her a look and said, "You better wait until the morning and we will get help. I would hate to insult them by wearing their clothes wrong."

CHAPTER 31

The morning came early because we both could not sleep. I was not sure of what time we were going to leave so I opened the door and asked one of the four men standing by. One answered by saying, "11:00." I waved them into the room and said, "Please, give us a few hints about the clothing."

One man exited and came back shortly with two women. The women took part of the clothing and Sherry to the bedroom. The men began to separate the reminder of the clothes and laid them on the furniture. We began with what must have been underwear and ended with the headdress. One of the men stopped and waved his hands, "Sir, the most important thing is the jambiyas, in your language the knife. Do you mind if I give you a bit of history about the jambiyas?"

"Please I need all the help I can get."

"Jambiyas are passed down generation after generation. Some are even centuries old. The jambiyas are rarely used as weapons of defense; rather they are a means of defining and displaying the status of a man in society. Jambiyas are also worn as a sign of patriotism and tribal loyalty. The brand of a jambiya is associated with the material with which it is made, its quality and its design. The most significant part of a jambiya is its handle. In most cases, the price of a jambiya is determined by its handle. The saifani handle is known to be the most famous, and is found on the daggers of higher class citizens. The saifani handle is made of rhinoceros horns which can cost up to 1500USD for 1 kilogram. Different versions of saifani handles can be distinguished by their color. Most other jambiya handles are made of different types of horns or wood. Apart from the material used for the handle, the design and detail on the handle describe its value and the status of its owner. In the majority of cases the double-sided blade of the jambiya is constructed of steel. The blade

258

is stored in a sheath, usually made of wood. The sheath is commonly decorated with various ornaments that signify status. These include silver work, semi-precious stones and leather. The sheath is fixed on a leather belt which is normally 2-3 inches thick. The belt is usually worn around the lower abdomen."

"Oh, I am afraid to ask if I need to wear the knife."

One of the men removed the jambiya from a piece of material and handed it to me. He assisted me with wearing it properly. I did not even ask if it was valuable.

We both were dress and Sherry was totally covered except for eyes. I had my Arab knife belted to my waist and it felt good. The funny part is that the handle looked just like the material the tools were made. I took my Nam knife from the suitcase and tried to scrape a small piece of the material from the handle. My knife would not even make a scratch and that had me worried. Well anyway I put the Arab knife back onto my belt and asked Sherry, "You ready?"

"As I will ever be."

We opened the door and were lead to a Mercedes SUV. There were four of them of the same color and were lined along the drive. We took the second one. Ten minutes later the Sheikh came out of the palace, took a moment to say hello to us and got into the third SUV.

We drove out of the city in a caravan and then to the freeway in the direction of Dubai. Dubai was about an hour's drive but we turned off the highway after forty minutes. The driver shifted into four-wheel drive and we were in sand. The wheels were spinning at times as we encountered dunes and soft spots but nothing stopped the vehicles. Our speed was not fast but after all we were in the middle of the desert and as far as I could see was sand. We continued for almost an hour and a huge tent came into view. The closer we got the more it looked like a camp with camels and goats boarded in an area near the tent. When I say tent it was not one you would take camping but one that was huge and from the outside it was decorated as a palace. I asked the drive, "What is all that?"

"Bedouins."

Sherry asked, "What are Bedouins?"

"Bedu, the Arabic word from which the name bedouin is derived and means 'inhabitant of the desert,' and refers generally to the desert-dwelling nomads. For most people, however, the word "bedouin" conjures up a much richer and more evocative image—of lyrical, shifting sands, flowing robes, and the long, loping strides of camels. These are the people that founded this land."

259

I had no idea what to expect as we stopped near the tents. The Sheikh exited his vehicle and all the people in or near the tents bowed in respect. I felt like I had gone back a thousand years in time as we were greeted by people dressed in typical desert wardrobe. Of course, Sherry and I were dressed in the same custom and it made us a part of what this meant to these people. All the men wanted to shake my hand and I was greeted with hugs and kisses on the cheek. The people were not soft and from their handshake I could feel calluses and a strong grip. These were hard working people. We were invited into the tent and offered a seat on carpets with surrounding pillows. Sherry was pointed in the direction along the tent wall while the men sat in a circle in the center. The Sheikh started with an introduction of the men around the circle. Food and drink was brought and placed near each of us. The drink was tea, well, I thought it was tea. It was powerful. It was late afternoon and the temperature in the tent was amazedly cool. More pastries were brought and I answered questions from the two men that sat next to me. After another thirty minutes of eating finger foods a man next to the Sheikh began to speak loudly. He was addressing all of us with broken English. Between words of the speaker came sound from outside of camels. They sounded in pain but I assumed they were just hungry or thirsty.

The speaker continued to give a brief history of the people of the desert and what the Sheikh had done for them. He stopped and picked up the tools that I had delivered years before. The circle of men began to cheer as he held the tools in the air. I was beginning to panic thinking I was in trouble. He speaker stood and stretched his arm high above his head with the tools in his hand. The cheers became louder. I turned looking from side to side and all were looking at me. I made a slight nod with my head and they continued to cheer. I think they were waiting for me to stand so I stood and held out my arms. They stopped cheering and I had no idea what to do next. I was saved by the speaker as he began with, "Mr. Taylor it is with great honor that we have you with us. Your bravery and integrity has been told to us many time by His Highness. We have you to thank for returning the instruments used by our fathers. These instruments are worth more than treasure and gold to my people. There were stolen many years ago and our hearts have been heavy until you returned them. Everyone here are leaders and all have agreed that we owe you a great debt."

I raised my hand and said, "Sir, I have been paid in full by His Highness. He is a great man to lead your country."

"No, we are not talking of money. We want you to lead the people of the desert. His Highness fully approves of such an act and wants you to be a part of us. Your honesty and leadership is known throughout this land."

The speaker reached for a flat wooden box and handed it to me. The box was hinged and lacquered. The wood was beautiful and I got a nod to open it. My heart skipped a beat when I saw a silver and gold vermeil jambiya dagger.

The J-shaped dagger measured about 10-inches from the handle to the bend. It was beautifully hand-crafted in silver thread on leather with gold sheeting at the handle and tip. The handle appeared to be silver on bone. The reverse side of the entire dagger below the handle was lined with green felt. The box was felt lined and inside of the top of the box showed the crest of the United Arab Emirates in gilt. I did not know what to say except thank you it is very beautiful.

The speech continued and it got a bit fuzzy for me. From what I caught he thought that I was going to live here in a palace. Maybe accepting the knife was a sign that I was one of them, I had no clue. I was afraid to interrupt thinking I would be insulting them. My praises went on and cheers got louder. I took a quick look at Sherry sitting against the tent and she shrugged her shoulders. I was not even sure what these people wanted from me or what they expected me to do. The talk continued for another half hour and then food came. The room was filled with mysterious smells and the sights of the food gave me as uneasy feeling. The food trays were position on a long table near the back of the tent. I was pushed to the front of the line and took food that that looked eatable. I took plenty of rice just in case. No women were allowed to eat until the men were completed. I felt bad for Sherry but she had a smile on her face.

We finished eating and most were not bad at all and some was delicious. There was a whole lamb or goat that had been roasted over an open flame which made it not bad at all. The men stood all and talked among themselves which gave a chance to speak to the Sheikh, "Sir, I am not 100% sure of what they are expecting of me or what I should do."

He almost laughed and then said, "The leaders of the desert tribes are asking you to be there ambassador, to give them honesty and bravery if disputes arise among themselves or from without. They want you to give them guidance in truths."

"Okay how would I do such?"

"You will live in the desert palace and you will receive guest similar to a judge. Not in a trial but as an advisor. It is a great honor."

"Is that your job and what if I tell them wrong?"

"You will have my greatest support and I trust you to be fair and honest."

"The desert palace, is it large so I could have my family here?"

"Very large, you will go there next."

My mind kept on track that I was missing part of the plan so I asked, "Will these people abide by what I say? How will they react if I go against what they desire?"

"I have had long talks with their leaders and they chose you as a fair and honest person. They respect your life as a warrior. There will times that you will disagree with what is told you and that is what they expect. Your judgment as a warrior will prevail."

I thanked the Sheikh and started toward Sherry but was stopped when the men sat down again. Women came into the tent dressed in what I thought was belly-dancer clothing. Men followed with musical instruments and the dancing began. Pipes were lit and the tobacco was very strong, maybe hashish, as they offered me a pipe. I took it and coughed as one of the men lit the pipe. They all laughed. Oh, the dancers were good as Sherry sat with her lips in the pouting mode. The dancers continued for another hour and the party seemed to break up as several of the men left. The Sheikh got into his vehicle and three of the SUVs drove off. I saw my driver and asked if we could go. His reply was a bit strange, "The Sheikh's Palace or your palace?"

I gave thought that I had better have a quiet talked with Sherry and replied, "Just a moment."

I walked to Sherry and asked, "What do you think?"

"I have never seen anything like it. You are the hero of the desert. I am so proud of you."

"But did you get what they want me to do?"

"What do you mean?"

"They want us to live here in a palace and for me to be their ambassador."

"Live here! Where? Not in a tent."

"Apparently, there is a palace or what they call a palace in the desert near here that we would live. I asked the Sheikh if it was large enough for our whole family and he said yes. Our driver is willing to carry us there now."

"Let's take a look."

I motioned to the driver and told him to take us to the desert palace. I asked how long a drive and he replied not far. He drove to a paved road that must have been recently built because it was as smooth as glass. Ten minutes later we came to a roundabout and turned right. Another roundabout and street lights on each side of the road made it look like daylight. Palm trees lined each side of the road. The lights and trees continued for about two miles and at the next roundabout we entered a gate. The lights changed colors to a golden yellow and a long fountain shot up water along the middle of the divided road. The lights of the palace could be seen in the distance and it was huge. We came to a large garden area that made a circle to a driveway at the front of the palace. Large marble columns stood at the entrance of the palace with steps leading to the front door. The vehicles stopped and the driver rushed to open the doors for us.

We walked slowly up the steps taking in all the stone work of the building. Carvings and statues were everywhere and gardens of flowers surrounded the front area. A man opened the front door for us and we took three or four steps inside. Marble floors and columns in the entry with gold trim on every detail of the furniture and picture frames of the entrance. The ceiling was stained glass with outside light sparkling through. Sherry gave a deep breath as her head turned in circles. The man offered us to come in and we followed him. The driver and the doorman had a small conversation in Arabic. The doorman spoke perfect English with a British accent as he said, "Please let me show you the palace."

"Thank you," I replied.

The man walked slowly as he talked, "The Palace has fourteen bedrooms, three dining rooms, six living areas, two libraries, and three recreation areas. The outside of the palace comes with two Rolls Royce, stables with horses and two pools."

He walked to the first living area and it must have been 50 by 50 feet with leather furniture and fine wood tables. Paintings and wall décor were originals from foreign counties around the world. It was overwhelming. We continued into other areas such as dining rooms and more living areas that were just as plush. Then we went to the largest recreation room. It was as large as our house in Texas with an indoor swimming pool and sauna. Exercise equipment took part of the room leaving huge areas for chairs and tables. Sherry tried to speak but she just turned in circles looking at every detail. We walked up the stairway running our hands along the rail feeling the texture of the wood. Upstairs were bedrooms and a recreation room. The marble flooring continued and the doorman opened the door to the master bedroom. Another gigantic room with a king size poster bed, chairs, sofa, desk and the bathroom was trimmed in gold and marble. By this time nothing was a surprise. Clothes filled the closets and they were our sizes.

We went down stairs and a staff of nine servants was there to meet us.

They were very friendly and offered any service. I asked to see the kitchen and was whisked off in that direction. Sherry talked with the staff and I returned shaking my head over the modern huge kitchen. My driver asked if we wanted to spend the night here or back in Abu Dhabi. I gave Sherry a quick look and said we would like to stay here. Sherry and I decided to have a drink in one of the smaller living areas. We sat in quiet trying to determine what had happened. After three or four sips I asked, "What do you think?"

She did not answer as soon as she should and I began to worry, "I like it."

"Are you kidding?"

"No, I sure you will miss the excitement of feeding the deer but I feel in my heart that you can support these people."

"Really?"

"Well if not, you will find out very soon."

I waited again before I said, "Honey, you know me better than I know myself. I like the people here and for us to be given this honor is hard for me to understand."

"You always have a passion for the underdog and these may be rich but they are surely not educated to all the outside vultures that will prey on them. You have a personality that is for the underdog and you are just too honest."

"So are you saying that I should take the job?"

"It looks to me that you already have the job. Welcome home."

"What about our family?"

"Let's see, is there room for them here? This place will house an army."

CHAPTER 32

My communication with the Sheikh continued and I had his full support. I called the kids and tried to explain what was happening. The kids had a hard time understanding and could not believe we would leave them. I made offers to my ranch hands to keep up the ranch and they could take any profits from the cattle and horses. I told them no hunting. After several days of phone calls, Jeff, Marge and both kids flew in for a visit. After a couple of weeks at the palace they began to feel at home. They ate and were treated like royalty and that must have been the part they liked the most because they stayed longer and longer.

I had a stream of Arabs coming to my door from all directions. Some even lived in Saudi. It seemed my reputation had gained popularity. Some of the problems were minor but others required research so they were welcomed to spend time in the palace. It seemed that I always had a camel parked in front of the palace. The position was not as easy as I thought but I stay more than busy listening and making judgments.

Once several enraged Arabs came and before I knew it there was fight in the main library. Words were flying and the only thing I knew to do was get in between them. I stopped the fight but got a few cuts in the process. I managed to calm them down and all was peace and love before they left. Apparently the word got around about the fight and people were bringing gifts to me for weeks. I never met a person that was dishonest and did not have a major amount of pride that came from the desert. Their religion played a most important part of their lives and I did the best I could at understanding and accepting the religion of the land. At times I called on a local religious leader for answers. The desert people respected how I used what resources that I knew and at times they would just come by for a visit. I became a friend.

Sherry was enjoying the desert or should I say the palace and the servants. That gave me a peace that she was happy. Every six months we flew back to Texas and sat on the porch feeding the deer for a few weeks. Maybe this was God's plan to have me make peace in the desert after all the killing and suffering that the war had given me.

People continue to ask about the Vietnam War and to give them details would hurt me and them. So when I speak of the war, I speak of it in general terms and avoid providing any more hatred toward any person. Sherry and I both made friends of the people and with family there is was a wonderful life. Funny, my dreams of the war stopped when I moved to the desert.